TO A DEADLY
CHASE

Published in the UK in 2023 by DR Enterprises

Paperback ISBN 978-1-7399182-6-2
eBook ISBN 978-1-7399182-7-9

Cover design and typeset by SpiffingCovers

Editing by Jessica Chapman

TO A DEADLY
CHASE

DOUGLAS ROBERTS

Lieutenant-Colonel Bernard Utting OBE
Commissioned into the Royal Engineers in 1940, decommissioned
from the XIV 'forgotten army' in December 1945.

Foreword

World War II truly became worldwide on 7th December 1941 when several of the great battleships of the American fleet were sunk in Pearl Harbour by the Japanese navy. Right up until that date, peace permeated the sedentary lifestyles in the numerous Pacific islands and other far-flung outposts that lacked running water. Some hadn't even heard of electricity they were that remote. Up until that date, the focus of war was firmly fixed on Europe, North Africa, and Russia, but the Germans had had global plans since well before the outbreak of hostilities. Their embassies were based in important cities, such as Buenos Aries in South America and Durban in South Africa, where they could steer and influence the local populace and nurture governments to adopt their way of thinking.

One such city was Cape Town, which had particular strategic value due to its geographical location directly along Britain's vital link with its colonies in the Far East, Australia, and New Zealand. Indonesia supplied rubber, Borneo crude oil, India tea (very important if you are British) and food came in the form of sheep from New Zealand. The list was endless. On the return journey back to India, ocean-going ships needed to round the southern tip of Africa, passing the Cape of Good Hope. Troops, equipment, ammunition, uniforms - as well as pay chests and other such vital items - all had to be shipped.

It would have been a grievous blow to the Allies if the Germans had been able to cut the one and only lifeline round the entire continent of Africa. India was still the jewel in the crown of the British Empire, but a little further afield lay Burma, now Myanmar, the Malaysian peninsular and, at journey's end, Australia and New Zealand. They supplied very necessary goods, all transported by ships that had to travel half-way round the world, a journey that took several weeks.

The Germans continued to pursue their world-wide domination plans, including the annexation of the Southern African provinces, while the Japanese followed their own agenda of expansion across the Western Pacific with an ultimate aim of isolating, and eventually capturing, Australia. If they had managed to break through into India, then the British Empire would have been cut in half and cease to exist.

Captain Stock's voyage round the South African Cape threw up its own problems, but they almost paled into insignificance when compared to what he would face in India and Burma. Before the end of the war, he would go on to create 22 airfields, several dams, bridges and railway lines, often out of dense jungle.

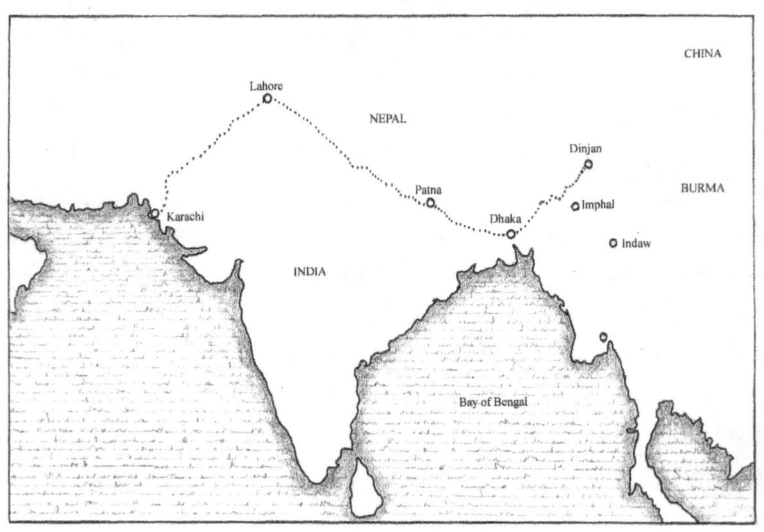

Chapter 1

The Warehouse

Winter 1941

They were stuck between the devil and the deep blue sea. Well, two devils actually and the deep blue sea was the Atlantic Ocean, even though it was admittedly not actually that deep just off the coast, although certainly deep enough to drown a man. There was even a third devil but they didn't notice their already parched throats and the almost overpowering heat that pervaded the inside of the giant warehouse. The sun beat down on the corrugated roof panels that seemed to radiate its intensity tenfold, and then trapped the air to a point where the sweat of a man could no longer cool the body as nature intended.

They had come to destroy the second devil and had primed their explosion more or less in the center of the huge pile provided by the German armament industry, and the words *Waffen Aufrustung* etched into the boxes attested to it origin. Not only did the crates of ammunition and shells reach higher than an elephant's trunk and included mechanized transport in the form of half-tracks lorries and motorcycles at one end, but at the other were the familiar forty-gallon drums and Jerry cans.

From previous experience, Captain Stock knew they really didn't want to be anywhere near these when fire took hold which was why he had chosen to stuff the petrol filler caps on two of the half-tracks with rags and opened the fuel drain off valves underneath them. There was a little slope to the warehouse floor. He could just about see in the gloom that the liquid merely puddled beneath the two vehicles rather than flowing in any particular direction and, now the fumes were beginning to infuse, they could all clearly smell it. It seemed there was enough material here to equip an entire corps, if not more. It was apparent that it had been stored in such a fashion as to facilitate rapid deployment; the smaller vehicles were at the front and, waiting behind them, the 88mm self-propelled guns. In the center was the ammunition, some already stacked in lorries. Adjacent to that were the small arms, uniforms and other such equipment. An aisle between the crates delineated the tinned food stores and finally, right up against the side of the building nearest the sea, the fuel, water and oils were stored that would power this particular part of the German military machine. It was a huge warehouse which Stock reckoned covered over an acre.

They had come, well, volunteered to be more accurate, to destroy this massive arsenal - but they couldn't. Not right now because they all knew that, if they set fire to the rags, it would start an unstoppable chain of events consuming everything and everyone within as well as the building itself. It would be the end of them. There was no way out, while the angry devils outside blocked their only apparent way of escape, and real blood thirsty devils they were too. They could hear them shouting and thumping the ground with their spears. It was difficult to tell how many of them there were but, as the last person through the small side access door, Stock had looked round to see that there were more than a hundred of them, armed with clubs, machetes, even bows and arrows, and more were coming. And now their axes were slicing through the big, corrugated iron doors at the front. Although the cuts were random, it wouldn't be long before the weakened iron gave way and let in a flood of savages who would hack them to death. And all they had to defend themselves with were golf clubs; the odds were at least 4-1.

Stock was nearest the hangar-type doors but looked round at his squad in a last desperate hope they had found a way out at the back, as Sergeants Day and Wisley trotted up to him from each side.

"No door at the back, sir."

"Not this side either and the buggers are round there now as well."

Stock forlornly looked at the other two for inspiration, Privates Needham and Tuffred, affectionately known as Needle and Thread in their platoon. He cursed himself for wasting time wondering why two such individuals had somehow managed to accompany each other on almost everything when it normally only required a one-man job. His mind was wandering. The noise of several dozen iron age weapons clattering off the metalwork focused his thoughts. He was about to turn back to face their inevitable doom when he realized the answer was staring him in the face. Weapons. They had all the weapons in the world right behind them. He felt such a fool for not realising it before. Not only that, but also they had their pick of whatever transport they wanted.

"Quick. Into that half-track." He pointed at one that already had a rag in the fuel filler as it was easiest to get to, while hoping that in the meantime an axe attack would not spark the explosive fumes before they escaped from the enclosure of the building. "Day, you take the driver's seat. Thread, Needle, you find some ammunition. Wisley, you man the machine gun."

As Stock neared the big machine he noted that there were two, not one, machine guns, one just above where the driver would sit and the other at the rear of the troop compartment. As Royal Engineers, they had not been trained in the use of enemy equipment and he prayed that Day could at least get the vehicle started. The guns were called MG30 somethings, like the car, but he'd never heard one fire so couldn't even begin to compare what the two differing machines sounded like.

Their way out was partially blocked by a pile of crates and he made a note not to be on that side of the vehicle when it knocked them down. As he hopped up into the cab next to Day, he heard someone cocking a gun just above his head. He looked up and saw Wisley looking down at him.

"Ready when you are, sir."

"How about the other one?" he had to shout as Day had managed to fire up the engine and was peering at four levers, wondering which one made it move forwards.

"Needle's on it, sir, and yes, he's ready too."

Three things happened at once.

Day managed to engage reverse; the half-track lurched backwards throwing them all forwards. This only exacerbated Day's situation. He put more pressure on the throttle pedal and the machine began to accelerate into the taller piles of crates behind them, toppling several of them into the troop compartment. It knocked both Needham and Tuffred off their perch and threw them to the floor.

Stock looked up in response to a flood of light as several of the corrugated sheets collapsed inwards. Not having the benefit of a steering wheel to hang onto, he found his chin making contact with the metal dashboard in front of him. He was momentarily dazed before Day managed to remove his hefty foot.

Wisley fared better. Instead of throwing his arms forward from the backwards inertia, he hung onto the machine gun's handles, lowering its barrel and pulling the trigger. Bullets spumed into the dusty ground directly in front of the half-track, just ahead of the surging crowd, bringing them to an immediate halt.

Day was now desperately shoving levers in opposite directions and playing with the accelerator pedal, knowing that they had to move forwards, and quickly; Wisley had ceased his firing and the swelling crowd was beginning to recover from the initial shock of being fired at. He found success at last and the half-track lunged forwards. As it did so, it nudged another pile of crates, throwing more of them into the rear compartment on top of Needham and Tuffred, but he wasn't to know that he had just crippled the both of them.

Even before Stock had time to recover and rub the blood from his chin, the back of his head thudded dully into a steel plate just behind him. He didn't have to issue any orders as he was aware that they were moving forward and out into the glaring sunlight but he heard Wisley's machine gun thumping away, presumably at the mob. It seemed a long time before he could think clearly again, but in fact it was only a few seconds before he looked out of the door to see that they were well clear of the building and that the crowd had fallen behind.

"Hold it here and give me your lighter."

Day's driving had not improved and Stock had just enough time to put his hand out to stop himself headbutting the metal dashboard again. With Day's lighter in his hand, he glanced at the crowd that were now pursuing them and threw himself under the vehicle to turn off the drain cock. Then he ran to the back of the half-track, removed the rag from the fuel filler and shouted at Day to move forwards. It was going to be close but he estimated he had just enough time to set fire to the rag and toss it onto the trail of fuel that ran down the slight incline towards the warehouse. He didn't smoke cigars or cigarettes and, although knew how to use a lighter, it took him a couple of extra seconds longer to produce a flame and set it to the rag.

The first of the mob was only feet away and coming at him with a raised machete, when he felt more than heard the bullets from Wisley's machine gun pass his right ear and chew up the rushing savage. Without any further thought for his own safety, he took two steps forward and carefully put the flaming rag where he thought the trail started. The intense heat rising from the loosely packed soil of the South African dirt was to Stock's advantage; it seemed that the trail had been waiting for just such an occasion as it leapt into action and released a tell-tale smudge of oily black smoke as the flames rushed back towards the warehouse like a flaming lance. Looking just long enough to confirm that it was still heading in that direction, he turned tail and ran towards the half-track before Wisley would have to use his machine gun again on the nearing crowd and shouted at Day to 'Go!' as he grabbed one of the rungs on its rear doors.

'This is going to be one hell of an explosion,' he thought as he eased himself further up the back of the now bouncing vehicle.

He'd only been in the Royal Engineers for a little over a year and already he had destroyed an airfield, including its fuel, and razed an oil depot to the ground. This would be a first when it came to ammunition, and this time he really did want to get well away from what would surely turn out to be the highlight of his army career. He mused to himself that he was moving up in the world.

As they crested a small rise, he looked back and saw that the local savages had given up the chase. He shouted for Day to stop, got down, and walked forward to the right-hand side to have a word with his sergeant, before realising that the steering wheel was on the other side. He opened the door.

"This ought to be good. Have a look," he said. Day had been with him when they had escaped from under the noses of the Germans in France the summer before. Like Stock, had nearly been killed when blowing up the oil terminal at Dieppe. He knew Day would appreciate seeing this one.

Day slid over to dismount on Stock's side, stood next to him and surveyed the pall of black smoke emerging from the front of the warehouse. "I reckon that other half-track's on fire by now but it's not putting off the locals. Look!"

They're bloody nuts," commented Wisley from his better viewpoint behind the machine gun on top of the cabin. "Don't they know it's about to go up?"

The locals were like a trail of ants servicing their nest, entering the warehouse empty-handed and emerging with boxes of whatever. But it didn't last long as the first 'crump' indicated that something else had caught fire. Two or three more 'crumps' followed closely, before there was an almighty 'boom' which had the effect of blowing off some of the roof sheets. Flame was now clearly visible through the thickening smoke. A staccato retort announced that the smaller boxes of ammunition were the next to submit, but their firecracker-like sounds were drowned out as the larger 88mm shells took over the concerto of explosions. And finally, the fuel at the back gave in as well, almost simultaneously. Even though they were nearly half a mile away, they felt a wave of heat brush over them and watched in awe as the building seemed to jump several feet into the air before disintegrating into a thousand pieces in all directions.

For over a minute they were speechless, all except Sergeant Day. "Proper job."

Stock looked at his fellow and joined his grin as black oily smoke gained height. "Damn. I left my golf clubs in there."

They all roared with laughter but it was Wisley who broke up the merriment as he jumped down into the rear of the vehicle. "Hey, Needle and Thread need help. Quick."

Both of the prone and unconscious privates were half buried underneath several crates and hefty boxes, and blood from one of them could be seen trickling down towards the rear doors of the half-track. It came from Needham's left arm which was all but severed at the elbow. Wisley found an almost clean rag that had been left lying around and wrapped it round the virtual stump of an arm while Stock took off his belt and tightened it around his upper arm to act as a tourniquet.

"Get us back to the ship. Pronto," Stock commanded. He looked over to Sergeant Day who was propping Tuffred up against the corner of the compartment and thought about giving him some advice about more careful driving, but then thought the better of it. If they didn't return to the ship in very short order and get the doctor to attend to Needham, the loss of blood might mean he wouldn't make it. As it was, he was going to lose the lower part of his arm. Just before Day jerked them into motion, Stock stood up and looked back down where the warehouse had stood and was gratified to see that it looked like almost everything that had once been inside it was now scattered outside. But it was the telltale column of black smoke riding high into the sky that now concerned him. If the Germans were within twenty miles, they would come running. He estimated that they couldn't be more than a couple of miles away from the docks where their ship lay at Port Nolloth. That was where the main part of his battalion was and where they had put in for emergency repairs. He hoped to God that the chief had managed to forge another propeller shaft cap because if he hadn't, and there were Jerries about, then it was likely there would be a few more casualties than Needham.

*****

Oberst Hartmann lounged opposite his counterpart, Oberst Sauer, and was feeling content as he sat with crossed legs resting on the top rail of the verandah, gazing out over the almost flat South African plain. It wasn't much of a view; in every direction, bar west towards the sea, there was little to look at other than scrubland, but he once again glanced over his right shoulder at the lines of dirty brown tents that housed his troops. His regiment at last. He watched the small group of officers who had just left the luncheon party trundle back to their duties. This natural bowl in the virtual desert provided the perfect place to hide and train over two thousand men so long as the desalination plant which they had disguised as a casual hut on the beach, kept going. Still, he had to admit he was worried about their supply situation, particularly the food,. Plus, the men's morale was beginning to wane since the Brigadegeneral, concerned that the element of surprise would otherwise be lost, had forbidden any contact with the outside world.

Kristof Hartmann had only been confirmed as Colonel a few days earlier. The previous oberst had managed to get himself killed in their warehouse when a stack of food crates had been toppled onto him by one of the drivers reversing a lorry. Hartmann was pedant, even by his own admission, and not over-loved by his troops, but at least he was efficient, one from the old school. Major Hartmann, who had in any case only been promoted a few weeks earlier, had now been further promoted to next in the chain of command, taking on responsibility for one half of the Kolonial brigade.

"What do you suppose our overworked general is up to right now?" asked Sauer, knowing that he was away in the town of

Springbok for the next few days.

Hartmann casually glanced away from his brandy glass and up in the direction of the afternoon sun. "Probably still in his birthday suit on top of someone's wife, but you can't deny the fact that he has earned it." He waited a moment for the predictable reaction from Sauer beofre continuing, "After all, we all have, haven't we?"

"Ha!" Sauer's exclamation held all the contempt he could muster after an alcoholic lunch. He was expressing the thoughts of most of the men under their command who had now lacked female company for nearly two months, other than the very few women who had somehow magically appeared and been round the camp several times. "If this carries on much longer, I may have to go and see Betti." They'd named one of the women Betti as they couldn't pronounce her real name.

"You'd never survive her thunder thighs more than two minutes. I hear she dislocated Corporal Fieller's pelvis."

Sauer was a slightly built man and concluded he was being ribbed. "Is Fieller one of your or mine?"

"Yours, I think. One of the communications team. Talking of communication, do you really think the *Atlantis* will come?"

"Of course, it will come." Sauer was one of those who had unshakable belief in Adolf Hitler and the OKW high command. Over lunch they had talked about little else other than the latest broadcast picked up by his radio team which said their cruiser *Atlantis* had sunk another allied ship, *The Tiara,* just off the coast. "It's probably just gone off to resupply before coming over to us. After all, it's going to need all the shells it can carry."

He was referring to the plan that Brigadegeneral Korstannant had revealed to them once they had reached the safety of their current location. They had travelled in disguised freighters captured from the Danish merchant navy and landed at the little-known harbour at Luderitz in Namibia some three hundred kilometers to the north. At first, the entire brigade had gone inland (so as not to reveal their true destination) before turning South and crossing the border into

South Africa. Now they were to wait undetected near Port Nolloth until the cruiser *Atlantis* was ready to proceed and rendezvous with them at Cape Town. Then they were to co-ordinate their attack on the small British and South African garrison, secure the strategically important harbor and with it, the entire city. They had initially been accompanied by a second brigade, making the entire expedition into divisional size – they'd even been named the 21st Motorized Infantry Division and given the nickname 'The Forderns' (Helpers), but it had been diverted for The Fuhrer's plans to invade England.

They had been told that this mission would strike a substantial strategic blow that would strangle the Allies' safer link with their Far Eastern Colonies since the route across the Mediterranean via Gibraltar and through the Suez Canal was still too dangerous for troop convoys. By taking Cape Town, the Germans could provide a secure base for their submarines and surface raiders to operate in the South Atlantic and ultimately force the government of the Western Cape to capitulate. There was already considerable German presence in the area, mainly left over from settlers pre-dating the Boer wars at the turn of the century, and their sympathisers would be called upon to help form a new government allied to Germany, not Great Britain and The Commonwealth. It was a great shame that their cruiser *The Admiral Graf Spee* had been cornered and scuttled in Montevideo late last year as this too had been part of the plan, but they would just have to manage without her.

They sat in silence under the shade of the thatched verandah roof letting the heat of the day gently waft over them, listening to the pair of junior rankers as they cleared away the clutter of their luncheon table inside. It was Sauer who first noticed the grey smudge of smoke in the distance. Frowning, he stood up. "What's that?"

Hartmann lazily open his eyes and gazed in the direction of Sauer's stare. "That's the damn depot." He jumped to his feet and nearly tripped over in his haste, just as they heard a first of a series of 'booms'.

"Oi, you two. Come with us - quickly!" he shouted at the pair inside and jumped down the two steps towards the staff car which was round the side of the building. Whatever the emergency, it would not be appropriate for a colonel to be seen driving a staff car, even though he was perfectly capable and wanted to. So, he and Sauer both sat in the rear waiting for the two rankers to assume the front seats. "Get us over to the depot. Straight line," ordered Sauer as the senior officer. As they passed close to the rows of tents, he shouted at no one in particular to follow.

They were both aware that there was a permanent two-man guard on the building some five kilometers away, hidden from their own view and the town by crests in the dunes. The guards were not dressed in their uniforms to avoid giving away the presence of their unit to any casual passer-by. All they had had to do was watch the hidden side access door and make sure nobody went in. It was impossible for anyone to go through the main doors as they could only be opened from the inside. It had only occurred to one bright spark some days after they had set the six-hour guard rotation system that the mere presence of a white face in a predominately black country would probably raise enough suspicion for further investigation. But the General had insisted on anonymity, so the guards had been told not to stand right next to the door, but to wander about and appear as casual as possible between the bushes that half-covered the ground, right up to the beach that led to the Atlantic. There was nobody around anyway as the inhabitants of Port Nolloth didn't tend to wander far from the town. Guarding the depot seemed almost superfluous although occasionally one or two locals with nothing better to do would wander out and converse with the guards. During construction of the warehouse, they had spotted it anyway, so the General had wisely bribed the headman of the town to keep all the locals on the side of the Germans and to retain their services should there be any problems.

They came across the prone guards in the shade of a bush. Sauer's first reaction was that they had somehow smuggled enough alcohol to drink themselves senseless, but as they closed on the somnolent pair, blood could be seen across the face of one who was stirring. Sauer ordered the car to a stop and stood up. "What the hell are you two doing here? You're supposed to be guarding the depot. Well?"

The one conscious guard had struggled to his feet and attempted a sloppy salute. "Herr Oberst, I have to report that there are Britishers here playing golf." With his saluting arm, he started to rub his bleeding head where it had been struck by a golf club.

Sauer was initially speechless. "Playing golf... Playing golf... Does that look like playing golf to you, dummkopf?" He pointed in the direction of the warehouse that was just out of sight, the pall of smoke revealing its location. "Get him up and follow us. Driver, go."

"The man's delirious," Sauer almost squeaked. "How can there be Britishers here AND playing golf? I'll have those bastards shot when we get back."

In less than a minute, they reached the top of the dune. Without instruction, the driver stopped. There was clearly no point in going any further. They could all see where the depot had been about half a kilometer away. He also stopped there because there was ammunition exploding and hurling death in all directions, as attested by several bodies that lay randomly around the depot. The two injured rankers breathlessly caught up with them, waited by the side of the staff car, and stared unbelievingly at the scene of destruction below.

Sauer was so furious it took him a while for the significance to sink in. Without their munitions, fuel, food, water - the list was endless - they were a toothless brigade. Their dreams of striking a serious blow to the allies ended and, with it, his chance for furtherment. He looked at the two rankers standing like sheep and went for his pistol to shoot them on the spot before he realized he had left it behind.

"WHAT......WHAT........" He could hardly control himself.

Hartmann took over. "Full report."

They both jerked to attention, staring at somewhere between

the two colonels. The first spoke, "Grenadiers Karfell and Schmidt, sir. We were patrolling the area as ordered and out of nowhere comes this golf ball, followed by a group of Englanders, five or six of them."

His friend butted in, "Seven or eight, maybe more, sir."

The first one continued, "One started talking to us but suddenly swung out with his gold club, knocking Schmidt out cold, and the others set upon me. I shouted at the couple of local kaffirs to help but they just ran off, and that's all I know until you arrived, sir."

They both stood to attention, hoping that their report would save their necks.

Sauer just stood there with his mouth open, amazed at the audacity of the story but Hartmann was already thinking ahead. If there was one group of British around, there would be others and he logically deduced that the only place they could have come from was the harbor at Port Nolloth. They needed to act fast. He virtually shoved Sauer out of the car and ordered the two rankers to return in it to the camp with instructions to deploy his entire regiment to the edge of the town abutting the harbor. Technically Sauer was in command of the two regiments, having served in his current rank longer, but to Hartmann that protocol took second place right now.

"Show me where this golf ball came from."

The car went off in one direction while the four Germans walked off in another towards a crowd of locals congregating near the top of a dune. None of them were armed.

Sergeant Day managed to negotiate the half-track round the few buildings without hitting them and approached the quayside where their ship, the *RMS Lady Oriana,* lay attached by several thick ropes. He pulled up in a plume of dusty gravel alongside a decrepit building next to where a football match was taking place, unknowingly blotting out a set of goal posts that had been drawn on the rusting tin sheets. The goalkeeper trying to ignore his approach as the opposition were pressing home their advantage. It was only

Sergeant Major Harries, as one of the many spectators from the far end, who brought order to chaos in response to the sudden arrival of a German half-track. He shouted at the referee to blow his whistle. There were forlorn looks on some of the players' faces, not understanding why the game between two rival companies had been brought to a premature end. Stock shouted his orders and Needham was carried away towards the ship via the gangplank, while Tuffred, who had come round, followed behind with some help.

"Bit of a big caddy-carrier, sir. Anything we need worry about?" enquired Harries as he ran his hand over the side of the vehicle.

During the short journey, Stock had managed to consider why there was such a large store of German equipment and had concluded that there must be a significant enemy presence in the vicinity. Now that Needham and Tuffred were being taken care of, he could concentrate on the consequences of his precipitous action. He told Harries of his suspicions and a runner was sent to Colonel Alfredson aboard the *Lady Oriana*. He turned his attention to other pressing matters.

"How is Wakefield getting on with the repairs?"

"Probably finished by now but he hasn't let us know." Harries looked around and shouted at a nearby squaddie. "Oy, Saunders, go and find someone to ask the chief engineer if we're ready to leave." There was a chain of command and protocol to be followed when requesting information. He turned back to Stock, adding, "Just about the time you left for your game of golf, he found a forge in the old part of town and melted down a few scraps of metal to make a new bearing cap. That was over three hours ago and the last I saw of him was when he disappeared into his engine hole trying not to burn his fingers. Here's the Colonel now, sir."

Colonel Alfredson was accompanied by Captain Lang walking a pace behind him just off to his right. Unlike most of the rest of the part-battalion, who were still milling around the makeshift football field, both were suitably dressed in their 'summer' uniforms. Stock and Harries saluted as they approached.

"Thought you might have something to do with that plume of smoke we saw a little while ago. Care to explain."

"Certainly, sir. But first can I suggest we post lookouts and get the men back onto the boat as there's probably some rather angry Germans about to descend on us. Oh, and I brought us back a present." He indicated the half-track. "Thought it might come in useful."

"See to it, Sergeant, and put armed lookouts on the boat, not on land. Ask the captain if he'd lend us some of his deckhands and, once it's loaded, get the men aboard. I suggest we continue on the foredeck." Alfredson was looking over Stock's shoulder at a growing crowd of locals who were beginning to show an unhealthy interest in their activities. Stock recognized their general demeanor as similar to those who had threatened them in the warehouse. They certainly had the same sort of weapons.

An awning had been previously re-erected on the foredeck to provide shade from the blistering sun which was just beginning to lose its intensity as it sunk lower in the sky. Before Stock apprised the small party of officers of his goings on, he visited the heads and grabbed a couple of bottles of tonic water. This was no time to be adding gin when a clear head might very well be needed.

Stock was the last to join the half a dozen other officers that constituted the 1st Battalion of the 6th regiment of Royal Engineers, attached to the XIVth Army en route to northern India. They had been advised that they would be supplying logistical support in the almost unheard-of province of Assam. The leaders of the other four hundred and twenty-three men crowded around a grubby chart that the vessel's captain had supplied, but it was a hopeless scale that covered most of the South-West African coast, and of little use.

Alfredson looked up. "Right, Stock. Perhaps you'd like to put us all in the picture." He had to raise his voice over the clanking noises coming from somewhere below where the half-track was being loaded.

Once he had told his story about playing golf and how he had errantly hit a ball in the wrong direction, way over the top of a dune, thereby discovering the cache of stores, he gave his opinion that there had to be a sizeable German presence nearby and that they had obviously bribed the locals to help guard it. "I am sorry I did not have time to make an inventory, but there were at least six 88's and about a dozen half-tracks, together with several jeeps and sidecars. Add that to the number of other crates and it all adds up to a brigade's worth. Those two guards we laid out were definitely German and must have come from somewhere close-by. They will have come round by now and are probably hot-footing back to their headquarters as I speak. Even if they are still out cold, someone is going to wonder what that plume of smoke is all about and it will not take them long to figure out where we are. Even if they do not have their supplies any more, they will still be armed."

"What the hell are they doing in the middle of nowhere?" asked Lieutenant Michaels. "After all, we're only here because we had to stop for repairs and there's nothing out there." He gesticulated with his arms out wide. "And you said you saw nothing other than that warehouse when you were trying to find your balls. How can you conclude there's Germans about?"

Stock and Michaels hadn't got along with each other ever since Michaels had discovered that he had been passed up for promotion to Captain in favour of Stock. He took every rare opportunity to belittle his superior. It didn't worry Stock one iota. "I think that is beside the point right now but we have to assume I am correct because if I am, then we are about to be overwhelmed." A fighting unit, even without its heavy weapons, would win hands down every time against an engineering unit.

Alfredson stopped what was about to become another contest between the two men. "Stock is right. We can't take the chance. Michaels, ask the captain how soon we can be underway, and to hurry him up tell him there's some Jerries coming over the hill. Lang, you get your chaps with their rifles lined up on that side of the ship with orders to shout out if they see anyone looking like a

German. Wavertree, you stick by the radio operator just in case. The rest of you, alert your men to the possibility of enemy action. Stock, you come with me. I've an idea."

The officers hurried off in opposing directions while Alfredson and Stock descended into the cargo area where all their battalion's equipment was stowed, together with the surplus for other units. Quite a haul if the enemy managed to capture the ship intact.

"Who was on the machine gun?" asked Alfredson over his shoulder.

"Sergeant Wisley. Good shooting as well."

They emerged through a steel door to see that the half-track was being half-driven and half-manoeuvred with the help of a winch between a D10 bulldozer and another bulkhead. Sergeant Major Harries was shouting coordinating orders at a squad. He kicked at a pile of ropes to see how many ends there were. "Soon have it secured, sir." He'd spotted the pair of them as they entered the gloomy hold, but Alfredson was looking up at the pair of machine guns.

"See if we can't dismount those and have them taken up top. They're the heaviest ordnance we've got. Get Sergeant Wisley to show others how they work."

Stock delegated the task of finding Wisley to a private who looked rather inactive, took a torch from another, then clambered up on top of the half-track through the driver's compartment. He could see the gun was mounted on a circular rail as though in a turret and would be able to fire through 360 degrees. All it would take to remove it was a pair of wrenches to loosen the nut and bolt that clamped through a shaped semi-circular claw. He shouted instructions at a private to get someone else to help him remove the gun and hopped down into the troop area behind, cursing as he caught a shin on one of the many crates that still littered its floor.

"Someone shine a torch down here." It was pretty dark in the hold anyway and, in the recess of the half-track, even darker. Someone produced a paraffin lamp so that he could make his way over the other machine gun mounted on the rear. This one didn't require any tools at all to remove, as it pivoted on a single steel upright, held in place by its own weight and what looked like a giant r-pin. He tugged the pin free and hefted the gun against his body.

"Here, take this and get it up top," he called to the private holding the paraffin lamp. It went dark again. He felt the half-track move under the strain of the man-operated winch and called out for someone to come to him with light and soon found the ammunition boxes, once again delegating their destination to topside.

'At least we now have something decent to fire back with,' he thought. He was well aware that they had Bren gun carriers elsewhere in the ship, but there was no ammunition to go with them. It was on a different ship that had been in their convoy. The MG34, nicknamed the 'Spandau', was a wonderful machine gun produced by Mauser for the German army. Although the bullets were approximately similar in diameter to that of the Bren gun, it had a far higher rate of fire and rarely jammed. Stock didn't know any of this, but the addition of a pair of machine guns to a battalion hitherto armed only with their Lee Enfield .303 rifles would be a definite bonus.

He found his way up to the main deck and temporarily had to shield his eyes from the lowering sun. He hadn't realized how hot it had been in the holds, so took a moment to wipe the sweat away from his forehead.

A private came running up to him and stopped with the briefest of salutes. "Sergeant Wisley asks if you can come to the front of the ship, sir."

As Stock approached, he saw half a dozen men crowding round Wisley who was showing them how to operate the MG. "No orders to fire, sir, but that crowd is becoming mighty restless and there's this chap who seems to be the ringleader. Running up and down and shouting all sorts. Egging them on, if you know what I mean. And the other thing is that there's no way to clamp the gun to the side. Here, look."

Stock instantly saw the dilemma; all Wisley could do was rest the barrel on the side of the ship. He thought someone, somewhere had told him they were called the gunwales but he couldn't be sure. "Get some rope and see what you can do. And don't open fire unless those buggers try to board the ship. What about the other one?"

"Corporal Wally's down the other end of the ship. He'll be having the same problem we do."

Stock was about to ask about extra ammunition but spotted a couple of boxes set against the side. Instead, he looked down at the milling crowd, then over the buildings towards the smoke that attested to his recent handiwork. The sun was behind him. While the ship cast a shadow over the dock beneath, it perfectly illuminated a dust cloud a mile or so away that could only come from vehicles.

"Looks like you will have to do without your rope."

Wisley stopped fingering the belt of bullets and looked at Stock who prompted him to look inland.

"Time to let Alfredson know."

He strode off in the direction of the bridge.

*****

Both Sauer and Hartmann had first gone down towards the burning warehouse but the waves of heat kept them away as one flammable substance or other submitted to the tongues of fire that were still spreading, mainly towards the shore. Groups of locals clustered around injured family. Women appeared from nowhere, crying out for help. Sauer shrugged off one tearful elderly woman who grasped his sleeve. He swore again, swore he would get revenge on the damn Englander who had done this.

"Come Sauer. Let's us get on top of that dune where we can see into the town. They maybe there… In any case, there's nothing we can do here."

Sauer swung round to face Hartmann in a fit of anger. "I'll shove an 88 up his arse and… and…" He calmed down just enough to understand what was being said, glared at Hartmann for a moment and stormed off up the slight incline that led to the top of the scrubby dune that overlooked both Port Nolloth and their depot.

"They're there. They're bloody right there." They gazed down past the ramshackle wood huts and past the more substantial buildings that led to the dock, perhaps a mere two kilometers away. They could see a large ship moored along the quay and just make out people moving but it was impossible to focus on any one thing as the sun was directly in their eyes.

"Where are our bloody troops?" Sauer flapped like an angry penguin and stared back at where their camp was. He was frustrated by the impotency of their situation and stood glaring inland and stamping up and down the top of the dune. He was looking for the telltale dust cloud that would announce that their troops were on their way. It seemed an age but it was in fact only a few minutes.

Captain Melwitz was heading the column of trucks in the staff car. He wisely dismounted when he saw the look on Sauer's face in particular.

"Binoculars," Sauer curtly demanded as he held out his hand. They all stood still while he assessed the situation, occasionally twitching the binoculars one way or another. He couldn't see the quayside adjacent to the ship directly because of the wharf buildings, but he could see British uniforms on its deck. To seize that ship they would need to attack from both ends at the same time. He looked over his shoulder and counted fifteen trucks, each with twelve men in. More were appearing in the distance.

He told Hartmann his plan, "You take the first ten trucks and approach from the north. I know it's longer that way round so I'll give you a five minutes head start and see if we can't coordinate our attack. Wait for my signal. I'll bring up the rest along the main road from the South."

He pointed about a kilometer away at the road that ran north-south and linked the entire South West African peninsular.

"We could wait an hour or so when it'll be nearly dark, "

suggested Hartmann.

"And they might be gone by then. No, I want that ship and I need prisoners. I want to find out how they discovered us here, so we move now."

Hartmann had already foreseen the situation on the quay: his men would fire up at those defending the ship, their bullets doing little damage, while the British fired down upon them, safe behind their wall of steel. And all the while, they had to gain access to the ship which would presumably be ready to repel them. Darkness would have made their job a lot easier but, then again, Sauer might be right and the ship could sail at any minute. Yes, speed was of the essence. He collected Captain Melwitz en route to the first truck. If only they had just one 88, but all they had were their small arms and limited ammunition.

*****

Stock entered the Bridge from the outside starboard door and waited for the captain to finish speaking to Alfredson.

"…and it's no good telling him there's an entire battalion of Engineers on board, he won't have it, however skilled they are. It's his engine room, he's in charge of it, and I'll be the first to back him up on that. No, your chaps can't help him and that's final." Captain Harridge took a breath and stared Alfredson directly in the face, daring him to argue further.

Stock took his cue. "If he doesn't get a move on, he'll soon be in charge of a German engine room. There are truck loads coming down the road from the ridge and another column through the town. They will be here any minute." Before he had stepped onto the bridge he had looked inland once again and seen the column split into two, a classic pincer movement that the Germans were famed for.

Harridge's face hardened. "I'll see if I can't hurry him a little, but he's a spiky fellow…" He turned and disappeared through an internal door - it led eventually to the engine room - and shouted at someone to get ready to cast off.

"This is going to be close. Harridge told me that the Chief needs another hour and in my experience that means two. I've met the fellow and, like Harridge said, he's a spiky chap but he seemed to know his stuff," Alfredson paused to look closely for a reaction from Stock, not as an officer, but as a friend of old, which is exactly what he was. The kind of look when someone says to you 'good luck' just before your brakes fail. "If it looks like they're going to take the ship we'll cut the ropes and take our chances drifting through the harbour. I've already told Wavertree to action that at my command. You keep an ear out too. If only we can hold them long enough."

"Just so long as they have not got anything bigger than machine guns or even light mortars, we ought to be alright but it will be tricky keeping them at bay when it gets dark. Dark… that gives me an idea," Stock trailed off. He shot out of the door to the outer bridge wing and looked at the Union Jack at the stern of the boat. It hung limply, but fluttered just enough for what he had in mind to work. In fact, it would be ideal. He didn't need to ask Alfredson to join him as he appeared at his shoulder.

"If we can spill some oil over the side of the ship and onto the dock and set it alight, the wind will take it directly into their faces and it will force them into the open where we can see them," Stock started to lay out his plan. He didn't need to add that it would have the effect of not only blinding them but also make breathing difficult. "That will make Wisley's job easier." He turned to face the bow of the ship where Corporal Wally was manning the other MG. "And if you look over there, there is not such a wide gap for them to get through and we can concentrate our fire on that point." The unloading area narrowed off the starboard bow where another warehouse had been built closer to the edge of the quay than the others.

Alfredson saw what Stock was getting at and grinned. "You'll be after my job next. You organise the oil at the back and I'll take care of the front."

As Stock descended the steep ladder to the main deck, has saw that Major Wavertree had assembled most of the men along the side facing the docks and had wisely had them sitting down below the level of the open side of the ship, out of sight of anyone on the quay. As enlisted men, they each had a Lee Enfield .303 rifle, which had been standard issue since well before the Great War, but as an engineering battalion - as opposed to an infantry battalion - they did not have copious amounts of ammunition, only what they had personally been issued with in England. It amounted to fifty rounds each. On the other hand, there were over four hundred of them, and that quantity of firepower could not be easily ignored. If each man fired a round every five seconds, they could cover the quay with over three thousand rounds a minute, but only for a few minutes.

"Can I borrow half a dozen men?" Stock asked. He knew the next job of getting a couple of drum loads of diesel-cum-oil from the bottom of the ship back up to the main deck, together with other easily combustible materials, would probably be rather awkward. As yet, he hadn't a clue as to how it would be done, but he'd pick the brains of one of the ship's crew on the way down. He didn't even know if there were any drums on board.

Wisley thanked one of the crew for the sturdy length of oversized rope that he had got from one of the lockers. It was far too long and they had trouble bending it round the barrel of the MG and through a gunwale outlet directly beneath them, but it was all they had at the time and would have to do. They left the surplus dangling down the side of the ship since cutting though it with blunt bayonets was not practical. At the other end of the ship, Corporal Wallis - better known as Corporal Wally for his knack for opening his mouth at the wrong time - was having just as much difficulty in securing his MG. One of his team had found a rusty piece of steel hawser and was busy trying to affix a shackle to it when Alfredson appeared.

"I presume you know how to fire it?" Alfredson asked

"Oh, yes, sir. Err, I think I do. Sergeant Wisley showed us and it seems quite straight forward."

"Well, we're expecting them to come through that gap there any minute now, so make sure you can bring it to bear. Captain Stock is arranging a smoke screen down the other end so don't be alarmed if you see it."

"Are we going to get going soon, sir?" asked an anxious youngster.

"If you mean cast off and get underway, the answer is yes, just as soon as the chief has finished repairs, which ought to be about the same time as Jerry makes an appearance - which is why you are supposed to be looking over there." He motioned with his eyes and head towards the gap. Although had been expecting it, was still a shock to see German soldiers running obliquely behind a rusty traction engine and taking cover. Within a few seconds, more came, about the size of a company, and ran straight towards the gap, but stopped short around the entrance to an open-sided warehouse. He couldn't see Wavertree from where he stood and sent a runner to warn him, just as another company of Germans appeared in the background.

"Hold your fire," he called and went over his preparations in his head just to make sure he hadn't missed anything. Wavertree had Companies One, Two, Three and Four up on deck. Coupled with the two captured MGs at each end of the ship, it ought to make the quayside a very unhealthy place to be. Below deck, Michaels had Company Five spread out and covering any other access including the big side-loading watertight door through which the half-track had been loaded. This was probably the weak point as it was the same height as the dock and, if the Germans somehow managed to get that open, then they could stream aboard. Both gangways had been removed and all that attached them to land were two thick mooring ropes at each end and he had ordered a squad, each armed with at least one axe, to stand by the fairleads, ready to hack away should they be boarded.

He leaned over the side and looked down the far end where other

Germans were amassing and wondered what they were waiting for. Then it came to him: they were going to attack both ends at once. Why wait until they were ready? Where was Stock?

"Open fire!" he bawled at the top of his voice.

Stock had coerced a reluctant crewman to assist, and his party had started to haul a forty-gallon drum of lubricating oil up the several narrow ladders that led to the open deck. It was dangerous work as it weighed nearly a quarter of a ton; should any one of them lose their grip on its slippery surface, then those below stood a real chance of being crushed. He had already sent two men ahead of them carrying a canvas tarpaulin. Once on deck, his plan was to soak it in oil before throwing it overboard and setting fire to it. With a final heave they managed to push it through the last door just as the forward MG opened fire.

"Quick! Roll it over there, out of the way," he shouted at several men from one of Wavertree's companies. Upon hearing machine gun fire, Wavertree had been about to order his men forward when Stock's party made an appearance. Before doing so, he refrained just long enough for them to roll the barrel along the deck and place it in front of his men.

The heavy tarpaulin was heaped about thirty feet from the rear machine gun and they up-ended the barrel on it. With horror, Stock realized they had no means of opening the drum. He looked beyond Wisley at a small group of men standing by the rear most tethering rope. They had an axe. He was about to shout across at the man holding it, but gave up when Wisley pulled the trigger on his MG. He wouldn't be heard so instead sent one of the privates, who was still catching his breath from hauling the barrel, to fetch it.

Within a minute, Stock had the axe in his hand. He was just preparing himself to heft it, when Sergeant Day put a restraining hand on his arm. "Best leave this sort of thing to me, sir."

Stock hadn't had time to consider where his big sergeant had been, but was glad of his interjection now, and almost casually stepped back to allow him plenty of swinging space. With practiced hands, Day struck the barrel squarely about two-thirds the way up. Under pressurization, and warmer than when it had been filled, the golden oil spumed onto the canvas. Hardly had the first drop hit the canvas, when Day swung the axe again, striking the barrel in almost the same spot. This had the effect of quadrupling the flow, but it inevitably started to glug. Day struck the top, opening up an air vent to allow the thick liquid to spurt out further.

Stock meanwhile looked briefly over the side and down the twenty feet or so at the mooring and saw that they would need to throw the tarpaulin as far away from the ship as humanly possible. The gap between the dock and the ship, created by old rubber tyres acting as buffers, was only a couple of feet wide. He didn't want it falling straight into the sea where it would be extinguished before it had a chance to catch alight properly. And that was another problem. They would have to set fire to it up on deck before throwing it down, not the other way round. He told his party what he proposed as the flow of oil started to ease. Once it was alight, they were to throw the lighter barrel on top of it.

As they heaved it up onto the side of the ship, they were aware that the tarpaulin had become considerably heavier now it had had some ten gallons of oil added to it. Stock started to doubt whether they could throw it far enough away from the ship, but there was no time left to reconsider as Wavertree's men had started their platoon fire in response to a rush of Germans.

"Light it." And two privates ready with matches struck them and presented the flaring ends to different parts of the lump-like canvas. Any Boy Scout will tell you that nothing happens at first and this was no different, except that when it did start to catch, with oil dripping onto the deck, it did so spectacularly quickly. They heaved it away over the side as the oil combusted, instantly producing black smoke, and watched as it dumped onto the quayside. Only one corner of it dangled near the water.

Bullets were now singing about their ears and they instinctively ducked down beneath the shelter of the ship's side. Stock counted to ten before standing up and risking a look down at their tarpaulin. He jerked his head back as flames licked up towards him, but he had seen enough; it was well and truly alight.

"Ok, lads. Let's get the barrel over the side," he yelled over the noise around them. Four of them struggled to lift it up onto the side and were about to toss it over when Day shouted again, "Stand back."

He only allowed a second for one of them to move out of the way before swinging his axe into the middle of the barrel at the untapped end and stood back while they continued. But the deck was now slippery with oil and one chap fell as the barrel did little more than roll off.

Stock took the time to look at the ensign that was fluttering a little more than before, and again sneaked another look over the side, but only for a couple of seconds as German bullets were thickening the air. He pictured what he saw as he crouched under the cover of the ship's side and concluded that the smoke screen he had hoped for was yet to come to fruition as most of it was billowing up rather than across. It looked like the barrel had landed on the tarpaulin and would therefore keep it burning for quite some time. But then a slight gust of breeze took it inland a little and he could tell that there were fewer bullets coming in their direction from the lessening of the clangs on the ships side. He took the chance to have a longer look, albeit not at full height.

Day appeared next to him, still holding his axe. "The buggers can't see," he grinned. "And look, the wind's picking up." It was indeed beginning to fan the flames exactly where Stock had hoped it would. The sweet sickly stench of burning oil would be getting into the enemy's lungs by now. Their only hope now was to try and outflank the black barrage but that would bring them directly abeam of the ship and right under Wavertree's rifles. The smoke had even made Wisley cease his firing as he couldn't see anyone to fire at, but occasionally he would let rip a burst as the wind took it in a different direction.

Stock was satisfied that his tactic had worked, at least for the moment. "You had better get back to your axe duty, but keep a sharp look out. They may try and rush around the side and throw grenades up at us. I have another idea. Get those same chaps to get another barrel of oil up front. I will meet them there."

"Right you are, sir." They parted in different directions. As Stock passed Wavertree, he found that it had gone quiet.

"Where are they?"

Wavertree pointed beyond the front of the ship where several Germans lay dead or dying. "Hiding in that warehouse mainly but there's some just behind that steamroller thing. I've got two injured men downstairs but otherwise we've repelled them. What with your smokescreen and my rifles, it seemed to unnerve them. Not surprising really; it would unnerve me. Oh, hello. Looks like they're getting ready for another attack." He lifted his binoculars and Stock waited for an update. "They're getting into a couple of trucks so I suppose they'll be using them as cover until they're right in front of us." He let his binoculars drop to his chest, cupped his hands and shouted, "When those trucks move, aim at the drivers! Aim at the drivers!" He turned and shouted in the other direction too just to make sure they had all heard him. "Alfredson's gone up to the bridge for a better view but, in case he hasn't seen them, would you be good enough to let him know?"

Stock departed and heard Wavertree ordering his men up to the side and to make ready. Nearing the top of the ladder, he looked back at his smoky handiwork which was by now in full flood and hoped once again it would last long enough. Another cloud overshadowed him and he looked up and saw similar coloured smoke emerging from the ship's funnel. It wasn't nearly as dense as his, and he assumed it must mean that the ship was about to get underway. Sporadic fire still came from dockside and he ducked as a bullet whined off the handrail just behind him.

"Ah, Stock, well done with that smoke. Even better news - we are about to leave." He looked past a happy Alfredson at Harridge who was nervously pacing up and down, awaiting his chief's call from the engine room through the voice pipe.

"Major Wavertree's compliments, sir. They're preparing to attack with their trucks from the north end."

The smile disappeared from Alfredson's face. "Better get yourself forwards then. We can't let them win now."

Stock turned to go but something caught his eye in the corner: the Very Pistol locker. He cursed himself in his usual manner for not thinking about the Very pistol as a way of setting fire to the tarpaulin, but he decided one might come in handy, so took one and loaded it. Harridge stopped his pacing "Oy, you can't take that." But Stock was gone.

He arrived at Corporal Wally's MG position and saw that they had been reinforced by a platoon from Waverly's men. He also saw four sweaty men rolling another barrel towards him.

"Have you seen those trucks?" he asked, pointing past the gap.

"Yes, sir. Nosey down there spotted them a minute ago." Wally was referring to a prone man he had posted right at the front of the bow.

"When they move, Major Wavertree's men will be aiming at the drivers, but I want you to shoot out the front tyres. Do you think you can do that?"

"I'll do my best, sir, but if they don't hurry up it'll be difficult to see." They both turned round and looked out to sea where the sun's lower rim was nearing the ruler line of the horizon.

'Maybe that's what they're waiting for,' thought Stock, and he turned to the four-man barrel party. "This time I want it so that it rolls towards that warehouse, so keep it straight when you push it over the side but wait for my command; we may not need it." Ideally, they should have been opening one of the access hatches on a lower deck, but Alfredson had forbidden anyone to open anything where the Germans might be able to take advantage. Most likely it would just land on the dock and not roll anywhere, but at least it was a potential source of fire that might catch the enemy out if the need arose. He couldn't use the same trick as he had done at the other end of the ship as the wind would blow the smoke in that same direction, and not affect the group that now threatened at the front.

They had broken the first attack, some using half their ammunition when 'Rapid Fire' had been called for by Wavertree. Now they were waiting for a more concerted onslaught. They waited in silence but could hear German voices in the distance, obviously being organized by their commanders to ensure success. A shout of command from the rear jerked their eyes away from the massing troops beyond the front. An instant later, the ship's deeper horn drowned out any other sounds and kept going for nearly half a minute. This was the pre-arranged signal that the axe parties were to sever the thick ropes that kept them moored to the dock. Alfredson would probably be telling Captain Harridge that his engineer had better have his repairs completed, otherwise they would be ending up on the harbour wall. He realised that sounding the deafening horn had also had the added benefit of preventing the Germans from issuing verbal commands. When they had made the plan, nobody had thought of that.

The first troops to appear came from the south round the smoke and this time they had donned their desert gear in the form of handkerchiefs and goggles, but they were in plain view of Wisley's MG, which chattered out its deadly missiles. Wavertree had split his command into two with half facing north and the other south. It was the latter companies that now opened fire on the mass of Germans. Almost immediately three trucks started to advance from the north but their drivers never stood a chance with the volume of fire being directed straight at them. One driver managed to duck down and keep going past the others before one of his front tyres blew, skewing the truck so that it flipped over and emptied men onto the quay.

The impasse might have stayed that way were it not for the German rifles that now started sniping from a warehouse rooftop. Almost immediately, the volume of firepower coming mainly from

Wavertree's companies fell away. The first casualty was Sergeant Wisley. With his MG temporarily silenced, the German troops rushed forwards.

From atop, Alfredson looked from one end of the ship to another, praying that his men would be able to keep the Germans at bay a while longer. They were definitely getting closer. He didn't know what they would do once they reached the ship's side, but he answered that himself when he spotted three or more squads coming from behind one of the trucks. They were carrying ladders while the men either side of them were providing good covering fire. He saw with chagrin that Corporal Wallis couldn't depress the MG's barrel enough and he spun to face Harridge.

"What's your blasted engineer doing now? You're the captain so tell him to start us moving and quick. No arguments or we're all done for."

Harridge bent over the pipe that led to the engine room. "Boyson, this is your captain telling you to engage the prop. I don't care if it's forwards or backwards but get us moving. There's Jerries swarming all over the place up here." He turned to his first mate, who was manning the wheel, and barked, "Hard to port. Slow astern."

It was customary for a ship of that size, without the help of tugs, to swing the stern away from the dockside first. Boyson would have known that and probably engaged reverse thrust first. The overriding issue was to enlarge the gap between the ship and the quay, so it didn't matter which direction they moved first.

The first mate handled the brass telegraph lever to 'Slow Astern' and turned the wheel to port. They all waited for confirmation from the counter arrow which was controlled from the engine room. It suddenly jangled loudly, catching them all out. They felt the vibrations as the propeller shaft began to turn.

Initially, the British had the advantage of the higher ground, but with the appearance of Germans on the rooftops - and coupled with their superior numbers - the ferocious firefight was now claiming a significant number of victims on both sides. Hartmann winced at the thought of so many of his men dying. He could see that his ladder details had reached the relative safety of the side of the ship and that the British had to lean out to shoot directly down on them. The first ladder rose and rested against the side and he was relieved to see that it was just long enough. A moment later, the first troops were scaling its rungs just as two more ladders followed the first, either side of it.

In the dying minutes of daylight, he saw a group of men at the top lift a barrel and release it so that it rolled straight down and knocked two of his troopers to the ground. He wasn't to know, nor could he see in the deepening shadow, that the barrel had split and its contents were now disgorging over the thin strip of concrete that marked the edge of the dock. Furthermore, his attention had turned towards the rear of the ship as it started to move away from the quay. 'Last chance,' he thought and urged more men forward to the ladder parties. Running with them, he wondered why no more men had scaled the ladders - after all, there was no reason why they shouldn't be going up it en masse. Only when he slowed as he approached the nearest, and slipped and fell along with some others, did he realize that the area was like an ice rink covered with oil. Only those around the bottom of the far ladder were making any progress. One man was half-way up with another close behind. He looked at his men around him. Any who tried to climb the two other ladders found that they were unable to grip the rungs. There was oil everywhere, coating everything.

Hartmann ran to the unaffected ladder, wiping his slippery hands on his trousers as he went, and pushed a man off the bottom rung, taking his place in a desperate attempt to encourage others to follow him. The man at the top was thrown back and landed on the ground besides him, dying almost instantly, but the man just above him kept going. Hartmann saw him disappear over the edge of the ship. His turn now, and he pumped his legs, slipping as much as anything else. As he did so, he felt the angle of the ladder begin to flatten out. He could sense another man on the ladder right below him, but he could climb no faster. Just as he reached the top, there was a loud splintering noise; the decrepit ladder had finally given in to age and excess weight. He threw both arms out to grab the side of the ship as the ladder disappeared beneath him and was wondering if it would be better to let go when two men above him grabbed his arms and hauled him on board. It was just as well that they had hold of him as his fingers started to slip off the rounded edge; he would have plunged into the dirty sea beneath and suffocated in the oil that lay on the surface.

By now, the stern of the ship was a good fifty feet away from the quay, and gaining more maneouvering space by the second. Under the skilled captaincy of Harridge, the front also began to gather more pace, as did forward momentum. But the Germans continued firing from the dockside, seeing their prey slip away from them quite literally into the sunset. Wavertree ordered the men stationed at either end of the ship to cease firing and duck down behind the protective cover of the ship's side. Those on the bridge didn't have that luxury since they still had to steer the ship out into the open sea without ending up on the harbour walls. The last of the German fire directed at the bridge petered out, but not before it smashed several sheets of glass, injuring the first mate in his right eye. All the while, the vibrations from below deck continued.

As Stock crouched against the side, the first German over the top was hammered into unconsciousness by a rifle butt and two men from his barrel party threw an officer on top of the man.

"I would stay down if I were you." He didn't know if the German understood him, but he would understand that bullets were still coming thick and fast.

Hartmann rolled over onto his knees, slipping on one of them as he did so, and looked across firstly at Stock, then at the too numerous British soldiers around him. Several of them trained their weapons on him, but he noted that Stock had only a flare gun in his hand and was watching him closely. It took him just a moment to realise the purpose of the flare gun. He started gabbling away in German, "Nicht…" He went to stand up but ducked down again immediately as unfriendly bullets clattered off the side of the ship and splintered paint around them. His English was poor, but as an educated man he had a basic understanding. His eyes pleaded with the British officer in front of him. "Please……. do not…… fire." He prayed he had said it right and would save his men.

The British officer smiled at him, hazarded a glance over the side, broke open the gun, removed the cartridge, closed it again and addressed him, "It was only as a last resort." Stock could see the man had clearly not understood him, so he tried again, "Not necessary now," and gestured with his hands. When Hartmann had appeared at the top of the ladder, he had indeed been preparing to fire down onto the dockside It would have committed the large number of Germans who were slithering around in the oil to a crispy grave. He meant it when he said it was a last resort; it would have been particularly indiscriminate and not something he could ever be proud of. He was glad he hadn't had to resort to it.

They waited a couple of minutes or so while the ship gained more distance from the dock and eventually the firing died out. They all stood up.

"Your pistol, please," asked Stock, indicating with his outstretched arm. Hartmann reluctantly went to surrender the one he'd taken from a junior lieutenant not so long ago. His still slippery hand had trouble opening the holster, and Stock took a step forward to help him undo the strap before taking the Luger.

"Oberst Hartmann." The German stood briefly at attention before relaxing back to his previous stance. Despite their enmity, there still remained protocol when surrendering. Stock didn't know what his shoulder epaulettes signified but he knew 'Oberst' was about the equivalent to a colonel in the British army.

"Captain Stock," he replied and also stiffened to attention momentarily.

He turned his back on the German and took a few paces to a knot of men who had gathered to watch the proceedings. "Any of you got any bullets left?" he asked quietly.

"Two, sir."

"Three," piped up another.

"Look after that chap and take him somewhere secure. I will take the oberst to the colonel."

Stock ushered Hartmann up the steep ladder to the bridge. They were passing the sea wall now. He paused to look back at the dock nearly half a mile away. In the deepening gloom of the evening, the glowing tarpaulin was the only real beacon that marked where they had been a few minutes ago. He felt a wave of relief pass over him now that they were out of harm's way.

They entered the bridge as Alfredson was leaving through the opposite door and followed him down to a large cabin that had originally been designated as the captain's Ready Room. For the past couple of weeks since they had left Liverpool it had served as the Officers' Mess. In spite of the steel surroundings and only two portholes to let in the light, Captain Harridge had made them feel at home. He had allowed them to make a replacement sideboard-cum-cocktail cabinet and build a sturdier book case from some teak they had found in the hold. After all, they were Engineers.

Stock now presented Oberst Hartmann to Colonel Alfredson, handing over the German's pistol as he did so. He had already replaced the Very Pistol in its cabinet with a nod of acknowledgement from the second mate. After brief formalities, Hartmann was led away to an adjacent room by two armed privates and locked in it while the Mess filled with the other officers. Reports came to Alfredson on the status of his battalion; eight dead, seventeen wounded (two seriously) and the first mate's eye would probably heal. 08.00 for burial at sea detail.

When Captain Harridge eventually made an appearance at Alfredson's request, he informed them that his very disgruntled chief engineer would not allow revolutions for more than eight knots and that it would take the best part of three days to reach Cape Town, where they would have to put in for more permanent repairs. Oh, and when they were there, would they mind repainting the stern quarter of the ship that had been blackened by the tarpaulin?

There was no formal dinner in the Mess that night, partly because morale was low over their losses, but Sergeant Day had one item of good news: he had a list of items found in the half-track and it appeared that several of the crates that had fallen into it contained food. There was enough tinned pineapple to go round. He left them with a dozen tins.

The officers were dismissed by Alfredson. Just as Stock was about to leave, out of earshot of the others and with only Wavertree left, Alfredson asked him to stay and take a seat. They had all agreed that they had been fortunate to escape but Lieutenant Michaels had raised the point that if Captain Stock had not insisted in trying out his set of clubs, then none of this would have happened. Although he was the only person to see things this way, it couldn't be denied that they had only won by a hair's breadth. Now the seeds of the suggestion that Stock had been to blame for the whole debacle had been sown, Alfredson needed to let Stock know where he stood, and quickly too before rumours started to spread.

"For whatever reason, Michaels doesn't have a very high opinion of you, does he? And don't go thinking I haven't noticed that he takes every opportunity to belittle you. I'm grateful to you for not rising to his comments, especially in front of the others. Wavertree here doesn't think he's going to last very long where we're going, so please don't do anything precipitous… and don't go mentioning that to anyone else." Alfredson took one of the three small tumblers of whisky offered by Wavertree before carrying on, "Whether or not those Germans would have found us had you not chosen to explore the dunes with your golf clubs is beside the point, but I have to write something that accounts for this action by the time we reach Cape Town. I expect your full report by lunchtime tomorrow. From what you've told me so far, it seems we - or mainly you - have inflicted considerable damage on the enemy, which is the real reason why we are where we are. From a military point of view, this probably rates as a minor skirmish, but to us as an engineering regiment, unprepared for carrying out the tasks normally associated with the infantry, it is significant. From my own position as the commander of this battalion, I think you did exactly the right thing, and have set a fine example." He paused for a swig. "And that's what I'll be putting in the regimental records."

Even though Stock and Alfredson were close friends, this sort of talk usually only took place between a colonel and his staff officer, in this case Major Wavertree, but he appreciated that he needed to be included as it would affect not just him.

"I'd like to know what those Jerries were doing in such a desolate place where there's no reason for anybody to be there, so over the next three days - before we reach Cape Town and he's handed over to the MPs - I'd like you to get some answers from our Oberst, gently of course. Butter him up, get his uniform cleaned, invite him into the Mess, that sort of thing."

As staff officers, it would not be appropriate for either Alfredson or Wavertree to be seen effectively befriending an enemy officer, but it could be argued that a captain was acting as a guard.

Stock looked thoughtfully into his whisky tumbler for a moment. "As we are short of space, why don't we start by bunking him up with me in my cabin? It has a spare berth."

"Ok. I'll leave that up to your discretion."

Wavertree leaned forwards. "Hang on a minute. Doesn't an Oberst command a regiment of over eight hundred men, as he would do in the British army? If so, where were the others? From my vantage point I thought I saw another officer with the same epaulettes down the far end of the quay. If I'm right, then there's over fifteen hundred Germans out there somewhere. What we saw couldn't have been more than four, perhaps five hundred men."

Alfredson looked at Stock without saying anything. Wavertree had a valid point. He continued, "And why would a colonel be at the front of a very precarious raid when normally he would be directing them from behind the safety of his own troops? Like the other one I saw."

Stock realised he was being prompted to find this out from Hartmann. He downed the rest of his whisky in one. "I suppose that is what we call luck."

Wavertree spluttered into his glass. "Luck of the devil more like, and if it wasn't for your shenanigans with the smoke at one end and the oil at the other, I expect we'd all be under a jackboot right now. You know, I saw you about to fire the flare gun onto the dock. What stopped you?"

Stock stood up and started for the door. He hadn't had the time to consider the answer to that question yet, but now it came to him. "Although we are at war, I have never killed anyone. I will always avoid doing so unless it's absolutely necessary. To fry twenty men at once for no reason other than the fact I could is not what I have in mind. I could not even see their faces." Before he shut the door behind him, he added, "Could you live with that? Good night gentlemen."

*****

Stock found the two sentries leaning up against the bulkhead outside a locker room. They quickly shuffled to attention as he approached. He looked in and found Hartmann sitting on a pile of dirty lifebelts looking rather sorry for himself. No doubt he'd spent the past hour or so trying to analyze how he had ended up in such an ignominious situation. Stock led Hartmann down one more deck to his cabin. Using pigeon English and gestures, he managed to convey that the German would have the bottom berth and to undress from his smelly and oily uniform. He ordered one sentry to remain outside the cabin, the other he sent to Sergeant Major Harries with instructions that only one guard would be necessary but that it was to be changed every two hours and that the oberst's uniform was to be cleaned, dried, and ready for wearing by 06.00 the next morning. He finally ordered a bowl of fresh water and two plates of standard rations, plus an opened tin of pineapples.

At first, a suspicious Hartmann didn't touch the tray offered to him but did so once Stock sat at his desk and started writing and eating at the same time. After the day's exertions, he found it difficult to express what had happened in such as way as not to betray that all this had come about because he had insisted on trying out the new set of golf clubs he had bought at Lingfield Park Golf Club just before they had been ordered to Liverpool. He found himself reminiscing about the circumstances that had led up to that morning.

The regiment had decamped suddenly from Horne Airfield, first by lorry, then train from East Grinstead into Victoria. They had marched across London to Euston station with only the briefest of halts in St. James's Park where they had been 'fed and watered' as the NAAFI sergeant had put it. The officers' personal effects had been transported by another lorry across London. The journey through the heart of the English countryside was pleasant, if not rather cramped, despite the onset of winter. Their immediate embarkation onto the *'Lady Oriana'* at Liverpool had not provided Stock with any chance to swing his new clubs. The convoy had consisted of about a dozen ships, including a destroyer and a corvette. Once aboard and at sea, having passed through the predictably rough Bay of Biscay and after an overnight refuel at Gibraltar, he had started by whacking his balls off the stern of the ship but soon desisted as he was fast running out of them. Their unexpected arrival at Port Nolloth presented an ideal opportunity. They had been at sea for some three weeks, during which time keeping the men occupied had been a challenge. Apart from the morning and evening roll-calls to see if anyone had fallen overboard, equipment practice and cleaning, the stripping down and rebuilding of lorry engines and gearboxes, they had invented games and inter-company rivalry had helped pass the time. By the time they arrived however, boredom with the monotony was beginning to set in. Oddly, his fellow officers did not show any enthusiasm for golf and so he had offered an excursion to four enlisted men who had not been involved with the football tournament Lieutenant Michaels had arranged. In fact, it was those same four, amongst others, who really did not get along with Lieutenant Michaels, and had suspected that somehow he would fix the games in order to blow his own trumpet.

It would have been easy to report that he had taken a detail inland to carry out a survey of the town's outskirts for future ordnance purposes but he knew Alfredson would frown on that, and in any case, everybody knew the real purpose of his outing. He even considered writing about hand grenade practice with golf balls or using his clubs as ranging sticks but in the end, he decided to amalgamate a survey recce and his golf clubs. After all, they now had intimate knowledge of the terrain just behind Port Nolloth.

Hartmann's uniform duly arrived on time. Stock was impressed with its freshly pressed lines and presumed that whoever had been responsible had probably used steam since it showed up their own uniforms. After breakfast in the Mess, Stock took the German on a tour of the ship, even into the hold to show him their engineering equipment but not into the engine room where he suspected they would not receive a welcome from the chief engineer. It was while he was trying to explain the workings of the Bailey bridge, something that the Germans didn't have, that they were overheard by a crew member who spoke German. He had once been stuck on a Dutch freighter for two years, manned mostly by Germans, and had picked up a fair understanding of their language. From then on, Will Smith from Bridlington accompanied the pair whenever Stock thought it appropriate.

The sea burial service for the nine they had lost was conducted by Captain Harridge. Even though orders had been passed down from Alfredson that the rank and file were not to show dissent against the two Germans, their scowling looks betrayed their thoughts. The hefty German whom Hartmann had landed on when he was hauled aboard was now sporting a very black eye and a head bandage. He was a corporal who Hartmann had not noticed before, but once the service was over, the two had been separated. The corporal was led away to confinement elsewhere on the ship.

With little else to do, ritually the officers usually settled down to their bridge school after lunch in the relaxing atmosphere of their Mess, but on this occasion Alfredson had set tasks for the others which left only himself, Wavertree, Stock and Hartmann. Will Smith had been seconded as their waiter and hovered in the background, occasionally being asked by Alfredson to translate. Bit by bit, and with careful manipulation, the German's story began to unfold. He was careful and wary at first but, with the conversation initially centering on their homes and loved ones, inevitably a few facts came out, even more so when he expressed an interest in the game of bridge. Alfredson decided that a session would be held after dinner that night.

The surreptitious questioning continued over the next two days, providing Alfredson plenty to put into his report, but it wasn't only Hartmann who was indiscreet, especially during the third night when the supply of gin and brandy was severely reduced.

Half way through the fourth morning, a cheer from the open deck announced that Cape Town had been spotted. Stock's initial hatred of the German as his enemy as demanded by king and country, was beginning to evaporate. He was at war with this man. Even so, it had transpired that he was an educated and decent man who would probably spend the rest of the war in a prison camp in South Africa or India where their destination lay.

Hartmann turned to Stock as the grim looking MPs started their ascent of the gangway. "Tell me, were you really just playing golf?"

Stock didn't reply, instead smiled and saluted before turning heel, leaving the German with the anguish of not knowing.

Striding back to the Mess, he cursed that he would need a new set of golf clubs.

Chapter 2

Karachi

The month or so that it took to reach Karachi from Cape Town was hard, at least for the men under Alfredson's command, and that included the officers. It would have been all too easy for him to allow them to laze about and become sunburnt as they passed the large island of Madagascar on their right, across the Equator and through the Arabian Sea to arguably Britain's foremost port on India's north-west coast. Stock also had time to reflect upon his military career to date as he lay in his bunk and totted up that he had so far destroyed considerably more than he had created. This was not why he had joined the Royal Engineers and he ironically considered if he would have done better by joining a bomb disposal unit. He still felt that his natural aptitude for building and creating things would be best put to use once they reached India and rather looked forward to being able to explore parts of that vast continent that he had only ever read about. He relished the opportunity to put all those practical ideas he had had on his Family's Norfolk farm to good use, hence his volunteering to join a construction unit rather than a fighting unit.

With the sun directly overhead providing heat, and Alfredson directing which machine was to be brought on deck for dismantling and re-assembling at the other end, competition between companies intensified. Deck quoits, volleyball, nightly quizzes, Morse code tests all helped to pass the time. This included swimming lessons in the makeshift pool that had been erected on deck. Captain Harridge put the exterior of the ship out of bounds when he spotted a pair of men climbing along each side of the outside of the ship in a race to the front. On the day they crossed the Equator, he presided on deck as King Neptune from a gantry that appeared to have no other purpose, and having primed the officers as to what to expect, selected half a dozen men from the winning company who were to endure the ritual.

"It's called Pollywog Day and we normally only initiate those who haven't crossed the equator before. Oh, I know we passed it on the way down, but our hands were a bit full then." He referred to the constant worry and lookout for German surface raiders as they sailed south past the West African coast. Now that threat had receded in the relatively friendly waters off the East African coast where only a pirate would be mad enough to challenge them, they could relax a little more, without distractions. Alfredson sat on the captain's right as 'Davey Jones'. Two of his crew either side made up King Neptune's court, dressed in grubby green suits and wearing mop heads. They dished out the punishment the poor men had to endure for daring to enter into the underworld of the sea. Harridge looked the part, donning a spikey crown made from brass and holding out the heavy trident also made mainly from brass which glistened in the bright sunlight in one hand, while nurturing a plaster mermaid on his lap. The six men were stripped to their underpants, covered in black boot polish and salt and tested to see if they could cross the pool, which had been filled with rotting and slimy food, using just a 4" pole. Inevitably the pole moved when jiggled from either end and none of the six managed to stay out of the smelly garbage. They were then hoisted onto one of the hold covers and hosed down. It was all good humoured fun which continued when one chap threw an eggshell at another who retaliated with some banana skins. Soon the entire compliment was dipping into the pool of rubbish and throwing it at each other.

Each evening in the Officers' Mess after supper, the customary bridge rivalry took place, just as ferocious as the enlisted men's activities during the day. It became clear that Stock had found his ideal partner in Alfredson. So much so that they were banned from partnering each other for the rest of the voyage, and instead rummy was as often as not called for. At first, the main topic of conversation was their narrow escape from Port Nolloth but, as time went on, speculation as to what part of India they would be sent to, dominated. A few nights earlier and under the influence of export strength spirits including pink gins, Oberst Hartmann had let slip their plans to occupy Cape Town and had become abusive when he realised what he had divulged. He even challenged Stock to a duel to ensure his silence, not realising that there were others in the Mess who had overheard his comments, but soon settled down in a rueful heap in one of the chairs. Nobody in that room could have known that, in the forthcoming half-century, those two thousand German soldiers, together with their offspring, would become the legendary and fractious mercenaries of Angola that were to plague the central African States.

"They wouldn't really have been able to take Cape Town, would they?" suggested Lieutenant Michaels on the first night at sea as they sat round the long table for dinner. They had spent just three days tied up alongside a jetty, taking on supplies while the chief engineer carried out a proper repair of the ship's propeller shaft bearing caps. The convoy they had left England with had departed a few days before they arrived, and they now had orders to proceed to Karachi on their own. As the two most senior officers, Alfredson and Wavertree had been the only ones to be granted access to the base's headquarters just off Strand Street.

It was Wavertree who responded, "Oh, I don't know. From what the colonel and I saw there were hardly any preparations for an attack from any direction, just a few sandbags round the guard post. From what we gleaned, there's only half a battalion acting as garrison, and those who we did see seemed rather lethargic. Nothing like back home. I think Hartmann might well have succeeded. After all, to these people this war is miles away and in another world. Why should they care what happens because it certainly isn't happening here, or at least it wasn't until those Jerries turned up."

Michaels couldn't be faulted on his blind loyalty to England and continued this line of conversation typical of someone of that ilk. "Perhaps at first, but surely the people would have been press-ganged into supporting our garrison and then there must be a South African army around here somewhere."

Alfredson decided to intervene and put an end to Michael's speculation. "You have a lot to learn, Lieutenant. Firstly, most of South Africa's army is fighting for us in North Africa at the moment, secondly I estimate our garrison in Cape Town to be only two or three hundred men, thirdly there's quite a ground swell of opinion that South Africa ought to be siding with the Germans and it wouldn't take much to sway the populace. Lastly, it only takes a relatively small military force to take over an entire country. One only has to look at the example of our destination, India. If you remember your history lessons at school, for decades the British and French fought for control of the entire sub-continent of millions, yet British dominance is only assured by a few thousand soldiers and some well-placed men. No, Wavertree is right, because if Hartmann had managed to move on Cape Town, his two thousand men would have taken over the entire region and, worse than that, it would have severed our safe link with India. Don't be too eager to jump to conclusions until you are certain of your facts. I think we should all be grateful that Stock here came across their depot, because otherwise the city may well have fallen to them. Without arms and ammunition, they are now toothless. Can you fill me up?" He briefly turned away from Michaels to ask the duty barman for another gin.

It was a double put-down for Michaels to be told that he was wrong, and that Stock had, albeit unwittingly, secured Cape Town's continued loyalty to Britain.

"Who knows what we'll end up doing in India. I hear they want to rebuild the railway down to Hyderabad so maybe that's where we're headed, but I also hear that they need some airfields in Assam. Until we reach Karachi and receive our orders, it's pure speculation, but when we do receive them, I expect you all to be professional and carry out your duties efficiently. Remember, it's us few thousand that will be setting an example to an entire nation. By the way, Stock, talking of constructing things, what's that thing your chaps are making in the hold?"

"Well, there are two projects on the go. One is a universal machine gun mount which any gun up to about a .50 calibre can be fixed to, the other I am making for Harridge so that he can load and offload quicker through the side access. It is a cantilever that does not require the current pulley system, but we will not be able to try that out until we reach Karachi."

"Now, that's exactly the thing that keeps men busy and keeps both body and mind active." Alfredson paused and looked at Michaels for a moment but decided against asking him what he was up to as he already suspected the answer. There was no point in demeaning the man further in front of Stock. He had also set a challenge that the day before they were due to reach Karachi: whichever company had made the most useful kite would receive bonus points on top of the football challenge scores. All in all, by the time they reached Karachi, he hoped that they would be a well-formed unit, capable of carrying out the tasks that were to be given to them.

They smelt Karachi before they saw it in the hazy pre-dawn. Wavertree even went down to the galley to see if the cook was having problems, but all became clear as they squinted into the rising sun. They could see rows and rows of drying fish on wooden frameworks, adjacent to the docks.

"Looks like we're having fish for the next few days, then," Commented Day as he stood next to Stock.

"I prefer kippers but those do not look anything like I have seen before."

"Cod'n'chips for me any day of the week. Soaked in vinegar. Parents took me to Cromer for my tenth birthday and I remember the vinegar dribbling down the pages of the Cromer Chronicle and dripping onto my new trousers. I got a real thick ear from my mum. Look, you can still see the scar where her ring caught it." Day shifted his head towards Stock who noticed the small indent. "Didn't put me off though."

Stock recalled when his parents had given him jellied eels on one of their numerous visits to the coast and how they hadn't told him about the 'hard bit' in the middle. "Well, we had all better get used to how they fry their fish here. Probably no vinegar though." He slapped Day on the shoulder. "Just make sure when they billet you that you are up wind of that lot."

"Thank you, sir."

Stock went down to the hold to check that his off-loading contraption was ready for securing in place when the side door of the hold was opened in a couple of hours or so. That's how long he reckoned, with the help of a tug or two, it would take them to dock. He took the opportunity to write a letter to his family. Without mentioning names and places, he described their rather tedious journey round the Cape, also adding that his new golf set had come in useful. He had started to write to Mary but had screwed up the several letters as he really didn't know the best way of portraying his feelings for her. With little time left before they docked, somehow he found it easy to let her know how much he was looking forward to receiving a letter from her. He then made sure all his belongings were secure and ready to be transported to wherever they were going before returning topside. As he left his cabin, he noticed that the door to one almost opposite was slightly ajar, the one that berthed two Lieutenants, one of them being Michaels. He was about to close it, assuming it had not been closed properly in the first place, when he detected muttering from within and quietly took one more step to put him in a position where he could just see inside. There was someone sitting on the bottom bunk and although he couldn't see most of the torso, the legs and hands clearly belonged to Lieutenant Michaels, one of those hands held what looked like a three-quarters empty Booths gin bottle at an angle. The muttering continued and he decided to stay still but out of sight for the moment and listen.

"Bastard... stupid... fores...," mumbled Michaels. Stock

couldn't hear much, but it continued for a minute, only interrupted when the gin bottle was lifted. The man was clearly depressed and seeking solace by way of gin, and Stock wondered if he ought to just let him alone. But they were about to disembark, and his men would need their officer when it came to their turn. Furthermore, it would not do Alfredson or the regiment any good if one of their officers was seen to be drunk on parade. He slowly pushed the door wide open and saw a dishevelled Michaels propped up against the cabin wall, quietly muttering to himself while staring into middle space. It took another minute and a swig for Michaels to notice that he was no longer alone, and his baleful eyes eventually focused on Stock in the doorway.

"You. It'ssh all your fault. Why don't you bugger off back to your farm in… in… wherever. If it wasssn't for you I'd be the captain now and quite rightly too. I wouldn't have gone wandering off into the African countryside and dug out a hornet's nessht. I wouldn't have shet fire to the dock and we wouldn't be going to BLOODY INDIA." His slurred speech betrayed his inebriated state and he tried to jump up and confront Stock, managing to catch his ear on the sharp edge of the bunk above, but instead slumped back down and covered his ear with his hand. Blood trickled through his fingers.

"Thissss bloody cabin is against me and always has been. Doesn't like me being in it. I shuppose you've got an answer for that as well, mishter bloody know-it-all. Or are you going to cuddle up to your buddy German and asshk him. GO ON… GO ON… ask the ruddy kraut what he thinks of being stuck on this schtinking ship."

Stock stood his ground, taking the insults without emotion, staying silent and watched as Michaels took a long pull of the almost empty bottle. He was trying to decide if he ought to help the man or lock him in his cabin, but he never got the chance. Michaels finished off the bottle, swung it so that it shattered on the iron frame of the bed, and tried once again to get up and instead sprawled into the desk opposite and ended up on the floor.

"Come here, you bassshtard, and I'll show you how a real man fightssh." He got on all fours and heaved himself upright using the desk with one hand but still holding the broken bottle in the other. Stock wasn't worried as the drunk officer in front of him tried to step forward but fell over sideways, knocking himself to the floor again and crushing the bottle with his own bodyweight.

"YOU SHOD. YOU CAN'T EVEN FIGHT CLEANLY," he screamed at the top of his voice.

It was enough for Stock, and he stepped forward, turned Michaels over and took away the bottle from under him. It had cut his arm slightly below the elbow. 'Why should I help you?' he thought. 'All you've ever done to me is try to put me down and no doubt will continue to do so.'

"Everything alright, sir?" A voice from behind made him turn to look at the door where Sergeant Major Harries stood.

"Not really, Sergeant. Can you give me a hand?"

They got a struggling Michaels to his feet and sat him back down on his bunk but were thanked by kicking and foul swearing.

"I don't think we can do anything for him this time, sir. He's turning violent. I've seen it before."

"You mean he gets drunk regularly?"

" 'Fraid so. Just last night we had to rescue him from the pool. Gets roaring drunk most nights."

"Oh, God, I never knew." Stock was genuinely concerned. His fellow officers knew Michaels knocked it back but never to this extent.

"Um, we tried to keep it quiet, me and the men, but we don't have any respect for him any longer and it wouldn't surprise me if the colonel doesn't know about it by now. What do you want to do about it, sir?" He looked at him as though there was one thing only that ought to be done. It took only a few seconds for Stock to come to the decision that Alfredson must be told. It would look bad in the records if the man was discharged for being drunk and could have even worse consequences for him; it would blight the rest of his life.

"You wait here for the moment, I will see what the colonel suggests. And try to sober him up," he added as he left the cabin.

*****

It was only the tall wire fence surrounding the docks, re-erected recently by another engineering company, that saved them from the local fakirs that hovered around its perimeter. Some clung on to the diagonal strands. Hundreds of them including children. The view from within the compound made it difficult to separate them from the genuine traders and their stalls beyond, that seemed to surround the entire docks. There were some who were legitimately allowed inside the big secure area, and they tended to their fetch and carry duties with diligence. There were patrolling guards on the inside there to ensure that it stayed that way, otherwise unloading their kit and equipment from the ship would have been impossible. The distraction of swarming locals proved difficult to the newcomers at first, but bit by bit over two days they managed to unload the ship which left for another dock almost as soon as the last item was gone.

Their temporary wooden barracks, although clean, were nowhere near the standard they were used to, and other than the officers, the entire regiment slept their first night on loose Indian soil. This was where had caught up with the rest of the brigade under the popular command of Brigadier General Hector Hobart-Smythe. Despite the fact that the enlisted men were not allowed outside the patrolled perimeter, local produce had inevitably found its way in, through a system of bartering with those the other side of the fence. Cigarettes, partly because they were one of the few items that fitted through the criss-cross wire, became the spontaneous currency to such an extent that the price of a packet soon rocketed.

It was no accident that Karachi was the main rail head in the northwest of the Indian sub-continent. Trying to emulate the British principles of industrialisation and trade, in 1859 the Indian civil leaders approached Sir Henry Frere, then governor of Bombay and renowned for his engineering prowess, to head a project to create the first railway linking Karachi to the interior of the vast region. It didn't take long for the wealthy investors in the East India Company and other luminaries of the then expanding British empire, to approve such a scheme but it took nearly five years before the track to the city of Korti was completed. Simultaneously, and the real reason why the line was constructed, a branch line was connected to the newly built docks, providing instant access from ship to train, thus minimising export costs, and those wealthy investors started to rub their hand with glee as oriental goods of all descriptions began to arrive in quantity in London.

The end of that branch line was where three trains now sat, the front engines quietly huffing and puffing occasionally, as they waited for their loads of men and military equipment, while the rear ones seemed to be sleeping. Their fires would be stoked before they reached the steeper inclines of the interior. As well as the aroma of drying fish, spices, obscure vegetables and the inevitable odour that accompanies hundreds of thousands of inhabitants, an air of expectancy permeated through the men who finished loading on the morning of the third day. Their comments to each other betrayed their eagerness to be away from the hot and almost airless city. The three heavily laden trains would depart in convoy across the very wide and fertile flat plain, irrigated by the River Indus. Unfortunately, it was also irrigated by the ablutions of over a million inhabitants of that part of India. Even though they had all been lectured on the consequences of drinking anything but that which was officially supplied, some of the rankers were already suffering from loose bowels. The price of toilet paper had gone up.

They learned from Alfredson that their regiment was allocated to the first train as they would be going the furthest east to Assam, while the other two trains were destined further south to the Ganges delta. It was likely to take them more than a week to cross over the top of the Indian continent to the terminal of Dhaka. Whereas on the ship free movement had been easy, this part of their journey would be cramped and rather unpleasant. The only exercise anyone would get was at the frequent stops when the engines needed to refuel with coal and water, and not only water for the steam furnaces that powered those engines, but vast quantities for the men, together with rations. It was not quite a logistical nightmare but it tested the British supply lines to the limit. Even as their train released its brakes and struggled away from the sea, they saw another convoy of ships approaching the docks. At least now there was a breeze that cooled them and provided much needed relief from the heat.

It was only the lieutenants who had to share berths. A carriage had been assigned for the officers, decorated with wooden panelling and oil filled lamps with armchairs at one end and a dining table at the other, creating quite a relaxed atmosphere. There was even a wooden shelf of books in a glazed cabinet. At one point during their journey, Stock took the opportunity to read a particularly boring but useful work by Jerome Bartley about the different types of tree that grew in various parts of India. What really interested him was their differing uses, so he memorised it as far as he could as he knew it would come in handy sooner or later. After all, they were heading for a jungle where trees would probably be the most likely source of construction material.

The previous night, Alfredson, along with other senior officers of the battalions, had attended a farewell dinner in the almost typical colonial building that served as headquarters, hosted by the incumbent base commander, Brigadier General Withers. The invitation was for lieutenant-colonels and above. Eight of them now sat round the remains of a five-course dinner and leaned back into their chairs while the decanter made its way round the table. They gained more insight into what the Imperial General Staff had in mind for them. Ever since the ignominious fall of Singapore a few weeks before, it had been stressed that no one, but absolutely no one, could discuss anything remotely connected with military matters outside of that room. The discussion inexorably centered around actions taking place in Burma and in the general area they were heading towards.

The large dining hall with its slowly revolving ceiling mounted fans provided just enough breeze to keep the flies on the move. Once the servants had been ordered out, and straight after the toast to the king, Withers pre-empted their questions.

"Yes, I can confirm you will all be heading beyond the eastern branch of the Ganges and not as previously ordered. I've received news that General Alexander has just ordered the evacuation of Rangoon and will be re-grouping around the city of Imphal. This is strictly confidential, but you'll soon find out anyway as your orders will be delivered to you in the morning before you depart," he affirmed and indicated the staff officer sitting on his left. "Colonel Grieves here will answer any further questions tomorrow but suffice to say that we're on the back foot right now. If the Japs manage to break through to Dhaka, then the entire northeastern frontier into India will be open to them. Just about the only thing going for us right now is the onset of the monsoon in a few weeks."

The newcomers had all heard about the monsoon. Although it had been described to them by others using words such as 'torrential', 'devastating', and 'incapacitating', none of them really had any idea of its crippling effect on that part of the world. In England, a torrential downpour might fill up the ditches for an hour or two and delay the cricket match until after tea, but in Burma it lasted for months. Driven by the Southern winds, trapped by the haughty Himalayas, and agitated by the high summer temperatures, for about three months every year from June or earlier, the heavens open. The rainfall was not measured in inches, but feet. Along with irrigation ditches and water-holding areas, houses and even entire villages could be washed away by mud slides so numerous that one needed a slide rule to count them. Even building on stilts half-way up a decent hill was often not sufficient as the quantity of water surging past would quite literally take the ground from under one's feet. But the indigenous population were used to it and accepted it as their way of life. On the one hand, the destructive power of water would take life, but on the other, it also provided life to the flora and fauna and, in particular, the paddy fields which provided their sustenance. It also incapacitated military movement to such an extent that no tracked vehicle, whether armoured or merely transporters, could move even a few feet from the road. And that was assuming that the road had not been washed away.

It was hoped that the oncoming rains would stop the Japanese advance through the jungle terrain, while the British brought up reinforcements by train from the rest of India. And that was assuming that the tracks had not been washed away.

The option of transporting men and equipment by air was also discarded very early on as there was neither the number of aircraft available, nor the fuel, nor the pilots. In any case, when the time came to land, the runways would have probably been washed away.

From the British military perspective, the monsoon presented the greatest problem that they had yet come across, while the Japanese were used to it and had carefully planned their timing around it. To a dispassionate onlooker from outer space, it would have been obvious but, to the unprepared British, what was an initial irritation was fast becoming their nemesis and needed to be dealt with - urgently. Otherwise, the jewel in the crown of the British empire would be lost. If India fell under the control of the Japanese, Australia would not be far behind.

Which was why vast numbers of troops and equipment were being sent by ships, halfway around the world.

Withers continued, "I am afraid that most of the news you've been picking up through the press is true and that the Japs really are spreading through Burma. They're like a cancer, destroying anything that doesn't look as though it might be useful to them, but they don't seem to care about upsetting the locals and this seems to be their weakness. For example, ever since the Indian delegation was captured and murdered by them in Singapore last month, we've had no end of volunteers come forward to enlist, but it's taking us longer to train them and organise them into fighting units. Your job,

Gentlemen, will be to ensure that the roads, bridges, railways and airfields are kept open so that we can transport the several hundred thousand men and their equipment to where they're needed."

He paused to sip from his glass and allow what he had just said to be absorbed. "On the bright side you'll have thousands of volunteers to help you do this. Believe me when I say you'll need their help, for when the monsoon hits, only men will be able to work where machinery cannot. Conversely, watch out for some Japs masquerading as locals as they have already infiltrated some areas, but so far they haven't managed to do much as they stick out in the local communities. There's been serious rioting and deaths in Calcutta driven on by sympathisers, no doubt financed by the Japanese. It's a serious problem. They call themselves the Indian National Congress and they do have significant power in certain provinces."

"Are there likely to be saboteurs?" asked one colonel.

"Only in the towns and cities at the moment, but who knows where they will pop up next. By the way, watch out for counterfeit currency. Although there's about 15 silver rupees to the pound, which is divided into pies, they're worth less than a farthing, and they're so poor here hardly anyone outside of the commercial areas can earn even one in a year - that's if they've even heard of money in some places. You can tell a forged rupee by its weight. Grieves will show you the difference."

"How many Japs are we likely to be dealing with?" asked the same colonel.

Withers shifted in his seat and delayed his answer a little, inadvertently showing discomfort at the question. "We're not really sure but it's certainly in excess of the five divisions that are currently working their way up the Burmese peninsular from Rangoon."

They all did a mental calculation to convert this number into men, which varied from fifty to eighty thousand, depending on how well maintained each division was.

"Alexander is keeping them at bay while he prepares his

defences around Imphal. It's the control of the coastal railway that seems to be the main Japanese objective and they've split their forces to pursue this. At the moment, your fuel and other supplies will be routed through the port at Chittagong as well as the route you gentlemen will be taking tomorrow, but I think you'll be safe until you near the frontier. By the way, talking about safe, I read your report on your excursion into South Africa. Do you think Cape Town is now safe or have they other forces in the area?"

They all looked at Alfredson and eagerly waited for him to reply, "We didn't actually interrogate the captured colonel. Well, not in the true sense of the word. One of my captains plied him with enough brandy to turn him into a walking distillery and he let slip what they were up to." They all chuckled at the age-old trick, even though they had already heard about the incident." Poor man was beside himself when he realised what he had said, but unless there was another brigade that he didn't know about, I think it's safe to say that Cape Town is securely in allied hands for the time being. By the way, he was a decent sort of chap. What's going to happen to him and his corporal?"

The authorities in Cape Town had considered it better if the two Germans were eventually imprisoned in India rather than locally, as they claimed that they did not have the facilities there, but really it was to stop rumours spreading. Two MPs had been detailed to accompany the Germans across the ocean.

"At the moment they're sweating it out in one of our jails, but due to be moved to our internment camp tomorrow." Withers stood up. "Here, talking of brandy, would you care to join me in the billiards room next door?" His invitation left no doubt that he expected them all to accompany him.

As they walked through the double doors and across the wide corridor, he took Alfredson to one side to ask, "Your captain, he wouldn't happen to be the same captain who I've heard blew up the fuel depot in Dieppe, would he? The same man who destroyed the arms dump at Port Nolloth?"

"Yes. Captain Bernard Stock. Why do you ask?"

"If he's the right sort of chap, I might have a small job for him before you leave tomorrow."

*****

A startled Stock was woken by Alfredson's batman while it was still dark, and he accompanied the man to General Withers' office. A sleepy Stock didn't notice the march, but the walk cleared his head of sleep and by the time they arrived, he was fully awake and wondering why he had been summoned. He didn't get the chance to wonder for long as he was shown straight in and saluted in front of the general who sat behind his desk. "Stand easy." He relaxed a little as the command indicated that this was no disciplinary matter, but Withers was eyeing him up and down as if deciding if his outward appearance really portrayed what was within.

"This is strictly off the record, and I assume you are a discreet fellow," Withers began.

This was certainly not the sort of line of conversation Stock was expecting, and it took him a moment to prepare an answer. "I've already been made aware of the official secrets act by an admiral, but I am afraid I cannot talk about that, sir."

It was a counter that Withers was not expecting, and he immediately smiled at the retort before starting to explain, "Perfect, and well done for your little escapade in South Africa, but what I have in mind requires a bit more subtlety. We have a problem here in Karachi. There's a nest of Germans passing themselves off as Dutchmen, whom officially we cannot touch because they have strong links in the community. I suspect you are rather ignorant of local Indian politics, and I won't bore you to death with the ins and outs, but suffice to say that we, us British, cannot just go and arrest them, even though there's only a few of them. If we were seen to act against them, it would likely stir up a hornets nest. The civic leaders are looking for exactly this kind of chance to rid themselves of what they describe as oppressive British rule. I'd love to go in there with a squad of men and have them locked up, but the governor has forbidden me.

"So, what we have is a building that houses some half a dozen or so Germans, who irregularly radio information about our movements to who knows where. I know this because I've listened into their morse transmissions and had them translated. Just last week one of our chaps found that the telephone exchange had been tampered with; it looks like they've been listening into our telephone conversations, God knows for how long. We haven't got a big intelligence section here as Karachi is considered a bit safer that other places on the other side of the country, so we rely heavily on the communications section to keep us up to date. Take the blackout we had last month. It was evident that one of the transformers had been sabotaged. It was easy to fix the following morning, but it cut off the supply to the police station and meanwhile someone had removed certain files, files relating to civil unrest cases.

"It's all down to these bastards. I suspect they have some small arms in their nest as well, so any attempt to arrest them would probably be bloody, noisy and more than a damn nuisance to the governor, hence the need for subtlety. I need to get them out of there and destroy their radio transmitter but I cannot ask anyone under my command, however secretive I may be. I have neither the calibre of man nor one whose face is not known around here and my only chance is to ask a loyal outsider - and they don't exist. Do you get the picture?"

Stock did. Withers allowed him a few seconds to digest the situation before continuing, "You see why I cannot ask our sympathetic locals under any pretence whatsoever to ransack the place. The minute they started, there'd be just as big a faction of anti-government dissenters trying to stop them, and we'd soon have a full-scale riot on our hands. I know there's little time as your train leaves in a few hours, but I'm asking you to have a look and see if you can't come up with some idea as to how we might rid ourselves of these blighters. Even if someone did accuse us of orchestration and you of sabotage, effectively drawing us into a lose-lose situation, you'd be long gone on your way to Assam."

That dreadful feeling you get when you're left with little choice but to attend to some unsavoury matter returned to Stock. From his perspective, he could either be a scapegoat - and lynched if he succeeded - and the same if he failed. Withers had altered his description of what had to be done from 'having a look' to 'having a go' soon enough. He was half tempted to rebut any suggestion that he, as a mere captain and newcomer to the city, would be able to help, but that was not in his nature. Besides, when a general officer asks you to do something, it inevitably turns out to be more of an order. He could clearly hear his old sergeant major shouting on the parade ground, 'I need three volunteers. You, you and you.' Withers hadn't even asked him to volunteer. Oh. God, here we go again.

"I'd need to look at the place first, sir. Do they patrol or have a lookout?"

Withers smiled again. "Not that we know of. I think they rely on their local supporters letting them know when something is coming their way. What have you got in mind?"

Stock looked at his watch. 03.00 and still nearly three hours before sunrise. "Can you get one of your men to show me where it is? I'd like to suggest we change into civvies. I think two army officers wandering about the streets at three o' clock in the morning would definitely warn them that something is about to happen."

Withers' smile broadened. "Better still, I'll show you myself. I haven't been for a night-time stroll outside of here for a while. Here, follow me. One of my suits ought to just about fit you." Withers was about the same height but a little more rotund than Stock.

Ten minutes later found Stock searching for an extra hole that didn't exist in the belt but, if he puffed his stomach out, they just about stayed up. He saw Withers put his revolver into his waistband, but when he came to do likewise with his own, he discovered that gravity tried to lose it down his leg, so put it in his right jacket pocket and covered its protrusion with his arm.

"There won't be too many people about at this time of night, but they have eyes everywhere. I'm hoping we will pass as European traders. Try not to walk too tall and certainly not in step with me."

They passed two sentry posts, Withers speaking to each in turn, advising them that they would be back shortly. As they left the outer one of the two, they overheard the corporal muttering something to his comrade about how desperate their commanding officer was.

Withers laughed. "If they think we are going out for the girls, that'll add credence to our cover and help quash any rumours, but I'll have to have a word with them when we get back. Make sure the wrong sort of rumours don't get back to my wife."

"Perhaps we ought to have brought a bottle as well?"

"Are you trying to get me into trouble?"

"I think we are both doing that very well by ourselves. How far is it?"

"Oh, about fifteen minutes, half-way up a small hill. Oy, break step." Stock had automatically fallen into step with his superior.

"Sorry, sir. Habit."

Neither of them could see very much under the half-moon and the only other light came from the rare utility building. Leaving the civilised and paved part of the city, Withers initially led them along a wide tarmac road. Stock was glad he had Withers as his guide as he couldn't imagine finding the place in daylight, let alone the middle of a dark night. Crickets, frogs and other unseen creatures called to each other and helped disguise their footfalls. Barking dogs somewhere in the distance continued their all-night-round duty and the occasional tinkering of a bell reminded them that goats also made up a fair proportion of the locals' diet. They took to the shadowed far side of one street to avoid a group of locals whose voices betrayed their presence and crossed over a half-tarmacked piece of road into a grove of trees that surrounded a small square.

"This is about the only decent road in this direction and our main link to the northern states. Your railway line runs just over there."

Stock peered into the gloom but couldn't see anything much, other than the outline of buildings and trees. "How long have you been here?"

"You know, I've not actually counted, but it must be getting on for a year or so. Only spent one Christmas here. Why?"

"Nothing important. Just wondering what it must be like to spend quite a significant part of one's life in this part of the world and have local customs rub off on you. After all, I cannot see this war ending that quickly and no doubt I will be closeted away somewhere in the middle of nowhere for the next year or so as well."

"I think you're asking me if I know my onions. Well, I can assure you it's worth it. Getting to know the locals is really quite worthwhile. They have a fantastic sense of humour. They're understandably savagely protective of their own, so not easily swayed unless the price is right. And you have to bear in mind that half of these fellows have been taught to believe that their duty in life is to rid themselves of the British yoke. The other half spend their time belittling the other half, particularly the Sikhs and Hindus, but that's another problem. Given the chance, one half would kill the other half and then there'd only be Muslims left. I can't but help feel we've got a tiger by the tail, although so far in the main we've managed to keep the peace. I consider us to be like the Romans. We've introduced electricity, hospitals, railways, and so on, but all they seem to do is try and get rid of us. Here, down this road. We're nearly there so hush. I don't think they give roads names round here, but I think this one's called Azam something or other."

The latter part of the road had been steadily rising up to that point and now became steeper. With the help of light spilling over from a large municipal building on the corner, they entered a gravelled road that sloped gently back downhill. With a quick look round to see if anyone else was about, Withers stopped in the faint shadow of a gnarled tree and gestured, "Look there. That's the building. First one down."

It was similar to others on the opposite side of the road. More of a bungalow but with the addition of another room in the roof space through an external stairway. A small passageway separated it from a row of almost identical houses that continued as far as they could see, which wasn't far. It looked like it was clad with wooden shingles and the porch was made from stone. More importantly, there was no sign of any light from within.

"What's behind and above it?"

"There's nothing there. It backs onto one of the reservoirs. They used to have a clear line of sight to the bund, but the plants grow so quickly around here when the monsoon hits it's a constant struggle to maintain it. One of the local markets is just across the road and there's a constant trading war between traders here and those in another market not too far away. Our problem is that these chaps are the ears and eyes of our German friends."

"Can we go and have a look over there?" Stock pointed to the gap between the reservoir and the bungalow.

"Certainly, but let's go round the pumping station," Withers suggested, indicating the far side of the municipal building. "Quietly."

Returning the way they had come and circling behind the building, they could clearly hear the constant hum of electric motors. Withers made sure they stayed in the shadows. On their right was a large earthen bund that Stock presumed to be the rim of the reservoir, interrupted only by a large sluice gate, and ahead was what appeared to be a corridor of open ground that ran behind the buildings parallel to the gravel street they had just been standing on. They stopped by the sluice since the sound of trickling water would usefully cover any noise they might make. Stock cupped his hands either side of his eyes to improve his night vision. Withers waited a while before commenting, "I know what you are thinking: if we could make an accident with that sluice gate, would the water behind it be enough to flush the buggers out? We've already thought of that one. The answer is yes, it would, but once again the Governor has pooh-poohed it. It would not only be too obvious but also starve this half of Karachi of water and then we'd have water riots on our hands. Besides which, they'd probably only set up elsewhere."

Had it been light enough, Withers would have seen the forlorn look on Stock's face as he looked around. He was thinking exactly that.

"Wait here a minute, sir." Stock disappeared for three or four minutes. He nearly made Withers jump when he silently returned. "I have an idea. Wait here again."

Five minutes this time, and Withers didn't know in which direction he had gone, but his reappearance nearly came as a shock once again. "Ok, sir. I have seen enough. Well, felt enough really. I am afraid I slipped over and probably ruined your suit. Back the same way?"

Wither waited until they were well past the pumping station before asking, "Well, come on then. What have you got in mind?"

"Can you wait until we get back to HQ? I am still formulating the plan, but I think it will work. Just one question for now -what time is our train due to leave tomorrow? Oh, em, I mean today?"

There was just a glimmer of the oncoming day on the horizon.

"12 noon I think, but knowing how efficiently the station masters can be, it wouldn't surprise me if that turned out to be more like 13.00."

It took Stock a little longer to undress than Withers, since most of the suit he had been wearing was wet. Withers picked the trousers up using forefinger and thumb and dumped them on top of the jacket in the corner of his room. "I'll have to have a word with my batman about this just to make sure other rumours don't start circulating. Now, tell me what you're thinking."

They were seated alone in his relatively bright office. the fan above them slowly revolving. Without warning, Withers picked up a stout leather swat and whacked it down on the flat of his desk. "Haaaa. Got the blighter." And he flicked the remains of a fly off to one side. The crack of the leather made Stock jump as he hadn't been looking in the right direction at the time, but he wiggled himself into the seat of the wooden armchair in front of Wither's desk.

"I have been working under a few assumptions so correct me if I am wrong. You're still holding the German colonel and his corporal?"

Withers nodded.

"Where?"

"In the military jail at the moment, just across this compound."

"Good. Have you any plans for them?"

"Yes. They are due for temporary transfer to our internment camp about six miles from here, a suburb called Malir, not far from the airfield."

"And how would you normally transfer this kind of prisoner?"

"We haven't had any German soldiers before, only political prisoners. If there's only a few, we take them in a truck, sometimes accompanied by another if there's more. There's a security detail in any case."

"How many have you got tomorrow?"

"I'm not sure, but I can find out. No, wait a minute, I think there's still those chaps from the docks who we arrested just before you arrived. Say five of them."

"Enough for two trucks?"

"If you want two trucks, no problem."

"How about three?"

Withers nodded, his head off to one side. "More if necessary."

Stock mused for a little, rubbing his hand over his unshaven chin. "I take it you have a hospital here?"

"As a matter of fact, it's almost adjacent to the jail, but only for military personnel."

"Right…….this is what I propose……."

*****

Withers sat playing with his swat as he watched the door close. He heard Stock marching down the short corridor and the sentries clip to attention as he left the building. Without realising it, he was beaming from ear to ear. 'Mischief' he thought. 'This'll give them a bit of mischief.' He hadn't had so much fun since he'd arrived in Karachi and was positively looking forwards to what would transpire over the next few hours. He'd have to keep a straight face of course when the accusations came his way, but it would be worth it, and with a little bit of luck, there wouldn't be a shred of evidence. It would be the sort of story he wouldn't be able to tell anyone about until the war was over. Well, maybe his wife. He spied another fly investigating the side of his desk and exuberantly had a go at it. "Haaaa!"

Stock hadn't heard the "Haaaa" as he was too far away by then. Even if he had, he wouldn't have registered the death of yet another fly. He was too busy thinking through the intricacies of his plan to notice such minor things. He hardly noticed that the sun had risen as he marched back towards his billet and certainly didn't notice the hustle and bustle of men moving the last of the equipment into the train's carriages. He reached his wooden billet and sat down on the side of his bed, held his head in his hands and continued going over the plan, step by step. He realised that the timing was going to be rather fine. That was his biggest worry. He reached over to retrieve his pencil and a pad of paper and started doodling a sketch of the site, inserting pointers and, on the far right-hand side of the foolscap page, a schedule of times. He had to re-work the timing again and again to get it right. Once it was completed, he sat back with closed eyes and went through the entire operation in his head again, all the while considering contingencies, of which there were few.

He dozed off but only knew it because later Sergeant Day told him he had. He jerked awake to Day's voice, "Colonel Grieves outside to see you, sir."

He looked at this watch and automatically wound with his right hand, noting it was 07.00, the time he had arranged with Withers that Grieves should attend. "Ask him in, will you, and stay outside until I call you in."

"Yes, sir."

The middle-aged, bespectacled Grieves adjusted his eyesight and left the door open to let more light flood in as he entered Stock's little den. Medium height, medium build and generally uninteresting, Stock's first impression of Grieves was that this was a man who would do well in a managerial position in a firm in the city. As it turned out, Grieves had decided to make a career for himself in the army and was well-suited to the role of a staff officer. He was rather efficient at it.

"Reginald Grieves and glad to meet you," he offered, holding out a hand before Stock had a chance to salute. "Call me Reg. Saves time."

"Bernard Stock. I suppose you had better call me Bernard."

"Oh, I know you're supposed to salute me because you're the junior officer but apparently not on this occasion. I haven't seen the general almost jumping for joy for a long time and he told me I was to put myself at your disposal. Highly unusual and he wouldn't tell me anything more, just that I was to be discreet and not tell anyone else about it. So, tell me more. Here, do you mind if I sit on your bed? Been getting too much cramp in my right foot lately." He helped himself.

Stock thought it better if he didn't join Grieves on his bed and remained standing. "I am not surprised the general did not tell you much because he needs to remain at arm's length. He cannot be seen to be involved should anything go wrong. I think the same applies to you, but what we have got in mind requires the authority from an incumbent senior officer and I presume the general chose you because he trusts you."

"Oh, we go back quite a way and you're right there. There's stories about the general I could tell you, but then again that would be rather indiscreet of me, wouldn't it? So, let's dispense with the whys and wherefores and get on with whatever you want me to do. I've delegated this morning's duties, but we've got another convoy arriving shortly and I need to make arrangements."

Stock realised Grieves was telling him that, although he would comply with his general's order to carry out Stock's orders, he was only happy to do so for as short a time as possible. He decided to be blunt. "The general asked me if there was a way to get rid of your Germans up by the water works without any come back on you and without causing a riot. I have found a way, but I cannot go round the compound ordering your men about. Only you can. The plan is straightforward but needs delicate timing and will not involve more than a handful of your men."

It was awkward telling a colonel what he would need to do, yet he had some comfort in the knowledge that General Withers had approved his plan. Still, he was in no doubt that, if it all went wrong, he would probably be on the next boat back home.

"Oh, those ruddy Germans. They've been a thorn in our side for months. I'm listening."

"Before I call in Sergeant Day, I need to know that your men will carry out your orders, however odd they might be."

"I don't think that'll be any problem." Grieves almost took this to be an affront to his leadership qualities, but the hope of ridding themselves of the Germans overrode any offence.

Once Day had, on Stock's order, come in and shut the door behind him, Stock continued, "We are going to blow up a house full of Germans, hopefully destroying their transmitter in the process, and make it look like one of their own is responsible. To do this we are going to use both of the captured Germans from South Africa and their half-track. I take it they have not seen your face?" This to Grieves.

"No, but I know they are in the cells at the moment and due to be transferred later this morning."

"That is what I am relying on. Everyone expects this transfer to take place. What time this is scheduled for?"

"In the past we've left at all hours, but normally at 10.00 hours."

"And can you confirm that the route you take goes right past the water works?"

"It does. It's pretty much the only route available to the internment camp."

This was the final piece of information Stock needed. They huddled round as he showed them the layout of the area surrounding the house which he'd sketched it on his piece of foolscap and started to elaborate, "OK, we will take four vehicles in convoy along the usual route. The first truck will contain the other prisoners - those you have already earmarked for transfer - together with the security detail in the back. Make sure that the flaps are down so they cannot see out. Sergeant Day and I will be in the next truck; that is the half-track He will be dressed in the German corporal's uniform and driving. Anyone who might be looking on will see a German driving a German vehicle and, if they look more closely, they will see a British officer sitting next to him. The third truck will be seen to be driven by two of my Engineers. It needs to be my Engineers because shortly afterwards they will be on the train to Assam, as will Sergeant Day and I, and none of us will be available for questioning. You, Colonel, will bring up the rear of the column in a jeep with only Colonel Hartmann for company. I take it you won't mind driving the jeep yourself and without an armed guard?"

"Not at all. Carry on." Grieves voice betrayed scepticism.

"It is perfectly natural for one colonel to accompany another colonel; an equal rank courtesy. Even if it is just to the internment camp. This is important as Colonel Hartmann will be our main witness. You will need to hang back a little, a hundred yards or so ought to do it, and if he asks why, say it is to avoid the dust cloud from the truck in front, miss a gear or something like that. Just make sure you are far enough away for Hartmann to see what is going on but not so close that he can pick out detail. The trick is to make it look like the German corporal - I cannot remember his name - is seen to be driving the half-track. This is vital, because it will divert off the road, catch fire, and explode as it hits the house."

His pause allowed the inevitable question from Grieves. "And why would it do that?"

"Because our 'German' Corporal Day here will clearly be seen trying to escape by onlookers. This is why you must hang back. It is about a hundred yards from the main road to the house in question, and you will come to a halt on the road about here," he pointed on his sketch with his pencil. "This is the same point where Day's truck will have left the road."

Grieves and Day looked worriedly at each other, but Stock continued, "This is just the outline of the plan so far and I'll go over it all again once I have finished. Now, here is the tricky part. Just before the half-track hits the building, I will set the fuse for the explosive that will detonate a few seconds later. With the front of the truck partially embedded in the house, when it does explode it will destroy the building and hopefully the radio that is hidden in there. Sergeant Day and I will naturally jump out of the truck before it impacts and run back to where the third truck has stopped. The third truck will initially follow the half-track but stop just by this small hut here next to the sluice gate, about half-way between the road and the house. My two chaps will jump out of the right-hand door, the side away from you and Hartmann, so that they cannot be seen by him. All eyes will obviously turn to the exploding half-track and this will be our compelling distraction. Meanwhile, our German corporal - that is you Day - will look like you are running away in a dazed state and disappear behind the third truck where you will join our two engineering friends and myself. The uniform you are now wearing will be in the cab of the third truck. Ok? Out of sight, my two engineers will take the real German corporal from the third truck and put him back into his uniform before placing him in the hut with his feet just visible from outside. Us four then get back into the third truck and go off in search of an escaping German."

Grieves was frowning and Day looked uncertain, but it was Grieves who asked how an unconscious German corporal was going to co-operate by being in the right time and place and not know what was going on.

"That is the easy bit." Stock was considering whether to keep them wondering and possibly leave them to work it out for themselves, but it was clear that neither of them had fathomed that part of the puzzle yet. "Shortly before the convoy leaves, we take the two Germans to the hospital, ostensibly for a check-up and a Malaria jab. This will involve them stripping down to their underwear. Hartmann will go in first, get his jab, and then be escorted by you Colonel straight to the jeep. Make sure it's parked some distance away so that Hartmann can't make out Day's features clearly. The corporal will see his colonel come out of the examination room looking fit and healthy and not suspect anything, but instead of giving him a Malaria jab, the doctor gives him morphine or something similar, so that he is then out cold. I am sure one of the doctors will be able to prescribe a suitable dose to keep him unconscious for at least an hour. Out of common sight, we put him into the cab of the third truck dressed only in his underwear. The half-track will not be in line at this point but parked at the far end of the compound and away from the other three. While you are sitting next to Hartmann in the jeep, Colonel, you will say something like 'he here comes now', just to make sure he sees his compatriot getting into the half-track. I will already be in it, but one of your armed squaddies, who has not seen the German corporal before and does not know what he looks like, will be marching him from the hospital."

Stock had turned over a leaf and was drawing out a rough copy of the compound on another sheet of paper.

"Afterwards, it will not matter how much he protests that it was not him who tried to escape nor that he cannot remember driving the half-track into someone's house, because there will be two colonels there to say that is exactly what he did. There will also be some locals who will have seen the incident and word will spread that it was all caused by a German in a German vehicle. More importantly, the Germans masquerading as Dutchmen in the house may not see the initial impact of the half-track hitting the building, but they will certainly see a German corporal running away. Whatever else they see it will not be for long, as the explosives in the half-track will soon divert their attention and they'll be busy trying to get out alive. They will be left with only one conclusion as to what happened. Just for good measure perhaps we can put some smoke grenades in as well."

Day was grinning in anticipation. He had been thinking that he was about the same size as his German counterpart. He only hoped that the boots would fit easily.

Grieves had a look of incredulity on his face. At first he was left speechless, his mouth open. Then he spoke, "You thought up all this by yourself and the general approved it? No wonder he doesn't want to be involved, it'll never work."

"Yes, it will work. It is a simple matter of deception." He could see Grieves was struggling with the concept of the entire operation. "Look, break it down into separate parts from the outset. The first is convincing Hartmann that his corporal is in the half-track, that is simple enough. Ok?"

"Er, I'm not sure the hospital will have what you need and…"

Stock wasn't about to tolerate a list of negatives from Grieves and put a steely edge to his voice. "Stop right there. I am not interested in what might not be possible and what cannot be done. This is something the general has charged me with, and I will be dammed if I cannot see it through successfully. I can see ways through problems whereas you just see barriers. I can go round or above them whereas you just divert off in another direction." He moderated his tone for the next part. "It is not your fault since I know the Luddite kind of establishment you are up against, and it alters the mind-set to think only along certain lines. Too much bureaucracy and pressure from other quarters may limit your options as a staff officer, but when something like this comes along, one has to find a way through the quagmire of military dogma. This falls outside that framework. Trust me when I say it will work."

Stock hoped Grieves would realise that his rebuke was aimed more at the establishment rather than the man and he let him mull it over for a few moments. "Alright?"

"Alright. Go over it again."

"From the start, then…" This time, he divided it up into sub-operations. The hospital visit, the march to the half-track with the armed guard pointing his rifle and in Hartmann's line of sight, the order of departure, the spacing and positioning of the vehicles on the road and, at the site, the crash and explosion, the subsequent 'escape' of the 'German corporal' and change of uniform, and finally their departure.

"Remember, Colonel, all you have to do is distract Hartmann at the appropriate times. You have the easy job with a grandstand view, it is Sergeant Day and I who will have the hard part."

Now that the operation had been sliced up into smaller parts, Grieves saw that it would probably work and felt more comfortable. "But it all depends on how accurately you can make the half-track go up. I've never dealt with anything larger than a hand grenade, but I know explosives can be tricky."

"All we need is a grenade and some fuel. Believe me, Sergeant Day and I know all about this, don't we?"

"Certainly do, sir." Day scratched his head with both hands as he was apt to do when getting excited.

Stock looked at his head. "I think you're going to need a visit the barber. A nice short back and sides, German style."

Day stopped his scratching and mournfully looked up as though he could see his hair.

"You see, little touches like this help." Stock was addressing Grieves who nodded in approval.

"Now, since nobody else in the camp will know anything about this, we will have to maintain the subterfuge, so do not warn anyone about what is happening, particularly the guard who will accompany Sergeant Day from the hospital to the half-track. You and I will go and have a word with the doctor shortly. First though I would like to go through the timings again."

It took them a further half an hour to iron out the plan and address minor points such as fuel cans in the cab section of the half-track. Perhaps Grieves could add a distraction and drop his lighter on Hartmann's lap when offering him a cigarette as he was watching Day impersonate the German corporal marching across the compound. Perhaps they should have a few reels of barbed wire in the back of the third truck as an excuse for delivery to the internment camp. Grieves didn't think there were any smoke grenades in the armoury, but would a bundle of oily rags suffice, and which way was the wind going to be blowing? Stock made another sketch of the house and surrounding area and was glad when Grieves asked to borrow the pencil to add a couple of lines indicating where he thought the first truck ought to stop. "Just a little bit further on as the reservoir bund will prevent anyone accidentally seeing your chaps when they change uniforms."

With the door closed and the rising sun beating down on the roof, the temperature within was becoming unbearable and sweat was apparent on all their faces. But they were at last finished and they re-congregated outside.

Grieves had totally changed his tune and was now eager. "Just one last item. You and your Engineers will still be in the third truck when it's all over. While I take Hartmann to the internment camp in the jeep, he'll think you've gone looking for his corporal. Go to Drigh, which is just past the airfield. It's a rail stop for locals. Your train will be passing through and I'll tell the driver he's to slow down enough for you to hop on and vanish from the scene."

Stock agreed and between them, preparatory jobs were allocated. Day went in the direction of the half-track while the other two marched over towards the hospital, all the while Grieves describing the orientation of relevant buildings and the direction they would be driving through Karachi. "Look, there's the jail. Oh, damn, I'd forgotten about the MPs." He spotted a pair of red-capped Military Police talking to each other. "They'll not release the Germans without a written order from the general. Their captain is especially unlikely to." He thought for a moment without breaking stride. "I'll arrange that after we've seen the doctor."

They crossed the open space towards a large white building which was in dire need of re-painting, the red cross on its wall portraying its use. Stock looked up. "Park the convoy just over there but place the half-track on the other side. That way Hartmann will be looking into the sun a bit more."

They found Captain Doctor Miller sitting with his feet up on his desk. He looked up from his files as they appeared in the open doorway. "Good morning, gentlemen. Neither of you looks very healthy so come on in."

"I forgot to warn you that Doctor Miller is renowned for his sense of humour." Grieves didn't attempt to lower the sarcastic tone of his voice. "Overrun with patients again I see."

"You chaps just don't understand the strain us educated types are under. You've no idea of the nefarious ways we manage to keep your bunch from itching, and no, I cannot hand out any more, we're running out of it." He referred to the persistent stream of men who came to see him after visiting the local whore houses.

Grieves ignored the jibe. "I hate to disappoint you and cause you any more anxiety than necessary but we're not here for that." He went on to explain what would transpire in an hour or so and, once he had finished, Miller slapped his files shut and stood up.

"Well, that's more like it, but I wouldn't use morphine. Oh, no, that'll just make the fellow delirious and if he's the violent type - and I presume he is - he'll only struggle and wreck the place. No, what we need here is something like a Benzedrine based substance, but we haven't got any of that. Ketamine would probably do the trick and I know we've got some of that here. It's usually reserved for animals and the like. He'll wake up with a thumping headache, but it'll certainly lay him out cold. Doesn't smell either so he won't suspect anything."

"Just so long as it doesn't kill him. Now, let's have a look around and find a suitable room for your, shall we say, administration, preferably nearer the back door so we don't have to carry him too far."

The telephone on Miller's desk rang. "Excuse me." He picked it up and listened. "It's for you." He held it towards Grieves, who also listened.

"Yes, that's correct, You may release the half-track to Sergeant Day and give him anything else he asks for. No, I haven't written the order yet. Yes, give him as much fuel as he wants. And oil. No, don't bother removing the ammunition or the guns. No, it doesn't need a service before it leaves, just let him take it. Yes, right now."

"That was Lieutenant Forbes, our eager newcomer. Pain in the backside but at least we get clean jeeps. Now where were we? Oh, yes." He handed the phone back to Miller.

They selected one of the examination rooms off the corridor towards the back of the building and left Miller in no doubt as to what had to be done.

"You're off one of the ships that docked the other day, aren't you?" he asked Stock.

"Yes. Why do you ask?"

"I've a couple of your chaps in the ward and, as you're here, perhaps you'd like to have a word with them."

Stock looked at Grieves who responded, "Time's short, but you've got a couple of minutes, I suppose."

As he entered the open ward he saw half a dozen occupied beds and heard a voice cry out, "Hooray, here's the captain." He looked over at where Needle and Thread had adjacent beds. It was Tuffred who had spoken out and was sitting on the side of his bed, apparently talking to Needham. The latter was still looking rather ill from the operation that had removed most of his arm. Aware that he had very little time, he told him he thought they would be going back home on the next available ship but that the regiment had been ordered to Assam. They were rather lucky that they wouldn't have to put up with all those gnats back in England. He wished them the best of luck, apologising that he couldn't stay longer.

Outside, Grieves suggested Stock return to his hut and prepare himself, while he would go and obtain authorisation from the general for the release of the Germans. "I'll collect you and Sergeant Day in, say, forty-five minutes. That will give you time to pick the two men you have in mind to drive the third truck. Oh, I'll leave you to square things with your colonel. I must say, I'm rather looking forward to this."

Stock was aware that he needed to shave and as he marched off towards his hut, the noise of an approaching vehicle made him turn his head. Day pulled up alongside him in the half-track. "Number thirty-nine stopping at all points near a pub. Hop in, sir."

The city of Karachi hadn't really cooled down much during the night, although the quickly warming land forced a breeze to develop from the ocean, bringing relief to the mild humid atmosphere. But the day was warming up in more way than one. Alfredson had shown no surprise at Stock's request, wished him luck, and suggested he pick the two men from Lincolnshire in Michael's old company, one having been recently promoted to corporal replacing the loss of one from the firefight in Port Nolloth. Corporal Ford and Private Cooke needed no encouragement as it meant that they were excused loading duties. Once Stock had explained what they would be doing, he made them go over the plan by repeating it to each other in turn. He left them with a sketch of exactly where they needed to be when the half-track veered off and was beginning to regret that he would not have a chance to show them precisely where, in advance. Even though they both assured him that they understood the importance of stopping right next to the sluice hut at an angle that would cut off any view from the jeep behind them, it still worried Stock.

But it was now too late to do anything more about it. From his shaded view from the half-track, he saw a grim-faced MP escorting Day towards him. One of his fears was that Day would look nothing like the German sergeant, but even in the bright sunlight, and parked less than a hundred feet from the hospital, he had to look twice. Without showing his head outside of the window, he glanced over at the jeep and saw Grieves point in Day's direction. There was no reaction from Hartmann. He looked down at the floor where there was a bag full of grenades at his feet, hoping that the MP would not want to look inside. The man held out a clip-board stiffly for Stock to sign, officially taking charge of the prisoner. A salute and an about turn was the last Stock saw of the MP and he thanked God he didn't have to have much dealings with their ilk.

Grieves hooted his horn twice, which was the pre-arranged signal for the lead truck to leave, and he watched Stock engage gear to fall in behind him. Within three minutes, the barrier to the docks was being lifted and the convoy was en route. Stock sighed. So far so good and grinned as he looked across at Day and commented cheekily, "Proper haircut, then."

"Now don't you start. I've got to live with this."

Stock yanked the wheel to avoid a stray cow that was threatening to impale itself under the front wheels. Their initial route took them the long way around through one of the busiest parts of Karachi. Although the roads were wide enough, the number of people milling about slowed their progress. Now that there was little more to do, it was at this point that Stock began to have doubts. He went through the process again, picturing in his mind how it would happen and what to do if anything went wrong. It would all happen very fast with no chance to stop and think of a way round any glitches. And if it all went wrong, then he would be responsible for the riots that would probably ensue.

As they entered a narrower street, his nose caught the waft of cooking, and the spiced food made him realise he had not even had time for any breakfast, but he quickly put that thought out of his mind. It would have to wait. There were no mirrors on the half-track, and he didn't dare lean out and look round to see how far behind the third truck was or if Grieves and Hartmann were following in the jeep. He wanted to stay hidden until they needed to make their hasty exit, but he did look down at the heap of rags behind him that surrounded a large open pot of tar. So soaked in oil were they that they exuded a powerful smell which until they had started to move, threatened to overcome them. Day leaned forward and checked the satchel crammed with grenades. They both watched them jiggle about as the front axle crossed a shallow drainage gully across the road. Day picked up one in his right hand and practiced putting his index finger through the ring.

"Not long now." He told Day as he recognised the small square they were passing, and he looked down again at the rags, wondering exactly where to lay the grenade. He looked up and saw that they were about to pass the road that they need to take.

"HEY, turn now." 'Christ…….. that was close' He thought with horror. 'Nearly missed it'. As he predicted, things happened fast but he was glad to see there were a few people about, going about their daily routines, some just sitting around with nothing better to do. These were the people who would later swear what was about to happen and if gossip was the same in India as back home, then the excitement of the crash would soon turn out to be an incredible event in their normally mundane lives. The truck would be going three times the speed, the bang would be heard from miles around, the flames would be twice as high and more vivid; there would be no end to what the spectators thought they saw. Stock noted, and as he had assumed, there was nobody in the area where the third truck would stop. He held his arm out half in front of Day, directing the angle at which the half-track should strike the house and for the second time in less than ten seconds, horror returned, trying to stun him into inactivity. "Brace yourself."

It couldn't have been more than ten miles per hour, but it felt more like fifty as they rammed into the back of the wooden structure and despite their arms and legs doing all they could to lessen the impact, succumbed to the sudden stop of forward motion by bouncing off the dash board. Without the help of a wheel to hang on to, Stock's head impacted with the windscreen, knocking his hat off his head and momentarily stunning him, but he looked at his right hand and saw he had less than seven seconds to exit and get away……..that was how long the delay on the hand grenade fuse was, because horror smacked him in the face like a sledgehammer and he subconsciously started counting.

Six. The seat next to him was empty and Day was gone.

Five. His senses returned and he tossed the grenade over his shoulder and threw open the door.

Four. He nearly fell over as his right foot touched the ground, his left already taking the first pace of a sprinter.

Three. The half-track was behind him now and he saw Sergeant Day ahead of him, leaning forward and arms pumping up the incline of the hill towards the truck that had just come to a stop in a cloud of dust. He thought he heard a cry from somewhere but he didn't turn round to see where it came from.

Two. He noticed that he still had the pin from the grenade in his left hand and he wondered what he ought to do with it. He also noticed for the first time since his exit from the truck that tar was dripping down his left sleeve.

One. Although a faster runner than Day, he felt he wasn't gaining much on him, but the truck was not far away now and Day was nearly there.

Zero. Nothing happened; at least not to begin with. He was expecting a big bang, but he heard the grenade go off and half-a-second later a much bigger bang. The tossed grenade acted like a primer for the rest in the satchel, and it took that half-a-second before the inevitable reaction took place; then there was a big bang and he felt the percussion push him forwards. He stumbled a few feet short of the front of the truck and it was just as well that he did as a flaming piece of debris landed just to his left. He got up and directly ahead in the shadow of the side of the truck saw that Day had already started to undress while Ford and Cooke were manhandling the prone German ready to receive his uniform. Another explosion from behind made him turn round and a wave of heat swept over his face. Though the thickening black smoke, he saw flames licking higher and higher, eagerly seeking out the house to consume, and with satisfaction saw a bulk of timber that looked like it might have once been from the eaves, fall down and bounce off the top of the remains of the half-track. People were running and a small crowd was gathering on the far side in the middle of the street, but with chagrin, he saw that from nowhere, buckets of water were appearing. Thinking about it again, he couldn't see that a few buckets of water were going to be able to douse what was now becoming an inferno; even if anyone could get close enough to administer it.

Before he turned back and trotted to the shaded side of the truck, he looked towards the main road and saw Grieves struggling to contain Hartmann in his seat in the Jeep. He hadn't thought of that one but was relieved to see that Grieves had him under control. Later, when he thought back on the situation, it would have been a perfectly natural instinct to try and rescue one's compatriot, but that hadn't occurred to him during his planning stage. He weighed up the angles and distance that the Jeep was from the truck and was satisfied that nobody in the Jeep would be able to see what was happening behind it and peeked a glance over the bonnet in that direction just to make sure.

The German's boot laces were now being tied up and Day was dragging on his trousers. "Give us a hand and open the door Sir." Ford looked up as he finished buckling the belt.

It took Stock a moment to realise he was being asked to open the door to the hut no more than ten feet away and held it open as Ford and Cooke lifted the deadweight of the German sergeant into it and dumped him on the stony ground within.

"Is he still alive?"

"Oh yes Sir. You can feel he's still warm." Ford volunteered.

Stock leaned down and adjusted his body so that one foot protruded when the door was pushed to, but it automatically opened fully again. He bent down and jammed a small stone under it, turned and took the few steps to get into the front of the truck. It was a tight squeeze with the four of them and as Ford released the clutch to turn the vehicle round to point back in the direction from where they had come, Stock ducked his head below the dashboard, dragging Day with him.

"We don't want Hartmann seeing us." That was something else he hadn't thought through and he silently cursed at his own error; but it would only be until they were on the road again. It wasn't for long as Stock peered out of the windscreen and told Ford to stop by some tall grass that obscured them from the scene they had just left. He got out and walked the few feet to the side and gazed down the hill, focusing easily on the main attraction. The gentle on-shore breeze was angling the billowing black smoke towards the adjacent building, preventing his assessment of the extent of the fire, but it looked like it was also alight and quite rightly, the crowd whose primary instinct was to try to put out the fire, was now easing back beyond an invisible circumference, away from the inferno. He felt, more than saw the others join either side of him and they stood admiring his handiwork, drawn by the primeval urge to watch fire.

Despite being nearly half-a-mile away, Stock focussed on the crowd encircling the houses nearest the sluice hut, and thought he saw the door being opened; sure enough the knot of people bought out the body of the German sergeant and laid him with his head propped on the rise of the bank just behind it. He was even more pleased to see that Grieves and Hartmann were approaching.

With a final look at the house which was spuming sparks high into the air, he turned to the others. "Time we were leaving I think……. And well done all of you."

"Proper job Sir."

He was getting used to Day's typical comment and returned his grin. "Yes sergeant. A proper job. Now, let's catch a train."

*****

The station at Drigh was hardly recognisable as a station, not at least to the Englishmen who were more used to the painted picket fences that surrounded their own countryside equivalents, and it was only by chance that Sergeant Day spotted a very corroded metal sign hanging sideways by one nail on a telegraph pole. There was a miserable looking corrugated tin shack with an awning that looked as though it was about to collapse next to a decrepit wooden ramp that was once used for herding animals into freight wagons. In fact, the best shade from the hot sun was in the back of their truck, and they rolled up the side canvas to benefit from the almost non-existent wind. Stock was thirsty but none of them had any water as they had all left their equipment behind. It would be on their train which was due to arrive in an hour or so and they sat in the back of the truck swapping their own versions of the extraordinary events from which they had just come from.

"You probably didn't see it, but the end part of the roof just disappeared over the house next door," Cooke was explaining to Stock and Day. He swung his arm in an arc by way of illustration. "And then the window nearly took your head clean off, sir." He was referring to the debris that had landed next to Stock. "If you hadn't have fallen over I reckon it would have had you."

"And then the door of the half-track disappeared into the house, taking out the side wall. That was something else watching that just go like that. Did you feel that heat? Like someone opening an oven door," Ford added.

"I don't suppose either of you saw if anyone made it out of the building?" Stock wanted to know.

Both Cooke and Ford shook their heads. "Couldn't see round the front and we only had a few seconds to get Herman out. Bleeding kraut was heavy."

Stock was about to ask if that was his real name but decided it was their nickname for anyone German.

"Do you get to do a lot of this sort of thing, sir?" asked Cooke. "Because Foordy and I heard you and the sergeant blew up half of Dieppe. And, well, you've got a bit of a reputation. The lads sort of look up to you as someone who gets things done. Like today, for example. If you don't mind me asking?"

Stock didn't mind and corrected the misconception that only half of Dieppe was still standing. It reminded him of their desperate escape from the much larger inferno that he and Day had caused at the oil depot. He was ingratiated to hear of his reputation directly from one of the rankers but didn't let it show. They were killing time, Day taking the opportunity to retie his boot laces correctly, when Stock's heart lurched as he saw a jeep approaching. He initially thought it was Grieves with Hartmann next to him, but as it neared he saw it was General Withers driving with a sergeant next to him in the passenger seat.

Day interrupted, "General approaching. Everyone out. Line up." They were out and lined up next to the truck before the jeep stopped. Stock led the salute as they stood to attention. Without his hat he felt naked in front of the general.

Withers acknowledged their salute as he walked over to them. "Stand easy, everyone. Nobody injured, then. Good. Stock, I'd like a word with you." He took a further few paces out of earshot of the others as Stock followed him.

"Bloody good show, I mean literally. I passed the site on the way here and it looks like you did a first-rate job. Of course, the governor was on the phone no more than ten minutes after I heard the explosion, wanting to know if it was us who had blown them up. Of course, I denied any knowledge, but I need to hear it from you before I go and make a bigger fool of myself, so please tell me it all went to plan."

The look on Withers' face said it all and Stock wondered if he would have had the courage to take the same course as Withers had done if the roles had been reversed. Probably not. This was clearly a man who had been in a desperate situation and, faced with the alternatives, he had had little choice. Besides which, if it had turned out differently, then the blame would have been squarely hefted onto Stock. He had taken all the risks and perhaps now was the time to blow his own trumpet.

Stock led him through the events starting with from the moment the German corporal was drugged. He watched the worry lines fade from Withers' face. "I do not think Colonel Hartmann saw what actually happen nor realised that his corporal's place was taken by one of ours, but as to what anyone else saw, I cannot say. As far as I am concerned, we switched their uniforms without anyone seeing. Have you heard anything to the contrary, sir?"

"Quite the opposite. In fact, it was your sergeant shouting 'Achtung' at the top of his voice as he fled the scene that clinched it. They must have a link with someone in the governor's office because the speed at which that little snippet of information reached his ears was far too fast for it to be normal. This means we can now concentrate our focus of attention in that direction. But these are only the initial reports and I suspect the rumours that it was an escaping German who caused the, shall we say, 'accident', will have reached the other side of the city by now. For the moment, nobody's pointing the finger at us and the only question that remains is who was responsible for letting the German take over the half-track in the first place." Withers smiled. "I think I can handle that small detail. I'll keep your name out of it."

"I need to ask - and suspect the answer - but was anybody killed?"

"Not certain yet and that might take a few days to come out, but don't let that worry you as I am sure that your actions today will have certainly saved some allied lives. I only hope that the truth never comes out." Withers looked at the other three who were chatting by the truck. "I am afraid I won't be able to report what really went on here today and it won't appear in your records as a job well done, but if things turn out as I think they might, you have my personal thanks. Just make sure your chaps keep quiet about it."

"I think you can say that the Royal Engineers have come to the rescue again, sir. But you will not even be able to say that either. Will you?"

"Best left there I think, Captain." Withers consulted his watch and ordered Wilson to take charge of the lorry. "Your train was just getting ready to depart when I last saw it, so you shouldn't have long to wait. Goodbye, Stock."

"Goodbye, sir."

Withers got back behind the wheel of the jeep but before he let the clutch out, he leaned sideways towards Stock. "You know, I almost pity the Japs where you're going." He let out a loud laugh.

Chapter 3

The Train

Everyone was happy and glad to be on the move, at least to begin with, and then it dawned on them that they were to be stuck on the train for almost a week. For most of the enlisted men, the excitement of travelling by train wore off soon after they left Karachi and they no longer took turns to look out of the windows. By mid-afternoon they reached the city of Hyderabad, and once again had their faces glued to the glass to look at the vast trading city that was the gateway to the Northwest Frontier. Some thought they would stop, but the veterans in the ranks knew better.

It wasn't until the sun was setting that they reached the town of Mipur where the engines needed re-fuelling, mainly with water, that they were allowed off the train, and then for only fifteen minutes. Most took the opportunity to visit the specially built latrines and line up to refill their own water bottles from the bowser. It was at this point that they learned that they would be receiving only one meal per day until they reached their destination, and the complaints came thick and fast, especially as they knew their officers had their own kitchen and dining carriage. Added to this, they discovered that the only toilet on the entire train was attached to the officers' carriage, from which they were barred. It took a bit more bellowing than normal from the sergeants to quell the discontent. Some were lucky enough to be in a carriage with horse-hair seats, but most had only slatted wooden benches. For the first night, they slept on whatever surface they could, including the floor. There was some initial bickering and bartering as to who slept where and the occasional swearing when someone's boot made contact with someone else, but they resigned themselves to another fact of army life.

The sergeants had orders not to call reveille as early as they recently had been doing so, as there was no longer any need for the men to be doing anything like loading. Yet for those awake to see it, the dawn was quite spectacular. As far as the eye could see in any direction, it was flat. Only wide-open brown space and the occasional field of crops in the distance where the river Indus meandered and irrigated. The night-time moisture in the air reacted with the heat from the sun's rays and produced an eerie layer of mist that sat close to the ground, like a velvet blanket in suspense just before it lands. The orange and lilac glow soon dissipated but in an otherwise boring time on board, it was a talking point for some. Then the cards and dice came out to help relieve the monotony.

Being allocated two carriages, the officers had an altogether better time of it, although not ideal. One carriage was taken up with sleeping quarters, while the other was a converted and well-equipped Mess together with a kitchen at one end. The routine that had started on the ship several weeks ago was all too easy to return to and with little else to do other than hone their bridge and rummy skills, their Mess accounts significantly increased. In an effort to restrain this, Alfredson made them spend time with their companies. Most men considered the daily roll call a waste of time.

At the end of the second day, they entered the Punjab Flats and stopped south of the city of Lahore and this time they were allowed a whole hour's break from the swaying motion of the train. At this major rail intersection, the second and third trains in the convoy drew in just as they were leaving but they didn't get the chance to talk to their comrades. What they did see however was a real eye-opener. As a local train arrived, they were amazed to see that it was not only full of locals but also the roof space was also taken, and more joined by clinging onto the sides so that one could hardly see any part of any of the carriages. It was a noisy affair with bags of luggage being thrown to and fro, but the train only stayed for a minute before it continued its onward journey. In that short space of time, the number of people alighting would have made a small football stadium proud and it created a hub of humourous conversation for the otherwise bored men.

The third and fourth day required the efforts of the second engine at the rear of the train as they traversed the foothills of the Himalayas and bypassed the kingdom of Nepal, although they never crossed its border. The had effectively crossed over the roof of India in a big arc and the tracks now took them on a more southerly direction beyong the city of Patna and on to the main terminal at Dhaka, which they reached on the fifth day. Although not directly on the mighty Ganges River, it lay in the fork of two other rivers and was the hub of all things in that vast region. It also marked the start of the jungle that smothered that part of Asia and continued for nearly two thousand miles right up to the China Seas. As they crossed the wide Brahmaputra River, the humidity became noticeably higher, causing sweat marks on their uniforms to be permanent. Despite the unusual scenery, it had been an unpleasant and generally torrid journey that most would try to forget.

At Dhaka, they were given a respite of six hours while the locomotive engines were changed for others. The original two would be returning to Karachi with half-empty wagons and carriages. For the first time in five days, the men were allowed a second meal in twenty-four hours. To their joy, there were showers and washing facilities. Once cleaned up and having attended the local headquarters with Wavertree, Alfredson addressed the entire regiment. He allowed them to stand easy as they gathered round. He stood on top of a small pile of railway sleepers.

"Not quite what we're used to back home, eh?" His reference to the last five days raised a smile and a titter but it at least showed him that the men were in good enough spirits. "And now most of you don't even know where you are." This time a laugh rippled. "Well, I can tell you that we're nearly there." All ears strained to learn. "General Blythe has just advised me that the other two regiments will continue south to the seaport of Chittagong but we will be going in the opposite direction to Imphal on the Burmese border. There, we will be supporting elements of the 17th division under General Alexander and the 7th armoured brigade under Brigadier Anstice as well as the Chinese expeditionary force which, as you all know, has suffered great losses at the hand of the Japs."

From the newspapers they were allowed and through the British forces radio service, they had all heard that the Burmese capital of Rangoon had fallen, causing a grievous setback to British and American aspirations. Effectively the southern part of Burma was now in enemy hands and the Japanese were advancing on Mandalay with a view of breaking through the eastern border with India, more or less where they were now. Alfredson chose his words carefully as he did not want to dispirit the men under his command. He implied that it was the Chinese who had endured an ignominious defeat, whereas in reality it was General Alexander who had come off very much the worse and was now retreating to Imphal. It would not do to let the men know they were about to support a beaten army in full retreat, at least not yet. They would discover the truth by themselves in any case.

"At Imphal we will be preparing forward bases from which to strike back at the enemy and our main role will be to build roads, airfields and the like from which we can launch our offensive."

Alfredson had been told their first job would be to construct defensive positions, but he wanted them to believe in a more positive outlook.

"I know the last few days have been rather unpleasant and we've got another two days of it yet but put your feet up and make the most of it because when we get there, you'll be working like Trojans. We've taken a licking from Jerry in France, built airfields in England, and enjoyed a very pleasant cruise half-way around the world." This raised a muted cheer from some. "But now it's time to knuckle down and prepare to strike back. Good luck to you all." As he dismounted his pedestal an instantaneous cheer went up.

All too soon, the monotony returned as they were back in the same carriages and traversing the flood plains of the Ganges Delta, but the terrain was changing and, the further east they went, the more it felt like the jungle was closing in on them. As the train commenced its long uphill struggle onto the plateau of Manipur on the final day, Wavertree announced that he had arranged a local cook from Chandpur to prepare a luncheon celebrating Alfredson's thirty-first birthday. Ankur Sabat had come highly recommended by one of the station masters in Dhaka and, as well as their normal rations being loaded, crates of local produce had found their way onto the train. It wasn't just one cook, but six of them, all from the same family and definitely subordinate to Sabat, who seemed to bark just one word orders to them. For their services, what had cost Wavertree under a pound was more like a month's wage to each of them, and they happily went about their business in the on-board kitchen, producing mouth-watering smells that none of the Englishmen had ever come across before.

Sabat's broken English was terse but accompanied by a genuine permanent smile, telling the officers to be seated at ten o' clock sharp and ordered them out of their Mess while the table was set. It only took ten minutes of waiting in the cramped space of the corridor but there was little else to do anyway, and when they were told to return, their eyes fell on an unbelievable sight. The bare wooden table from which they had been eating during the past five days and which had also doubled up as their card table, was transformed by a sheer white tablecloth, on it the requisite number of place settings was laid out, perfectly spaced. The silver-plated cutlery gleamed, the crystal goblets sparkled, and there was a plethora of accompanying accoutrements symmetrically set around the candle chandeliers. In front of each chair were two stacks of plates, one larger than the other, and at the far end of the room stood two of Sabat's sons, attired in crisp waiters' uniforms and each holding an oversized napkin draped over their left arms. From a pair of rose water bowls with bright pink flowers in the centre, arose a sweet scent which wafted through the carriage and suppressed the previous cooking smells. Or perhaps the aroma came from the scented candles, but whichever, it was a heady atmosphere that dispelled their experiences of the past five days. The sideboard, which up to then had been cluttered with packs of cards, half-read books, pencils, used ashtrays and the like, was also covered with a flat white cloth and on it at one end stood methylated burners while at the other stood ranks of bottles as well as pitchers of lemon infused water.

It was such an unexpected sight that, at first, the officers were speechless while they filtered around the table to a seat, Alfredson at one end and Wavertree at the other. Their silence didn't last long.

"By Jove, you've done well this time."

"A feast fit for a king coming up."

"This looks wonderful."

"Can't wait to get stuck into this lot."

"Must have cost a small fortune, where did you find this fellow?"

"Hope the food's as good as this looks."

"Look. I've counted fourteen plates each."

The compliments came thick and fast and even though they were not attired in their dress uniforms, it was clearly a formal occasion, so they stood chatting behind their chairs until Alfredson indicated silence for Grace.

"We ask our Lord to bless those who have provided us with this food and wine and thank Him for our continued health. Amen."

It was indeed a feast, even more so compared to the previous few days and there were indeed fourteen plates, one for each course. Sabat entered and lined up his entourage, introducing each of his sons in order of importance and announced that although it did not happen until next month, they would soon be celebrating the Polia Boishakh, a festival which highlighted the culture of the Bengali people. He and his family were honoured to present a sample of their traditional dishes. Barking just one word, he made his sons sprang into action, some serving out drinks while others scurried back to the kitchen to retrieve the first course. Fried with goat's butter on one of the burners, it turned out to be a small portion of red spinach leaves on flat bread, and whetted their appetites for what was to come next. Sabat announced each course as it was served, describing in detail how it was prepared and cooked. Inevitably, some of his translation was misinterpreted yet the officers soon warmed to Sabat's earnest attempt at proper English. He proclaimed that his proudest moment had been when he had prepared and served the Viceroy of India and his good wife, Lord and Lady Willingdon, on their visit to Dhaka in 1936, and from the folds of his jacket, produced a letter of thanks.

Memories of their recent hardship dissipated quickly and stories from home circulated among the merry throng, helped with liberal amounts of gin. The courses did not follow each other quickly; Sabat had explained that, if their banquet was to be enjoyed to the full, then time must be allowed to savour each delicacy. Next to come was grated bamboo shoots, pickled in a secret recipe of spices and mixed with rotten potatoes. His sceptical guests needed reassuring that the bamboo would not pierce their guts and most needed to wash it down. Sabat produced wines from Thailand, not really up to the standard of what they were used to, but it sufficed. Hot lentil soup was served in bowls, prawns steamed in banana leaves, mango and papaya salads, red ant chutneys accompanied the succulent lamb set on a bed of black rice. The courses kept coming. None of them noticed the time of day passing by, nor that they were thoroughly enjoying themselves. The wines were now palatable, and their voices rose as they bounced memories of their escapades off each other. Alfredson and Stock had the advantage over the others since they were the only two who had grown up together.

"Hockey," Alfredson retorted to one comment. "Hockey's a girl's game." Stock's sister Jean had played for England at one point. He he had watched her play and knew it was anything but. He thought it better not to interrupt Alfredson in full flow.

"Compared with the rugby we played on tours. Stock, you'll back me up with this won't you? That year we visited North Wales. Where was it? Dolgellau, that's right. One end of the pitch backed downhill onto a slate factory where they threw out all the defects and it was the devil's own job to avoid playing in that half, but we pinned them there and drew more Welsh blood than English. Come to think of it, I think I've still got the scars to prove it. And they cheated. I'm sure to this day that they had a double-headed coin specially minted. We never cheated, did we?"

Stock thought this one over before speaking. "The Vandals might have bent the rules a little now and then."

Alfredson spluttered into his goblet, not caring about the repercussions.

"Who are the Vandals?" Asked one of the braver lieutenants opposite Stock.

"You tell 'em Stock and don't miss the part about the smoke screen." In between coughs and laughter, Alfredson delegated the job. It was one of his favourite stories that had come from one of their matches and now seemed as good a time as any to initiate the others in what went on in the world of club cricket.

Stock looked round the table to assess how receptive they might be and decided that although they were all well down the alcoholic road, none were too far gone. He decided it would be worth telling.

"We have all played one part or another in the sporting world. You Roberts like tennis and golf, Wavertree here is more of a snooker man while the colonel and I prefer rugby and cricket, and we all belong to a team, much as we are now around this table, and each team has its base - a clubhouse. The alternating fixtures that revolve around the practice of home or away form the basis of where matches will be played, and it had been that way for as long as anyone can remember and a team that has not got a base is suffixed with the description of 'Wanderers'. For example, there's a rugby team near just north of London called 'The Mountfitchet Wanderers' who do not have a clubhouse but they spend their season wandering between other clubs and play all their games Away. The Colonel and I formed such a wandering club in 1932. Good grief, I've just realised: The Vandals are ten years old this year."

The Colonel was on his feet first. "To The Vandals."

They all rose to their feet. "The Vandals." And followed their colonel's example of finishing whatever drink they had in front of them at the time. The hovering Sabat indicated to two of his sons to refill the empty glasses, but before they had a chance to sit back down Alfredson held their attention.

"Gentlemen, while we're on our feet, I think it's time to toast our king." He waited briefly while glasses were replenished. "King George the Sixth. May he see us victorious through these turbulent times."

They repeated the loyal toast and again followed Alfredson's example by finishing their charged glasses in one, knowing that if they did not, then it would be noted.

"I think it's smoking time, gentlemen. Sabat, be kind enough to offer that box of cigars round, will you?"

They re-seated themselves except for another captain who excused himself to the toilet. "Carry on, Stock. I won't be long." Captain Tiffery shuffled past one of the waiters down the corridor.

"Err, if you don't mind I need to visit the toilet as well." The young Lieutenant Risley, who was feeling rather unwell at having just downed half a pint of Thai wine, followed Tiffery, bouncing off the door jamb in his hurry.

Stock noted they still had four plates in front of them, yet it was past two o'clock. They had been eating and drinking for over four hours, but he didn't feel bloated. Well, not too bloated.

"Come on, Stock, we all know about the home and away principles but what has this got to do with The Vandals?" asked another lieutenant.

"It is simple now that one looks back on it, but at the time, it was the only solution. Several of us in Dereham had a fondness for cricket, especially as England had just won the Ashes back from Australia. We looked up to the all-rounder Gubby Allan whose family came from Dereham, and he often popped in to our local to see how we all were. It was at his suggestion that we formed our own team, but we did not have a ground or a clubhouse, so he suggested we became a wandering side. The only problem with this was that established clubs would look down their noses at wanderers, so we came up with the idea that we ought to give ourselves another name and thus The East Dereham Vandals were born. He even played for us in our first game against Bury St. Edmunds and it was only when we won by over a hundred runs that someone on the other side recognised him in the bar afterwards. There and then we did not let on that we had no home ground but, rather deceitfully, led them to believe we were a new team in the process of upgrading our clubhouse and would need to play Away for the rest of the season. Well, word got round that we were a team worth playing and we were soon receiving invitations from not just Norfolk but as far away as Somerset. It was an idyllic situation. People would come to matches hoping to watch Gubby and we had to explain his absence with one excuse or another. Apart from the colonel and I, the rest of the team were hopeless and only came along for the laugh and would often still be hungover from the night before, but without Gubby there was no chance of winning anything."

"I think that was the only match we won, and I think you too will admit we were both hung over on one particular occasion." chuckled Alfredson.

"Yes, I was coming to that, but first you have to understand that, as the season progressed, our reputation nose-dived and we were soon playing the lowest echelons of the cricket world. Team managers who had spent hours painfully rearranging their schedules to accommodate playing us, were obliged to honour the fixture. They produced their lowest ranking teams against us, and they were mainly comprised of unfit, middle-aged or even elderly drinking players who only attended to escape their wives for the day."

Stock paused as Sabat announced the first of three courses of dessert and ordered the first to be served: Chum Chum, a doughy ball made with cottage cheese and saffron, to be accompanied with a sweet wine, again from Thailand. The train master came in from the far end and announced that they were now on top of the Dailong mountains and from here on in, it would be downhill all the way to Imphal which was about four hours away. They would be picking up speed and there was just one more ravine to cross over a new bridge, but they should not worry if the train rocked a little more. Nobody had noticed that for the past four hours the train had been struggling up the steep incline and had barely been doing more than fifteen miles per hour.

Tiffery rejoined them and sat down. "Risley's not feeling too well. Being sick all over the bumper, but I told him to show a brave face. He'll be back soon."

Stock cut into the small dumpling with his spoon and was surprised at the deliciousness of it, like ice cream but without the cold part. "Right at the end of the second season, we ended up playing a fifth-rate team from Robertsbridge in East Sussex on a small pitch surrounded by trees and downwind of a farm which stank of cattle and manure. The night before, we all stayed in a local inn, The Black Dog."

"The White Dog," corrected Alfredson.

"Oh, yes, The White Dog but the governor had a black labrador, that's right. It turned out he was the captain of the Robertsbridge and District cricket club, who we were due to play the following day. The pub was full of players from both teams, and we somehow ended up in a drinking contest well into the small hours. Even his wife joined in. I seem to remember it was actually daylight by the time we eventually got to bed, cramming in three or four to a room and you can imagine how we felt the following day."

He had to pause to let out a silent belch, covering it discreetly with his hand. He had opted not to smoke as he considered it a bad habit, but he did enjoy the aroma and watched the smoke from others following the breeze through the carriage.

"Sounds like a good time was had by all, then," offered Tiffery.

"Oh, yes, we were having a wonderful time. Those were the heady days when we would carouse until late into the night and work our overindulgence off with a bit of exercise on the cricket pitch the following day, despite this one being very hot and sweaty. Anyway, we batted first and surprisingly managed to reach over fifty - fifty-eight I think it was - and we put this down to their bad bowling rather than our batting prowess. Lots of wides, though. After tea, which was served early due to our comparatively miserable score, it was their turn to bat, and it soon became clear that we were going to lose. We had not won a game all season and our captain," he nodded towards Alfredson, "decided that we really ought to have at least just one victory to our credit in a season. I cannot remember who spotted it first, but just behind us on the boundary, the farmer's manure pile was merrily smoking away. It made our eyes water. There were a couple of pitch forks standing just there and we stoked the smouldering heap so that it burst into flames and once we had added a few fronds of bracken, the thickening smoke billowed into their batsman's eyes. We started to move the pile to a better position for maximum effect. Remember, it was a small pitch, and the crease was not far away. The very next ball, we got a wicket, clean bowled as their batsman couldn't see a thing through his streaming eyes."

When Stock had mentioned the smoking heap, his audience had guessed the outcome and started nodding and laughing at the ploy.

"Good move…"

"Not really cricket, was it?"

"A proper smoke screen then."

"Nothing in the rules…"

Stock quietened them down. "Quite right, there is nothing in the rules, but it was their captain and number one batsman who we had got out. Jim Grace, the governor of the White Dog, and he took umbrage at this ungentlemanly play, came striding over to the colonel and I, and started remonstrating and threatening us with all sorts, including his bat. There he was, standing right in front of us, cartwheeling his arms about with tears streaming down his face and I think matters would have taken a regrettable turn for the worse had it not been for a change in the wind."

They were all heartily laughing at such a daft situation and Stock's description of the scene of an irate batsman complaining in such a fashion.

"He took a lot of convincing that there was nothing he could do about it, and it was only when we pointed out that they were likely to win anyway, that he stormed off in a huff. he even threw his bat at a passing pigeon."

They were all hooting in mirth now, Alfredson thumping the table in approval. He went to take a drink from his goblet - empty. "Gentlemen, I must apologise, and this is very remiss of me. We've overlooked the port but don't worry. I've been keeping some for just such an occasion. Sabat." Even before he looked over his shoulder, Sabat had the decanter in his hand and was handing it to Alfredson, while two sons cleared away the penultimate plate and distributed suitably sized port glasses. Just one plate remained. Alfredson began the pouring etiquette himself, before the decanter would make its way in a clockwise direction round the table, when there was a particularly heavy jolt, causing him to spill some of the fine red liquid onto the table. "Damn." The heavy jarring toppled over one of the candelabras on the sideboard.

"Not to worry, sir." Sabat was there in an instant with a napkin. "That was the union of the old line with the new line on the bridge. There'll be another one in a minute at the other end. If you wait, it will be better."

Alfredson didn't want to wait and continued his pouring before setting the decanter down on the table to his left. "There's another when this one runs out and then I believe Wavertree has some brandy for us as well?"

"Armagnac actually, and it ought to be good."

"So, what happened? Did you win or lose?" Tiffery asked.

Stock let them settle. "Well, that is not the end of the story yet because, just as the next batsman was facing his first ball, the wind shifted again, fanning our smouldering piles and blowing the smoke directly towards the wicket. He too was out first ball since he wandered down the pitch too far, our wicket keeper stumped him. He couldn't see a thing. The poor lad could not have been more than sixteen years old and was a last-minute stand in to make up the eleven. I think we had nicknamed him 'Gracy' after the singer Gracie Fields because of his squeaky voice. And it was his first match as well."

The train suddenly braked hard and interrupted their laughter. They felt the bang as it jumped a little more than before as it crossed back onto the older track.

The port now continued its journey round the table and Stock carried on.

"Quite understandably, Jim Grace was livid and, as the next batsman was walking into bat, we could see him gathering the rest of his team and they disappeared round the back of their clubhouse. We wondered why the batsman was taking so long to walk to the crease and talk to his partner at the other end, when they appeared from behind the scoring hut trawling a giant roller. You know, the sort that flattens out humps in the ground, but this was no ordinary roller that one or two people could push. No, this was a really heavy monster about five foot high with a bar that ran all the way round it so that half a dozen men were needed to make it move. Must have weighed well over a ton and it was coming our way."

His silent audience were perplexed as to what was coming next and Stock made them wait while he poured himself a glassful and passed on the decanter.

"It was only when they came within about ten feet or so that we realised they planned to put out the burning piles with the roller and I remember Jim shouting out 'Ramming speed.' They put on a spurt and simply crushed the first of our three piles. The colonel and I had enough sense to get out of the way sharpish, but their momentum carried them into the brambles beyond the boundary and we fell about laughing as they tried to dig their heels in to stop the juggernaut to turn it around and aim it for the next pile.

Alfredson cackled and was thoroughly enjoying Stock's tale as were the others.

"They were quite a way into the undergrowth, and we could hear them cursing the spikey thorns as they edged themselves to the far end to push it back in the same direction. When they did emerge, ripe blackberries had stained their whites and they looked like they had been at the far end of a shooting gallery. Our hilarity at their dishevelled looks only enraged them and they put their backs into the machine trundling it towards our next pile." Stock laughed heartily with the others at the ridiculous situation and caused even more mirth when he said. "They missed."

It took them a while to quieten down enough for him to continue.

"While all this was going on, our bowler announced he was ready and started his run up, while their batsman was waving his hand around in front of him trying to clear enough smoke away so that he could actually see the ball coming. The umpire did not see it, but the colonel and I learned afterwards that our bowler did a double flip with his arm and when their batsman offered up his bat to hit the ball which wasn't there, the real ball came in slow and hit the stumps."

Stock had trouble containing himself with the outrageous memory. "It was a hat trick, the only one we ever achieved."

"By the time Jim's party had steered the roller to point in the right direction, their next batsman was on his way in, but Jim had set his mind on at least winning his own battle by extinguishing our smoke screen. We could hardly let them just put out our fires as a matter of principle so the colonel and I grabbed the bar at the opposite end and started to push back, but against six or seven of them, we could not hold them. One of our fellows fielding not far away, Johnny Dean, came to help out and soon we had nearly as many pushing against the roller as they did. It was about this point that the match became secondary to the control of the roller, as more and more from each team joined in on one side or another, trying to get the thing moving. We let them roll over the second pile and, just as they put in their best effort, we let go, and off they went into the undergrowth again."

They were all howling with laughter at the silly scenario. Because both Stock and Alfredson had each other to back up the story, they took it to be true, which indeed it was, and this only made it altogether funnier.

"I have not finished yet." This increased the laughter even more as in disbelief, they couldn't imagine it getting any worse.

"Jim was calling from the wood for everybody to come and help get the roller back onto the pitch, which they did, and for the sake of continuing the new game we had invented, we let them. By now the only people left on the pitch were their batsman and our bowler. Even their second batsman at the other end had abandoned his post to come and help. Their batsman could not leave his wicket unguarded because our bowler would have simply bowled him out, and the two of them assumed ready positions. The bowler threatened to bowl occasionally, trying to trick the batsman with a dummy run up, and the batsman pretending not to notice through the wafting smoke."

The port decanter was nearing empty as it made it way round and Sabat offered up the second to Alfredson.

"As they emerged from the wood, Jim's rolling party managed to aim it at the third pile which, more than the other two, was well and truly on fire. He was telling them to stop the roller on top of it instead of rushing over it. Even so and with us pushing less or more to upset their plan to stop the roller exactly where they wanted to, they overshot by three or four feet, just where the roller bar was."

Stock paused to swig from his glass and to let the significance dawn on them, which it did to some of them.

"Right on top of the fire, they hopped around as red-hot sparks covered them and flew up their trouser legs. Of course, we could not control ourselves watching grown men trying to stamp out the fire at the same time as taking off their trousers or patting out smouldering bits of hay that landed on them and in their hair. By now, even the two chaps on the pitch had given up their positions and had joined up between the two wickets and were hanging on to each other. We were bending over, resting on our knees in laughter as one chap sprinted towards the clubhouse with smoke pouring off his trousers. He dunked them in the water butt and nearly fell in."

Stock had to stop and join in with the others' infectious laughter which continued for some minutes, some of them repeating snippets of what Stock had said and commenting on the impossible scenario, but there was more to come.

"And to make matters worse, the roller had somehow disturbed an underground wasps' nest and the little blighters were buzzing all around us.

"Grown men with tear-streaked faces, gallivanting half-naked around a cricket pitch in the middle of the English countryside, with their grubby whites now brown and spotted with blood, most of them laughing their heads off or swatting invisible wasps, could hardly be described as a typical village cricket match. Afterwards in the pub, the two dozen or so spectators who had come to watch a sedate and probably rather boring Saturday match, would verify the extraordinary events of that day. To remind them, they pinned the burnt pair of trousers to the bar ceiling once they had dried out."

Tiffery persisted, "What was the official outcome of the match?"

Stock was about to reply when the door at the far end of the carriage burst open.

Chapter 4
Groundrising

A corporal who nobody could put an immediate name to, marched up to the merry party, his eyes darting from one side to the next, taking in the contrasting scene in the officers' carriage. He stopped to attention and aimed his salute at Alfredson at the far end of the table.

"Carry on, Corporal." Alfredson didn't bother returning the salute and instead waved his hand while his elbow still rested on the table.

Corporal Jones lowered his hand. "It seems that Lieutenant Risley has fallen overboard, sir, and I was sent to ask your permission to stop the train."

It took just a second for his report to sink in and when it did, most eyes turned momentarily to the empty chair in the hope it wasn't true. Alfredson asked the inevitable question. "How do you know it was Lieutenant Risley?"

"Private Hopper was taking a riddle between the carriages when he says he saw what looked like Lieutenant Risley rolling down the embankment on the right. Says he got up again but fell over, sir. Sergeant Major Harries sent me to…"

Alfredson held up his hand indicating him to stop and turned to Tiffery. "Go and look where you last saw him. Blithering idiot," he muttered to himself. Then he addressed Corporal Jones, "If it's true, go and tell the train master to stop as soon as he can." He looked at his watch and then outside, assessing the amount of daylight that was left. Less than three hours, probably only two.

Tiffery returned but didn't sit down. "No sign of him, but you can see where he was. Must have been that last jolt over the bridge that dislodged him."

Alfredson raised his eyes to Jones. "Off you go, then, and be quick about it." He fingered his half empty glass of port, rotating it with his fingers while he contemplated what needed to be done next. Losing an officer from a moving train that was miles from the nearest enemy activity would certainly not look good in the regimental records, but his main concern was for Risley. His options were rather limited. To bring the heavy train to a stop downhill would probably take a good mile or so. If Risley had fallen off when Tiffery said he had, then that might mean the bridge was getting on for ten miles behind them. Backing it uphill at a painfully slow speed might take another hour, if not more. There was no telling if Risley would have the sense to stay near the track or go wandering off into the jungle by which time it would be dark. He could picture the scene as another train came over the bridge, not managing to stop in time.

"Stock. You know how to ride a bike. Take one of the Enfields back up the line and retrieve Risley. We're going to carry on to Imphal, so you'll just have to make your own way there the best you can."

"Do you mind if I take Sergeant Day with me on a second bike, sir? If Lieutenant Risley is injured, it may take two of us."

"Not really what I had in mind, but I see your point. OK."

Their carriage was more or less in the middle of the train. With apologies, the trainmaster arrived and verified that Alfredson really wanted to stop the train. Almost from their invention, there had been a cord inside each carriage designed to alert the engine driver to stop if pulled. Although their particular carriage was rather old, it was still equipped with one which rang a bell in the engine cabin. The train master tugged on it several times and they could all feel the immediate but slight deceleration. It was linked to both engines, and a moment later the train slowed more significantly as the second driver shut off the steam and applied his brakes. Even so, and as

Alfredson had predicted, it took an awful long time before they came to a halt, since they had picked up speed with the slope down into the Imphal valley.

The alcohol-fuelled merriment of the past five hours dissipated as the officers begrudgingly gave up their chairs. They had been looking forward to relaxing in the pleasant atmosphere of after dinner proceedings and more light-hearted banter, accompanied by Wavertree's Armagnac, but now had to attend to their duties, thanks to Risley.

Stock and Day were ready to leave, sitting astride their Royal Enfields with just the minimum of provisions, but plenty of water when Tiffery almost sauntered up and over the rhythmic thumping of the 250cc engines and asked, "Just one thing Stock. What was the bloody score?"

Stock gunned the engine to warm it up a little more and waited until it returned to tick over. "It was a draw - and went into our records as 'smoke stopped play'." He nodded to Day, engaged first gear and headed back up the track.

"Good luck."

To begin with, it brought back memories from their French escapades, but this was worse, much worse, and was taking far too long. On a normal road it would have taken twenty minutes or so to return to the bridge, but they had to stay on the loosely-packed large stones at the side of the tracks due to the invasion of the jungle that hemmed them in on both sides. At one point, Stock led them between the rails but the evenly spaced sleepers made it almost impossible to gain any momentum and threatened to dislodge them from their bikes. If they gunned the engines too much, the rear wheels would spin and dig ruts so they gingerly tried to maintain a constant modest speed, often not much more than a fast-walking pace, all the while clenching the heavy machines between their legs. Interrupting the dense jungle on occasion were rare signs of animal tracks but none could be seen, and their only company was the evenly spaced telegraph poles. After an hour, Stock stopped them for a rest at a small flat clearing that disappeared into the forest.

"I'm bloody knackered," announced Day as he adopted the stance of one who had been in the saddle for a whole day. "Can't be much further. My guts can't put up with much more of this." They were both covered in sweat which oozed freely over their bodies, and Stock was feeling rather uncomfortable after the protracted meal that was still settling in his stomach.

"It better not be. Night is on its way." Stock mournfully looked beyond the tall trees on either side as he gulped down water from his flask. Unlike England where the evenings are drawn out and twilight takes time to appear as the sun gently sets at an angle, closer to the equator night comes in a hurry. One minute the sun is up, and the next, it is gone. The transition between day and night is abrupt and Stock wasn't looking forward to having to negotiate the track with only the headlamp to show the way.

"Wonder where that goes?" asked Day nonchalantly as he stretched his arms above his head and looked down towards the end of the clearing. "There's nothing out here, but there's some tyre tracks over there."

Stock had missed Day's observation and wandered over to them but didn't follow the direction from where they came. He turned around and saw that they followed alongside the rail track in the direction of the bridge. He stood and thought for just a moment. "Come on, back on the bikes. These are fresh. No bigger than a jeep but some sort of car and it looks like there is a beaten track. Look."

Sure enough, and now that they knew what to look for, they could just make out the tyre marks. Less than two minutes later along the smoother track, they followed them round the bend in the line, and could make out the iron superstructure of the bridge ahead. Next to it was a gleaming Lagonda shooting brake.

Stock and Day parked next to it, stalled their engines, dismounted and looked around hoping to find the owner of such a fascinating machine. Stock casually looked inside out of curiosity and was startled to see Lieutenant Risley and another gentleman lounging in the back. He opened the door and stood back, leaving space for Risley to exit, but he didn't. He just sat there until Stock had to prompt him, "Would you care to explain yourself?"

It wasn't Risley who replied but the rather rotund gentleman, wedged in the corner, clutching a hip flask in one hand. "Ah –ha, there you are. We've been waiting for you. I'd offer you a seat but that would make it a bit crowded in here, wouldn't it? Ha," his deep voice boomed in a nonchalant way. "Here, help me out of this." He held out an arm for Stock to grab hold of and crouched out through the open door, eventually managing to lean up against the bodywork on his own. Half a head shorter than Stock and dressed in smart plus fours with a matching waistcoat that helped retain his stomach, his beaming but veined face accentuated clear blue eyes which studied Stock and made him feel a little uneasy. "I know what you're thinking. What's a man dressed like this doing in a car like this in the middle of nowhere? Well, don't worry young fella, all will be revealed shortly. Here, care for a drop?" He held out the flask.

When Stock replied that he didn't, the man took a swig before putting it away in his waistcoat pocket. "Come on then, let's get going before it gets too dark. Here, shut that door before he falls out again."

Stock did as he was told as the man shuffled himself behind the wheel and started the sweet-sounding engine, and before he knew it, the Lagonda was off in the direction they had just come, following the tyre tracks. A bit non-plussed, he briefly looked at Day who was returning his stare, but he didn't need to say anything, and they both hurried over to their Enfields. As Stock engaged first gear and looked up, all he could see was a cloud of dust that showed where the Lagonda had gone, and he nearly stalled as he let out the clutch in a rush. Whoever the gentleman was, he seemed to know where he was going and, try as he might, he struggled to keep up. They returned to the clearing they had stopped at a short while before and followed the dust along the narrow track through the jungle at the far end of the clearing.

Their route was twisty at first and they started climbing. The dust was thinning under the overhanging trees, yet he still couldn't see the Lagonda on the short straights. He didn't need to look over his shoulder to see if Day was managing to keep up, as he heard the occasional reverberation from his sergeant's machine, but he was having to push his own quite hard. The last thing he wanted to do was lose the thinning dust trail. They crossed over a shallow but stony ford, and at last he caught a glimpse of the car as it bounced over a crest. He hardly had time to think about their destination as he needed to concentrate more and more on keeping the Enfield under control. Mercifully, there was only the one track. On any other day he would be enjoying the challenge, but today he was having to work hard to keep up and his muscles started to complain. Worryingly, the light was going fast under the jungle canopy causing him to slow down, but now the track flattened out and just as he was thinking that he wouldn't be able to continue at this breakneck speed for much longer, they emerged into an open field and followed a smooth wider track along one side. The choking dust was back again. He slowed enough for Day to pull alongside of him and nodded to confirm that they must continue. Easing himself on the saddle to relieve his stressed muscles, he was glad to see that the slight wind was taking the dust off to one side and, as it did, he could make out the shape of a building not too far ahead.

The track was suddenly so smooth and straight that he had time to notice that they were now between two fields of crops and he could see several workers off to his left walking with baskets on their heads. He assumed that this might be one of the colonial tea plantations he had heard and read about. No doubt they would find out shortly and he slowed as they approached a gap in the perimeter stone wall between the field and the building. Pulling up alongside the Lagonda he realised the handsome three-story building was far more substantial than he had first thought and so far behind had they been, that Lieutenant Risley and the gentleman were already at the top of the half a dozen wide steps that led to the verandah traversing the breadth of the building and disappearing along each side.

"Come on, you two. Stop dawdling or you'll miss it," urged the gentleman and ushered Risley to a set of chairs that were arranged on one corner of the verandah. He motioned to Stock and Day to sit as they approached.

"Not there - here," he ordered as Day went to sit in a facing chair.

All four of them were now sitting in comfortable cushioned chairs with their backs to the building, looking out over the rail of the verandah which was absurdly low so as not to obstruct the view. 'Breathtaking' was the first thought that came to Stock's mind. From their elevated position near the top of the mountain they were looking out over mainly forested hills that undulated into the misty distance with a setting sun on the horizon. A handful of locals were heading back to their huts having worked all day in the fields and above them a few black birds circled over nothing in particular.

A servant dressed in white apologized as he briefly blocked their view and served each of them with a tumbler of light brown liquid adorned with a leaf. By the time he had departed, they watched as the lower rim of the sun seemed to bounce off the edge of the Earth.

"Haven't missed a sunset in years. Now be quiet and watch."

They were mesmerized by the changing shape of the sinking orange orb as its altered hue seemed to eat into the Earth by making its own arc below the horizon. It gently reached its half-way point and, as it did so, a clear horizontal line of yellow light momentarily accentuated the rim of the world and spread towards them, bathing them in a radiant atmosphere. What came next took them by surprise as they gazed into the shimmering sinking ball. The last rays reflected off a layer of mist, a stiff breeze hit them directly in the face, and along with it came the distinct aroma of ripe strawberries mixed with a healthy smell of earth. They heard the rush of the wind before it reached them. At first, they dismissed it as just another breeze, but this one was special and unique to that particular part of the mountain due to its topographical location.

Stock shut his eyes for a few seconds and breathed in the heady air that lifted his spirits. When he opened them again the sun was all but gone, but the bouquet of the plantation lingered in the softening breeze. It brought back happy memories of England at that distinctive juncture just after the evening rain has stopped and the ground breathes a sigh of gratitude. Stock had rarely had the chance to experience the groundrising phenomenon back home in Norfolk and certainly not as intensely. It evoked a oneness with the land. Now he understood the gentleman's urge to absorb its magnificence. Sitting there enjoying the magic of the moment and reflecting upon the uplifting experience had a calming effect. Soo, the silence was disturbed by the first of the invisible night creatures as it limbered up for its ritual call. It was answered by a second, a third, and then a myriad of others joined in.

"Frogs," announced the gentleman quietly.

Their rhythmic chirping surrounded them and occasionally struck up an inadvertent musical harmony.

"That was beautiful, really beautiful," Risley sighed like a love-struck puppy.

"Stunning, isn't it? And now you know why I rushed to get back here. I must have seen a thousand of these sunsets and each time it's slightly different but it still has the same wonderful effect. It brings back fond memories of my wife. We used to sit here every evening for an hour before sunset and take in the extraordinary event. I've not come across this anywhere else in the world but no doubt someone will correct me. Come, gentlemen, drink to my departed wife because it was her idea that we should make our home on this spot."

As he raised his glass, Stock looked at the transparent light brown liquid. It felt slightly chilled. Nosing the leaf out of the way, he took a reasonable sip. Yes, there was an element of alcohol in it, yet not so much that one would notice immediately. The aroma that permeated up through his mouth before he swallowed did justice to the concoction as it trickled down his grateful throat. He took a satisfying, longer pull.

"Now that my evening ritual is over I suppose it's time I introduced myself to you chaps. Major General Hobart-Smythe of the Royal Bengal Lancers. Retired, naturally, but don't let that fool you. I've still got what it takes in the saddle. If any of you ride, I can offer you a wonderful picnic on the far side of the mountain tomorrow. Need to pay my respects to an old Magi who probably won't last much longer," he chuckled. "Mind you, we've been saying that ever since we got here. Now, tell me about yourselves, I haven't managed to get much out of your lieutenant here. I suspect he's eaten something nasty. I can see you're all sappers and no doubt heading for Imphal, but I only get news once a week all the way up here. I send a couple of my chaps down there on a regular run to pick up supplies and deliver whatever we've produced during the week and they bring me back the local papers. Do any of you speak a local dialect? Not even Nepali, Urdu or Hindi? No?"

As the introductions were made, Stock was fairly certain that Risley was suffering from too much wine, but the general had planted a seed of doubt in his mind so he decided to give Risley the benefit of the doubt. A series of wall lights were turned on from somewhere inside, bathing the verandah in a warm glow.

The general cut him short with a summons as Stock was describing their part in the evacuation in France. "Ravi."

A well-dressed Indian gentleman appeared. "This is my head of house and estate manager, Ravi." The three guests could not understand the language that the general and Ravi now spoke, but the brief conversation between them came to a sudden halt.

He turned a little in his chair to face Risley. "Ravi and I agree you're suffering from *jipta* - that's a local expression for someone who's eaten what they shouldn't have. Happens all the time, but we've got a cure for it, so you go with Ravi who'll sort you out. Don't worry if what he gives you smells a bit, but you'll be alright by the morning. Sergeant, would you mind going with him?"

An ashen looking Risley shakily got to his feet and was ushered inside by Ravi.

"I don't suppose you noticed if he has eaten any dried fish lately?" asked the general. "Because that's what it looks like. You can smell it."

Stock was taken aback at the thought of anyone being able to smell such a malady but, then again, he supposed he would be in for a few more surprises yet in India.

"Ravi's a first-class fellow and looked after the house ever since Sheila passed away. Been here since he was a boy when we took him in after the floods in '21. His entire village got washed away and we found him half-starved, wandering around aimlessly. It was a great sadness that we lost our only son who was killed in the last days of the great war, and Ravi was the closest we came to replacing him, so we brought him up as if he were our own. In the English tradition of course, here at Groundrising."

Stock quickly cottoned onto the relationship between the name of the estate and the heady atmosphere that still pervaded.

The general continued while looking down at his shoes that he symmetrically waggled from side to side, "At the time, my wife was distraught and it took her several years to get over the fact that she would never see her son again. That suddenly changed when Ravi came along. Her maternal instincts got the better of her. He's a very bright chap. Once she had taught him to read and write, Sheila had little difficulty introducing him to the joys of poetry, music and teaching him to appreciate the finer aspects of being an Englishman, such as etiquette. By the way, Sheila's my shortened name for Ashellinasmi which roughly translates to 'flower of the mountain'. Believe me when I tell you that she really was a blossom to behold."

He stopped his foot waggling and looked to see if Stock was paying attention. "She was a princess, you know. Before you ask, no, I wasn't forced to marry her. She was the eldest daughter of Maharaja Rashama and he was so grateful that I, well, I mean my troop, rescued her from a local bandit, he offered me her hand in marriage. Not that I was reluctant, you understand, as we had met before. If he hadn't, we would have probably eloped anyway. He endowed us with part of his kingdom." He waved his hand in an arc. "Almost as far as you can see on a clear day from here down to the Jin River."

He paused to take a final sip from his glass. In the relative silence - interrupted only by the frog song - Stock heard a clock chime from somewhere inside.

"Here, I was forgetting my manners. We always serve dinner here at half past seven and you need to clean up first. Yuti ."

Stock rose from his seat with the general. Yuti must have been waiting just out of sight as a small girl appeared in an instant. "Truth is that we don't get many visitors up here but, when we do, I tend to get carried away. Yuti is Ravi's daughter and she will prepare you for the dining room. Let her take care of you."

The General abruptly turned and marched off into the house, leaving Stock with the realisation that more food was on the way.

"Please, sir. This way."

He looked down at a smiling Yuti who held her hand out, indicating for him to follow in the general's footsteps. She couldn't have been more than twelve years old, but she held herself with grace and waited for him to take the first step before following at his side. Passing through the wide double doors into what he could only describe as an atrium which ascended to the top floor, he was faced with a pair of symmetrical staircases directly ahead of him. On either side were plain white walls, interrupted only by doors. Yuti led him to one of them off to the right. She opened it inwards for him to pass through ahead of her, took two steps and stopped.

"Please sit down, sir." She clasped both hands across her stomach and stood directly in front of a pair of fine wooden chairs. Stock did as he was told. She crouched down without her knee touching the stone floor and held out her hands either side of his right foot, waiting for him to offer it forwards and began to untie his laces, then removed his sock. Stock remained seated while she stood up and placed the footwear items on a shelf, opened a cupboard and produced a pair of slippers, which looked and felt like they had been made from some sort of carpet material. They felt wonderful on his feet, freed from the confines of army issue.

She led him up the first flight of stairs that curved round on itself to form one wider one ascending up through the middle. Surrounding the cavernous atrium as he reached the top were the most unusual ornaments Stock had ever seen. At the head, a pair of imposing, carved, full-size bull elephants stood on each side as if on guard, their tusks almost reaching the floor. He had the unnerving feeling that he was being watched by their life-like eyes which seemed to follow him as he passed between them. He recalled the old adage 'elephants never forget' and hoped they would remember him as a friend. He looked up at the massive glass chandelier that hung centrally from the lofty ceiling and reached down almost to the first floor, marvelling at the beauty of the rainbow effect from the electric bulbs as they played their random patterns off the walls. But he was taken aback when Yuti led him past a pair of what looked like stuffed sabre-toothed tigers sitting each side of the entrance to the balcony overlooking the entrance on the ground floor. He had to stop and examine them more closely.

"They're black panthers, sir. Very rare."

He had only read about the almost mythical beasts and had wondered if they actually existed, and right in front of him was the proof that his schoolday teachings were correct. He couldn't help reaching out and stroking one on the head between the ears and was surprised to feel how soft the pelt was. So life-like, except it didn't respond to his touch, but it appeared to be grinning back at him, perhaps in anticipation of lunch.

Yuti had moved off towards one of the doors which she now held open for him. "Your bath is ready for you, sir, and Dulal will be pleased to help you with the razor." With a slight bow of her head she abruptly turned away, closing the door behind her, and left Stock standing just inside the oversized bedroom. The opulent furnishings bedazzled him and it took him a full minute to cast his eyes over the room. There was a large, delicate porcelain bath on the opposite side of the room to the magnificent mahogany four-poster bed with silk trappings. A polished walnut dressing table, a changing screen with inlaid ivory and gold veins, and an octagonal stone table stood in the centre, with a stuffed strutting peacock with its plumage fanning out behind it in one corner. A pair of interwoven gold and white curtains, separated by an overhead pelmet, framed the doorway to a balcony. The floor was a highly polished stone on which a Persian rug was perfectly positioned, but there were other furnishings he didn't have time to take in straight away because a small boy appeared through a side door that he hadn't noticed and stood directly in front of him.

"Good evening, sir. I am Dulal and your valet for tonight. I will help you in the bath, shave you, dry you off and get you ready for dinner. Can I help you get undressed?"

Stock didn't know it but his mouth was wide open. All he could do was nod his assent. Five minutes later, he had his arms outstretched, resting on the sides of the bath, as he looked up at the decorated ceiling that depicted a jungle river with fishermen in their boats. Dulal started to lather his chin with scented soap in preparation, and Stock closed his eyes out of habit. His thoughts wandered over the extraordinary events of the past hour or so, and he had to admit he was now receiving royal treatment in palatial surroundings, courtesy of Major General Hobart-Smythe. He had not previously had the time to assess the man whom he had first met down at the railway line, but perhaps this was because he had been difficult to pigeon-hole. He looked like he was approaching his eighties yet still managing to keep a reasonable figure, perhaps because he still maintained his estate on horseback, or because he kept driving his Lagonda at breakneck speed. His bushy moustache, typically Victorian or Edwardian, didn't need to hide the few wrinkles on his face, yet still perfectly matched his thinning, light brown hair. And then there were the obvious trappings of wealth. Had this all come from the Maharaja or was he prosperous in his own right? Had he carved his estate out of the jungle for himself?

How long had he been there? Once the war was over, perhaps he too could emulate the general's idyllic lifestyle and make a home for himself in another unknown part of India. His dreams drifted further into the future but were interrupted by Dulal gently shaking his shoulder.

"Sir, sir.It's time to wake up, sir."

For some reason he looked down at his fingernails and saw that they had been manicured. 'Crikey,' he thought. 'How long was I asleep for?'

Dulal held up a towel for him with both hands. Before he was hardly dry, he saw that Dulal was holding out a cream robe for him to wear. Naked underneath it, he felt its soft fibrous material sensitize his skin, goose-pimpling his neck.

"Over here please, sir." Dulal steered him towards a full-length framed mirror, adjusted the lapels and belt so that they were perfectly centered, and stood on a short stool to attend to his hair with a brush and comb. He hopped down to take a look at his handiwork. Stock stared back at his dapper self in the mirror. He put his shoulders back, standing to attention, and decided he had not felt or looked this good for a long time, probably not since well before he had joined the Army.

"I will escort you to dinner, sir. It will be served shortly. Your slippers."

"Dinner dressed like this?"

"Yes, sir. The general insists on it every night."

Stock was initially shaken at the thought of attending dinner in only what was in effect a glorified dressing gown, but readily accepted that the general's house rules were probably completely different to any others. As they reached the top of the stairs, he saw Day emerge from one of the other doorways, similarly escorted by a young boy and wearing a similar coloured robe.

"I see you've had the full works as well, sir. Feels great, doesn't it?"

"Never come across anything like it in my life."

"The lad even did my nails. Look, I don't think they've been this clean since I was born."

Stock had to clench his toes slightly to stop his feet sliding out of the slippers as they descended the stairway. The two boys led them back under the stairs, through a decorative archway that opened out past screens adorned with green leaves, and into the dining room. Here the boys stopped and waited either side of the doorway as they passed through. At one end, adjacent to what looked to Stock like a long low cocktail cabinet, the general stood talking to a gentleman and an extraordinarily tall woman, all dressed in similar gowns. Suddenly he didn't feel out of place at all.

"Blimey, this takes the biscuit," remarked Day, looking round at the vast room as they covered the fifty feet or so to join the trio. The general had spotted them and interrupted his conversation to welcome them over, which didn't provide them with any chance to take in the glory of the decor.

"Ahhhhhh, there you are. Glad you could make it for pre-prandial drinks." He turned to the couple. "Yuti really does work wonders round here, you know. These chaps arrived here not two hours ago and looked like they had been trekking through the jungle for days but she's topped and tailed them just in time for dinner. Oh, and here's my favourite, Ravi."

As Ravi joined Stock on his right, he assumed that he would be joining them for dinner as he had also donned the obligatory gown but, instead of standing still, he briefly bowed his head towards the couple. Stock was trying to figure out what to make of them. Both were handsome, in their mid-twenties, and obviously refined by the way they held themselves. The man was shorter than Stock with almost a Roman nose and a clean-shaven face. The woman had an inch or so on him, and that didn't include her coiffured hair which perfectly augmented her delicate facial skin. Her ruby earrings and neckless matched one of the rings on her finger, displaying an element of wealth. From the way the man stood, he couldn't see if he wore similar jewelry on his fingers.

The two young boys that had attended to Stock and Day joined a pair of young girls who were lining up along one of the walls with their arms clasped in front of them. The general said, "Pini," and the two girls went about offering the newly arrived guests glasses of clear liquid which they poured from a small silver ewer they took from the cabinet.

As they did so, the Major started his introductions, Maharaja Vindu Rashama, Maharani Pashena, may I present Captain Stock and Sargeant Day of the Royal Engineers. Captain Stock, Vindu is my late wife's great nephew. Technically speaking, that makes me his great uncle in-law, but I've been around here for so long now and I know the locals affectionally call me Uncle. I don't mind, especially at my age. Here, try your water while it's still cold and before you ask, we've a natural spring under here which helps keep things cool."

While the general had been rattling on about his relations and the temperature of the water, Stock had been furiously thinking how to address Royalty. As part of the British Empire, only the king would be a 'majesty', so it wasn't that, but the dress code was, to say the least, informal so perhaps protocol was not to be at the forefront of etiquette. Instead, he settled on the only other option he knew, took a bold step forwards and nodded his head.

"Your Highness, Ma'am," he said with a smile.

"Relax, Captain," the Maharaja smiled back. "We do not stand on ceremony when we come here. This is more like a family reunion to us." He held out his hand and shook first Stock's and then Day's hand. His English was impeccable. "Please call me Vindu. After all, that's what they called me at Oxford."

"And how ought we to address your beautiful wife?"

"You can call me Shena and, no, I did not learn my English at Oxford. I have the general to thank for that." Stock detected genuine sincerity as she flashed a smile at the general to reveal a model set of white teeth.

Stock still inclined his head just a little in recognition of her status, but Day muttered the word 'Ma'am', as he couldn't think of anything else to say.

"And how do you like to be addressed, Captain? If you are going to call me Shena, then I must know your first names."

Stock realised his social status was being elevated by her question and wondered if this was out of politeness or a genuine inquisitiveness. Probably a bit of both, he thought as he responded, "Please call me Bernard."

"And I'm George. My mother once told me I was named after King George V because I dribbled a lot when I was a baby, but I'm pleased to say I've grown out of the habit." Day blushed as the others laughed. He turned to Stock and added, "Don't go telling that to the lads, sir, otherwise I'll never live it down."

"Don't have to worry about nicknames the older you get," declared the general. "They used to call me 'Hoofer' when I first joined the lancers as a young subaltern. Something to do with my horse tending to lose more shoes than the others." He was about to continue when a gong sounded in the background. "Aaaaah, splendid, dinner is served."

Their chairs were pulled out for them as they approached the laid table. Stock really wasn't quite sure if he would be able to manage an entire large meal so soon, but in such elevated company he would just have to do his polite best. At first, the conversation happily wandered between trivial topics, giving him the chance to look round part of the room as laughter echoed off the lofty ceiling. It was undoubtedly a common sight to them, but he had never before been in such an elegant room. Even the cutlery was solid gold, or that was what it felt like from the weight of it. Mercifully, the numerous courses were small and Stock's appetite coped.

Day managed to chip in here and there and it was clear that the general was enjoying the company. He saw Stock fingering his glass. "In case you're wondering, we only serve water with dinner. The local wine's not really desirable and spirits tend to clash but more importantly, it's cold and has something in it that the mosquitos hate."

Stock told them about their long luncheon on the train earlier that day and agreed that the local alcohol left a lot to be desired.

"By the way, I had a shipment of those new refrigeration units on order from America to help preserve the fruit etc., and was hoping to have them installed by now, but I think the Japs sunk the boat in the Philippines just as they declared war. I've ordered some more from Kelvinator but God knows if they'll ever arrive. I was quite looking forward to having some ice on tap. If they do turn up, I'll let you have one," he addressed Vindu who gratefully acknowledged the offer of a gift. "Now that really would be a first in this part of India, eh?"

The general's mention of the war depressed the levity of the atmosphere and it wasn't helped when Day asked the inevitable question to no one in particular. "Do you think the Japs will get this far?"

The initial silence was broken by Vindu who stared directly at Day. "I was hoping you might be able to tell us that. After all, it is you who will be fighting them, not us."

Day realised he ought not to have mentioned the subject, but it was too late now. A man in his position in the army was used to taking orders without question, not asking them, and he decided he really ought to leave the questioning to his captain.

Stock came to his rescue and decided to add a little humour to diffuse the situation that was on the cusp of turning maudlin. "I think it is inconceivable that we would abandon India to the Japanese. After all, where else would we English get our tea from?"

"And who else would I sell to?" retorted the general. "Very profitable, along with everything else we produce here. Remember the next time you're out in the field and you brew up, that it's us planters who keep the British army fed and watered. Don't produce any sugar though, more's the pity, as it doesn't seem to want to grow round here." He turned to Vindu. "Do you remember old NcNish, had a plantation down by the Jin and got flooded out a few years back? Lost a fortune over it. Now, if that was me I would have…

The war was forgotten, the courses came and went and Stock began to fill up again. He now knew the wisdom of dining in loose-fitting attire as the fans gently rotating above wafted cooler air around him. He wasn't envious of general who had undoubtedly earned his position as one of the more prosperous tea planters of India. Furthermore, he had a family he could call his own, admittedly not of his blood, but certainly well-placed. 'One day', thought Stock, 'maybe one day I too can enjoy such an idyllic lifestyle'. Mercifully, dinner was a relatively short affair compared to lunch and he let out a silent belch as the last plate was cleared away. He realised Shena was addressing him as the conversation had somehow drifted to the musical arts.

"And do you play anything, Bernard?"

"I really do not think you would enjoy my rendition of 'Chopsticks'. We have an out-of-tune upright piano at home and the three of us, my two sisters and I, once tried 'Chopsticks' all at the same time." He laughed at the happy memory. "We were bashing away, leaning over each other and tangling our fingers so much that we broke one of the ivories. My father was furious and gave us each a thick ear." He could still feel the sting of his father's hand. "It taught me to stay away from trying to become a virtuoso."

"I usually listen to the gramophone when there's no one else around, but as you're here, I'm sure we'd love to hear your delicate touch once again," the general asked Shena. "I had it tuned again a few weeks ago, but my skills are no match for yours."

"Of course. I would love to. Still in the drawing room, is it?"

"Where else?" The general's flattery was not lost on the others. "Ravi, would you mind getting it ready and tell Yuti we'll be taking drinks there?"

"No problem. I haven't heard Shena play since she was half her size and I am sure she can now reach all the pedals. Excuse me for a moment."

"I hope you haven't forgotten anything Sheila taught you?" ribbed the general.

"Of course, I have not," Shena replied almost indignantly. "She was a wonderful teacher but I have surpassed her and play our piano at home all the time. Perhaps you and Bernard can give us your version of 'Chopsticks'?" She led the laughter as the general huffed.

A few minutes later, they wandered into the drawing room. A decent floor to ceiling library spanned the wall opposite the bay windows. It was richly appointed with a stone floor covered mostly by a series of matching thick rugs down the center on which were placed several winged, high-back chairs arranged round a concert-sized grand piano with its lid already open.

Shena trotted over to it ahead of the others. "This is my favourite." She ran one of her fingers over the fine black wood, enjoying the silkiness of the Steinway, before sitting on the stool which she adjusted. Yuti waited for them to sit before offering them each a brandy glass from a silver platter.

"A special occasion demands a special drink," the general beamed as his picked up the balloon glass and dipped his nose in to savour the aroma. "Armagnac de Montal. A fine spirit to match a fine couple and my thanks to you for coming over tonight. You've made an old man very happy." He raised his glass to Vindu and Shena in turn before taking a decent sip.

"I know exactly what to play for you," said Shena with a wicked smile, and struck up the 'Major General's Song' from Gilbert and Sillivan's Pirates of Penzance. She watched as the general reacted with glee. Nobody was well versed enough to remember the words but they all knew the chorus, even Day, and led by the general, they all joined in, " I am the very model of a modern major general."

Shena stopped after the second chorus with a few loud contra-notes. "More than one of us is out of tune and it definitely is not me," she laughed. They all laughed, happy and oblivious to whatever else was going on in the world. Her delicate fingers continued to play lively but classic tunes that most of them recognized, her head and upper body occasionally arching back in sheer enjoyment. She stopped to take a swig from her glass and looked outside.

"Yuti, can you turn off the lights?"

The initial darkness soon dissipated and she waited for her eyes to adjust to the light of an almost full moon that flooded that part of the room. She kept the silence lingering, stretched out her hands and played Beethoven's moonlight sonata. The slow rhythmic tune had them all enraptured, accentuated by the moonlight shining off her robe and highlighting her hair in a misty halo. Her face was in shadow, but that didn't detract from their memories of her beauty. It was a magical few moments that, with her expert playing, opened the soul to let peace and calmness pass through in both directions. Stock's subliminal thoughts were led by the notes as they reminded him of fond memories of home, friends, the happiest of times, his aspirations, and the few regrets that he harboured in his life. He was in seventh heaven, listening to the most wonderful piece of music he had ever heard, being played by an exquisitely beautiful woman, sitting in a plush chair clasping a glass of the finest Armagnac, amongst those who he could now call his dear friends. He was crying, crying with joy, and the tears freely ran down his cheeks as he absorbed the music that pulled at his heart strings. Somehow it also stiffened his resolve to be a better man, to be true to himself, others, and to make the most of his life.

All too soon it came to an end and Yuti turned the lights back on.

"You really have surpassed Sheila. That was exquisite," remarked the general. Similar accolades came from the others, but Shena had noticed the tear streaks on Stock's cheeks.

"And now something for you, Bernard. Would you care to join me?" She squeezed over on the stool to make space for him. At first Bernard was reluctant in the knowledge that his skills couldn't match hers, but he could hardly refuse such as request.

"Ready?"

"Ready."

She started 'Chopsticks' but not too quickly, allowing Stock to familiarise himself. He smiled at her choice with the knowledge that she was not belittling him, but now she sped up, and although Stock did his best to rise the challenge, he had to give up well before her deft fingers did. She finished with a loud crescendo and a laugh. The others clapped, more out of politeness to Stock.

"That was fun," she announced. "And thank you for reminding me. I have not tried that since I was a little girl."

"Neither have I, and your lead was just right, but I am not sure I am ready for the next lesson yet."

A clock in the corner started chiming and the general stood up. "Good God. It's midnight and we've an early start if we're going to reach the Magi in time. Can I suggest breakfast at four?" he asked Vindu.

"Four o'clock sounds fine to us."

The general turned to Stock. "It's going to take us the best part of the day to reach the Magi on horseback and I'm afraid I won't be here to see you off, so I'll say cheerio now." He held out his hand, first for Stock, then Day, to shake and wished them all the best of British luck. "I've asked Ravi to take you down to Imphal. Your motorcycles can go in the back of the Bedford when you're ready, and if there's anything you need, just ask him."

Goodbyes and farewells were said to Vindu and Shena. As Stock was about to leave the room, she called out to him, "Bernard. Next time we meet I expect you to keep up."

"The next time I will have learned something else."

As they ascended the stairway Stock told Day to make sure Risley was ready for breakfast at 06.00.

*****

Their journey in the Bedford lorry took them nearly six hours. A healthier looking Risley opted to sit by himself in the back. The fact was that he had chosen the back so that he could lie down as he still wasn't feeling his normal self. Stock had been summoned to the temporary regimental headquarters, even though he had been about to leave for it in any case. He had pu together a brief and hasty written report.

It had nearly finished raining and raining hard enough so that one could almost watch the ground being washed away from under one's feet. Stock was led by a corporal along a pleasant tree-lined avenue interspersed with large huts on each side and could hear sporadic rifle fire coming from up ahead. Stock enquired what this was.

"Target practice for the Indian volunteers, sir," replied the corporal. "But they haven't got enough meat on their bones to hold a rifle steady for long enough and when they do fire, they rarely hit the target. There's at least three of them yesterday had to visit the MO with broken collar bones. They don't seem to understand that they have to hold the butt into their shoulder. Here we are, sir." He saluted Stock at the bottom of three wooden steps that led up to a rickety-looking porch at the entrance to one of the huts. Alfredson was finishing a telephone conversation as Stock knocked on the open door before entering one of the rooms.

"I hear you found him. Alright, is he?"

Stock surmised that Alfredson was under pressure from his terse tone. "He'll live. For the record, I think he was suffering from food poisoning. Nothing other than that." He placed the one page of his report on the desk.

Alfredson looked at him with suspicion. "Really?"

"Really."

"Right, then." He took Stock's report and placed in on a pile of other papers. "Now, down to business. I've just received confirmation that we're heading north to a place on the Brahmaputra River called Dinjan. Seems that the Americans are trying to fly supplies to the Chinese over the top of what's being called 'The Hump' but they can't seem to keep their airfields from being washed away." He allowed himself a wry smile. "Looks like they're in need of some experts so we'll be on our way at first light. Just our regiment, though, as the rest of the brigade is being attached to the XIth Royal

Armoured Corps down south. Our equipment's still on the train which will take us to Jorhat and from there we'll be taking a ferry upriver. Before you ask, we can't take the train directly to Dinjan as the Japs have cut the link by bombing the line. Apparently we have to get a move on before the monsoon floods the river, so once we arrive at Jorhat, make sure your men know what to do."

Stock thought he was keeping a straight face but Alfredson could read the obvious look of concern.

"Other than in France, we'll be as close to the enemy as we've been so far. Once we get there, keep your chaps on their toes. Good day."

As Stock saluted, he realised he was leaving behind a puddle of water on the wooden floor boards and was about to turn around when Alfredson stopped him.

"Oh, by the way, I don't suppose you know anything about that chest do you? It's got 'Groundrising' stamped on it." He pointed to the corner of the room.

Stock walked over to inspect it and smiled. "Tea, sir. With the compliments of Major General Hobart-Smythe. Something else for the Mess."

Chapter 5

Assam

Autumn 1942

"We have to wait a little while longer, Sahib." Despite being only a few feet away, Pranab had to shout above the rain and the cascading waters so that Stock could hear him.

"What is it this time?"

"One of the wives is having a baby and cannot move. Ujjal says it's going to be a boy."

Stock finished tying another knot combining the ropes that they had lassoed to one of the larger trees. He stood up and prayed it would not be torn out of the ground. He really didn't care if it was going to be a boy or a girl, just so long as it came quickly, but no doubt a boy would be more valuable to the mother. He wiped the rain away from his eyes again as he tested the tension on the rope that reached across the narrow but deep ravine, and waved at the men on the other side indicating that they could now feed the second rope across with the help of a much thinner rope.

"And what if the ropes give way before she has given birth? It will not matter if it is a boy or a girl because they will end up as fish bait fifty miles downstream." He realised he was being unfair speaking to Pranab like that but it had been a long, wet day and his patience was being tested to the limit. He didn't have time to be polite because if they didn't secure the second rope in the next hour, while there was still enough daylight under the forested canopy, then in all likelihood, the village would be washed away, birth or no birth.

"I am sorry, Sahib, but she wasn't expecting for another week yet."

He wished he could tell him to send a runner back down to the village and tell her to hurry up, but refrained as he knew he might be taken literally. Nature would not be hurried but it seemed like it was now doing its best to upset his plans to save the village from the monstrous floodwaters that were rising almost by the minute. 'Just another two feet, please……..just another two feet'. While the villagers organized themselves and prepared the second rope, he looked once again at the water level behind the dam they had been building during the past two weeks, and hoped for the umpteenth time that his mad idea would work.

He hadn't found out yet how Ujjal had become chief of the nameless village of about a thousand souls a mile or so further down the valley, nor exactly how many wives he had. All the women seemed to be his 'wives' and he would certainly not appreciate Stock's efforts if one of them was washed away. In fact, Stock would probably fail in his promise to Alfredson that it could be done, and it wasn't just Alfredson he would be letting down. He wearily leaned against the tree and watched the slow progress of the rope as it was pulled across by numerous hands and reflected on how he came to be there.

While supervising the distribution of equipment from their ferry on their arrival at Dinjan, Alfredson had sent for him, and as he entered the shelter of the quayside warehouse, spotted Alfredson talking to another colonel in the far corner. Two colonels in discussion over a large map set on the makeshift table meant that something was afoot and he hoped he was going to be a part of it, whatever it was. His footfalls betrayed his approach but it was only Alfredson who returned his salute.

"Just in time. This is Colonel Wingate of the newly formed 77th brigade and he has an interesting proposition."

Stock saw a lithe bearded man a little older than himself staring back at him, looking him up and down as if counting his limbs and was surprised when he held out his hand, His grip was startlingly firm, but he returned the gesture.

"Orde Wingate," he announced. "And from what Alfredson tells me, you're his construction expert."

Stock pondered the fact that he had spent more of his army life destroying things rather than creating them but had to admit to himself that he probably was the regimental expert. "Depends on what you want built."

"A runway, in the middle of the jungle but invisible to the enemy. By the end of the month."

At this point, most people would have laughed and said it was impossible, but that wasn't Stock's attitude. One of the reasons why he had volunteered for the Royal Engineers was so that he would have impossible challenges such as this to rise to. What was being asked probably was impossible, but then again, he had never tried.

"Right then. Where do you want it?" He certainly didn't expect the reaction he got from Wingate, whose face broke into the widest possible smile his face would allow.

"God's teeth and little fishes. You know I'm asking the impossible and in the middle of the monsoon rains, yet you say you can do it. If I asked this of anyone back at headquarters, they would automatically say it can't be done, and send me away with a flea in my ear. What makes you think you can do it?"

"I am not sure it can, but then nobody has said it cannot be done, so until I try and find that it can't, the answer is yes. If I fail, then the answer is no."

Wingate put his hands on his hips and laughed out loud. "You'll go a long way with an attitude like that and it's one that I admire. Come over here and look at what we've got."

The three of them bent over the table and looked down on a pair of maps centering on the densely forested mountain some fifty miles or so to the south east of their current position in Dinjan.

"General Wavell has asked me to investigate the possibility of mounting an operation into northern Burma. Two reasons for this.

One is to divert some of the troops threatening Imphal and the other to recce a supply route through to Kunming in China. For this I need a series of airstrips along the route but it is the Americans who will be dealing with this. Naturally the Japs will strafe and bomb them, which is why I need one airstrip off the beaten track that they won't find. Somewhere in the Patkai Range. Look here." He picked up one of the two pencils and sketched in an approximate route that would later become known as The Ledo Road. "The first section up to the Burmese border is relatively easy and so is the next, but the closer we get to Myitkyina down here, the more Japs there will be. If I'm going to take troops down there, I'll need regular air-drops without excuses that they can't deliver because they have been bombed or whatever. So, what I want is a forward airstrip somewhere around here." He circled an area further to the south and looked at Stock. "We're going to be out on a limb without the chance of being re-supplied by road until it is built and in the meantime, I need to be certain that I can count on a second source of supply."

What Wingate didn't tell Stock was that it was his own plan for an incursion behind the Japanese lines. That he would keep to himself. He allowed Stock half a minute to study the terrain. In some parts it rose above 5,000 feet along a series of ridges that continued for several hundred miles in a southerly direction. Its northern end connected to the eastern arm of the Himalayas and acted as a natural barrier between India and Burma and, beyond that, another even higher range into China. The map was mainly shaded green, denoting that the vast region was very heavily forested, interrupted only by the occasional river and even rarer dots that highlighted a town or village.

Stock looked at the edge of the maps. "Who surveyed this and how long ago?"

Wingate stood upright and frowned. "Good question and one that I am afraid I can't answer. Nobody's been there for years as far as we know, so it was either a missionary or possibly some expedition." He looked closer at the notes scrawled on the side." By the style of the writing, I'd say it was made well before the last war or even late last century. I see now why you ask, but I'm afraid it's all we've got."

Looking at the maps again, it dawned on Stock that he wouldn't have the benefit of any of the earth moving equipment the regiment had brought with them for the simple reason that they wouldn't be able to get it there. and even if they could, it would most likely take them the rest of the month to do just that.

"How many men can you let me have?"

It wasn't Alfredson who answered but Wingate, "None, I'm afraid. You see, this operation must be kept quiet for reasons I won't go into now, because it's the Americans' airfields that officially have to take priority and we have to be seen to be building their runways." He looked at Stock to gauge his reaction and realised he would have to explain further. "There's political forces at work here, namely the Chinese, and it seems that General Sitwell has promised them hundreds of tons of supplies in return for their allied support. If we can't get those supplies to them, some of them may well side with the Japanese. You see, this part of China is so remote from the rest of it that their militia is governed by the Mandarins in the provincial cities. They don't really care two hoots about the age-old enmity between their two nations once their palms are greased with money or supplies. It's not a clear cut 'us and them' situation, so you can see why we have to be seen to be doing all we can to expedite the supply route into China."

Politics had so far not featured in Stock's life, yet he could see the logic behind Wingate's report. He hadn't a clue as to how many men or brigades were being talked about but if significant resources were being used to keep the Chinese happy, then it must be significant.

"Give me a minute or two, will you?" With his hands clasped behind his back, he walked aimlessly away from the two colonels and considered the conundrum. He was sure Wingate wasn't telling him everything, otherwise he'd have his brigade carry out the work, but then again they may be being utilised elsewhere. He decided not to speculate why Wingate was being circumspect right now and instead concentrate on the problem before him. One thing was certain, though; he couldn't do it on his own. He paced up and down and round in circles for a full five minutes, hearing the colonels talking quietly to each other in the background, all the while picturing how it could be done. When he stopped, the colonels fell silent, and he strode back over to them.

"Given a bit of luck, I may be able to do it, but I'll need a jeep, a lorry, a squad, a radio and someone who knows the area."

Alfredson looked briefly at Wingate. "I'm sure we can let you have that, but we'd have to ask about for the local. There's a regiment of Gurkhas temporarily stationed here but they're ordered down to Imphal tomorrow. Perhaps they may know someone. What have you got in mind?"

He leaned over the table to look closer at the map. "This town here, Laju. Is that more or less where you want your airstrip?

"Ideally beyond the ridge and a bit further south, but at a push, yes."

"And do we know where their sympathies lie? Because if we can utilise their manpower and knowledge of resources in the area, then we stand a chance. I take it you need a runway long enough for a DC3?" Stock asked, referring to the most common form of air transport, the Douglas Dakota which was famed for its short take-off and landing abilities on almost any reasonably flat surface and was the mainstay of the logistics corps, courtesy of the Americans.

"We don't really know what lies beyond the Patkai Ridge but, if the locals round here are anything to go by, they won't have any love of the Japanese. The further you go into the hinterland, the more you'll find they probably speak any one of a number of tribal languages, still wear loincloths, and hunt with spears. Maybe this is your chance to discover a new tribe. Let's hope they're not cannibals, eh?" Wingate chuckled. "And you're right about the Dakotas, so you'll need a runway at least 1200 feet long, preferably 1500 or more. How do you propose going about it?"

"I have one or two other ideas and I won't bore you with the nitty-gritty right now, but I may need help picking up some equipment. If you can accompany me to the stores, sir?" He looked at Alfredson who nodded.

"Right then, I'll leave you two to work out your nitty-gritty bits but come and see me before you go. I have some radio protocols to go through with you. You'll find me over at General Sullivan's Headquarters on the airfield." Wingate clapped Stock on the shoulder, abruptly turned, and marched off.

Stock's daydream was punctured when a coil of thick rope rubbed against his leg as, pulled by half a dozen villagers, it snaked its way towards a large boulder a few feet away. His measured eye had already ascertained that it would be long enough but now he had doubts as he had forgotten to add the extra thirty or so feet to go round the boulder and back onto itself. Under the watchful gaze of a semi-circle of villagers, and with the help of Pranab, he secured the knot before turning and looking at the crowd of villagers who lined the vertical bank opposite.

"Ask these two to stay here and shout if anything moves when we pull the rope tight but bring the others over to the other side. Ok?"

Pranab rattled away in the local language – there were so many of them, a chap couldn't keep up - and Stock led the way back over the top of his rocky dam. As he did so, he looked down at the second rope to satisfy himself that it was in the right position.

There were twenty or so villagers waiting for him with deadpan faces. 'Probably hoping I will fall in,' he thought to himself as he strode up to the big tree he had selected earlier and turned again to Pranab.

"Tell them again that we're going to take the first rope round this tree, pull it as tight as we can then tie it off to that tree over there. We are going to need most of them pulling on this side of the rope, not that side. Oh, and they need to wait for my command."

He didn't want them to waste their energy with premature tugging. As Pranab barked out the orders, Stock decided he had better set an example and picked up the rain-sodden rope that squelched under his grip. It immediately reminded him of his tug-of-war days at school as he started to take up the strain and was quickly joined by the others, who jabbered away. With their bare feet and curling toes gripping the ground, they had the advantage over him as they weren't wearing boots. He left them to it, and went to check the rope across the face of the dam was staying put and supporting it. Testing the tension and satisfying himself that it was just about as taut as it was going to get, he trotted over to the rope's end, fed it round the chosen tree and tied it off so that it would self-tighten.

"Now the other one," he shouted and pointed simultaneously. He didn't need Pranab to translate. The villagers, now flushed with success and knowing what was being asked of them, started to show a smile here and there as they ambled over and picked it up without prompting. Stock stood back to keep one eye on where the rope crossed the ravine, watched as they organised themselves, and started to heave. Up until now, they had been doubtful and shown little enthusiasm towards Stock's plan, but once shown what was required, adapted readily. He was tying the final knot when a shout made him turn. One of the two villagers on the other side was jumping up and down at the same time as pointing at the top of the dam exactly where the ropes crossed.

Pranab, who was helping with the knot translated, "He says the dam's starting to move but the rope is holding it back, Sahib."

With a final tug on the rope, Stock trotted over to the edge of the ravine, nearly slipping over, and saw that their timely intervention with the ropes was working by restraining the top couple of feet of the stones and boulders they had previously put in place. He wasn't worried about the lower part as he considered it thick enough to withstand the huge buildup of water pressure. It had stood successfully for years, but the top two or three feet was much thinner. As the water rose, the danger was it would topple into the ravine fifty feet below. The ropes were working and he prayed that they would be strong enough. Quite a bit of water was now spouting from the dam face as more pressure forced it through the gaps that they had been unable to plug at short notice, but it was an insignificant amount compared to what was falling from the skies.

He walked over the small ridge and down the slippery slope to the pathetically small channel they had dug out the previous day. He stood still for a moment trying to discern how fast the water level was rising. It was only inches away now. His plan was simple enough. To divert the waters from one valley to another, and by doing so, save their village from being washed away. It all depended upon the water lapping over into the small channel and then cutting its own way through the ground to form its own route down into the next valley. Stock respected the power of water from first-hand knowledge back in the flat lands of Norfolk. Only three years before the war during one particularly wet winter which threatened to flood the entire county, he and his family had had to divert one of the larger drainage ditches away from the very productive fields. The winter crops had been sown but, if flooded to the point that the topsoil was washed away, then over a hundred acres of prime arable land would have had to lie fallow for several years. His father had sketched out his proposal. Despite the Family's howls of scepticism, his plan of making a small cut in one of the banks to allow the water to make its own enlarged aperture and flow where he wanted it to flow, had worked.

Now it was Stock's turn. With delight he saw the first trickle of water breech the top of the channel. The principle was sound and so was his engineering, but it all relied upon the dam holding out until the water cut enough of the soil away to relieve the pressure. He had chosen this specific spot because it was directly above a fissure in the mountain. Once the water level dropped, then he would be able to breathe a big sigh of relief. He took his hat off but hurriedly put it back on again as the rain splattered into his eyes. 'Please let it work, please'. If it didn't work, then all his labour from the village would probably dissipate and he would never get his airstrip built. He reflected once again how important this was to him, his career, Alfredson, Wingate, and all those others who were relying on him to build this hidden runway.

He wanted to see the muddy water actually cut its way wider and deeper. He wanted to take the opportunity to show the villagers what he had learned from his Father: that water can be used for one's own purposes. He went back over the ridge to tell Pranab to get them to follow him and watch nature in motion. They were all standing around watching the ropes and the dam.

"Tell those two fellows to come back over this side and ask the others to follow me. I want them to see this," he ordered. Pranab rattled away at the top of his voice as Stock started to walk back up to the ridge. He had gone but half a dozen paces when a shout made him turn his head round. The two men had crossed two-thirds of the way along the top of the dam, but now Stock could only see one of them. From the excited cries from the other villagers, who had stopped following Stock and were now looking down, he assumed one of them must have fallen. He ran as fast as he could without going over on the treacherously slippery ground. As he stopped next to the dam, he spied one of the villagers clinging onto the straddling ropes, his colleague jabbering away to Pranab.

"He says the top of the dam moved and he fell over."

"Tell him to climb along the ropes to this end," Stock barked. He could see that the dam had indeed moved a little and more water was beginning to spout through. 'Not now,' he prayed. 'Not when we're so close'.

"Quickly. Get him to make his way onto this bank."

More jabbering between the dangling man and Pranab. "He says he's frightened of heights and can't move Sahib."

Stock looked at the petrified young man, who was pretty much still a child he realised, with his feet on the bottom rope and his hands wrapped round the top one and covering his head. His terror was quite understandable really when the option of letting go would mean a few seconds fall before being pulped to death on the flat rocks below.

They all heard as much as felt the top of the dam move another inch but it was still restrained by the ropes. Some of the villagers moved back a pace away from their vantage point along the edge. If the ropes failed, it would be the demise of this lad, along with a birthing woman and baby. He had to do something because nobody else was going to.

"Here." He took off his hat, Sam Browne and holster, and handed them to Pranab, knelt down, grasped the top rope, swung his feet onto the bottom rope and started to edge himself towards the stranded figure. He was only twenty feet or so away but he immediately felt terribly vulnerable as a squirt of water from between the stones soaked his already wet chest. It was loud, not just from the rain but the hiss of water as it was squeezed through ever slowly widening gaps. Ten feet now and he scraped his hand on a sharp rock as the rope pressed against it. It was certainly taut and holding back the dam, but because the spray temporarily blinded him at one point, he had to feel for the next handhold on the rope where it didn't rest against two flat boulders. He made a conscious effort not to look down as he inched his way across, reached out and touched the fellow's elbow and realised that that was the easy part. Getting him to let go and cling onto him before traversing back to dry land was going to be the hard part.

"Look at me," he shouted. He knew the boy didn't understand English but trusted his meaning was plain enough as he tapped the terrified chap hard a few times on the upper arm to get his attention. His eyes wide, the lad jerked his head round. 'Christ, how am I going to get him to grab onto me?' he thought. But he was saved from the dilemma when suddenly the small rope, which they had used to drag the larger ones across the ravine, appeared from above. He looked up and saw Pranab and three others standing on top of the dam just a few feet above his head, dangling the rope within reach.

"Tie it round him, Sahib, and we will pull him up."

Easier said than done as far as Stock was concerned because it meant he would somehow have to keep one arm looped round the top rope while attaching the thinner rope round the lad's waist. It meant he would have to lean out. He felt another vibration from the top rope as it stretched a little more under the strain of holding back the dam and heard the grinding of rocks from somewhere within. He had no choice but to ignore this and position himself so that his stomach was against the man so he could reach round him with one end of the rope. It took another minute before he had the end in his other hand. He knew how to tie a slip knot but for a moment his mind went blank before he went into automatic. It was going to hurt the fellow a little when it closed around his chest when those above him took the strain, but that would be a small price to pay in exchange for his life.

He slipped the knot as close as possible and looked up to see Pranab and the others staring back at him. "Right. Try that."

The slack rope straightened out and the lad let out a cry of abject fear as he realised what was happening. He wound his arms round the top rope even more.

"Tell him to let go," Stock shouted. Pranab responded and the boy jabbered back and shook his head from side to side.

"How do I say 'let go'?"

Pranab had to tell him twice before Stock shouted the message straight into his ear.

More head shaking from the lad.

'We haven't got time for this,' Stock thought. He grabbed his fingers and started to uncoil them. All the while the lad was wailing for all he was worth. Fortuitously, one of the man's feet slipped and he grabbed onto Stock's shirt in place of the rope. A second later, his other arm snaked around Stock's neck. Stock immediately felt the strain of his weight being taken from above and had to wrench his arm away from his throat. Then he was gone, his feet kicking wildly, missing Stock's head by inches.

Stock took the opportunity to rest for a few seconds and wipe the water away from his eyes before starting back along the ropes. He had hardly reached the end when hands reached out and pulled him to his feet and he looked round to see he was surrounded by the villagers who, without exception, were all smiling at him and clapping him on his back, touching him on his arms, legs, body and jabbering away.

"You are a hero, Sahib," Pranab declared as he forced himself to the forefront of the crowd. "Nobody else would have done that and he would have fallen to a long death." Stock knew what he meant. Behind Pranab stood the lad with tearful eyes, but he stepped forward and hugged Stock round the middle.

"He says he owes you his life and he will be very pleased to do what you ask of him from now on. And he says he's sorry for not letting go."

Pranab shouted a few words at the crowd, who responded with jubilant shouts, some even dancing in circles round each other.

"You're one of them now, Sahib, and your brave deed will not be forgotten. They're calling for a feast tonight and you will be their honoured guest." Pranab looked up. "It will be dark soon anyway."

"Before they go, ask them to follow me."

They arrived at the channel that was unrecognizable from when Stock had last looked at it a few minutes ago. Just as the last man peered round his colleague to see, a large boulder finally gave up its perch, tumbled away and disappeared over the edge. All the soil around it that had held it in place had been eroded away by the force of the water. Immediately a thundering torrent took its place, throwing spray high into the air, cutting deeper and wider. Then a significant section of the channel wall collapsed, allowing yet more water to release its energy. It was all up to gravity from here on in as more and more soil, rocks, and gravel succumbed to the power of the muddy waters and cut their way towards the fissure.

"It is getting night soon, Sahib, and we must go," Pranab's voice urged.

Stock wanted to stay and watch but it was certainly becoming gloomy. As they passed the dam, he stopped briefly for one last look and was gratified to see that the level had fallen, not much yet, but he would come and check again in the morning.

On their way back down the narrow trail in amongst the chattering villagers, he reflected on his achievements. Now that he had secured the safety of the village and earned their trust, he hoped that more of them would volunteer to help him prepare the landing strip. Over the past few days, only a handful had come forward. At the rate they were clearing the jungle, it would take them months. He would ask Ujjal tonight.

The news that the dam would stand, and subsequentially their village, had somehow got ahead of them. As they entered the small arena more or less at the heart of the place, flaming torches encircled the throng that had assembled and everybody wanted to touch the man that had made it all possible. Stock was jostled as he made his way over to his fellow compatriots standing outside one of the stilted huts. There were only four of them, led by Sergeant Day.

"I hear you've worked one of your miracles again, sir. 'Fraid I can't lend you a towel that's any drier than mine, but at least it's stopped raining."

"Are you referring to the dam or the lad I saved from falling into the ravine?"

"What lad?"

Stock started to explain but was cut short by the quieting of the crowd that parted to let Ujjal through. Their previous encounter two days earlier had been a bit frosty as Ujjal had reluctantly negotiated pay for his villagers to work on the runway. This time it was a different story. Background jungle noises, dripping rainwater and flaming torches were all that could be heard as the Head Man of the village stood in front of Stock.

Pranab translated as he broke into speech. "He says that it was his grandfather who once warned him long, long years ago about the dam. He said that should the monsoon rains come early and finish late, as they have done this year, then the village might be swept away by the floods. This is why he asked you to make the dam higher and save their home. This is his test of trust. Because you save one of his sons, you have proven yourself worthy and will be the boy's godfather, the one who keeps evil spirits away. Do you accept?"

The thought of being a stranger's godfather caught Stock by surprise but he quickly assessed the consequences if he refused. "Tell him the honour is mine."

Ujjal cried out a single word and the villagers cheered and whooped with delight.

Pranab continued once the jubilant crown hushed enough. "Ushmi is his third wife and has just given birth to his fourth son who, thanks to you, will be brought up here in this village. To celebrate, he has ordered that four male goats will be killed and eaten tonight."

Stock thought that the previous shouts of jubilation were loud, but they were nothing compared to the frantic noise that now surrounded them. Yelling, singing, and dancing started immediately and the crowd opened to allow themselves space. While the noise abated a little and the villagers went about their preparations for the feast, Ujjal took a step closer to Stock. Pranab was certainly earning his keep.

"He is offering help with your task from everyone in the village but asks that you pay with rice instead of rupees.

Stock tried not to show his delight at the proposition but couldn't resist a smile. Once the runway was finished, it would be simple enough to fly in enough bags of rice to keep this village fed.

Accompanied by Alfredson and his superior authority, Stock had browbeaten the quartermaster into letting him fill the lorry with everything non-mechanical that would be needed. Ropes, mattocks, adzes, sledgehammers, rams, wedges, axes, saws, the list was comprehensive and enough for a hundred men. For the first two days, Ujjal had only allowed a few of his sons to assist, but now with his promise of several hundred hands, the task of clearing a runway would be possible - and on time.

Stock had chosen a fairly even, and for some reason unknown to him, a less densely forested area, at the bottom of a valley adjacent to a small river. He had given this a lot of thought. His logic for siting it next to a river was fourfold. Firstly, if an enemy plane flew within sight, at first glance they might assume the cleared area was part of the river and just ignore it. A rectangular mud-brown clearing in the middle of green jungle would have stood out for miles around. Secondly, being at the bottom of a valley, an enemy plane would need to be more directly overhead to see it. Thirdly, rocks and stones from the riverbed were readily at hand. Fourthly, the valley sides funneled any wind nicely to create a headwind. The single most important factor when building an airstrip was its positioning. Above all else, this governed every other element of construction. He would remember this valuable lesson if he was ever called upon to build another.

First to be cleared would be the bigger trees, followed by the brush, much of which was bamboo and although it grew back quickly, it was fairly easy to chop down. The slight natural slope would act as its own drainage, thus necessitating just one gully along its length instead of one each side. Using the sledgehammers, wedges and spikes, bigger rocks would be broken down, mixed and crushed with smaller ones under the heavy rams to form the runway's base. He didn't know how many planes would be parked up at any one given time, and had to assume a maximum of three, so had to clear a semi-circle off to one side at one end to enable turning. He was rather pleased with himself that he managed to create most of this area under the higher branches of some taller trees.

From a pilot's perspective, it would be a tricky approach down a fairly narrow valley with a rough landing on the broken stones, trees on one side and a river on the other. The length of the runway would mean he would need to put the plane down right at the beginning of the strip and apply his brakes vigorously, but the headwind would help. In all circumstances and around the globe, a plane will both take off and land into the wind, and Stock assumed that the incoming Dakotas would be laden, but much lighter taking off. He had been assured by Ujjal that the wind always blew in the same direction, which was why there was only the one turning circle. Pilots would have to put up with taking off with a tail-wind - besides which, that would be downhill.

It was nearly midnight by the time Ujjal declared the feast over. Stock met with his men under the moonlit shadow of the back of the lorry.

"I do not know how many of Ujjal's chaps will be helping tomorrow, but if the whole village turns out, we are going to have to organise them into gangs. You men will have to lead them and I am going to allocate you your different tasks for the morning, but make sure you do not offend them, otherwise we will still be here for Christmas. First thing in the morning, I am going back up the trail to check on the dam because I want to make sure there's still a village standing and somewhere for these people to live. Sergeant Day and Private Brockington, I want you to arrange the biggest party to concentrate on those trees we marked out, starting at the village end. Corporal Clews, you start by tackling the bamboo with a smaller gang at the other end, much as you were doing today. Madigan, you take a dozen or so down to the river and start breaking up the rocks. Make piles of different grades. We will be putting the heavier stuff down first and filling in the gaps with the smaller ones. Ok? You need the exercise anyway."

They all laughed at Stock's reference to Private Geoff Madigan's stout frame. Stock was glad they had so far been keen to get the job done. He had chosen them because of their attitudes, but he knew that when the physicality of the job started to tell, he would somehow need to perk them up.

"Look. It is going to be hard work but set an example to these fellows and maybe they will follow your lead. You know I promised the colonel we would have this up and running by the end of the month. That only gives us a little over two weeks, but you too will be given the credit if we can finish in time. Not only will we be the first to build an airfield this side of the mountain, but once we get back, I will make sure that every engineering regiment gets to hear about it, so let's show the Yanks how the British succeed. Oh and, as ever, no fires. I do not want to give away our position with any smoke."

*****

It was a struggle because not only was it steeper than he remembered, but also the radio Stock had strapped to his back felt like it was getting heavier the higher up the trail he went. He had to stop as he neared the dam and took the opportunity to palm some water from a rivulet. Eventually he reached it and pride swelled as he surveyed the previous day's handiwork. Not only had the water level fallen well below the top of the old dam, but his diversion was working perfectly. He put the radio down and sat on a rock overlooking the small reservoir to wipe his brow. This was one of the reasons why he had volunteered for the Royal Engineers; to make something worthwhile. He hoped his legacy would ensure the safety of the village for decades to come.

Because of the overhanging trees, he couldn't see much from where he sat, but he looked up towards the summit of the mountain anyway. To make the radio transmit, he was going to have to get up there. It made all the sense in the world to have made an early start. Not only was it the cooler and less humid part of the day but also the driest. He was fast learning that during the monsoon season, which by all accounts should have finished by now, the heavens opened up every afternoon during the hottest part of the day. He was hoping to be back down in the village before that happened. In any case, he was due to radio in before midday today. With a quick glance at his watch, he hoisted the radio onto his back and set off up the almost invisible trail, going over in his mind the set of radio instructions Wingate had given him.

The trees weren't exactly thinning out but there was slightly less scrub at this altitude. He didn't have a map showing contours but estimated he must have climbed over three thousand feet. The relative coolness of the air and his rasping breath attested to that. He couldn't go any further anyhow because right in front of him was a chasm. He chose a vantage point where a rockfall had naturally cleared an area. While the radio warmed up, he looked down the valley stretching out of sight through the misty mountains - nothing but trees in every direction. It made him very aware of the isolated remoteness of his predicament. Remembering his instructions, he returned the dial to the pre-arranged frequency and picked up the handset.

"Peter calling Wishbone," he repeated several times while adjusting the dial.

"Wishbone here. Repeat your callsign and authenticate."

His authentication was his service number backwards. "Peter 530118. Message for the chaplain." Again, he had to repeat at the same time as adjusting the dial for a clearer signal but managed it in the end. Why Colonel Wingate had chosen the codename 'the chaplain' was a mystery.

He had been told to keep any messages short as the Japanese might have a listening station, but also not to refer directly to what he wanted to say. Instead, he would have to be circumspect with his choice of words. He was also told that he would have to go through a relay station as the range of his set was limited and unable to reach Dinjan directly. He waited for several minutes before Wishbone replied, presumably while they fetched Wingate.

"Chaplain ready. Please relay your message."

This was his first time using a radio for real and he had always wondered what it would be like. The wonderment quickly dispelled as he concentrated on making sure his message would be understood by the recipient.

"Pitch found and being rolled ready for the bowler from the Pavilion End only. Short balls and bouncers only. Over."

A nasty thought occurred to him. What if Wingate wasn't conversant with the cricket ground at The Oval in Kennington? He'd certainly understand the first part of the message, even if he didn't play cricket, but would he understand the part about the Pavilion End as opposed to the Vauxhall End?

"Passing message on now, Peter."

He suspected what was coming next and was prepared for it. Additionally, he would somehow need to let Wingate know where he was. Even though he didn't know his exact location, had already decided to give Wingate a compass heading from Dinjan. At least that would provide the pilots some idea as to his whereabouts, but as far as distance was concerned, he was helpless. He would need to use flares when the Dakotas did start circling, or as a last resort, the radio.

"Wishbone to Peter. Message reads are you on target for a first innings victory? Over."

"Target is 150 by end of play and beyond expectations. Over."

He waited for Wingate's response hoping that he would understand that they were 150 degrees from Dinjan, ahead of schedule and in the ideal area.

"Wishbone to Peter. Your message understood. The chaplain is asking about the crowd and if they are all supporting the home team. Over."

Stock presumed he was referring to the villagers. "Our home supporters are doing all they can to egg us on but looking forward to tea and supper. Are you able to arrange a long-grain table for five hundred straight away?"

"Message being passed Peter."

Stock hoped that his reference to long-grain rice as well as a table would be clear to an Englishman, but not to a Japanese eavesdropper, and he waited nearly two minutes before the radio squawked into life again.

"Wishbone to Peter. Message reads only have floating-grain and will do best to provide before rain stops play tomorrow. Next transmission when the last batsman reaches the crease."

Stock translated the surreptitious message to mean that his next radio contact would be the day before the landing strip was ready. That would be the last day of September. More importantly, bags of rice would be air-dropped by parachute before lunchtime tomorrow.

"Thank you, Wishbone. Out." He switched off the set but sat there for several moments holding the handset, gazing out at the wonderful vista around him and wondering once again if he would really like to settle down in this part of the world when the war ended. So far, he had liked the country and the people who lived off the land. Compared to him, they were as poor as church mice, yet happy and content with their lot in life, and their ignorance of worldly matters kept them that way. What would they care about whatever happened outside of their valley, and in any case, there was little they could do about it. But it was he who had dragged them unknowingly into the war and if the Japanese did succeed and find the airstrip… He stopped thinking about the repercussions and instead swatted an insect that was threatening to crawl up his sleeve.

He thoroughly enjoyed his downhill hike, taking time to take in the landscape whenever a gap in the trees allowed. He inevitably stopped at his dam, sitting on the same rock again. Now that the water level had fallen, the thick ropes would no longer be needed and he would have to send someone up at some point to retrieve them. Someone who didn't suffer from vertigo.

He nearly made it before the afternoon's torrential downpour started and ran the last few hundred yards to put the radio in the back of the lorry before it got wet. While he was there, he opened a tin of bully beef before setting off towards the airstrip. The nearer he got, the louder the singing, not just one song in unison, but several, as though in competition with each other. He stopped at the edge of the clearing that only yesterday had been jungle. Everywhere he looked, there were villagers of all ages armed with their own tools as well as those he had provided, cutting, sawing, digging, felling. It was a veritable hive of activity, and for over a minute he stood behind a large rock and watched their progress with a critical eye. As Private Brockington spotted him, came over and stood beside him, he noticed that there were also several women helping to clear the ground and tackle the smaller branches. This came as a bit of a shock to him, as in his own mind this was more like man's work but they were being very useful by removing the rotting and decaying flora from underfoot.

"I reckon they've done this before, they know what they're doing alright. Look at that team over there. They're working together to uproot that big tree."

Stock watched as half a dozen villagers on each end of the coils of tree twine, wrapped round opposite sides some twenty feet up the large trunk, alternately slackened and tightened, creating an irresistible oscillation. This time they sang in turn as the tree swayed from side to side until it gently reached an angle of natural repose, balanced by the vibrating twine. Those on the slack side rushed round to grab hold of the taut twine, took their lead from one voice, burst into a different song and pulled together. As the great tree gathered pace towards the ground, they scattered in all directions except directly away from it, chattering and shouting loudly. A cheer went up as it crashed to the ground and almost immediately a few armed with saws started to attack the thicker boughs, while others axed at the thinner branches.

"See what I mean, sir. If they keep this up I reckon we'll reach the far end in five or six days, although there's that stand of bigger trees about three-quarters of the way down which might hold things up a bit. I don't think it's the same wood as these trees, so can you come and have a look?"

As they headed off towards the far end Stock paced out the clearing, having already estimated about eighty yards by eye, and smiled to himself when he trod the eighty-third. If they could manage a hundred yards a day and reach his projected five hundred or minimum of fifteen hundred feet, then Brockington was right. The happy sounds of the villagers receded as they made their way through the undergrowth. It took them nearly ten minutes of fighting their way through the vegetation before Brockington pointed up at the first of a clump of trees with darkly shaded bark of and strands dangling down around the main trunk. Stock's suspicions were confirmed when he ran his finger over a fissure which oozed a milky white fluid.

"They're rubber trees."

Brockington gave an exaggerated look of surprise, "What, sir, are you saying they bounce?"

"No. Not made of rubber, but where rubber comes from," Stock laughed at the deliberately goofy look on Brockington's face. "Alright, alright, very funny. Here, feel this." He pointed for Brockington to rub his finger over the same fissure and squeeze the milk between his finger and thumb. "Sticky, eh?"

"Yes. I'll bet this is the same stuff they've used in their huts. You know, between the timbers. Corporal Clews had it all over his hand on the first night. Haa haa. We really ribbed him about that one, if you know what I mean. Haa haa."

Stock did know what he meant. "Better that than seducing one of the village girls. Just remind the others to keep their hands off."

"Will do, sir." The brief moment of humour had gone.

"Now, where is the boundary from here?"

"Just over here." Brockington took a few steps, rounded a fronded thicket and stood on the invisible edge of where the new runway would be.

Stock pondered for a moment. "Leave these until we have a clearer idea. With all this jungle around we may even be able to keep them here. Right. You go back while I go and see how Corporal Clews is getting on."

Without an interpreter, the corporal was not making as much progress as Day and Brockington. One villager had been bitten by a snake and another had cut his hand badly. Down at the riverbank, a shirtless Madigan was showing off his muscular prowess by swinging a twenty-one pound sledgehammer, while a cringing villager held the chisel firm against a small boulder. As it cracked asunder, the villager hopped smartly to one side.

"I know it's too big for what we want, but I've been wanting to have a go at it all morning. It's been right in our way. This is where we want to put our stockpile."

Stock could see several piles of stones that had been collected from the edges of the riverbed, ready for distribution once the flora had been cleared.

"Want to have a go, sir?" Madigan held out the heavy hammer at arm's length. Stock made him wait for his response to see how long he could hold it there. He knew he was being challenged, not so much his authority, just his ability. His standing would diminish slightly if he refused, but even more so if he tried and missed the chisel. He stepped forward and relieved the weight from Madigan's arm, which had begun to quiver.

"You're on. But you hold the chisel."

They held eye contact for a moment, Stock searching for any sign of fear in Madigan's eye, but there was none. They both knew that if he missed, Madigan could end up with a shattered wrist.

He selected one half of the innocent boulder and took a couple of practice swings at it. The wooden handle was more slippery than he realised and he had to concentrate on keeping a firm grip on the shaft. Both times he hit the spot he'd chosen, but only he knew this. He decided to twist Madigan's tail.

"Just off to the left a bit, but I think I have got it now. You had better stand on the right. Ready?"

Madigan did his best to hide his concern but his nervous swallowing was not missed by Stock who knew he had won the gamesmanship. Stretching out Madigan's agony, he took his time looking over the small crowd that had gathered around them, assumed the position and nodded to the corporal.

The last time he had swung such an instrument was back on the farm in Norfolk, knocking in fence posts. and that was over three years ago, but he still felt confident he could hit the chisel square on.

He had spent hours practising, first with a claw hammer and four-inch nails by hitting them with one blow, flush into the end of sawn logs. Then he would line up three or four nails and sequentially attempt the same, pausing only to raise the hammer to a suitable height, and succeeding more often than not. Stock was glad that Madigan didn't know this.

CLANG. The rocky hemisphere split wide open as the tall chisel drove directly through it into the ground. Madigan let out the breath he had been holding.

Stock stood the hefty hammer upright. "Easy enough. The rest is up to you, Private." He walked away, not letting Madigan see the smile on his face.

*****

His blisters were so bad that he cursed in the local Assamese dialect, which he'd been picking up a bit, as he trekked up the mountain, but this time he had the young lad carrying the radio, the same lad he had saved from falling into the ravine two weeks earlier. Rubrat was his name and, predictably, it had been changed to Rugrat or Ratty by his men. Over the last two weeks and presumably out of gratitude, he had embarrassingly latched onto Stock and appointed himself his personal slave, but Stock had drawn the line when it came to his personal ablutions and sleeping. At first, it was more of an embuggerance as every time he turned round, the lad was there and, as often as not, in the way, but Stock had used him as a runner, as one who could hold the other end of his home-made level or keep a pole upright while he took measurements. On top of this, they were teaching each other their languages, and now he freely cursed in both at the aggravating blisters that tore into his feet. He was not looking forward to going back downhill either, after he had made radio contact with Wishbone again. The sores on the back of his right foot would suffer the most, but it was something that only he could do, and not delegate.

He took his mind off his abrasive injuries and instead thought of those working below him in the valley. His own men had suffered, no, were still suffering, particularly their feet as their footwear never had the chance to dry out, but at least it had not rained for the past two days. Ujjal had told him that the monsoon had now ended. The one good thing that had come out of the heavy afternoon rains had been that it had helped to level and settle the finer stones on the runway and had also shown Stock that his drainage system worked. With just the turning circle to finish clearing, they had finished the landing strip the previous afternoon and, better still, he had one day in hand. It was now the 29th of September and he would be able to report that he had achieved what everyone, except Colonel Wingate, had said could not be done. The villagers had intensified their efforts the day after the Dakota had parachuted a load of rice bags. One of them had split open upon landing, but that hadn't deterred them from scooping virtually every last grain into baskets. Ujjal had announced that they now had enough rice for months and there would be another feast that night. They happily gorged themselves on a concoction of rice, goat, and leaves, while the villagers talked excitedly about the noisy bird that had provided them. Afterwards, Sergeant Day had introduced them to the joys of arm wrestling.

Once they had cleared the forest and laid the stones, Stock had them cut some of the fallen straighter branches where boughs protruded and upended them to use as rams for flattening the stones into the ground. There were two villagers to each ram, one line abreast the strip, with a second and third row following on behind. He had also distributed twenty of the metal rams he had purloined from the stores. These were much lighter than the logs and needed only one villager to operate easily. It was slow and tedious work in the heat, and he watched from the sidelines as the three rows made their way ever so slowly to the far end, calculating that it would take well over a day to complete this final part of the operation, possibly longer. Indeed, they were making particularly slow headway but, after nearly two weeks of intensive laboring, he could hardly crack the whip over them. After all they had made stunning progress even if now they were wilting. They were not singing any more, nor were they as happy as at the outset, but he had had Ujjal assure them that this would be their last major job.

He listened to the rhythmic thumping that vibrated the stones into place and was about to turn away from the somnolent scene when something caught his eye in the middle of the third row, and instead he walked over to take a closer look. The villager was a small man with his back half-turned against his direction of approach and he continued to raise and drop the metal ram onto the ground as Stock neared. Unlike the others however, he was not shuffling his feet forwards but continuing to lift the ram just a few inches off the ground before letting it drop back in exactly the same place. Stock looked at the flattened ground and was baffled as to why the man continued his ramming in exactly the same place each time. He craned his neck enough to look into the man's face. His eyes were not only shut, but he was oblivious to Stock's presence. The man was asleep.

He looked round at the rest of them and saw he had a somber audience, although most of them continued with what they were doing while looking over at him. The fact that the man was three-quarters asleep but still continuing to try to carry out his job, displayed an eagerness, but his actions were really rather unhelpful in getting the job done. Stock wanted to shout at the man and berate him for being a slacker and was about to do so when he had another idea. He quietly laid himself flat on the ground and stretched out his hand, palm down, so that it was directly under the man's ram and waited for a reaction. The man continued his pathetic ramming without hurting Stock and the frequency of each lift became less and less over the next thirty seconds or so. The others slowly realised what was going on and gradually stopped their own efforts and started laughing at the absurd scene. Soon they had all joined in and still the man slept. It may have been the bead of sweat or the fly that landed on his cheek, but it was probably the sound of laughter and comments that woke the man.

At first, he continued his ramming as he looked around at his fellow villagers but then realised they were all laughing in his direction. He let his ram fall a final time before looking over his shoulder to see what was worth looking at, and still he had not seen Stock at his feet with his hand now trapped beneath the flat head of the ram. The blank look on his face epitomised one who had just woken but it turned to horror when he eventually looked down and saw the prone man. With shock galvanizing him into action, he took a step backwards, tripped over his own feet, and landed on his bottom, letting out a cry as he did so, mainly because he had landed on the point of a stone.

This was too much for the other villagers, who found the entire scenario so funny that they roared with laughter and whooped with delight at their friend's embarrassment. Stock joined in their laughter as he lay there with his hand still stuck. He could have easily lifted the ram off with his other hand but left it there emphasizing the absurd situation and watched as the man hopped to his feet and lifted the ram off. Stock decided to be even more theatrical. Standing up, he lifted his flattened hand out with his other arm and let it dangle as though it had just died. As he jiggled it about and it flopped lifelessly from side to side, the villagers reacted predictably, some squatting down or hanging onto the logs to contain themselves, others jumping up and down. Stock could see his own men in the first row clapping and cheering and he knew he had handled the situation just right.

The apologetic man in front of him was jabbering away so fast, he could only catch one word in ten and it was Pranab who came to his rescue.

"He says he is very sorry, Sahib, and hopes your hand will live. He promises to be a better ramming person and will do bigger rams from now on. He asks for your forgiveness."

The worried look on the man's face showed sincerity and Stock took his dead hand and placed it on his shoulder.

"Tell him it is not his fault but that if he manages to stay awake until we reach the end, then I will forgive him," Stock said.

The man's face broke into a smile as Pranab translated, "He promises to do so, Sahib."

Other villagers had gathered round to join in, and now started chanting.

"They are renaming him 'Deadhand' in honour of you, Sahib."

Stock called a half-hour break, deciding it would be better to have alert labourers than dozy ones. He thought again about taking a breather himself. It would take them about another half-an-hour to reach the same perch from where he had previously transmitted, but Rubrat wasn't showing any signs of stress and he didn't want the lad to think he was the weaker one of the pair, so he kept going.

The view was the same as it was two weeks ago but clearer than before as he took a swig of water from his canteen while the radio warmed up. He went through the same 'Peter and Wishbone' formalities before reporting that the rain had not stopped play and that the batsmen were ready to receive new balls from the Pavilion End.

"Wishbone to Peter. The Chaplain is not available to pass on his blessing but his verger suggests your team to return to the clubhouse. Over."

Stock interpreted the message to mean that Wingate could not be reached and that Alfredson had left orders for them to return to Dinjan. He was about to ask when the first bowler could be expected, but then thought the better of it. If their transmissions were being monitored by the enemy, it would be a foolish thing to ask and even more foolish to respond. He signed off by saying they would start the long walk back to the clubhouse in the morning.

As they sat round the fire in the centre of the village that night, Stock looked round the circle of their friends, for that was what they had become. He thought his own men looked a little gaunt but by comparison the villagers looked rather healthy and he realised that after they had left the following morning, their life would carry on as before. Ujjal had promised they would keep the runway clear of weeds or anything else that might hinder the planes when they came and had named it George after Stock had explained that that was the name of their king. He had to laugh at their attempts to repeat the name George. As he rolled over in his camp bed, he reflected that it had been very hard work, but at last he had created something worthwhile.

*****

It was only when he reported to Alfredson at the airfield on the outskirts of Dinjan three days later, did he learn that Wingate had been recalled to Dhana where the 77th infantry brigade was training, and that his plan for incursion into Burma had been postponed.

Alfredson continued after the orderly serving tea had left the room, "It's somewhere in the middle of the continent and miles away from here. Wingate didn't tell me much before he left, but he was fuming. He even broke his cane over the general's desk when told that his operation had been put on ice, but I'm rather glad that he's out of our hair, though, because he was starting to cause a nuisance of himself. Even tried to tell me how to organise this regiment more efficiently. Imagine that."

"He did seem a bit of a character. Do you think he will be back?"

"Oh, he'll be back alright. Men like that don't grow on trees but I suppose it makes a change from the usual dogmatic approach some of those at headquarters seem to breed. Anyway, tell me what it was like. How did you really manage to build an operational runway with just coolies?"

"I do not think you could call them 'coolies' even if they were rather cut off from the rest of the world." Stock described an accurate picture for Alfredson and proposed that news of his team's success be published for the benefit of the regiment.

"I'm afraid that won't be possible, but I'll see you get a mention in dispatches. You see, the Americans are going full tilt trying to supply the Chinese with airdrops and your runway is just too far south for their purposes, but I'll certainly let the general know what you achieved. I suspect that once he hears about your prowess you'll be delegated more of them. Even the entire regiment. How do you feel about that?"

Stock hadn't considered what lay beyond the next bend in his army career. Alfredson was being kind, perhaps as a reward for a job well done, but then he realised he was being asked if he could do the same again. 'Crikey,' he thought, 'I'm actually being asked what job I want to do instead of being told.' If he told Alfredson he could do it again, then he would probably be asked to do so, but if he responded negatively, then he may just as well remain an ordinary captain for the rest of the war. In other words, Alfredson was asking him if he wanted his name put forward; unheard of in the British army. But then again, they were lifelong friends.

"If I had to do it again, I would be far better off with more men and above all else, decent equipment. We were lucky that the villagers were so compliant and skilled, and that the jungle was not very dense just there."

"Luck has nothing to do with it," retorted Alfredson jovially. "Well, maybe just a little, but it was your skill in finding the right place that made all the difference."

"Getting earthmoving bulldozers to wherever we go next will be the most important factor. Once we have those, then we can really make headway, but they cannot cut down large trees. That can only be done by hand. Remember, there were nearly a thousand men helping us. If we uprooted even one battalion, that is about half of their number, just think of the supply problems we would have just to sustain us. Those people live off the land and do not require food, water, fuel, ammunition, etcetera, etcetera. And that amount of personnel would be bound to attract the enemy. No, I think if I had to repeat the operation, then just one squad or a company would be enough to train the locals, providing we have the equipment."

"Ummmmmm. I'll let the general know your thoughts," Alfredson paused and considered his next words. "Keep this to yourself for the moment: I hear they are planning a move on Mandalay once the Japanese offensive against Imphal is rebuffed, and make no mistake, it is being rebuffed. We can't let them anywhere near, but they're now trying to push towards Chittagong. That won't help them very much because the river's far too wide there. Miles across."

Stock tried to remember the geography of the region and recalled that Chittagong was more or less on the banks of the very wide mouth of the Brahmaputra River, and much further south than where they were now.

"Your runway's pretty much in a straight line between here and Mandalay, and will probably become very useful once things kick off, but in the meantime we're still helping the Americans - apart from Tiffery's company who are helping to repair the telephone exchange which got hit the other day."

Stock felt deep sadness that his runway wasn't going to be used, at least not straight away, and then maybe not at all. After all his efforts, it was a bit of a come-down.

"You and your men recover the rest of today and tomorrow, then report back here. There's a problem looming with the way they are constructing the culverts on the west side of the main airfield and I want you to look at it."

"Not the latrines this time, then?"

Chapter 6

Burma

Christmas 1943

Captain Stock was laughing. Certainly not out of politeness, but an uncontrollable belly laugh that made his ribs ache. He unknowingly moved both of his hands down each side of his body to support the tender sides of his torso and gasped for air as the heaving racks of mirth rippled in unison throughout his entire body. Had there been a mirror nearby that he could have squinted at through his tearful eyes, he would have seen that his contorted face resembled the darker colours of a disorganized rainbow. And then, just as he was beginning to regain control, he glanced to his right and involuntarily doubled over to help keep himself upright on his own two feet. Every sinew in his body demanded more oxygen. As the last dregs of air were expelled from his lungs in a pathetic wheeze, that part of the human brain which unconsciously controlled his basic bodily functions took over and allowed him to inhale enough to continue his self-inflicted torture. For torture it was.

It seemed like half the population of that part of town had crammed themselves into the rickety looking two storey building that galleried the open mud pit. The only barrier between them and it were flimsy looking bamboo rails that looked like they would give way with a decent push. Those at the front had the dubious honour of having to use their legs to complete the barrier below the bottom rail, while those at the back derived great pleasure with the occasional push forward to upset their balance. Those with wiser heads had opted for the low gallery, accessed by a single steep uneven set of steps that one would have heard creak if there had been even a half-modicum of silence. Incessant chattering and the random raising of voices, coupled with the odour and cigarettes of several hundred people, exacerbated by oily smoke from the dozen or so lanterns, turned the atmosphere thick to a point where those at the back we almost invisible in the shadows.

More than just a whiff of alcohol and incense had welcomed Stock and the two other officers as they had jostled their way through the throng that encircled the bamboo arena. A definite hum of animal was also present but, as yet, they couldn't see from where this emanated as they wormed their way through the crowd towards a slight gap adjacent to the pit. Shuffling their physical superiority between the locals, the trio discovered that the gap straddled a small but effective rivulet that drained the spring-fed mud pit. Narrow it may have been, but it was too awkward a size for the smaller locals to stand with ease, and so the three of them had ended up with a ringside view of the proceedings which had already started.

Stock blamed Day for his predicament as he rested his arms on his thighs and tried to focus on his now muddied boots, partially submersed in the slime that oozed between them, but that only added to the comical characteristics of the entire proceedings. He stood upright and saw his two fellow officers had managed to find a dry patch of ground just off to his left, but they too were obviously experiencing the same problems, as one was coughing violently while the other was just howling with laughter. The modest amount of alcohol they had consumed just prior in the Mess may well have contributed, or maybe the mere fact that they had been released from the staid surroundings of military dogma. It could have been that they were now well rested and had time on their hands to consider matters outside their usual routine, or even the surety of relative safety that came with decent billets, comfortable beds, hot water, and passable food. Having spent months mainly in the heavily forested foothills of the Himalayas, to now find themselves 'on leave' with the prospect of spending Christmas without being soaked by the monsoon, bitten by innumerable insects, the absence of an unseen enemy, complaining troops, disease and everything that goes with it, all seemed to culminate to this one point in time. Their pent up anxieties now released themselves and liberally manifested the relief that they all needed in the form of laughter.

Stock watched a fist-sized lump of liquid mud fly up from the pit and land squarely on his belt buckle and ironically looked at the person responsible, floundering about in the mud just in front of him. On his almost naked skin, only the man's eyes were visible, his lips parted just enough to breathe through gritted teeth, conveying the struggle that an unrecognizable Sergeant George Day was having. He maneuvered himself onto all fours, craning his neck to peer towards the crowd through the viscus slimy mud that completely covered him and dripped from the end of his nose. Stock thought he detected a plea of help from the look he was receiving. The response, if it could have been heard over the general racket, would not have the right one and Day knew it. Instead, he swiveled his neck to look for the slippery little so-and-so that blended into the brown surroundings and spotted him a few feet away. This was going to be one of his last opportunities to catch the little blighter, because he knew he couldn't keep this up for much longer. He aligned his body, felt with his toes to find any sort of grip and, with a final intake of breath, launched himself at the piglet that was momentarily looking away from him. Elation surged through him as at last he managed to get a firm grip with one hand on a fore leg. He was stretching out his other to grasp the other when, with the now familiar high-pitched squeal, the young pig used his other three trotters still on the shifting ground to slip free from the grasping hand. Its snout, temporarily ploughing a decent trough in the mud, snorted out the compacted slime over a couple of onlookers' legs, and its body bounced off an adjacent pair that prevented the very worried animal from returning to the safety of its mother's teats.

Day dropped his head, immersing it into the quagmire, and blew out a sideways spume, indicating that this task was almost as impossible as it was futile. He lay there gathering the last vestiges of his strength as the piglet slithered out of arms reach again and continued its slippery trot inside the circle of legs. What had started out as what looked like a fairly simple task, was, in fact, quite the opposite - and time was running out. He looked up at the wooden board of coloured beads that showed he had less than two minutes to complete the task of catching this suckling pig and placing it in the tantalisingly close head-height bamboo cage that dangled from a rope in the arena's centre. He decided that, after nearly ten minutes, using brute force was not the answer. By constantly slithering around, he had all but drained his own strength. But might not the little piglet also be weary? He sat up and looked at the now static animal in the eye, noting that its front trotters were more splayed apart than they were when they had both been thrown into the ring. He picked up a handful of mud and threw it at the poor animal, trying to goad it into tiring itself out, and was rewarded when one of its back legs collapsed under itself as the startled pig tried to accelerate in any direction it could. More muddy clumps, and the wide-eyed piglet was becoming more and more confused as mud hit it directly in the face, momentarily half-blinding it. Another thrown clump contacted with its rump and half-spun it round so that it ran in his direction. Day lunged with both hands outstretched, simultaneously grabbing its hind legs.

He let out a whoop of joy, knowing that all he had to do now was stand up, throw the piglet into the open end of the cage and shut the door. Supper beckoned. He looked over at the man in charge of the beads and saw him raise a hand to flick the last one to the end of the rail, indicating that time was up. Without any further hesitation, he stood up, lifting his catch while its front legs paddled uselessly at the air and was just inches away from the door, when he felt his feet slip away from under him. It all happened so fast, and the realisation that he was not going to be able to put the little swine to bed, came too late for him to react but he wasn't going to let go. Falling backwards into the soft mud, he kept his arms outstretched, which for a brief moment meant that the piglet was directly above his head, mucus dribbling into his eyes. Day inevitably slackened his locked arms, snout and face contacting in an upside down kiss, and eventually he released the piglet so that it landed belly up on his stomach, before skidding away out of arms reach. He never heard the sound of the gong nor the roar of the crowd due to his mud-plugged ears and instead, just lay on his back looking up at the empty cage with his one eye that was still able to focus.

Had he looked to his left, he would have seen Stock doubled over and the two other officers hanging onto each other, while the rest of the crowd was grinning, laughing, or exchanging money. A dejected Day went to get up, slipped, and decided it would be better to crawl to one of the bamboo uprights that marked the edge of the arena. Even with a firm grasp, his hand still slid down the shiny pole as he ducked between the rails just to the right of Stock's location, but all he could see through his partial vision was a British officer assuming a crouching position as if on a toilet. He had no trouble in recognizing Stock, but it was certainly not reciprocated as he resembled more of a swamp-encrusted log than a human being. When Stock eventually did stand upright and looked at the tree trunk with one-and a half eyes at the top end, it brought on another fit of laughter, and the other two officers weren't helping much either.

Day, chest heaving, waited for the mirth to abate a little. "I suppose you think that's funny," he shouted as this was the natural thing to do with blocked eardrums.

Unable to say anything coherent, all three officers blurted out with more laughter at this innocent comment. It was a full half-minute before the banter began.

"What a performance. Is that you under there, Sergeant? Don't stand still for too long, a dog might want to relieve itself. A slippery customer if ever I saw one. Just don't sneeze in my direction. No, keep away".

At last Day saw the funny side and decided he needed to get his own back. He lifted his arms out, opened his palms as if emulating a monster and took a pace towards the three of them and let out a roar. It worked. The three officers turned and ran, not wanting to be embraced by the muddy man and even the locals stepped smartly back at the sudden appearance of a relative giant as he stamped his way through the crowd.

The heady atmosphere immediately dissipated as they emerged into the clear evening air outside, and this by itself initiated the ending of the game of chase as the three officers stood their ground a few feet in front of Day.

"Well, that was worth every penny we lost on you. It cost me a hundred khats, or ought we to rename them pigs?" one officer offered with glee.

The other retorted, "Probably the best dollar I've ever spent, but I'll bet you, you won't be doing that again."

"Wouldn't be the same if it had been a goat."

"Or a sheep. Baaaaaaaaaa."

"But at least you're mosquito proof now," said the first as he flicked away a piece of drying mud that caked Day's body.

Day let them laugh at him as there was little alternative and now that he had got his breath back, he too grinned. "Your turn next, sir, and there's a few tips I can give you if you like."

"Oh, you won't catch me in there. Not after seeing where the little fellow shoved his hooter."

"Obviously love at first sight," offered the second man. "I'd like to say that sports like this are plainly beneath us officers, but, then again, it was the other way round with you, wasn't it?"

As they guffawed at him, Day instinctively rubbed his arm across his mouth and spat out the muddy dregs and pig spittle. "How am I going to get this stuff off me and where's my clothes I left you looking after?"

Stock walked off in the direction of the doorway where Day's pile of clothing lay on the floor.

"I suppose we'd better chaperone you back to the barracks. The way you smell right now you might well attract the wrong sort of mate. Do you think the Doctor's got anything that might help?" The first fellow addressed the second but looked at Day. "You can grunt in approval anytime you like, Sergeant. Haaaaa haaaaa."

"Just don't tell them any porkies at the guard post. Hooooooo hooooo," offered the second.

"Just trot along now."

"Here look. The mud's crackling on him. Haaaaa."

Stock reappeared with Day's pile of clothing, adding, "You swine are making a real pig's ear of these bad jokes. Gamon, let's go. Here, mind your footing, Sergeant."

The short uphill walk back to the compound left the four of them breathless by the time they arrived at the pointless guard hut. Pointless because there was no fence surrounding their quarters adjacent to the small airfield but, nevertheless, the Americans seemed determined to maintain an official point-of-entry. The young guard watched them approach from his small hut in the gathering gloom, and recognised three of them. His jaw dropped when he spotted the fourth walking several paces behind the trio.

"Don't worry, Trooper. You're not being invaded by a heard of hogs. It's only Sergeant Day disguising himself as Christmas dinner."

"Yeah. What a fight the filthy swine put up."

"You could say we're bringing home the bacon."

The three officers stopped but ignored the guard who continued to gawp at the muddy man as Day trudged up to him. He clearly thought it about time he contributed to the dreadful jokes that were being made at his expense. He stopped squarely in front of the guard and said, "Oink."

"That's not the password, Sergeant, but it's no good telling that to a Grunt."

"Wasn't the password 'Chop Chop'?"

"No. That's tomorrow's."

"With stuffing?"

The mirth of the trio was totally lost on the bewildered guard, but Day wasn't finished, "You see what us under trodden types have to put up with. Bellyache."

The guard took a step back to get away from Day's pungent odour as the sergeant turned and grabbed his clothes from Stock before stomping off towards the shower block, leaving the officers to revel in their own euphoric world.

He was still within earshot when two boys carrying a basket between them came running up to the guard post and jabbered away.

"Now, this really is dinner," pronounced Stock. "A pair of suckling pigs."

"But I though Sergeant Day lost."

"He did, but I paid for these two little fellows by betting against Sergeant Day. Cost next to nothing."

Day ceased his trudging, turned and glared at Stock. "Do you mean to say that I went through all that for nothing?"

"Not quite nothing. You see, so you can decide which one will be tastier, you now get to choose which one you sleep with tonight."

*****

Christmas day was turning out to be rather merry in the Officers' Mess at Fort Hertz. It wasn't the kind of fort one would choose to make one's last stand as it was more of a palisade made from the trunks of local mahogany and bamboo. Nor were there any ramparts, and the bamboo gates were barely high enough to keep out the occasional marauding tiger, but nonetheless it was a place of relative sanctuary in an otherwise desolate forested region. In fact, the walls of the dozen low buildings made up most of the outside. The poles were only held together by sturdy twine. In the late 1800s, those same trunks were the brainchild of William Hertz who had established this minor and hardly significant British outpost. He had been directly responsible for the expansion of the township as a trading centre.

The addition of a brace of suckling pigs to the menu made all the difference, as otherwise, apart from a few local vegetables, their only source of food was the rations flown in by the American Air Force in Dakota DC3s. Initially, these supplies were parachuted in as the pathetic runway was totally unserviceable, but with the arrival of Stock and Day as experts in airfield construction to guide the unit of American Engineers, together with a few mechanical items, the DC3s were able to land.

"Cheer up. You'll only need to be there a couple of weeks and then you can catch a ride back on one of the Americans' planes in time for Christmas. Leave the rest to the Yanks once you've got it up and running." Alfredson put his arm round Stock's shoulder in an avuncular manner while sporting a wide grin. He knew Stock would rather be involved with the creation of yet another airfield in the depths of the jungle nearer to the brigade in the south, but someone had to be tasked with the Americans' request.

"I have heard that one before but keep the Christmas pudding warm for me. I will take Sergeant Day if that is alright with you, sir."

That had been nearly a month ago and, although they had managed to make the runway serviceable, hitching a ride back to their own battalion was proving more difficult than had been first imagined. The simple truth of the matter was that the supply planes flying over the eastern arm of the Himalayas were just not stopping at Fort Hertz. The new model of DC3 had a greater range yet did not have enough fuel to land and take off again on their return journey from Kunming. Stock and Day were therefore left to their own devices until either someone remembered that they were there, or a plane put down there with a mechanical fault that they could fix. They were still waiting for that one plane.

Sergeant Day wasn't worried about their predicament, while Stock, as was his usual manner, made the most of the situation by learning more about the local Kachins and their way of life. One of the things he discovered was that they liked to gamble, which was why he had put Day's name forward to wrestle the baby pigs. He was so glad he had, as he sat at the makeshift table with succulent juices threatening to dribble down his chin. As a non-commissioned officer, Day was ensconced with fellow sergeants from the Americas in an adjacent building, while Stock was sharing his Christmas dinner with seven officers of the 114th Airborne Reconnaissance Brigade, mainly from Michigan. Their colonel had been recalled to Dibrugarh soon after Stock and Day had arrived, so Christmas day formalities were left to Major Wisden who now waved an almost bare rib in Stock's direction.

"I wish I'd been there to see it as from what these two described, it was a hoot, and tell me, how did you know he was going to lose?"

Stock masticated over the mouthful as well as his answer, wondering how gullible these Americans might be, especially as Day was not there to be cross-examined. The outcome had been pure luck, but he kept them waiting as he swigged from a beer bottle. "I do not claim to be an expert but I was born on a farm and spent most of my life weighing up what kind of temperament an animal has, or will have as it matures, and one learns to be able to assess its qualities from an early age. How long it is likely to live for example, or will its markings fetch a decent price at market. Whether or not it is suitable for breeding or, in this case, for consumption. One can gain a lot by looking into its eyes and watching how coordinated it is. In this instance, I assessed that it had just about outgrown its mother's teats and was particularly agile, so I simply placed my own bet on it escaping from its captor. On what basis would you have bet?" He picked up one of the small meaty ribs and eyed it before putting one end in his mouth, thus providing him more time to think about how to answer their next question when it came.

"That's fascinating," S

said Lieutenant Linney. "And you saw all that from when we walked in?

"This guy thinks he knows what he's talking about and he's the one we have to thank for anything but K-rations today, so you'd better believe it. Where in England did you say your farm was?" This from another lieutenant that Stock had already decided he would never be able to get along with. He had a cocky air about him and had generally talked down to Stock whenever their paths had crossed. "Wesley P. Minster's the name and if you think I'm gonna tell you what the P stands for, you better think again," had been his opening gambit.

"In Norfolk. About a hundred miles north of London. Been in the family for generations." He didn't add that they hadn't had pigs on their farm ever since he could remember. "It has been a tradition in our family to have turkey at Christmas and it usually fell to me to slaughter one that we had picked out earlier in the year." He paused in recollection. "The trouble was that my sisters used to name some of the birds with endearing qualities such as 'Sweet Tooth' or 'Whisky' and one year they would not let me kill 'Pussums' so they chose another. When their backs were turned, I simply swapped the birds and we ended up eating poor 'Pussums' anyway. But I gather you Americans prefer your turkey in November. Why is that?"

His comment raised a united titter around the table, and then he realised that they really didn't know the answer. Major Wisden was the first to respond. "That's because there's so many of the goddammed birds at that time of year. They're so heavy they fall out of the trees."

"That's if they can get up into them in the first place," piped up another Captain.

Another lieutenant joined in, "I reckon it was because they couldn't catch pigs."

This last comment raised genuine laughter.

"My grandma is a churchgoer and when we were small, she once told us it was so they could use the feathers to re-stuff their pillows, and that they'd grow back in time for next year. We never really believed her but we sure never went hungry on Thanksgiving."

"I was told it was because our founding fathers thought it was a wholesome meat, but I guess it's also because they didn't have enough cattle at the time."

"Whatever the reason, these locals have got it right as this sure beats the hell out of turkey."

"I've got a cousin in Manchester and a few years ago one Christmas he sent me over a case of beer. Boddington's I think it was called. Not only did it look like washed out old socks but it tasted like it as well. How can you British put up with that compared to the likes of Falstaff Blue Ribbon. You ought to try it if you ever go over there. Like nectar it is, especially after a hard day's fishing."

A couple of officers who both lived near Detroit close to Lake Erie and were keen fishermen formed a trio with a third to discuss the merits of what was the better type of rod and reel to use when catching freshwater trout, while Stock somehow became ensconced with Wisden and the others on the subject of baseball versus cricket.

"It is more a social game than a competition in England. You see, it is the taking part that counts more than the winning and at local level it helps bind the community together," Stock chuckled to himself recalling one particular moment. "We were playing the next village and were in desperate need of runs to win, when one of our batsmen hit the ball for 'four' over the boundary so hard it became wedged in the spokes of a passing cyclist. You should have seen the other side chasing after the poor man down the road. When he turned round and saw half a dozen hefty blokes catching him up, it only made him pedal faster and by the time they had caught him to retrieve the ball, we had scored enough runs to win."

The conversation rattled around the distinctive likes and dislikes of the individuals and inevitably returned to the differences on each side of the Atlantic, but unsurprisingly resumed to their own predicament in that particular part of the world. Toasts were made to the president, the King, Churchill, and one lieutenant's mother, who, he announced, was a hundred years old that day. "Her name's June."

"The simple truth of the matter is that they're outnumbered." Wisden's statement to those at his end of the table received concurring nods. "And the longer the war goes on, the greater the victory. Now you take the latest action in The Marshall Islands. They've run out of carriers and with that they can't bring up either supplies or reinforcements, and from what I've heard on the radio, we've just got one more island to take before we move onto the next bunch. MacArthur's got it right, taking island by island until we reach Japan itself. But they're feisty little fellows and as we've all seen, damn difficult to dig out of their foxholes. And that reminds me, why did you get our guys to move that gun pit on the southern perimeter fifty feet to the left?"

Stock had only been half-listening to Wisden as his other ear had picked up raucous laughter coming from an adjacent building where most of the enlisted men were enjoying their own celebrations. He had been wondering if it would have been more fun joining them instead and had nearly made up his mind to drop in on their proceedings on his way back to his own quarters. His mind still half on this, he replied, "Whoever put it there in the first place probably found it easier to dig it just there as the ground was softer, but if you look at the terrain, you can see that the sand around it had been washed away from the course of a stream that will undoubtedly return with the monsoon. I just placed it on the slightly higher ground so that it will not get flooded out next year. Besides which, there is a closer small gully that one can run along at a crouch to get to it in a hurry." To Stock's trained eye, this had been a simple decision made soon after he and Day had arrived and inspected the place, but to others, it was not so obvious.

"I don't know why we bother 'cos this place's the back end of nowhere and there's not a Jap within a hundred miles. I volunteered to fight, not dig holes in the ground. I have to ask you, Major, when are we gonna get our orders to move on?" Wesley P Minster was griping, not just on his own behalf, but also reflecting the thoughts of the men in his company.

"You'll have to ask the colonel when he gets back from area command tomorrow or the day after, and you and your sergeant may be able to grab a ride back to your own unit if his plane's going that way."

This was news to Stock who too was starting to become bored

with very little to do. He had been half-way through a letter to Mary, but had screwed it up into a ball, as he felt that it's tone was too military-like, describing what he had been up to the past few months. It wasn't that it contravened the code of giving away information to the enemy but dwelt too much on the disadvantages of living in the jungle where jaundice and malaria were rife. Instead, he had prepared another, recounting the wonderful scenery and how relatively happy the local population were, once they discovered that the allied armies did not treat them the same way that the Japanese had. All he needed now was somewhere to post it.

Just before he and Day had left for Fort Hertz, it seemed like two years' worth of letters had been received by the entire battalion and news from home was generally good. The men's demeanor changed for the better, at least for a short while, but there were those who had lost either kith or kin, or in some cases both. Mary's letter to Stock described the living conditions during her short posting to Liverpool and how she felt that she was growing webbed feet as it had incessantly rained, and he wondered how it would compare with the annual monsoon that they has all endured in Assam. She said that while the food rationing was still as unpopular as ever, there had been benefits to living in proximity to where the convoys docked at Liverpool, and she had managed to persuade the concierge in her hotel to let her have some nuts. '….and the wretched man gave me monkey nuts.'

At the mention of the word 'Limey' by Wesley P Minster, Stock's attention was wrenched back to the table as they were discussing the progress, or rather the lack of it, made in retaking of Mandalay, several hundred miles to the south. Somewhere in that direction was his own battalion.

The party broke up soon after midnight and Stock was glad that he had not needed to show off his staying power when it came to out-drinking the Americans. Besides which, the stuffy atmosphere was stating to give him a thick head anyway and the relatively bracing wind outside was literally a breath of fresh air. The short route to his quarters took him almost past the enlisted men's revelries and he paused outside the crude wooden door wondering if he ought to see how Day was getting on. A s he did so, two soldiers came out through it and almost bumped into him in the gloom.

"Sorry, pal."

"Hey. Watch where you're going."

Stock took a pace sideways letting the pair past en route to the latrines. "No problem."

"Say, you're that British officer, aren't you?" One had paused while the other had trotted off.

He guessed it was his accent that gave him away and instantly dismissed the idea of telling the man to salute his superior. "That is correct. Why do you ask?"

"Just curious, sir. You weren't thinking of going in there, were you?" He jerked his thumb over his shoulder. The man was standing directly in front of him and attempting to peer at him. Stock could smell liquor on his breath. "It's just that it's a kind of unwritten rule that officers don't come into our Mess. That's all." He started to jiggle from foot to foot, whether from nervousness or from his need to relieve himself. Stock decided it was the latter.

"No. Just passing."

"Well….. good night, sir, and Merry Christmas."

Stock did not have time to reciprocate the seasonal wishes before the man disappeared. Now, lying on his bunk and closing his eyes, his thoughts went out to Mary once again. This was his third Christmas away from her. Even though her letters sounded genuine and depicted her happiness, he wondered if she would really wait for his return or be swept off her feet by some other. Next Christmas… Perhaps I'll be home next Christmas.

Two days later, walking round the unmarked perimeter of the runway and lost in thoughts of his future, he caught the far-off sound of an aircraft. There were at least two engines from the drone that struggled to betray its direction. He played the guessing game of where it might first appear in the early morning sky, took a bead on a distant peak and scanned first to the right, then hearing the muted sound of engines wafting on the gentle wind, to the left of it. He nearly thought that he had been mistaken as he stood very still for over a minute, trying to make out anything mechanical such as the glint of metal in the sun, or the return of engine noise, but all he heard was the light rustling of a small creature in the nearby undergrowth. He looked down and noticed the branch of a mellowing fern twitch briefly and thought he saw a marsupial like tail disappear along an almost invisible trail. He was about to retrace his path back to the compound when he definitely picked up the distinctive sound of aerial engines and breathed a slight sigh of relief that he had not been imagining things. He increased his pace across the runway, arriving at the side nearest the quarters, and watched as the three-engined aeroplane began its final approach. He had not come across a plane with three engines before and later learned later that it was one of the rare trimotors produced by Henry Ford, nicknamed 'The Tin Goose' due to its ungainly struts that splayed at a wide angle from under the wings.

The medium sized aluminum-bodied transport aircraft looked just the type that would ferry about a dozen personnel and he hoped that the pilot carried orders to collect Day and himself. He was standing halfway between the compound and the fascinating three-engined aircraft when he was joined by Major Wisden and two other officers.

"Good morning, Captain. I see you've been inspecting the perimeter early again. Anything to report?"

"Absolutely nothing, sir, and yes, the machine gun posts were properly manned."

Major Wisden smiled as this was exactly the kind of report he could present to his commanding officer.

The plane taxied round to face the direction it had landed and came to a stop less than a hundred feet away from the small crowd. The side door opened and out jumped a man with a set of small steps, followed straight away by a tall man who made his own exit in a far more dignified manner, despite his need to duck out of the narrow aperture.

Colonel Rees adjusted his dress and marched towards them.

"You'd better stand at the end of the line as you're not really part of the 114th," Major Wisden addressed Stock. All he needed to do was look at his fellow officers who automatically took their cue from him and lined up in order of seniority.

The step man had jumped back in the airplane taking his steps with him and, before he had even closed the door, the pilot was already moving back down the runway to prepare for take-off into the wind. Stock was naturally disappointed and wished he could recall an appropriate swear word in Assamese.

Both noise and wind from the aircraft abated as it trundled its way along the runway. Stock took his cue from Major Wisden's salute, doing likewise as Colonel Rees neared. He gave a brief salute in return.

"Well, gentlemen," he greeted them, " at least down here I'll be able to hear myself think. I couldn't hear a damn thing in that old noise bucket," His accent had more of a twang about it than the other Americans but Stock did not know enough about the subject to guess which part he came from, but he sounded rather jolly to him. "I presume you've got a fire going inside." He strode off trailing the rest of them, in need of warmth after his chilly flight.

As a foreigner, Stock wasn't sure if he ought to attend the gathering of American officers in the Mess, but he had little else to do. In any case, the worst that could happen was that he would be told to leave. He needn't have worried. As soon as Colonel Rees had divested himself of his greatcoat, laid his cap on an adjacent table, and acknowledged the presence of his juniors, he addressed Stock, laying steady eyes on him.

"And you must be the British sapper."

"Yes, sir. Captain Stock, 14th army, Royal Engin..."

"Yes. Yes. Yes. I know all about you." Rees centered himself in front of the fire so that his backside received its full effect. "Colonel

Wyngate had nothing but compliments for you when I met him, and I see you've done a fine job here." He motioned his head towards the runway. "If you were wondering why you're here, you can blame him, but I suppose you want to know what else we've got in store for you, eh? Well, don't worry; I gather GOC has another project for you down south, so you won't have to put up with being stuck in these backwoods for much longer. That deathtrap called a plane is doing a tour of forward airfields and will be back in five days to collect you, so meanwhile you might as well enjoy our company. Perhaps we can show him how we carry out recon American style, eh?" His fellow officers joined him in polite laughter.

"Major." Rees looked briefly at Wisden, indicating that he should follow before walking off through a door that led to his office, leaving the others to await the outcome. Stock was mulling over the statement Rees had made regarding the reason why he been posted, albeit briefly, to this remote outpost in the first place. It wasn't as though the Americans couldn't create a runway themselves; from the way they had worked under his direction, they were perfectly capable of doing that, but his expertise had been needed when it had come to levels, drainage, soil, direction, everything that came naturally to him, but not to others. He knew they had a renowned engineering corps that was currently building the Ledo Road into China and surely they must have their own experts to hand, yet he and Day had been summoned instead. Wingate. It must have been on Wingate's initiative, and if that was so, then there must have been a political reason behind the thinking. There was going to be very little to occupy his mind and he started wondering how best to do this over the next five days, other than visiting the local gambling den again. And of course, keeping warm.

He needn't have worried as ten minutes later Colonel Rees and Major Wisden both emerged back into the Mess, the latter carrying a rolled-up map which he spread out on one of the tables.

Rees waited until everyone had gathered round before beginning, "I've just received orders over the radio to root out a nest of Japs near a village called Nawngmun about 30 miles from here." He pronounced it Nowgum in his mid-American accent.

Wisden placed his finger on a circled point on the map, adding, "Seems that there's only a few of them but they've brought down one of our Dakotas and badly damaged another carrying supplies over the Hump.

"Linney," he looked up at the lieutenant who had taken post off to his left, "it's about time you got out and about, so I want you to take your company down this road here via Machanbaw, then up this valley to Nawngmun and bring back as many of the enemy as you can. See if you can't locate where our plane went down and find any survivors. Clear?"

"Yes, sir." Lieutenant Linney straightened himself out, happy to be pleasing his colonel. This would be his first recce in charge without being overseen by a superior.

Rees glanced at his watch and continued, "Take five, no, six trucks and one of the jeeps but leave as soon as you're ready. By 11.00 hours at the latest. You won't get lost as there's only one road in and out of that valley. Rations for three days. Be back here as soon as you've got them."

It took Linney all of three seconds to realise that that was the end of Rees's orders. He saluted and turned to go, knowing that he was being watched by all in the room. He had less than one hour to get moving. Once he was out of the room, Rees cast eyes on Lieutenant Minster who now stood where Linney had been a few seconds earlier. "As soon as Linney's gone, you'll take your company on foot down to this village Machanbaw and carry out a recce. Make sure there's no enemy there and stay there until Linney returns. You'll be our mid-point relay and back-up if he needs help. Take one of the .30s and set it up, presuming Japs will be coming this way." Rees smiled before his next comment, "I expect your men will be glad of a ten-mile hike after Christmas anyway."

"Yessir." Minster knew exactly who was going to carry the .30 calibre machine gun.

"In the meantime, Major, I'd like to take a look round the airfield, just in case there's other Japs about. Stock, you can accompany me."

"I would rather go with Lieutenant Linney if you do not mind, sir."

Rees had half-turned to return to his office, paused, and thought before answering, "Now, why would you want to do that?"

"Well, sir, the airfield is in good condition, the drainage will work properly when the monsoon returns in the summer, what little perimeter fencing there is in good order, and the machine gun posts are well sited and dug in. I can report that there is little more that I can do to enhance this airfield. The aircraft that will be collecting my sergeant and I will not be returning for another five days and besides which, I thought I would take advantage of your offer to see how you carry out a reconnaissance."

The last part was a little cheeky but in his estimation, Rees seemed to be the sort of man who would appreciate a pertinent retort. In any case, it was in his nature to volunteer rather than shirk an opportunity and there was no doubt in his own mind that he had said the right thing. He half suspected that Rees wanted his company so that if there was anything amiss, he could judge Wingate's recommendation.

Rees turned back to look Stock squarely in the eyes while considering his request. "It's not often I come across someone who's willing to volunteer, but I take your point that otherwise you'd be kicking your heels here. Go on then, but only as an observer, and I don't want you getting in Linney's way. He's in charge. Clear?"

"Yes, sir."

*****

Standing at an elevation of over five thousand feet in the south-eastern Himalayan foothills, Nawngmun felt like it was miles from anywhere else in any direction, but was still the local administration centre for that locality in northern Kachin. It was the last town almost at the top of a dead-end valley that eventually abutted the Chinese border, surrounded by vast chasms that governed the course of rivers. Why a township had ever grown up there was a mystery as there appeared to be no industry and little agriculture nearby, but it had once been important enough for Genghis Khan to have stopped there. According to the incumbent Buddhist monks, he was quoted as saying, "If there's nowhere else to go, Nawngmun is the place to be."

At first glance at a map, there seemed to be no reason why this small town had any military importance, as there was only one road that led to the flatter cultivated lands in the south, while directly north and east was an almost impassable mountain range. Upon closer inspection, it overlooked a natural tear-drop shaped bowl from which other minor tracks disappeared into various gorges and ravines. A wooden bridge dissected the adjacent village and crossed a very lively river, especially in the springtime when the snows melted. The indigenous population of just over a thousand souls paid their paltry dues through a feudal-type bureaucracy and would have continued to do so, had it not been for the arrival of the Japanese soldiers. From the outset, the Kachins couldn't understand why their new masters had demanded that all gold and silver be collected and delivered to the commandeered prefect's house: to them, the otherwise valueless shiny metal was just another way of adorning the several holy shrines in the area. What they could understand was that their stock of food had been denied to them, and this was of far greater value. Which was why the Japanese had come.

The Japanese supply route from the south had been severed by British forces in the main and had brought on a lack of rations, forcing them to live off the land. They had learned that the harvested vegetables and meats from the lower valley were taken higher up to a village beyond Nawngmun where the air was colder and the temperature in the caves rarely rose much above zero. What was there in the caves wouldn't have fed an army, but it would do very nicely for the Japanese half-sized battalion and remnants of the 18th

Division, which had strayed north after being cut off by the newly built Ledo Road nearly a hundred miles to the south. Even if they could have traversed the haughty mountain passage at the height of summer, sooner or later they would have come across elements of the Chinese army stationed in that part of the world. For the time being, their small pocket of relative peace had been overlooked by the Allies as it was so remote as not to warrant any action. that was until the Americans noted that too many of their supply planes were being shot at while ferrying supplies to the Chinese.

Their leader, Major Hashimoto, had died from a snake bite several weeks earlier and command of the unit had fallen to Captain Kimura. He did not have the same callous attitude of his superior and, coming from a family of farmers in the county of Shirako within two day's walk of the capital Tokyo, held a certain amount of sympathy for the local Kachin. Rather than pursue a policy of 'slash and burn', as the now senior captain he had ordered his troops to be more fraternal with the inhabitants and to assist with the growth and transport of the local food. After all, the delivery of their sporadic supplies had completely dried up, and they were forced to survive on what was available. They certainly weren't loved or trusted but the demise of his predecessor relieved tensions to an extent where they could at least learn the local dialect and discuss more efficient ways of harvesting. The local Buddhist monks engaged with these foreigners and some of their ethos was beginning to rub off on many of the rank and file.

There was little to occupy their minds, other than the almost daily flights of American aircraft that carried supplies over what was generally known as The Hump in that part of the haughty mountains. To counter this, Major Hashimoto had positioned his three machine guns posts as high up the mountains as was prudent, whereas he had had his troops billeted on both sides of the river. Now in command, Captain Kimura had taken over the houses, most of which were more like shacks, on the eastern side of the bridge. This helped him facilitate command and maintain unity within the half-battalion while leaving most of the locals to rehouse themselves on the western shore. Besides which, it was far nearer and quicker for changing the duty rota on the machine gun posts, which were well over an hour's hike up the walls of a ravine.

With the ending of the monsoon, starving foot soldiers from the 18th Division started to arrive, bedraggled, partially armed, and usually in twos, threes or fours. Having been separated from their normal chain of command, those few who had evaded capture had wandered north and ended up in the desolate looking valley. These were hardened but weary troops who at first, in exchange for food, gladly obeyed Captain Kimura, but with the arrival of another captain of equal standing from their own brigade, begrudged his seemingly pointless orders not to molest the Kachins. Their own Captain, a certain Yoshida, was soon at loggerheads with Kimura. After a shouting match late one afternoon heard by many, he set up his own headquarters on the western side of the bridge. Most of the inhabitants of Nawngmun rehoused themselves again on the eastern side under Kimura's protection and it became necessary for each faction to place an armed guard at either end of the bridge. Nearly all of the food stored in the caves was on Kimura's side and he was determined to ration it out, rather than let Yoshida's men run through it in short order. Fortunately for Kimura, not only did his men outnumber Yoshida's nearly five to one, but they were also fully armed with an adequate amount of ammunition and had three machine guns. All things considered, Kimura assessed that, although they were cut off, his little command could maintain itself until the rest of the division ever managed to break through to them. The news that Yoshida's troops brought with them was not good and he mulled it over with his senior sergeant, one Saito, one morning as they sat on a large protruding boulder overlooking the river.

"So. We're really cut off, then."

"Looks like it, sir. They all said just about the same thing and that last bunch that came in a few days ago just confirms it. What I don't understand is how they managed to cut our supply line so quickly. I mean, our high command has been telling us that we are winning, yet whenever we move, it always seems to be backwards. But look where we are now. We certainly can't go any further backwards from here, and winter's just about on us anyway."

"Well, what would you do, Sergeant, from a military prospective only I mean? Look at our situation. On the negative side, our morale is barely adequate and waning further, especially with the weather deteriorating daily. We have no radio communication and no hope of being resupplied. We're surrounded by either mountains or the enemy and we're tens of miles from our nearest units, who by the sound of it are also cut off. There's very little timber up here to help keep us warm and our medical supplies are nearly finished." His dejected tone of voice reflected his real feelings. "And then there's a handful of our fellow zealous countrymen over there, who, given half the chance, would murder us for what's in those caves. On the positive side, we're still a coherent unit with enough food to see us through to at least spring if we're careful, enough ammunition and grenades to still fight, and of course, there's always hope. Hope that our forces in the south will break through to us."

This was the first time Captain Kimura had spoken his thoughts out loud to the sergeant who was rather taken aback but felt that he was being asked to contribute. "Don't forget what our major told us when we arrived here - that we're only here while the American planes continue to fly over these mountains. There hasn't been a single one for two days now but they'll probably be another flock of them tomorrow, or the day after. That's their usual pattern. Perhaps we ought to move the guns again so they're more underneath them?"

"That's half the problem, Sergeant, and that's what's demoralizing the men. We move them to one location and the Americans fly over where they were yesterday. So, we move them back and once again the Americans pass over the old spot. But you're missing my point. What happens when we do run out of ammunition? What then? We'd be like a clawless cat." He threw one of the two small stones he had been playing with into a quiet part of the river and watched the ripples dissipate. "I wish we could shoot down one, just one plane, and then I'd feel like we were doing something useful, but otherwise, we're only kicking our heels here while our armies are battling it out for us."

"We'll get one soon, sir, I promise. After all, the men have had enough practice and sooner or later one is bound to come over us a bit lower and then we'll get him."

They both sat there watching bubbles foaming at the waters' edge and listening to the soporific sounds of the river.

Kimura broke the silence. "Sooner or later, we're going to have to leave this valley but the question is when. Do we leave now before winter fully sets in or wait until spring?"

The sergeant realised why Kimura had asked him to come this secluded spot and was horrified. "We can't leave without orders, sir."

"And who's to give those orders, Sergeant? We've been abandoned and I doubt anyone knows we even here still."

It was this last statement that brought home the reality of their situation to the sergeant. He went to open his mouth but then shut it as it dawned on him that without any way of communicating with headquarters, those orders would never come. Their eyes made contact with each other in mutual understanding.

Kimura continued. "While we're carrying out our orders to intercept the American planes, and we haven't got a single one yet, I'd be happier if, when we rejoin, we can report that we downed at least one. So, what I propose is this." He turned and looked up at both top lips of the ravine and pointed at one. "We get most of the men with their rifles up there on the eastern ridge, clumped together but bracketed by the machine guns. They can be the firing party. Then we place only one section as far west as they can go to act as lookouts on top of the western ridge. They can warn the others which route the aircraft will be taking and, as long as they're in visual range of each other, they can signal either left or right. With an additional two hundred rifles firing, we ought to hit something.

What do you think, Sergeant?"

"A brilliant idea, sir. When do you want to try this out?"

"Let's get them up there for first light tomorrow morning and tell them to use mirrors to signal the firing party." A wry smile came over Kimura's face. "The lookouts can use the rising sun as it will be directly facing towards our guns. A good omen, yes?"

"Indeed, sir." The sergeant also smiled at the thought of their nation's own flag that depicted a rising sun. "Can I leave one section down here to guard the bridge and supplies?"

"By all means, Sergeant. I think I'd best stay down here as well. You go up and enjoy yourself. It'll be bitterly cold up there that time of the morning, but the long climb will soon get you warmed up."

"And what if we do shoot down the Americans? Can I tell the men that we'll be leaving after that?"

Kimura looked at the one pebble he was playing with in his right hand. "No. Probably best not to tell them yet, but I think we ought to leave soon after. And I don't think we ought to tell that lot over there either."

"When we do get out of this valley, sir, where will we be going?"

"We can't go north or east because of the mountains and the Chinese, we can't go west because that's where the Allies are coming from and to the south they've cut our route. Yet that direction is our only option. I'll make you a deal, Sergeant. You get me that plane and I'll buy you and the men all the sake you can drink when we get back home."

"Yes, sir." The sergeant stood up to attention and saluted with glee. "I'll be glad to tell them that, sir."

He watched Sergeant Saito make his way back across the pebble strewn shoreline, hoping that he had done the right thing in taking him into his confidence. If he lived to regret it, then he would look back on the chance meeting he had had with one of the monks yesterday on that very same rock. He had been on his way to check the guard at their end of the bridge when he had spotted the monk sitting alone, as though fishing but without a rod, and his curiosity had compelled him to investigate what he was doing there. The monk was staring at what seemed to be middle space and didn't move as Kimura stood directly in front of him, blocking his view. But as Kimura looked closer at his face, he saw by his opaque eyes that he was blind. He looked around to see if he had missed something that was obvious to the monk but not to himself and acknowledged that it was a picturesque setting. The gentle sounds of the babbling river making its way through its own rock-strewn course, with a backdrop of snow-tipped mountains, made for a very peaceful scene, but he still couldn't see what had drawn the monk to this spot.

"What are you sitting here for, old man, if you cannot see?" Kimura had muttered the words more to himself than the monk, and stood there shaking his head in sympathy.

Still the monk did not move, but as he went to return to his bridge the monk spoke in Japanese, "One does not need eyes to see."

If he had had any, the hairs on the back of Kimura's neck would have stood on end, but instead his jaw dropped. The monk was clearly blind yet he had to make sure. He thought about threatening by drawing his sword or throwing a pretend punch, even a kick, but instead ended up waving his hand a few inches from the monk's face. No reaction whatsoever.

"I know what you are doing but your time will be better spent if you join me. There is room for two," the monk said calmly, and moved over, gesturing towards a space to his left with his arm.

Kimura looked around to see if he was being observed by anyone, half suspecting a trap, but the nearest person was a guard leaning against a rock overlooking the bridge nearly three hundred yards away. He adjusted his sword sheath and took a similar pose next to his host. "I did not know anyone here spoke Japanese."

"I am the only one. Before you ask, I was sent to Mount Moriyoshi in the north of your island by our elder over forty years ago. I spent three years at that monastery studying the unique ways of Zen . It is one of the deeper meditation paths of Buddhism, helping others to overcome their own unhappiness. I am truly sorry to know that you are unhappy within yourself.”

“And how can you know that? We have never spoken before.”

“Everybody suffers from a degree of unhappiness at some point during their lifetime. By realising one’s own state of mind, one has taken the first step. We can only take one step at a time, but knowing in which direction to step is another matter entirely. For example, this river in front of us is happy. Why? Because it is going in one direction only and does not have to make any other decision. It is therefore glad to be going in that direction and because it cannot go in any other direction it is happy to be going towards its destination. It does not have the choice of being unhappy and therefore accepts that it is happy.”

Kimura masticated over the logic for a while. “Are you trying to tell me that I am unhappy because I have a choice?”

“No. You are unhappy because you have to make a choice. Let me help you here. Imagine two identical pebbles in your hand and you have to discard one of them. Once you have thrown away one, you are happier because you have made the decision. Now imagine a fist full of pebbles and you can only keep one.” He let Kimura think about this before continuing, “The same thinking applies. I t is easier to discard what you have to, because a moment ago you had already been through that same thought process. That is one step followed by another step and all steps are easier when one considers this simple conundrum.”

Kimura nodded in agreement.

“In your own mind throw that fistful of pebbles in different directions.”

“I did.”

“Good. That is the next step. Now tell me, did you include up and down when you were throwing your pebbles?”

“No.”

“Why not?”

“It did not occur to me.”

“But you had the choice?” The monk let that comment hang

a moment. "And now you are unhappy because you realise that that was yet another choice you could have made, but do not berate yourself because that will only compound your unhappiness. After all, we are only talking about imaginary pebbles, even if they represent our choices in life."

"This is more difficult than I first thought."

"Sometimes we have to make choices we do not want to make but always think back to those pebbles and you will find your answer in the one you are left holding. That will make you more contented and free you from misery."

Kimura felt that he had just been given a valuable lesson in life and resolved to apply the monk's thinking when he was next presented with a conundrum. "Are you ever unhappy?" he asked.

"I haven't been for a long time, not since I was able to apply the thinking of those who taught me. I detect you are now more at ease with yourself. That is good because you can now elect which choice to make first and then take the next step with ease."

Kimura didn't feel as though he was being taught how to organise his own thoughts but recognised that the monk was being helpful and asked why, "You don't like us being here, do you, so why are you being so helpful?"

"You are correct, but it makes no difference. If it were not you, it would be the Mandarins or the Mongols and who knows which race will come next. We carry on as we have done so for thousands of years. Does it make anyone wonder why a blind man cries? We are isolated here like that blind man but nobody would pay any attention if we were to cry, so it is pointless. You will not be here for much longer anyway and then we will revert to our own contented way of life and you will pursue your own."

Kimura was shocked that the monk thought he knew that less than an hour ago that he had decided to leave as soon as honour would allow. "And how do you know that?"

"It is obvious. There is absolutely nothing here for you and the war that encircles us all beckons you. A man soon becomes unsettled if he has no end to pursue and there is nothing here for you to pursue. Beside which, the food here will run out before winter's end and then your hold over your men will cease, so you must surely depart soon."

Initially he bridled at the idea that he had been out-thought by a simple monk, but then again this particular monk possessed an ethos whereby nothing seemed to disturb him, even the temporary dominance of Japanese troops. He realised that other than the food issue, this monk would not be too concerned if they either stayed or went and had nothing to gain by putting such a suggestion into his own mind. He saw no harm in confiding further with the monk.

"We have but one task here and I intend to see that we accomplish our duty. Once we have done that, yes, we will depart."

"If you have made that choice, then you will bring you enemies down upon you, rather than go out and face them. That will be your fate."

Kimura's legs were beginning to cramp on the cold rock and he stood up. "It will be an honour to face my enemy whatever form they take."

The monk suddenly stood also and stared past his shoulder with blank eyes. "Consider this: your enemy has the same choices to make as you do, so put yourself in his place."

By the time Kimura blinked, the monk was already taking his first paces in the direction of the village. He could now see that there was a slightly worn pathway through the boulders. Blind or not, the monk knew his way back.

*****

Lieutenant Linney was popular with his men, attested to by the way they had sought to cover his retrieval from his exposed position, but the medic who attended to his bleeding shoulder was shaking his own head in uncertainty. "The bullet's lodged somewhere near his main artery and I don't think I can fish it out without nicking it. Not here anyway."

"Do what you can and get him into one of those trucks," Company Sergeant McCaulin ground out the words between his teeth in chagrin as he stood over his lieutenant behind one of the larger rock protrusions not too far from a bridge. "He's not bleeding too badly, so that's a good thing."

As gently as the uneven ground would allow, three privates carried the unconscious Linney to the rearmost truck, passing several of their comrades who took the opportunity to crane their necks.

"I know why he didn't listen to me. You can tell this is his first action by the way he wanted to lead from the front," he commented to nobody in particular in the small group that had gathered round. "Godammit! I suppose we'll just have to do this the proper way.

"Corporal!" he shouted over at another rock. "Get your BAR teams up there and cover us. Patchy, your platoon on the right. Myson, yours on the left. I'll take the middle. Time for some bayonet work I think."

His eye fell on Stock a few feet away, and added, "You choose your own ground, sir. Here, you may as well have this." He kicked a foot at the unused Tommy gun lying on the ground that until a few moments ago had been in Linney's hands. "Not sure what you're doing here but leave this to us."

It was clear to Stock that the sergeant knew what he was doing and he had no intention of letting an unknown officer mess up. Stock picked up the Thompson machine gun and propped it against a wheel. In the absence of any other officers, he was technically in command but had no intention of imposing rank. "I'll observe from here, Sergeant. Carry on." There were no salutes, just the merest acknowledgment from McCaulin as he turned to attend to the situation.

Above him, four pairs of men with their Browning light machine guns scrambled up the rock-strewn side of the mountain that overlooked part of the village where enemy fire had come from. The rest of the company dispersed in a professional manner, fanning out in an arc with the river on their right, and took cover behind the numerous boulders. Stock moved to a higher platform and surveyed the three hundred yards or so that separated them from the nearest house.

Linney's injury had been so unnecessary but he supposed that it had been his pride that had urged him to show his men that he had the same amount of courage that they did. Only a few bullets had come their way when they had dismounted from the vehicles but it had been Linney who had wandered towards the village. He made a mental note not to emulate that kind of bravado if it ever came to it.

Stock was surprised that no enemy fire interrupted the Americans as they scuttled left and right between boulders, slowly but surely advancing. The final hundred yards would be more difficult as there were no rocks large enough for more than one man to hide behind. He wished he had brought his binoculars with him as he focused on the closest building and blinked as, at last, rifle fire flashed from within. This provoked fire from two of the BAR teams, who took it in turns to splinter the wooden façade. He heard McCaulin's shout and watched the sixty or so men rise from behind their protective rocks and charge the village. This must surely be the crux of the engagement - if superior fire suddenly came from the enemy, then McCaulin and his men would be caught in the open. If not, then they would reach the relative safety of buildings that could provide them with a chance of cover.

From Stock's perspective, what actually happened next was a text book example of taking an enemy position. Rather than a desperate stream of bullets, it looked like there were only three or four rifles firing back at the Americans as they jinked forwards. While a few held their positions behind rocks, firing at the rifle flashes and acting as back up should the need arise, the main body of the platoons surged forward and all of them, bar one, reached the start of the village and began filtering between and into the various buildings. At the same time, two of the BAR teams made their way down the steep slope and repositioned themselves to provide additional fire from a different angle.

There was now very little for him to see from his vantage point but he could tell the difference between the sound of a Japanese rifle and an American Springfield rifle, which had more of a snap to it. The enemy was no longer returning fire. He heard some gruesome screams coming from further back and decided it was about time he went to look for himself.

"If you're going forward, sir, you better take this." One of the privates who had been left behind to guard the convoy held out the Tommy gun.

Stock looked at the youth, who hardly looked old enough to be fighting, then at the weapon. It was heavier than it looked and he hefted it while feeling for the safety catch.

"Sir, all you have to do is pull the trigger, sir."

"Thank you, Private."

He crooked it in his right arm, making sure his fingers were nowhere near the trigger guard, before setting off towards the village. He was about to pass the entrance to the bridge on his right when he noticed that there was an enemy soldier on the far side of it, a mere fifty yards away. As far as he, and probably everybody else was concerned, the Japanese were only on this side of the river, but the mere presence of another on the far bank could mean there were others, and ultimately they could be cut off if there were enough of them.

He hurried his pace to put a large boulder between him and this new enemy, lent against it, and gingerly peered round to take a closer look, wondering why he had not been shot at when he was in the open. After all, it wasn't a long shot for a rifle. He looked round to see if any of the others had noticed this lone soldier, but the half dozen truck guards had congregated several feet away from the jeep at the front of the column, their attention on the village. He looked back across the river to see that the soldier was now, like him, shielded by a rock, occasionally poking his head round it too. Stock wondered if this man had run across the bridge when the column first appeared or if he was part of another group. He looked past the far end of the bridge and the other lone soldier, stationed towards the second half of the village a short distance further on, but saw no sign of any other Japanese. He asked himself again why he had not been shot at. Maybe the soldier was under orders not to give away the fact that there were more of them hiding in the village on that side of the river. Perhaps he was just too scared by the overwhelming size of the American force. He might be out of ammunition. Ammunition! That might be it. He looked again at the western part village on this side of the river, noting that he had not heard any shots fired for quite some time, and saw that the Americans were herding prisoners out into the open. In fact, most of the Company was now coming out into the open. This could just be the opportunity that an enemy on the far bank had been waiting for.

"Private," he shouted at the nearest soldier, who was smoking. "Private. Come here." It was the same youth who had handed him the Tommy gun a few minutes earlier. "Hurry."

The private dropped his cigarette and trotted towards Stock, all the while an easy target for the Japanese soldier just across the bridge, but no shot came.

"Yes, sir?"

"Stand just here." Stock indicated to a point where he would be in the shadow of the rock from across the river. "Go and find the sergeant and tell him there might be more of them on that side of the river. Tell him, no, respectfully ask him to deploy his BAR teams on this side of the river but to aim at the other bank."

"Yes, sir."

"Private."

"Yes, sir."

"Make sure you ask him respectfully."

"Yes, sir."

Stock only watched the private for a moment as he set off, before reverting his attention to the far bank. He had to wait almost a full minute before the lone soldier poked his head up again briefly. He thought of the Tommy gun that he still cradled and how effective it might be if there was a sudden rush of the enemy across the bridge. From what little he had heard about it, he couldn't remember if it held forty of fifty rounds. He wondered whether, like the British Sten gun, it would jump upwards and to the left when fired. He glanced to his left and saw that the private had found the sergeant. Then concentrated on surveying the rest of the village beyond the bridge for any sign of more of the enemy. If only I had my binoculars, he thought to himself again and made a mental note to make certain from now on that they would accompany him wherever he went. However hard he stared across the river, he could not see any movement other than the occasional helmet appearing from behind the rock.

Sergeant McCaulin had obviously delegated the corralling of the prisoners to another soldier because he and a corporal had joined him. Stock was pleased to see that the BAR teams had indeed taken up positions where he had suggested, and not only that but at least one platoon had spread out between them, all facing across the river.

"What gives?"

Stock explained.

"Right. It's too far for a grenade so here's what we'll do."

It involved one platoon charging across the bridge while another plus the BAR teams provided covering fire.

"I have an alternative idea, Sergeant. Have you got anyone who speaks Japanese?

"Yeah. Pearson knows a bit, but he's over there with the prisoners. Why?"

"Get him to come over here and tell the Jap across the bridge to surrender. After all, there might be a horde of them hiding in those buildings just waiting for such a move. Why take the risk?"

McCaulin thought about this for a moment. He had only lost one man up to now, but he could see the logic behind Stock's thinking; this could turn into a massacre as they crossed the bridge. "Ok. Louis, go and fetch Pearson."

"Better get a white flag ready," advised Stock.

"Are you sure you haven't done this before?" asked McCaulin. "And how come you saw the Jap when we didn't?"

"Just being observant, Sergeant. As ordered by your colonel." This last comment provoked a concentrated stare from McCaulin as it emphasised that there was a chain of command and that Stock was letting him know that it was he who actually had command and not the American. "If you like, Sergeant, I'll be the man to hold the white flag."

Stock had thought this through rather too quickly, but it gave McCaulin an easy way out if things did go awry. He could claim that the British Officer had stuck his own neck out too far. The fact that the Jap had not fired earlier was probably the main factor why Stock was volunteering. In any case, his father's advice always to volunteer was by now a natural instinct.

A panting Pearson came to a halt next to McCaulin. "There's a Jap behind one of those rocks over there. Tell him to surrender or we'll come and get him."

"Do you mind, Sergeant?" Stock made sure that McCaulin could look directly at him. "Also ask him if there are any others."

"Go ahead, Pearson, but keep behind this rock. Let's wait with the white flag for the moment," McCaulin shouted off to his left towards the nearest BAR team. "Hold your fire."

Pearson cupped his hands and shouted, then - in the absence of any response - repeated his cry after half a minute. Everybody watched the rock which the Jap was hiding behind and saw a tentative figure emerge from behind it and take just one step sideways. He still held his rifle but the barrel was pointing towards the ground while he and Pearson exchanged shouts.

"He says he cannot surrender without his captain's orders. Didn't we just kill one of those over there?"

"Yeah. Vicious bugger."

"But is it the same captain?" Asked Stock rhetorically.

"Ask him where his captain is."

After another exchange they saw the Jap turn his head to his right and look towards the village.

"Shit. I think we have our answer. White flag time." McCaulin looked at Stock who lent the Tommy gun against their rock and took the rifle with the grubby white handkerchief from the corporal.

"Is it loaded?"

"It's loaded."

Stock had hardly taken one pace when a shout came from one of the BAR teams.

"Hold it." McCaulin held his hand out against Stock's midriff and looked over the river to where more than one of his men was pointing. One of the doors had opened revealing a Japanese officer who took two measured paces down the steps. He held out his arms, one of them exposing what looked like a dirty white handkerchief after taking one more pace.

"Show time," McCaulin said to no one in particular.

"American." The clipped accent of the Japanese offer barely reached where they stood and he repeated his cry. "We talk."

"I think I'd better join you." McCaulin wasn't going to let Stock take over all by himself. "Here. Let me have that," he nodded at the Tommy gun which was handed to him by a nearby private. "I reckon we can go about half-way across the bridge and dive off it if things turn nasty. How're you at swimming?"

"Whenever I can, Sergeant." Stock was now nervous. On the face of it, the Americans had overwhelming superiority and an excellent defensive position, but he was worried that there may be an entire battalion hiding in the rest of the buildings. It could even be that the Japanese officer was going to ask them to surrender, not the other way round. "I suppose we ought to see what he has to say for himself. Together?"

McCaulin knew that protocol stated that the officer would normally lead. That's what they get paid for he thought, but this Englishman seemed to have a grasp of reality as opposed to the superior manner of others that he had heard about. Their eyes briefly met in acknowledgement of the potential danger they were about to walk into. "Together. Pearson, stand by in case we need you. Keep an eye on the store until we get back." This to Sergeant Myson as they slowly passed him by on their way to the bridge.

They didn't march, more like strolled, but automatically broke step as their first strides took them onto the wooden bridge. All the while, they searched for any clues as to what lay in store for them in the direction of the village. The both noted that the Japanese officer was walking towards them but it was abundantly clear that they would reach the centre of the bridge well before him. It was easily wide enough for the two of them abreast but, although it looked solidly built, they felt it sway just a little as they came to a halt.

"I'll keep an eye on our friend on our right, you concentrate on the officer. Do we speak first or does he? Aren't you going to unbutton your holster?" McCaulin coughed before speaking, clearly as nervous as Stock.

"Contrary to what you might think, I have not done this before, but I think maybe *he* has, since he offered the white flag first," Stock replied. The Japanese officer was still well out of earshot and would be for the next few seconds. "If it comes to it, I suspect he can draw his sword a lot quicker than I can draw my revolver. In any case, if we do have to jump off this bridge I would rather not lose it. Oh, and by the way, do not dive-in."

"Why not?" McCaulin looked directly at Stock.

"Because you are more likely to smash your two front teeth in rather than break a leg. It is a bit shallow." Stock nodded to the rock-strewn river below them in an avuncular manner.

Two seconds passed before McCaulin burst out laughing and it brought a smile to Stock's face. "I can't even swim."

It was Stock's turn to laugh out loud and they shared that precious moment as if it may have been their last. For just a moment was all that it was. The Japanese officer had taken his first steps onto the bridge and came to a stop a mere six feet away.

They saw a fit man, slightly smaller than both of them, tuck the white piece of cloth under his belt and stand to attention. Neither

Stock not McCaulin were that formal. One was standing 'at ease', while the other stood with his legs apart cradling the Tommy gun. The awkward silence extended and only intensified the babbling of the river beneath them. Even the slight breeze seemed to have paused.

McCaulin shifted slightly. "Do we ask him if he speaks English?"

Before Stock could answer, their enemy replied slowly, "Yes. I can speak English. Which one of you speak Japanese?"

"He's over there." McCaulin motioned with his head but kept his eyes on the man in front of them. Stock felt that the first parry in their negotiations had been won by the Japanese officer.

"I suppose we must continue in English, then. I am Captain Kimura, Commander of the Tenth Detachment of Horii Division." Three half-faded stars on each collar attested to his rank.

Stock knew that Japanese army units were generally smaller than those of the British and American armies. Whereas a battalion of an allied regiment at full strength would have some eight hundred men under a lieutenant colonel, divided into companies of eighty to one hundred men each, it was believed that the equivalent Japanese battalion, called a detachment, would have only five hundred and be commanded by a major. He wondered if he really was the enemy leader or had been sent by his unseen major. He looked across at the village trying to see if they were being observed but his action wasn't missed by Captain Kimura.

"I assure you, I am in command here. Major Hashimoto died from infection. You must tell me who you are."

Stock had been trying to think about this ever since they had left the safety of the rock but hadn't had the chance to think this through. With the immediacy of needing to reply, it suddenly came to him that there was a distinct advantage to be had here. The fact that two soldiers from different units were addressing this Japanese officer must surely indicate to him that there were more of them close by. Furthermore, if he were vague enough, perhaps he would be able to bluff the opposing captain into thinking that there weren't just some more of them, but considerably more of them in the form of an entire division.

"Captain Stock of the Fourteenth Army and this is Sergeant McCaulin of the 114th Armoured Brigade. His commanding officer was injured only half an hour ago by your men over there."

It immediately dawned on Stock that he may have made a gross error by inferring that McCaulin's men were from an armoured unit. He fervently hoped that their own insignia would not be recognised. If Captain Kimura could see his own shoulder badges, it would bear his own part in the ruse out, but he couldn't remember whether McCaulin's signified just reconnaissance or airborne reconnaissance and he dared not glance at them to find out in case he gave the game away. He hoped the sergeant was bright enough to go along with the ploy. He'd seen it in a film at The Roxy but couldn't recall the name of it, where the two sides met and discussed surrender under a white flag of truce. Perhaps it was a Western. He'd even read about it in a book, but which one escaped his memory. No, that was it, the Last of The Mohicans by James Fenimore Cooper. The British had been slaughtered as a result. That too had been a bluff, hadn't it? His heart thumped as his thoughts returned to the issue in hand.

Captain Kimura had started talking again, "You must know we outnumber you more three-to one."

"Well why the white flag then?" McCaulin was direct.

"It is simple to give you opportunity to surrender. Why waste useless lives?" The meaning of his imperfect English was understandable. "As we speak, machine guns are ready on you." It was as much of a threat to them both as the entire company. "I give you one hour to decide."

Stock saw an opening. A whole hour? Why not straight away? He's stalling, but for what? He looked at McCaulin and from the look on his face saw that the same thought had entered his mind. He was furiously thinking on his feet knowing he had to respond, and just to gain a few seconds for more thought, took a pace and a half forwards so that he could have almost touched the Japanese officer with an outstretched arm. In the instant before he spoke, he recalled another such incident when he had been confronted by a French policeman on the dockside in Dieppe. Then, by virtual willpower and an overbearing attitude, he had managed to force his antagonist to back down, and perhaps, just perhaps, he could do the same again. He decided to keep that ploy up his sleeve if it came to it. Instead, he'd try to see if he couldn't smoke out the reasoning behind the proposed delay.

"We can surrender to you now, but I must have your assurance that the terms as set out in the Geneva convention will be followed. We have an injured officer who needs immediate medical attention. Do you have hospital facilities here?"

McCaulin was appalled and joined Stock by his side. "What are you doing, Captain?"

Stock's face was like thunder as he looked directly into McCaulin's eyes. "I will decide what happens here, Sergeant." It was enough to silence him and he returned his stare to Captain Kimura. What he saw was a flicker of uncertainty and he knew then what the outcome would be.

"We have no hospital but good,errr, nurse. He is away now but back soon."

That's it thought Stock. They're all out on patrol and there's only a handful of them here. Or maybe it's just this officer and his man by the rock? Let's find out.

"In that case, Captain, where would you like us to surrender? This side of the river or on that side? We cannot move our injured officer."

McCaulin was about to complain in as colourful language as he could manage, but then realised exactly what Stock was trying to achieve and shut his mouth with a clunk.

"You may keep your men over there." He pointed to where the captured Japanese were assembled, close to the parked trucks. "But I want them to put down their arms and release our prisoners first."

"We can do that before your guards cross this bridge." Time to draw him out. "Where are they?"

"They are hidden, Captain."

Now to put the knife in. "How do I know you are not bluffing?"

Kimura hesitated. His eyes darting from one to the other. "I do not know this word."

"It means we do not believe you." Both he and McCaulin were looking slightly down on the beleaguered officer, the latter smiling as they waited for his response.

"My detachment is ready to…"

"Spare us the agony, will ya?" McCalin drawled and stood abreast of Stock. "You're all alone and now we know it. One hour, my arse. Have you got anyone else other than your sidekick here?" McCaulin thumbed a hand at the bridge sentry who had moved to the end of the bridge to try and hear what was being said.

"I am in command of over two hundred men who can cut you down…"

"I've heard enough," McCaulin spoke over the Japanese officer. "Just give up while you still can."

Kimura made one last attempt. "My men will…"

McCaulin jabbed his Tommy Gun into Kimura's midriff. "I'll watch this character while you sort out that chap. Myson, get your platoon over here now," he shouted over his shoulder.

It took Stock all of two seconds to react. He unbuttoned his holster and pointed it directly at the sentry, who, understandably, didn't know exactly what was going on as he had not managed to overhear much of the conversation. He'd had his eyes on his commander but his attention was drawn by the onrush of Myson's charging platoon over the bridge. By the time he had made his mind up, it was too late as Stock was upon him. He dropped his rifle.

There were only four other Japanese soldiers watching from the nearest hut who had seen the sentry drop his rifle and assumed that they do must do likewise. They emerged holding their hands up as Myson's platoon neared.

Captain Kimura was stunned at the sudden turn of events. With thoughts of glory in his mind, one minute he was about to accept the surrender of an entire company of Americans, the next he was being disarmed by a swarthy sergeant who shoved him towards his fellow prisoners.

Stock holstered his revolver as he rejoined McCaulin in the middle of the bridge. "And not a shot fired."

"Jeez, Captain, but you had me going there for a minute."

"I never had any intention of surrendering, but at least we now know how it is done."

"I'll remember that for next time, if there's a next time." He looked around and up at the sky. "I suppose we had better make camp here tonight as we've still got to search for those missing airmen tomorrow. It'll be getting dark soon. Hey, how was that Jap going to get us to surrender in the dark anyway?"

"Now that you mention it, I have no idea."

As they meandered back to the trucks, they both laughed at the realisation that they ought to have thought of that a few minutes ago. Relief that it was all over was in their hearts. One of Myson's privates came running up to them.

"Sarge. You'd better come and see this."

"What?"

"In the huts. There's quite a bit of stuff. Sarge reckons there's enough for half a battalion, if not more."

"Any sign of anybody?"

"No, Sarge. They've all gone and it doesn't belong to that lot over there."

"Damn. They're still out there." He turned to Stock. "What do ya reckon, Captain?" McCaulin had built up enough respect for this British officer that he sought his opinion.

Stock gritted his teeth together a little too hard and thought back to what Captian Kimura had said on the bridge before replying, "Well, he did tell us he had over two hundred men and that explains why he wanted the delay. They are probably out on patrol now but no doubt they will be back soon and probably before night. I think we ought to set up a defensive position."

McCaulin turned his neck left and right, his trained eyes taking in the detail that might betray from where this latest threat might emerge. "Yes, but they could come from anywhere. Over there looks like a dead end." He pointed past where Kimura's men had surrendered. "And which side of the river do we defend, 'coz we don't want to have to cross that bridge under fire." He could see Stock thinking the same thing; if they chose the wrong side of the river, they could well be pinned against it.

"Time to have a word with our captured prisoner I think, but in the meantime we must assume they will be coming from the far side. We did not pass any on the way here, so they must be in that direction."

"But there's nothing there except for those mountains and they look pretty impassable to me."

"Here, wait a minute. If you intended to shoot down an aircraft, where would you do it from? Not from down here, so they must be up there - or there." Stock looked at both sides of the valley.

McCaulin pondered this for a bit as he rubbed his bristly chin while looking up at the mountains. "Yeah, you're right. You'd have to get damn close to bring down a Dakota. Even with a machine gun and he said he had some of those, but he may have been bluffing about that as well."

"Since we are here to rescue an aircrew, we must assume that they do have more than just rifles. I am betting that those machine guns are on their way back down here as we speak."

They were both looking for signs of movement among the rocks higher up one of the ravines but there was nothing.

"If they are up there, they will be able to see us well before we will be able to see them. Look, until I speak with Captain, er, Kimura, why not assume they will be coming from that side of the river down, say, that ravine there." Stock chose the more likely one of three. "Can you hide most of your chaps in the huts on that side of the river and get the trucks and prisoners moved out of sight round that bluff?"

McCaulin appreciated the way Stock had asked rather than ordered the disposition of the men and in any case, he agreed with his suggestion. "Yeah, no problem. Let me know what you get out of the Nip. If you're right, then we'd better move it. Sergeant Patchford," he shouted towards a group of men and strode off in their direction.

Less than ten minutes later Stock rejoined Sergeants McCaulin and Patchford in one of the huts closer to the chosen ravine. He had Captain Kimura in tow. Before he ducked down through the doorway, he looked back over the river and was pleased to see that there was no sign of their trucks or even the other prisoners who had been herded out of sight. He also had a good look up at the threatening sky.

"Watch this fellow, will you," he addressed one of the privates, moved a lantern closer and left Kimura in his care. The hut was one of the smaller ones but had the advantage of being more or less in the centre of their line of defense.

"We cleared out the locals into a couple of the far huts but what worries me is that we're not sure that the Japs are going to come from that direction. The rest of the men are spread out in huts either side of us." McCaulin pointed through a shuttered opening towards a line of various shaped huts that had a good view. "But Myson reckons there's a clear trail leading that way and he's posted a couple of men up there so that they can give us an early warning. "I've put two of the BARs in that temple place with extra grenades and a few sticks of dynamite from the trucks. Whadda he say? Anything?"

Stock could see why the temple had been chosen. Although it was more exposed and set some distance apart from the rest of the village, it had the benefit of height and would provide an additional angle of fire. "I only asked him once and he is not saying anything, but if we can put him where he can see what is about to happen, he might have second thoughts."

All eyes in the room turned to Kimura for a moment before McCaulin stepped towards him. "Listen, you stupid Nip. Your men are about to get wiped out. They're all going to die. So, you gonna tell them to surrender?"

There was no reaction from Kimura but Stock thought he saw a narrowing of his eyes and the slightest uplifts to the corner of his mouth. He tried to put himself in Kimura's shoes and wondered what he would have done in his position. "Unless he has already sent someone to warn them."

You could have heard a pin drop. Of course. The obvious thing Kimura would have done when the fighting first started across the river, would have been to have dispatched one of his men to get the rest of the detachment back down to the village as soon as possible. Until Stock had spoken those words out loud, nobody had thought of that.

"Shit! That's why he wanted an hour's grace on the bridge. That's why he didn't care if it was going to be dark or not, as long as his men could come to the rescue in time. They're going to come down ready to take us on, and like he said, they probably outnumber us. Oh, the clever bastard. Never trust a friggin' Nip," McCaulin spat out the last in disgust.

While Sergeants McCaulin and Patchford continued to curse their luck and the Japanese officer with equal disdain, Stock concentrated his thoughts on how to gain some sort of advantage. With the bridge and the river behind them, if it did look like they were going to be overwhelmed they would have a hard time crossing back over without serious loss of life. He had already discarded the possibility of wading across the lively river and wished that there had been a second bridge, but no such luck this time. Bridge, he thought. The card game that was often described as 'making the best out of a bad hand'. What have we got in our hands?

He eased the shutter to one side a little and looked again at the chosen ravine. "Sergeant, how much dynamite have we got?"

The two sergeants paused. "There's a few more sticks in one of the trucks. What you got in mind?"

"Would you say that ravine is narrow enough just past the temple there?"

McCaulin gave Stock a speculative look, turned and took three paces across the room to join him looking out. "Yeah. Just before it opens out onto the flat there."

"If we can bring down that large vertical chunk next to it when they are almost through the gap, and then let the rubble fill it up, they would have nowhere to run to, would they?"

"Yeah. But that might just make them more fanatical."

"But if timed right, we can split them in two. Those on this side will be at our mercy while the rest of them who have not been crushed or are still on the other side, will not be able to provide support. Will they?"

McCaulin thought about this as Stock spoke. "I guess so."

"Have you ever been near a large explosion?" Stock didn't wait for a response. "I have - twice - and I can tell you that you really do not want to be anywhere near it when it goes off. You are thrown to the ground and lose all sense of direction. You are deaf to everything but your own survival. You struggle to breathe and your heart races so fast it paralyses you. You are blind because of the smoke and dust, and your comrades become blurred figures in a foggy distance. If that is not enough, there is an enemy firing at you." Stock was emphasising more for the benefit of Captain Kimura than the others in the room. "If you are lucky, you will be able to stand up after a minute, and thus make a perfect target. So, I think we can safely say that we need not worry about numbers if we can place a few sticks of dynamite up there at the base of that rock and I suggest we do it sooner rather than later."

Stock had made his point well, attested to by the looks on the faces of the others. Even Kimura's face showed a slight reaction.

McCaulin turned to the corner of the room. "You, Private. What's your name?"

"George Gaddion, Sergeant. GG for short." The private had

been following Stock's order by watching Captain Kimura.

"Go and tell Sergeant Myson that's what we're going to do. Tell him to fetch that dynamite from the temple and get someone to shove it into the base of the massive boulder next to the path."

"Yes, Sergeant."

"If you do not mind, I think it best if I join you." Although Stock was looking at McCaulin, he was addressing Private GG. "After all, I am the only Royal Engineer around here."

This produced a smile from McCaulin. "Good luck to you, Captain, but watch it if those Japs suddenly appear. If they really are coming, it won't be much longer."

"Come on." Stock led GG out of the hut and they ran towards the temple. "You can carry the dynamite."

*****

Despite the incessant cold, Sergeant Saito was happy enough and so were his men, until a runner had come up from the village. This was the third and final day that they had been camped out along the three-mile-long windswept ridge that straddled two lofty peaks. It was ideal for their purpose as it ran perpendicular to the route the American aircraft had been taking and, naturally, the Dakotas had chosen the lower altitude of the ridge to cross. The conundrum for Saito had been to guess where they would intersect. West, across the vast chasm that stretched nine or ten miles towards another similar crease in the Himalayan range, was their section of spotters, who had split into two groups almost five miles apart. Their ideal siting meant that any aircraft approaching from virtually any direction would be easily seen. Using mirrors, they had set up their own form of code based on the recently popular game of Japanese or richii mahjong. Such was the dominance of their panoramic all-round view, quite often both groups would send the same signal: 'nan' if the plane looked like it would cross Saito's ridge to the south, or 'pei' to the north, followed by numbers. To help the initial boredom while waiting, they had refined their own colloquial code and started to play games across the expanse, but this became too much of a task for most of them as the messages became more and more absurd. At that altitude, what clouds there were didn't stay in place for long as they raced eastwards, but Saito's system worked well as long as they had adequate visibility.

On their first day, the sun had just passed its zenith when the mirror flashes told Saito that six aircraft would be taking the more northerly route, and he tersely ordered the entire detachment in that direction. His men, understanding why they were on the ridge and knowing exactly what was expected of them, needed little encouragement. From their mid-way location on the ridge, hefting the machine guns and copious boxes of ammunition over the snow-covered rocky terrain northwards did not take overly long. Their passage along the frozen ridge resembled a steam train as their breath and sweat evaporated in the thin air and was swept away by the breeze.

They had been told to lay still and flat until given the order to fire. Saito hoped they wouldn't be seen so early that the pilots would have time to alter course to avoid them, and it looked as though his wish was about to come true.

"Ready. Aim for the one on the left. It's lower than the others," he ordered.

The two pilots in the cockpit of the C47 Skytrain were oblivious to what was about to happen to them, as were the two cargo handlers in the rear. For the pilots, their initial task after take-off was to gain height and, as they approached 'The Hump' of the Himalayas, they would need a minimum altitude of twelve thousand feet to clear one of the ridges. Without cargo, they could have managed this with ease, but today they were once again overladen with forty-gallon fuel drums. Fifteen of the unwieldy drums would have amounted to the manufacturer's recommended weight capacity of six thousand pounds but now they had eighteen. Just about twenty percent over. Four days earlier and under political pressure from above, the major of logistics had strong-armed them into taking seventeen and they had returned to base to report that they thought just one more would be the absolute maximum.

Much above thirteen thousand feet and they would need oxygen. Some crews automatically donned their masks as the altimeter needle approached this mark, but the two seasoned pilots knew that, once over this ridge, they could drop down to an easier eleven thousand feet until clear of the mountainous range.

They could hear and feel the engine notes change as the propellers scrabbled in the thinning atmosphere and they needed their wits about them to maintain not just height, but also stability, due to the ever-changing winds. The captain pulled a little further back on the stick to bring the nose up, adjusted the propeller pitch on both engines, and looked out of the angled side window at the rising face of the mountain. With his left hand, he automatically altered the trim wheel and told his co-pilot to keep a close eye on the ground as well. With their attitude of nose up at fifteen degrees, they had sacrificed speed for precious altitude, whereas they would normally cruise at about a hundred and fifty knots. Their airspeed indicator showed that they were managing a mere hundred-and-five and although it was well above their stall-speed, they didn't want to go any slower.

It was a little nerve-racking as they closed on the ridge, and they held their breath. They saw that they were going to clear it, but it would be by little more than a hundred feet. Just as they simultaneously exhaled, the last thing they saw through the side windows were tracers coming up from the top of the ridge.

*****

It was an ankle-breaking journey downhill, literally. In their haste to return to the village, one man carrying a pair of ammunition boxes had no time to put a hand out to prevent his ankle from being broken as he caught his right foot on a protruding rock, and another had fallen over, knocking himself out. Sergeant Saito had detailed two riflemen to stay behind while urging the others on down the steep side of the mountain. But now he told them to stop, to keep low to the ground and be quiet as just ahead was the final crest before the village. Joined by another sergeant, they eased themselves up the slight incline and, with Captain Kimura's borrowed binoculars, surveyed the village beneath them. It was starting to get gloomy and they didn't want to be caught in the middle of nowhere when the sun set. They could already feel the temperature beginning to drop and, without the tents they had left on top of the mountain, would suffer from the elements without them.

"Can't see anything moving. Can you?" They passed the binoculars back and forth between them.

"Nothing. Perhaps they've already gone."

Saito focused in the distance where the only road disappeared behind a knoll. "Not even a sign, but I see that our bridge sentry is missing, so either they're hiding or they've all gone."

"But it would be difficult to hide that number of people in the huts, so we must assume they've gone. After all, there's nothing to keep them here, is there?"

"I agree with your assumption, but I'd rather go down prepared, so this is what we'll do. You see that tall rock where the gorge narrows?" He waited while the other sergeant steadied the binoculars. "You set up the machine guns each side of the entrance and I'll take the men into the village, fanning them out left and right. Once we have ensured this side of the village is clear, get one of your machine guns just this side of the bridge, the other in the village facing across the river, and I'll continue to the other side." He looked up. "We'd better get a move on. It'll be dark in a few minutes."

The first few snowflakes began to swirl round them, yet despite suffering from the cold, they dispersed efficiently, many eagerly looking forward to a warmer night's sleep than the previous two. This in itself spurred them on and, although not quite reckless, they were not as diligent as they might otherwise have been. They certainly did not notice that there was a small plume of smoke travelling along the side of the ravine, nor the two enemy soldiers, all but invisible as they cowered some distance away in a vertical crevasse.

It happened very much as Stock had described earlier, but Private George Gaddion still wasn't ready for the ear-shattering blast. He had thought that their hidden hidey-hole would have protected them, and it did, from all except the initial noise. By the time he had opened his eyes, he saw Stock striding off towards the village. He was shouting and holding his hands up to his mouth to throw his voice further, and in response, saw his comrades emerge from the huts and charge towards the rubble at the entrance to the ravine. He looked to his left where there was once a smooth vertical rock but was now nothing more than boulders and dust clogging up the entrance to the ravine. Dust was everywhere and still spreading in his direction, indeed, in every direction he looked.

He couldn't see any Japanese as he followed in Stock's direction and was rather surprised at the amount of destruction caused by those few sticks of dynamite. Then he remembered he'd left his rifle back at the hole he had just come from and rather sheepishly returned to get it.

The Americans had formed a rough semi-circle but had nobody to fire at, quite simply because of the dust. Even when figures began to emerge, it was evident that they were in no condition to fight. They were rounded up and shepherded to a holding area just short of the bridge. McCaulin had ordered one platoon to climb the treacherous rubble and check the far side, but when they returned, they reported that all they found were some soldiers that had already been injured.

"That was pretty neat timing, Captain. We thought you had left it a little late, but hey, look what we've got. A whole heap of trouble that we've got to get back to HQ."

Stock was considering whether he ought to tell McCaulin that the timing had been little more than a stroke of luck, a guess at best, or to wallow in the deception. He decided on a neutral retort, "I was wondering the same thing."

*****

The next morning's weather was overcast, definitely colder, and looking decidedly nasty. It would take two days or so to march the prisoners back to Fort Hertz, and despite Lieutenant Linney's condition, Stock offered to accompany him ahead of the others in the only jeep. Besides which, if he lingered too long, he might miss the flight back to civilisation. It ought to take a few hours unencumbered by trucks and prisoners. There would not be enough space in the trucks for everyone, and it was an easy decision to make the Japanese prisoners walk. Although Linney's injury wasn't overly serious for now, they all knew that infection could take hold at any time and McCaulin insisted they take a driver. "I'm giving you Hux, but don't believe a word he says. That's if you can get a word in." He half turned and kicked a stone that was an easy target. "Listen, Captain." He was clearly embarrassed. "We really appreciated what you did for us here. I mean, if it weren't for you I have a lot of ID Tags to account for."

Stock looked at the half a dozen faces behind McCaulin and saw they were all grinning at him. One man gave a half salute.

"Well, I am glad I had you lot to back me up. I doubt I could have managed it on my own."

It raised a ripple of laughter and Stock took McCaulin's outstretched handshake.

He was half-lost in kindly thoughts of the Americans he had spent the last couple of days with when Corporal First Class Huxley Ristervero suddenly let the clutch out and jerked them forward. Even though Lieutenant Linney was heavily sedated in the back and probably wouldn't have felt a thing, Stock still told Huxley to try to be a bit gentler with his driving. McCaulin was right; Huxley talked almost non-stop, at least for the first half of the journey until they reached Machanbaw where Lieutenant Minster's company was temporarily stationed. Huxley had an opinion on most things but specialised in where the best places to eat in Chicago were, and where to find the best ingredients for a pizza. It soon became apparent to Stock that his knowledge was a little skin deep and limited to that particular part of the United States.

A little over an hour later, they pulled up outside the hut that had been designated as the Field Hospital at Fort Hertz. Stock made sure that Linney was being cared for before marching over to the Mess to give Colonel Rees his report.

"Over three hundred of them!"

"Three hundred and fourteen, sir, including their injured."

"All armed?"

"Happily disarmed now, sir, and on their way back here. Ought to arrive sometime tomorrow afternoon."

Rees was taken aback. "Only one fatality and Linney's shoulder you say?"

"If you will allow me, I would like to put this all into my report." Stock felt that if Rees pushed him for more at this stage, he may end up regretting saying something in haste. "Sir, I can let you have it in a couple of hours and then you will have an accurate tally for HQ." He hoped Rees would grasp the chance to have facts and figures at his fingertips when he contacted his superior.

Rees looked at his watch. "Twelve hundred hours, then."

"Yes, sir." Stock turned to go in search of some hot food, a decent amount of foolscap, and another pen, but turned round when Rees called to him.

"By the way, if what you say is true, someone's going to get a medal."

Stock was about to reply that Sergeant McCaulin ought to be the recipient, but instead tactfully retorted with, "Sir," and continued on his way.

Chapter 7
Mid Burma

A mere forty-eight hours or so later, via two different aircraft, a short train trip found Stock back with his regiment. Well, almost. He hadn't quite got there yet, but they were bivouacked a just few hundred yards away. He stood rigidly to attention in front of a brigadier general who sat easily behind his desk, while off to one side stood a staff colonel who shuffled papers within a buff folder. He leant over the desk and made some notes once Stock had finished reporting.

"That's quite some claim you're making. Three hundred and…" he referred to the file but not quickly enough.

"Fourteen, sir."

"Three hundred and fourteen it is, then." He looked skeptically at Stock. Up to that point in Assam, allied successes had been rather thin on the ground, especially when coupled with the lack of losses on the Allied side as was the case in this instance. "And if we can get hold of a copy of Colonel Rees's report, it will bear that out, will it?"

"Yes, sir." Stock kept his answers short, preferring the two senior officers to refer to his own report that was virtually identical to the one he had given Colonel Rees two days earlier. Indeed, he had transposed most of it. What this report included over and above his earlier one was his assessment of the condition of the airfield at Fort Hertz as well as his efforts in bringing it up to scratch.

"Stand easy, Stock. I think you've earned it." It was the first time the brigadier had spoken.

"Thank you, sir." He relaxed by spreading his feet a little and clasping his hands behind his back but was still a little apprehensive in the presence of a general officer.

"What do you think, Colonel?" The brigadier looked at the staff colonel who closed the file.

"I don't see why not, subject to the usual paperwork. Although his record shows he's more than capable and has just about put in enough time, he lacks the seniority and it goes against the procedures." They were both looking at Stock who naturally felt a little uncomfortable being spoken about as if he wasn't there.

The brigadier was clearly trying to make his mind up in the prolonged silence, other than the hum of a convoy of passing lorries not too far away. The silence became a little uncomfortable. At least, it was for Stock who felt he was certainly the subject of their comments. "Right then, let me explain. While you've been gallivanting away in the Himalayan foothills, Lieutenant Colonel Alfredson's gone down with a bout of jaundice and won't be fit for duty for a week or two. Maybe longer. Ordinarily, Major Wavertree would take over temporary command, but it seems he too has contracted something akin to jaundice. On top of that, with you being away these past two weeks, your battalion has been lacking in leadership, and we are in desperate need of a prime engineering unit to carry out what might turn out to be an awkward task. In fact, I know it's going to be an awkward task. As things stand at the moment, you're the senior captain and technically in command, but as Colonel Bradford quite rightly points out, there are certain administrative obstacles that need to be overcome and God only knows how long that might take."

Bradford took a pace forward. "That's why I'm here and in my opinion…"

The brigadier suddenly stood up and went round the side of his desk to stand directly in front of Stock. "Enough. We can't wait any longer. How do you feel about leading the battalion while Colonel Alfredson's away?" He jutted his neck forward as if in a challenge.

This was something Stock hadn't been expecting. Commanding a battalion of what ought to have been some eight hundred men - but was probably down to a little above six hundred by now - would be totally different to commanding a company a tenth of the size. Relatively simple orders were issued to company commanders, which by now, Stock was well versed in carrying out. Important decisions were made by colonels and above, but it was up to the captains and lieutenants in charge of their respective companies to achieve the objectives of their commanding officer's demands. Life would become more complicated and it would be his responsibility to not just to issue those orders he would have normally been given, but to ensure that they were the correct ones. Just one mistake would be ten times more costly. Only just recently and with spare time on his hands while he had been at Fort Hertz, he had wondered what it might be like to be promoted into a position where he would be in command. After all, he had been an officer in the Royal Engineers for over three years and knew he was a competent sapper, but commanding an entire battalion? When he had left the Americans, he hadn't made his mind up if he would take promotion when it became due and if it was offered, but now, out of the blue… and it was only going to be temporary until Alfredson got better, wasn't it?

"Certainly, sir." Stock didn't add that it would be no problem because he suspected it would be quite an onerous undertaking.

The brigadier held Stock's eyes for a few moments, possibly to make sure he had not made a mistake himself, turned, and sat himself back down in his chair. "That's settled, then. Until Colonel Alfredson returns. I expect Colonel Bradford here will be putting the wheels in motion to see about a permanent promotion for you, but in the meantime you'll be in command of your current battalion. Isn't that so, Bradford?"

"In the absence of Colonel Alfredson, will you be sponsoring Captain Stock, sir?" Bradford was clearly uncomfortable at being put in the position of having to accede to the brigadier's decision.

"Most certainly. We can't have officers the calibre of Stock languishing where he is just because of red tape, can we?"

"I'll see what General Scoones has to say about it, sir." Bradford was still hoping that he would be able to assert the grinding wheels of the military establishment over a brigadier's whim.

The brigadier chose to move on rather than dwell on a subject that had already been decided. "Now. There'll be a briefing at eighteen hundred hours in the hut next to the canteen that I want you to attend, but don't present yourself until eighteen thirty hours. I need to finalise a few details with other commanders first and you don't necessarily need to know about those. If you don't know where your battalion is stationed, you'd better ask my adjutant in the next room. Good morning."

Stock struck to attention. "Sir," he said, about turned, and let himself out of the brigadier's office. Once outside, he paused and breathed a little easier, glad to be away from the conflict between two senior officers. He grinned to himself, realising he'd been volunteered.

Cleanly shaven after a tepid shower and dressed in his uniform that had been brushed down by Sergeant Day, he stood outside the meeting hut and waited for the requisite time, all the while watched by a sentry who stood beside the only door. He'd told his fellow officers of his appointment by the brigadier and had surmised that it had been a popular decision, not that any of them disliked Alfredson. Even while he had been showering under the makeshift tinny head that leaked as much as anything else, he'd been thinking through how best to resolve the several problems that had been evident at company level, now magnified at battalion level. Each company was to prepare a list, in order of priority, ready for him after he returned from brigade HQ. That way, when he eventually did get to go to bed, he would have a chance to mull the issues over in his mind. Typically, they were problems such as the state of their uniforms, which were partially dissolving in the permanently humid conditions, and the everlasting complaint about their boots and how they seemed to wear out where the laces threaded through. He knew some of the men used the straps on their gaiters to…

The door half-opened and a head poked round it, interrupting his train of thoughts.

"Captain Stock?. In here, please."

The only real noise came from the sentry, who, startled out of his own thoughts by the silent opening of the door over his left shoulder, dropped his rifle as he attempted to come to attention. Neither Stock nor the head in the open doorway moved while the soldier bent down, collected his rifle, and finished his movement.

The door opened a little wider. "I'm not even going to comment on that, you grotty soldier."

"Sir." To Stock, the sentry looked rather sheepish.

Stock obliged by following the officer through the door and into a brightly lit room that did not appear to have any windows.

"Sit down, Stock."

He recognized the voice as that of the brigadier's but he didn't have time to see from where exactly it came. He chose one of the two vacant seats off to the right-hand side of the large rectangular table, round which were gathered a dozen or so senior officers, some of them smoking.

"I won't bother with introductions as we'd be here all night, "the brigadier began, "but suffice to say that Captain Stock here is in temporary command of our sappers and it will be his job to ensure you have an easy transition."

Eyes turned as he seated himself and casually as possible. He returned the looks but couldn't manage to glean if their stares held any message. There would undoubtedly have been some who were curious as to why a relatively lowly captain, rather than a colonel or a major, was in command of an engineering unit, but then again, this war had been throwing up some most unusual situations and they were all fairly well used to anything out of the ordinary.

"Major, do you have that sketch?"

A rough piece of paper was unfolded and spread out in the centre of the table. Obligingly one colonel reached out to hold an edge down while the major attended to the other as they all craned their necks for a better look.

"This, gentlemen, is the bridge you will be crossing and as you can see from Major Gillard's drawing, it may be a little on the flimsy side. Have a good look, Stock, as it'll be your job to shore it up and ensure our armour can cross the river without getting its feet wet." He looked directly at Stock. "Speak to Gillard here directly afterwards as he personally drew this sketch and can give you details."

Gillard and Stock's eyes briefly met in acknowledgement. The brigadier continued.

"Once across the river…," he waited while Gillard removed his drawing to reveal a detailed map of the area, "you'll be pushing south and east towards Mansi here." He used a shortened length of cane. "And you'll be joining up with Lowry's brigade who will be advancing on your left. By the way, they have a far more difficult job of crossing the same Ayeyarady River since their sappers have to rebuild the bridge that our RAF friends kindly destroyed two days ago."

He didn't exactly glower, but his momentary gaze at the wing commander liaison officer seated on Stock's left was not missed by most. "I'd be grateful if you can inform you pilots to leave ours intact for the time being."

"Group is aware, si,r and I'm sure it wasn't intentional."

"Hummmmm. Very well. Just make sure they all know otherwise we may as well start building our own retirement homes here because these are the only two bridges for the next fifty miles to the south." He paused to take a sip of water. "Now, taking this bridge intact ought to be straight forward as you've already heard, but rumours of the Japs moving in some anti-aircraft guns on the far side may well be true. If that's the case, then they'll need to be dealt with before the sappers can start work on the bridge." He looked up. "Ocky, can I ask you to attend to that?"

"Certainly, sir."

"We'll fix timing later once we know exactly when division want us to proceed, but that's likely to be the day after tomorrow. Oh, and make sure those boats actually float this time," he grinned and three of the other officers grunted a small laugh, but the joke was lost on Stock.

"Windy and Patric, you get the prime job of pushing down this road here but no further than Lashio which, as you already know, is your objective, but we expect Lowry's brigade to get there ahead of you. Now, logistics have come up with…"

Stock was only half-listening as the brigadier continued his oration. He supposed that he had been omitted from the earlier part of the briefing as there were manoeuvers and other details that he and his sappers either did not need to know, or should not even know about. He looked a little more closely at the unmarked map, seeing a medium sized river meandering in a rough north east-south west direction. Where they were now was a few miles to the north of it and Lashio looked like it was nearly fifty miles the other side to the south and east. The bridge Lowry's brigade would have to cross was way off to their left, while the one that Stock was interested in not only looked to be on the more direct route, but, on the face of it, the more major one.

The thought crossed his mind that while they might have been happy with Alfredson in charge, they may have doubts as to his own capabilities. He would just have to rise to the challenge and prove them wrong. He now grasped how vital it would be for him to make certain that the bridge would be strong enough to take the tanks, transports, bowsers, and other ensuing vehicles. Without that bridge, not even one single lorry, let alone a tank, would be crossing, and the entire operation would flounder. Those who had crossed over in the boats could well be cut off if there was any counter attack by the Japanese. Failure would mean some two and a half thousand men would be looking to him to explain why they were on the wrong side of the river, at the wrong time, and that way he would remain a captain for the remainder of the war, knowing that he, and only he, bore the responsibility for this. Not only that, but the other brigade would probably be depending upon their timely arrival and they too would be pointing their fingers in his direction.

He decided he'd best take some advice. For some reason, he

found himself looking at the colonel who had opened the door to him. What had the brigadier called him? Ockky?.Oakey?. He liked the way he had handled the dozy sentry. Perhaps he was someone with a practical frame of mind, someone he could glean some useful information from. He would have to wait until the briefing finished. A colonel at the far end of the table was coming to the end of his report on the long list of items they were lacking. Stock assumed he was part of the logistics corps.

Then suddenly the brigadier was looking at him again and speaking directly to him, "Talking of which, once you've finished with the bridge, you'll move on to somewhere in this area here, say five miles short of Lashio, and make a runway so that Johnson's lot can fly our supplies in." His cane was hovering over a point on the map. "But make sure you don't get too far ahead of our lead units unless you want the glory of being the first into Lashio and probably the first to be captured. Ideally, we want that runway up and running within a week. OK? Right then, I want to talk about contingencies and possible moves the Japs might take by way of a counter attack. Intelligence suggests that…"

Stock studied the map again to see if there were any indications as to where might be a suitable siting for another airfield, but apart from a few sporadic spot heights, it didn't show anything but a couple of roads and minor tributaries running through what he supposed was mainly jungle. Lashio itself was set in a valley where he hoped, from previous experience, the jungle might give way to sparser vegetation, and he made a mental note that just to the north would be a good place to start. He heard the brigadier bringing the assembly to a close with a comment about the new bombs for the Stokes three-inch mortars not being available yet and sought out Colonel Oakey three places down from his own seat. As he stood, Stock could see that he was not too much older than himself, and looked like he was in excellent shape. Introducing himself, he admitted he didn't know his correct name.

"Actually, not many do. I have a rather unusual middle name

so I'll keep that to myself if you don't mind, but in the meantime it's Clarence Ockham. ~I'm delighted to hear you've got command of the sappers. By the way, when is Alfredson expected to return. Before he left, did he mention anything about when we can expect that return rugger match or the small wager we had on it? I'm rather looking forward to taking another bottle of Black and White off him again."

He spoke almost without pausing, leaving Stock unsure as to which part to comment on first. He'd heard about a rugger match some three months ago while he had been posted elsewhere and now realised that it had been Oakham's lot who had soundly beaten his own regiment. He decided to take a stab at provocation.

"Well. We did not have as many ringers in our side as you did."

"HA!" Oakham's loud guffaw was noticed by all in the room that temporarily hushed. "So, you heard about him did you? Well, all I can add is that Scotty Prentiss was, shall we say, temporarily seconded but has now moved on. He was worth his weight in salt and turned down my offer for a permanent posting to the battalion. Great shame really, but I gather he's fit and well and still serving in the artillery stationed further down south. Now tell me more about Alfredson."

There wasn't much to tell as he had been away and thought best not to show his ignorance.

"Well, pass on my good wishes for a speedy recovery, won't you. Now, I suppose you want to know how we're going to coordinate rooting those Japs out from the far side of the river so that you can get on with repairing your bridge without getting shot at. Umm? Well, it's fairly simple. If it's AA guns, they won't be able to depress them enough for us to worry about, but the brigadier's concern, and obviously ours, is that there'll be a number of support troops that go with them so we ought to be faced only with small arms. We've got a dozen or so canvas boats that we can fit eight men in each, so that means I'll send across one company at a time starting at say, 04.00. It's a round trip of about twenty minutes so by, um, 05.00

we'll have the best part of two companies on the far bank ready to sweep it clear while the rest of us will simply cross the bridge on foot, if we can. You hang back until I give you the all clear. Here, I hope you've got plenty of hammers and nails because from what I hear you're going to need them. Have you spoken to Gillard yet? He's rather good at carrying out a recce and always seems to know exactly where, when, and how many of the blighters there are. I think you'll find he was down there yesterday so he can let you have the latest gen on it. Hey, here he is now, so I'll leave you two to it."

Stock saw Ockham look over his shoulder and by the time he had done likewise and turned back to thank him, he was en route to a group of other senior officers. He had felt entirely at easy while being addressed by the colonel and instinctively knew that they would get on when it came to taking the bridge, but now he was confronted with a dour looking man in the form of Major Gillard. Half a head shorter than himself, with a slight stoop and lips that seemed to meet in the wrong places, he immediately put Stock on the back foot.

He took Stock by the arm, led him a few paces to one side out of earshot from the others, laid his sketch on a stack of ammunition boxes, and indicated that Stock should hold down one side.

"Bit of a hard act to follow, taking over from Alfredson, so do try to keep up. I expect you have your hands full at the moment, so I'll keep this simple. The bridge is a little over three hundred feet long and was built there by somebody's ancestors. This is the narrowest point for miles but that means it's also the deepest where it cuts through a range of hillocks. Every other year the monsoon washes part of it away and every other year, once the level's dropped, the locals re-build it. Part of the problem is that the Japs have prevented this year's re-building and it has fallen into greater disrepair than normal. Look here." He paused briefly. "We're fortunate that it is a bridge of two halves dissected by a mid-stream rock on which the centre stone support stands, and I estimate that the northern side is slightly shorter that the southern. That means we have one half that's about a hundred and eighty feet supported by suspension cables and chains, the other, say, a hundred and twenty feet made from local tree trunks and also suspended by a mixture of whatever the jungle's provided. This end's not my main concern as it stays fairly well intact and needs minimal repair, but it's the longer half which dangles close the river when it's at its highest and gets destroyed by the floods that'll need all your efforts."

He paused again to let Stock take a closer look at his drawing which showed what he had described. It looked as though Gillard had used charcoal but it still showed the presence of cables and chains across the span, dangling without anything attached. Stock was formulating several questions when Gillard continued.

"I know what you are about to ask but we had this crossing in mind months ago and finally last week, our requisition for that amount of bridging equipment came through. The trouble is that it's too high to float on water and the longest section can only span forty feet, even then it still needs support at both ends. So, we have some rather useful cabling supplied by the Navy which, so they tell me, will be more than adequate to string new suspension hawsers across from which we can attach drops every forty feet for the base bridge. All you have to do is suspend these twin cables, one end from the rock in the middle and the other anchored on the far bank, before you build your drops on which the bridging bases can be set. As to your next question, the bank is fairly steep at the far end so you ought to have a sufficient vertical height from which to swing your cables. Colonel D'Burrard is our man in the logistics corps with all the new equipment you'll need and he's stationed a couple of miles just up the road from here. He's been told to expect you. Any questions?"

Stock was shocked at the gunfire speed at which Gillard delivered his description and had little time to prepare his numerous questions in order of priority. One, however, stood out above all else. "How long have we got before we go?"

"I'm afraid that's privileged information at the moment, but it won't be tomorrow." Gillard caught Stock out by smiling at him after looking at his watch. "I think we can give you a little more than nine hours' notice. Just be ready when the call comes through Captain."

"Sir." He didn't add 'Thank you very much'. So, this was what it was like to be a lieutenant colonel. In the past, orders had been clear and concise. Easy to follow. Now he had to interpret them before issuing his own and the onus would be on him if he got them wrong. He didn't notice his march back to his quarters as his mind was totally ensconced with forthcoming events. How long and heavy was the cable? Did it come in a drum and how would they get it to where it was needed? What kind of cleats would they be? What could he use as piling to attach the cables to on the far bank? How taut would he need to make it? What was its breaking strain? What…… the questions were endless and he decided he needed to see Colonel D'Burrard first thing tomorrow morning. Meanwhile he would convene his company commanders tonight and prepare them as much as he could.

"Sir….. Sir." he found himself standing outside of a neighbouring regiment's headquarters being addressed by a corporal on guard. He had no idea as to how long he had been standing there and quite rightly, the corporal had challenged him, then put him on the right track to his own battalion.

*****

"I was told you would be coming." Compared to his own quarters, D'Burrard's was positively palatial, even to the extent of what looked like a cocktail bar complete with high chairs in one corner, but without a waiter standing behind it. "Oh, do sit down and make yourself at home. Have you breakfasted yet? Evans makes a good brace of scrambled eggs on toast and although he tells me they're chickens', I'm not always so sure."

Stock eyed up one end of a comfortable oriental looking sofa, realising that not only was he being offered breakfast, but virtually told what he would be having. "Not yet, and yes I will take you up on your kind offer." He had driven himself in one of the jeeps a few miles and wondered what kind of person he would be meeting. He had half been expecting the colonel to have a French accent, but his English was perfectly pronounced. Not only that but he looked typically English. Tall, moustached, debonair, dressed in something akin to a smoking jacket and on his feet what looked like wooden sandals.

"Evans. Breakfast for two." His shout produced an acknowledgement in the distance. "Now, tell me about Alfredson." He sat at the other end of the sofa, crossing one leg on top of his knee.

"There is not much to tell, really. When he became ill, I had already been posted to Fort Hertz, helping the Americans repair the airfield there, but before I left he seemed in rather good spirits. Come to think of it, his pallor did seem a bit off and it has since been confirmed he is suffering from Jaundice quite badly. I suppose it will take another couple of weeks or so before he is back in charge of the battalion again."

"Well, we've no such worries about jaundice round here as Evans has a cure. More of a preventative really. He puts radish leaves in the tea. Personally, I think it's an old wives tale, but I have to admit, we've hardly had a single case since he started doing it. I must say, you're looking rather healthy yourself. What are you taking for it?"

"Apart from the occasional gin and tonics whenever I get the chance, nothing out of the ordinary. Our American friends didn't really believe me when I told them that the Fourteenth lived on G&Ts but I left them with the idea that they ought to at least try it." He chuckled out loud. "I prescribed them half a pint of gin a day each and I would have liked to have seen the look on their supply officer's face when the requisition chit came through. Of course, I didn't tell them that it countered malaria and not jaundice, but I expect it will do them some good somehow."

D'Burrard was smiling at the believable story. "Well, I'm your supply officer and I can tell you right now, if you're thinking of ordering that amount of gin for your lot, then you better think again. Oh, we've got plenty around here somewhere but we'd soon run out if the whole division started drinking that amount on a daily basis. Here, talking of which, Alfredson asked me for a bottle of Black and White scotch and I suppose you ought to take it as he's not here in person. Do tell him it was the devil's own job getting hold of some." He stood up and retrieved a bottle from behind his bar. "Any idea why Black & White in particular?"

"Something to do with a wager he had over a rugger match."

"Ha! Well tell him to lower the stakes next time. Now, I suppose you want to see this bridging equipment for crossing the Ayeyarady. Well, I can tell you it's there's lots of it. Brand new as well, but somewhere along the line it's all gone rusty."

Stock knew the name of the river they were about to try and cross. "How rusty?"

"Ummmm. Not too bad considering, but some parts will need a sledge hammer to get them hinging again. I'll show it to you after breakfast. Talking of which…" he indicated with his hand. "I suppose you've got more of that radish stuff in our tea again Evans."

Evans sat a tray down on the bar counter. "Not today, sir. Radishes have gone off, so it's mint."

"And what's that supposed to cure this time?"

"Good for your joints, sir. You know. Elbows, knees, and the like."

"Nothing wrong with my joints."

"Also helps keep the larynx free of nodules."

"What the hell are nodules?"

"They're the small white fungus-type growths that attract spores on your tonsils."

D'Burrard gave up. "Evans here ought to have been in the

medical corps as he seems to know some sort of cure or another for everything. Come on, then. Let's get stuck in. We haven't got all day."

They perched side by side on their bar stools in the bell tent, Stock thoroughly enjoying what was obviously more than just a brace of nicely scrambled eggs on some sort of toasted bread. "Would you happen to know when we are going over the river? I would like to have time to study and prepare the bridging equipment. Any Bailey in it?"

"Ummmm." D'Burrard wiped his mouth. "It doesn't surprise me that they didn't tell you. They're not too keen on divulging high-level secrets to mere captains. That's a job for us colonels, you know, but I really don't see why you oughtn't to know. It's the day after tomorrow. Morning, that is. There's not much new Bailey Bridge stuff and there's no plates or side supports but quite a few transoms. Here, you may be interested in some steel plates that look like they hook and maybe hinge. I believe they call it Marsden Matting but I suppose you'd know all about that as it looks more like what you'd use on an airfield.

Stock groaned. Marsden Matting was made from perforated steel plates about ten feet long and a little over a foot wide and, when laid on unfirm ground, made a good relatively flat surface for aircraft. It could be hooked together to create anything from a long strip or an area for manoeuvering but it certainly wasn't made for suspending across rivers. "I suppose this is a gift from our American friends?"

"Most likely as we certainly haven't got any. The funny thing is that they left it all on the lorries."

"What? Still on the lorries?"

"Yes, I believe they call them trucks where they come from. Bit of a godsend, that one - it'll make transporting it an awful lot easier. Huge great flatbeds. Here, this tea's alright but I'm not sure about the milk."

They both stopped sipping their tea with exactly the same

thought in mind but it was D'Burrard who said it first, "It's in the milk. Evans!" he shouted. But there was no reply.

Ten minutes later, D'Burrard was suitably dressed, the swagger stick completing his superior look. They were accompanied by his sergeant who took up station three paces behind the pair of them as they marched through mountains of stores that serviced the division. Camouflage netting covered some if it and tarpaulins a little of the rest, but by and large, it was mostly out in the open. After several minutes' walk, D'Burrard slowed and finally halted behind a vast tower of crates marked with different regimental insignia.

"Well, there they are on the left. Sixteen lorry loads of matting and the like. Bailey Bridges off to the right, cabling, hawsers, rope and tools more or less in the middle and girders etcetera Where are the girders, Pritchard?"

"Behind the Bailey Bridges, sir." Sergeant Pritchard consulted a ledger he had previously tucked under one arm. "Ought to be a hundred and eighty-six of them, sir."

From the look on D'Burrard's face, Stock could see pride that he ran an efficient unit. "Mind if we have a wander round?"

"Help yourself, Stock, and if you don't mind, I'll leave you in the capable hands of Sergeant Pritchard here. There's the small matter of overseeing the distribution of ammunition for the guns before tomorrow night."

Stock was stunned at the sheer amount of equipment stockpiled. It wasn't prettily laid out as one would expect to find in an English depot, as every so often - with all the toing and froing of the front lines - the whole lot would have had to be moved either forwards or backwards. Recently it had all been forwards. He eyed up the row of large transporters, each marked with T980 and each connected to a flatbed trailer to which the Marsden Mats were lashed. His first thought was that they were big enough to carry a tank each and as he walked round the side of one, saw that the back angled down a little, with ramps stowed underneath, which confirmed his initial impression. He wondered if they had been diverted from the Ledo

Road project. He did a mental calculation as to the number of mats and came up with a frightening figure that he would re-check again with pen and paper. Nearly three acres of the stuff but useless for spanning. Followed by Sergeant Pritchard, he wound his way in and out of various heaps, noting roughly what was available. He ended up standing in front of the stacks of the favoured Bailey Bridge elements. He started to count but was interrupted by Pritchard, ledger open.

"Sixty-four incomplete units and an additional fifteen side panels. Plenty of pins, bit short of planks and cases of nuts and bolt,s sir."

"What about this cabling the navy's supposed to have delivered?"

"That's been put behind the beams and there's, hang on..." he thumbed several pages, "four drums of one hundred yards each." He could see Stock thinking about lengths. "How much length do you need, sir?"

"Two hundred feet," Stock replied as he still counted up.

Pritchard left him alone for half a minute and continued his thumbing. "Would it help if I told you they also delivered eighteen chains of chains?"

Stock ceased his calculations, absorbed what he was being told. "Eighteen chains?"

Pritchard didn't need to reply.

"Where?"

"Follow me, sir."

They had to pick their route through the rough ground. The standard length of a chain was sixty-six feet and three of them together totaled just short of two hundred feet. It all depended on how thick the links were. Pritchard stopped and scuffed one boot over the vegetation to reveal some very rusty, but sturdy, chain. Stock bent down and, with the help of the sergeant, had to heave to pull it away from the undergrowth that now intertwined throughout its length. Each link was some six inches long, deep red with flaky rust that came away in their hands, but he immediately knew it would do the job nicely. "How long has it been here, Sergeant?"

"Arrived soon after the monsoon ended, sir."

"Much longer and it would have disappeared forever."

Pritchard gave Stock a hard look as if to say, 'Oh, no, it wouldn't.'

"What size cleats are there?"

"Standard six-inch towing cleats and I believe we have over a thousand of those."

"Why so many?"

"Why indeed, sir."

Stock smiled at Pritchard and clapped him on the arm. "That will do nicely, Sergeant. I think we are finished here."

They were marching back towards D'Burrard's headquarters when Pritchard suddenly broke into a run off to one side and disappeared round several piles of tyres. Stock followed at a quick pace and, rounding a corner, saw that Pritchard had managed to catch a large boy and had him by the ear. How he had managed it without dropping his ledger, Stock never knew.

"We'll take this one with us I think, sir."

"Pilferer?"

"Get 'em a couple of times a week but we send 'em back with a little more than a flea in their ear. We cane 'em, sir. Seems to put 'em off for a short while."

*****

News that there was to be an attack over the River Ayeyarady was rife throughout the battalions and Stock felt a little miffed that nobody had told him officially. It was as though he was the last to know. Other than that, he was feeling pleased with himself and confident they could manage to rebuild the bridge in the time given, but there was just one caveat: the Japs. If Oakham's lot couldn't clear the far bank, then the whole show would be a non-starter and they would be kicking their heels on the north bank until somebody found another way over the river. Sitting at Alfredson's military desk in the battalion's bell tent, he was going over what he had already set in motion and what would happen the next morning, when Sergeant Day appeared with a staff officer in tow. Once he had read and understood the sealed orders, he called Day back in.

"You can let everybody know now without fear of being court marshalled, because it will all happen tomorrow morning, which means there is the devil's own work to be done between now and then. Do you know if the transporters are at the assembly point yet?"

He had ordered the bulk of the battalion over to D'Burrard's logistics headquarters to fetch the transporters, complete with their matting, as well as several lorry loads of other items they would need. In the opposite direction, he had gone with the one remaining company towards the river where he had found Oakham with his battalion in the assembly area, less than a mile from the river. He and Major Gillard stood alone in discussion but they fell silent as he joined them.

"Got everything you need, Stock?" asked Gillard.

"There will be an awful lot of equipment and we may need to temporarily block the road because the trailers are more likely to beach themselves off it."

Gillard turned sharply to look at him. "Not a good idea blocking our one and only major route out of here, just in case things go wrong. How about we clear those few trees over there?"

"Not possible given the time, but if I had had a little more notice…" His pointed comment aimed at Gillard was not missed by Oakham, who emitted a badly disguised cough.

"Captain, may I remind you that you are here only because your colonel is temporarily unavailable. If you had taken the time to recce this area beforehand, you would have realised the problem and taken the appropriate steps. If you cannot foresee this type of problem, then perhaps you really are best suited to remain a captain."

"Which problem are you referring to, sir?" Stock decided

he wasn't going to take this slander lightly and chose his words carefully, hoping that Gillard would be too busy belittling him rather than facing up to the reality.

"The problem that goes with the assembly area marshal which you are obviously not conversant with."

"What would you recommend, sir?" He could see Gillard hesitate and that was all he needed. "Would this be the problem of transporting over a hundred tons of equipment along a pot-holed road over ten miles away in less than twenty-four hours, or that the assembly area is not large enough? Or were you referring to the fact that the bridging units you told me about are not actually bridging units at all and are unusable as such?"

Gillard's mouth was gaping, but Stock hadn't finished. The confrontation with this pedantic staff officer focused his thoughts regarding such men. Incapable of expanding their own thoughts to encompass further aspects or to ask the 'what if' question. Those who are too ready to pass the blame onto someone else because they have not done their own homework properly. It made him angry that indifference to this kind of detail was left in the hands of those above him when he was perfectly capable. Oddly enough, he realised he had his own failings, but kept those to himself.

"From your description and rough sketch of the bridge, I have to assume that the longer span is in excess of your hundred and eighty feet and that the shorter part of the bridge is in a bad state of repair, and all this flying several feet above a river that we don't know the speed of, with banks at either end consisting of unknown soil. Nor did you tell me of the condition of the centre support, which, if it cannot take the weight, will probably end up in the river along with most of the rest of the bridge when the armour tries to cross it. You will have your bridge on time once all our equipment arrives which ought to be within the hour, providing you have left somewhere to put it, sir."

Stock saluted smartly, turned and marched back towards his jeep before Gillard could reply. It took several seconds before

Oakham broke the silence between them.

"Well, there goes the next general."

Gillard was fuming. Nobody had spoken like that to him before. Well, certainly not while he had been in the army. And to rub it in, Oakham was not backing him up. He stormed off towards his own jeep, deciding to delve into Stock's records and see if he couldn't find something that might put the scuppers on any further promotion. Part of him hoped the bridge would collapse and then Stock could take all the justifiable blame, but his overriding sentiment was that this attack must succeed. Damn bloody jumped-up captain.

Stock wondered if the assembly area hadn't been designated too close to the river as when the MPs had eventually allowed him further down the forested bank once night had fallen, was shocked to discover that it was less than half a mile from the river. Just the other side were the enemy who may have been able to hear the engines of the transporters as they had arrived and parked up. As usual, the military police were trying their best to be efficient. The noisy tracked Stuart tanks had wisely been corralled further back and behind Stock's transporters as they were being saved for when the bridge was completed. Nobody had told anyone not to shout too loudly, nor to keep any sort of noise to a minimum. If the Japs heard almost any kind of mechanical noise coming from this side of the river, then they must surely draw only one conclusion, and prepare themselves.

Binoculars in hands, he lay on the ground overlooking the bridge next to Oakham, but there was little to see in the dark other than there was actually some sort of bridge flying across the river. He briefly glimpsed up to see if the waxing half-moon was likely to help in the near future and decided it was more likely that dawn would break first, and that wasn't so far away. Other than the usual night noises from unseen creatures and the distant sound of trickling water, it was silent enough to make one want to hold one's breath. Those noises included the frequent high-pitched buzz of mosquitos and they both knew that within a few hours, their faces would reveal where the little blighters had landed on their exposed parts.

"There they go now, over to the left." Oakham had nudged him gently on the arm with his elbow and he peered down on the second tranche of small boats as they imperceptibly made their way across. "Didn't hear a thing. Did you?"

"Nothing."

Stock was reluctant to put one eye to his luminous watch face as it would destroy his night vision, but it felt like they were running to schedule. In less than an hour's time they would all know if Oakham's raiders had managed to secure the far bank by the cessation of shooting, if indeed there was going to be any in the first place. That would indicate that they had achieved their objective. "I had better get back."

"Don't make any move until you hear the first shots or see the sign."

"Of course not. I would certainly not want to steal your thunder."

Following the faint path as he stumbled back avoiding the trees, he tried to remember if the Very Pistol signal was to be red followed by green or the other way round. Still, he remembered that two white flares would mean that they were in trouble and would need covering fire for their retreat. He knew that repairing the bridge would be the greatest test of his mettle yet and although he had it all planned out in his own mind as to how it was going to be done, he hoped that the way he had explained it to his fellow officers had not been too ambiguous. Now, waiting for the signal and surrounded by his company commanders, he was reiterating and answering almost asinine questions. They all paused as the first sounds of gunfire and grenades reverberated from across the river and heard the nearby whistle that galvanized the rest of Oakham's battalion to cross over the untested bridge. Almost instinctively, they look down at their watches and it literally dawned on Stock that night was fast becoming day.

"Right. You can start the lorries now." He turned to Sergeant Major Harries who saluted and double-timed it away from the party just as Sergeant Day came running towards him.

"Sir. There's a major up there asking why we're not moving yet."

'Supercilious bastard', thought Stock. "Tell him it is because the mosquitos have pissed in the fuel tanks and we are going to hang them at noon."

Day was about to reply 'Yes, sir' and had jerked his right hand about to salute when he stopped himself.

"No. Probably best not to tell him that as he will only go and try and find them." In the distance, they heard the first of many engines cough into life just as the sky was lit by red and green flares. "I think you can ignore that, Sergeant, but let him know we are on our way."

"Sir."

Neither of them had noticed that there was now no firing from the other side.

*****

If Stock had had more time, he would have appreciated just what a fine day it was. Cloudless skies with a hint of a light breeze which would have reminded him of a splendid day's cricket on a typical English village green. One didn't mind getting hot and sweaty when there was a marvelous tea break just round the corner and the promise of a few pints of bitter at the end of the day to slake one's thirst. No such luck this time. The men had his permission to remove their serge shirts, revealing their glistening torsos as they laboured furiously, preferring the risk of mosquitos to enduring the prickly heat, not that it was excessive but just preferable. He had wanted to remove his own shirt as, along with half a dozen others, he heaved on one end of a thick rope, but he was under the gaze of the brigadier who had set up a temporary command post overlooking the bridge. He wasn't trying to impress anyone, least of all that interfering major or the other staff officers that milled around on the nearside riverbank. No. All he wanted to do was make sure his plan for spanning the river would work properly. Right now, that meant they needed to pull the rope close enough to attach it to a winch on the front of one of the lorries. He breathed a sigh of relief when the big D-shackle's bolt screwed into its keep and they all relaxed their grip. Pairs of steel piles ten feet apart had been driven deep into the rocky ground on both banks and would eventually act as anchors. A set of pulleys had been attached to those on the far bank and the twin ropes across the river doubled back on themselves, one end attached to the winch and the other to thick chains that would pay out from their revolving drums. Another pair of piles only six feet apart would provide more anchoring for the lower pair of chains.

He was about to shout over to the far bank to ask if they were ready when he remembered that he was now the commanding officer and delegated the task to a junior.

"Make sure they keep an eye on the block and tackle on the far bank, will you, and to shout out if it moves. Get that winch turning."

Lieutenant Tiffery obliged by shouting and waving.

The tricky part would come when those on the far bank had to unshackle the rope from the chain and attach it to the piles. Stock had ordered men to stand at eight feet intervals along the rickety bridge to support the immensely heavy chain while this was done, and he prayed that the newly welded links would take the strain, and that it would be long enough.

Throughout their initial preparations, Oakham's battalion had been crossing the river over the bridge and in the small boats. Stock reckoned that, by now, most of them would be across the other side. They'd been at it for less than two hours when Sergeant Major Harries reported that he wanted to take one squad to distribute drinking water and another one armed to deter the roaming crocodiles that were threatening the company shoring up the central pillar.

"Nearly had Creasy's whole right foot and it was only because he hadn't tied his laces properly that he only lost a boot. In the old days we would have docked his pay for negligent loss of equipment, but instead he's on his back at the Doc's, having a few stitches." He could see Stock's thoughts were really elsewhere and decided to jog his attention to what he had just reported. "Can I drop a couple of hand grenades in the water if they become a real pest, sir?"

Stock was indeed deep in thought as he watched the second set of chains being clamped to the nearside piles just a few feet away. Now that the top pair had been secured, he was repeating the procedure for an identical pair to run some four feet beneath the upper pair but only six feet apart. It would be these he would attach the Bailey Bridge transoms to. There were not enough of them for the entire bridge but he planned to intersperse them with stout tree trunks that were being felled not far from where the brigadier stood. On top of the transoms would lie the Marsden Matting, doubled up, overlapped, and bolted to provide a stable base. He became aware that the sergeant major was still standing next to him and realised he had mentioned something to do with crocodiles. He looked down at the far bank to see more than ten of varying sizes sunning themselves close to the river's edge.

"Hang on a minute, Sergeant. Did you say hand grenades?"

"Yes, sir. They'll probably make a tasty meal as well if we cook 'em right."

"Carry on." They both looked up as they caught the drone of an aircraft engine someway off to the south. In fact, nearly everybody not engaged with whatever task they had been charged with looked up, but there was nothing to see. Yet.

Sergeant Major Harries returned his stare to the bridge, stiffened, marched off and shouted at the men to get back to work. Stock prayed it wouldn't be the enemy, but from what little engine noise he had heard in those few seconds, he feared the worst. The pitch had been just a little too high for his liking. He looked over towards the brigadier and wondered if he was going to order any preparations in case it turned out to be the enemy, but the brigadier and the staff officers were craning their necks to scan the sky in all directions. More worrying was that he hadn't seen any anti-aircraft batteries. Even if there were some, they would probably not be near enough to the river to make any difference.

He strode over to where the men were pulling on the last chain, helping the struggling winch reel it nearer the waiting pile. He joined the long line of men keeping the strain, like a massive tug-of-war team, while new links were welded into place round the pile. A cheer went up as several men collapsed to the ground when Tiffery yelled for them to relax.

"Transoms, sir?" enquired Sergeant Major Harries.

"Yes. Start laying them but get the lower chains fixed to the central pillar in the meantime." Smiling, he watched the bellowing sergeant major striding off, before refocusing on the brigadier and Major Gillard as they approached, returning the lazy salute.

"I've been watching you, Stock, and I must say I'm impressed. Alfredson's obviously built up a good body of men but I'm intrigued to know why you're not utilizing what's already there. This end looks stout enough, if not a little narrow."

He didn't reply that it was quite simple to work out why since it had taken him a little time to figure it out himself. Instead, he decided to take the opportunity to show Gillard up, just enough to put a seed of doubt in the Brigadier's mind.

"Well, sir, this end of the bridge may be sturdy but, without enough time to carry out a full recce, I would not like to rely on it, and it would have taken as long to shore it up as replace it. As you can see, we are utilizing the central pillar but adding steel girders to brace it. The far end is hopeless in any case and there is not enough of the Bailey Bridge equipment promised by Major Gillard. What there is of it is being utilized. Given the little time available, I considered this to be a better method than that suggested by the major."

He let what he had just said sink in, but only for a moment before turning to Gillard. "By the way, sir, you did not mention there was enough chain, which is turning out to be ideal as you can see. Would you like to inspect our work before the armour crosses or are you content to leave it up to us sappers?"

Stock knew that Gillard was caught in his own cleft stick and that was exactly where he wanted him. And in front of the brigadier as a bonus.

Gillard could hardly criticise Stock now that he had received the brigadier's blessing, nor could he claim to take any of the credit himself as it had been pointed out that there had been several errors at the planning stage. Stock inwardly smiled as he saw Gillard grit his teeth.

"I can see perfectly well from here. You will of course have it ready on time, won't you?"

Time, or rather lack of it, was the one factor that Stock had been uncertain about. "The impossible we do at once. Miracles take a little longer. We will do our very best, sir."

Stock had quoted the unwritten motto of the Royal Engineers in a rather cheeky manner, but it was not lost on the brigadier.

"I will let you know 30 minutes before it is ready, sir." He turned back to the brigadier and added, "But when the vehicles cross, may I suggest that you restrict it to one at a time?"

Gillard went to open his mouth, but stalled as they all clearly heard the returning drone of aerial engines, much closer this time and from behind. A few seconds later, an explosion sounded some distance away.

"They're after the bloody armour." The brigadier was the first to turn and run back towards his marquee, closely followed by Gillard.

Stock shouted at Sergeant Major Harries, "Rifles!" and watched as the order went across the river down the lines of men, who stopped whatever they were doing and made their way back to the nearside bank where their rifles had been stacked. "Line them up in firing platoons along the bank, Sergeant."

It seemed to take forever for the last man to pick his way across the not even half-built bridge. Meanwhile, Stock had been scanning the skies and saw at least three Japanese Zeros occasionally appear behind the tall trees that restricted his view somewhat. More explosions interspersed with machine gun fire. He counted four of them and was grateful that they only had one bomb each, but now they were circling the area in wider arcs before returning to their targets with machine guns. He couldn't understand why they had gone for the tanks and artillery rather than his bridge. After all, if the bridge was destroyed, then the armour would never be able to cross the river.

All of a sudden, one Zero appeared over the tree tops directly in front of them. He didn't have time to shout 'Fire!'. Even had he done so, his voice would have been drowned out by the staccato of several hundred rifles. The Zero jinked directly above them before turning sharply in the opposite direction and heading back towards its original target, seemingly unaffected.

Stock watched the men reload and redraw their beads on the fast-moving plane, most managed a second shot before it vanished behind the treeline. While everybody was looking in that direction, some instinct urged him to turn back round. What he saw were a pair of aircraft higher in the sky heading towards them, directly in line with the bridge. His gut churned, as they were perfectly placed to deliver bombs on his bridge, and he foully cursed the enemy for thwarting their plans. He was about to shout the order himself to 'About Face' when he had second thoughts and was jolly glad that he did. As the two single engine planes neared, they turned out to be British Hurricanes. Somebody must have been on the radio already. Either that, or they had been patrolling out of earshot, and a cheer went up from the men as they roared overhead.

"Silence!" he heard the sergeant major roar. "Stand Ready!"

The men almost immediately assumed their firing positions again, heads following the line of their rifles as they sought the next target, but it seemed as though they were going to be denied the sight of an aerial battle as the gunfire receded. Eyes peered to their left as the sound of an engagement reached them. Then, without any further warning, a Zero appeared, following the line of the river, with a Hurricane in pursuit.

No one had ordered or even asked Sergeant Major Harries to take command of the firing platoons, but he had naturally done so, and he now gave the order to fire on the first plane only as it passed over the central pillar. The Hurricane also fired at the same time with its Hispano cannons. Stock watched. It seemed that most of the shells had missed, instead spuming the water not too far below and ahead of it, but something must have made contact with the Zero because smoke immediately trailed behind as the Japanese pilot turned away from them and disappeared beyond the trees on the far bank.

For a moment there was silence. Only the dull boom of something minor exploding off towards where the armour and other transports were parked broke it. The men slowly realised that they were no longer under attack. A few still looked up at the sky, but most now grounded their rifles and, chatting about their latest close encounter with the enemy, started shuffling into groups. It would have become a joyous melee but for Sergeant Major Harries cry of 'Attention!' Immediately the silence returned as they all stood still. He marched a few paces towards Stock and addressed him formally.

"Back to work, sir?"

"Wait another minute, Sergeant. Just in case. Then you can get them to check their rifles before returning to their duties."

"Yes, sir." He saluted, turned and had taken only one step when Stock called him back.

"Well done, Sergeant, and tell the men the battalion may be able to claim its first enemy aircraft."

"Sir."

*****

Stock thought he was being clever by having two jeeps brought up and parked on the bridge so that their headlights could provide illumination when night made it too dark to carry on working. They had made excellent progress. The first half was just about finished as the sun disappeared behind the trees, but Lieutenant Tiffery presented him with the next problem.

"They need a decent break, sir." He waited while a prone Stock finished inspecting a series of links welded to the central pillar steels.

"What do you call a decent break, Lieutenant?"

"Two hours ought to do it, three if possible."

It was fortuitous that Stock had had to lie down to look closely at the welds, as he stood to answer Tiffery, he felt a twinge in his back. It made him change his mind. If he had felt it, then he supposed some of the men must also be suffering.

"Go on, lieutenant."

"Well, apart from the two short breaks they've already had, they've been at it for nearly twelve hours now." He paused. "We can work them until it gets dark and then we can let them catch up with a bit of sleep after a hot meal." He waited for Stock to make his mind up but added, "Less likely to have accidents or produce shoddy workmanship if they've had a respite."

Stock looked over Tiffery's shoulder and watched a gang hefting more matting into position. He had to admit they looked about all in.

"Which companies do you think have had the easiest tasks?"

"E & F on the far bank. E's had a bit waiting around for one thing or another."

"I agree. Right, they can take over moving the matting and trunks to the far section while the others take three hours. Then swop them around but wait until it gets dark, which'll be in about, er, looks like less than half-an-hour." He wondered what the brigadier would think if he suddenly made an appearance and found that nothing was being done, but at least two companies were making at least some noise in the dark. Bloody mosquitos were coming out in force.

It was around midnight when Major Gillard made an appearance, just as Stock had sat down on the stub of a tree on the nearside bank with a cup of luke-warm tea. He had removed his boots and socks. Sergeant Major Harries stood in front of him holding a torch over a sheaf of papers, reading out a list. "The problem here is that we're running out of spanners to do the nuts and bolts up with."

"Why?"

"It seems the men keep dropping them into the water." He let him think about that for a moment. "It's rather awkward working on the underside of the mats. We're down to just four of them. Two working on top and two underneath, but if we lose another, we'll be down to just one effective pair, so I've sent a runner to ask around for some more."

Having not taken a break himself, Stock felt very tired, Hence the need for a cup of tea on the tree stump. Even so, an idea came to him. "Get them to use lanyards. If you cannot find any, get them made. Use bootlaces, socks, or cut up some gaiters if you have to."

"And Sergeant Day is asking how you want the steel hawsers attached to the piles on the far bank."

Just before the last light of day had disappeared, Stock had gone to inspect the big piles on the far bank and decided that, due to the sandier nature of the top layer of soil before it became rock, additional cables would ensure that there was no movement when the heavy machinery strained them. Smaller piles would need to be driven into the ground twenty feet away and attached by steel hawsers to act as secondary stabilisers to the main piles. "Loop them round and use the chain ratchets to tension them. Next?"

Gillard approached and interrupted in a terse tone. "The brigadier wants to know when. I might remind you that the schedule calls for this bridge to be operational by 06.00."

Stock decided to keep him waiting. "Anything else, Sergeant?"

"Nothing that can't wait, sir." Harries took his cue and vanished into the gloom, leaving Stock and Gillard peering at each other.

He was too tired to retort with a smart answer but wondered what Gillard had been doing these past few hours. "Tell him I can let him have a verbal report at 04.00."

"That's not good enough. He wants to know now."

Stock doubted the brigadier had put his question in that way and suspected it was Gillard who wanted an answer so that later he could say that it was Stock who had provided the wrong information. "I cannot give you an exact time, Major, but tell the brigadier that we are optimistic. Now, if you leave me to it, I can attend to the thresholds at the far end." He tipped the rest of his cup on the ground and attended to his footwear, hearing Gillard stamp away.

*****

Stock had gingerly driven over the nearly completed bridge in one of the empty Bedford lorries and parked next to the other two jeeps on the far bank. In the wash of the headlights, he recognised the shape of Colonel Oakham directly ahead, hands on hips. "I suppose you think that was funny."

He strolled up to the colonel. "Right now I could do with any kind of humour. What have you got in mind?"

"Those hand grenades your chaps were playing with earlier. Had us looking over our shoulders and wondering if we were going to be attacked from behind. What was that all about?"

It seemed ages ago, but he recalled the crocodile incident and told Oakham.

"That accounts for the funny smell. What did they taste like?"

"I still have no idea but they tell me it has got a bite to it."

"Haa haa. Very funny. I see you're ahead of schedule and that'll upset Gillard. What have you got in mind for the road ahead? There's a section not too far away that's looks like it has been washed away some time ago. Virtually impassable for lorries and the like."

"How far?"

"Oh, only half a mile or so."

"Thanks. That will be my next job. Tell me, how many Japs were there? We heard some firing but not for long."

"Dozy blighters were literally caught napping, but one of those ruddy Zeros crash-landed into one of my platoons and killed three men. Real shame as otherwise we got off scot-free."

Stock looked at his watch in the headlamps: 03.50. He looked around and spotted Lieutenant Tiffery standing over a box of nuts and bolts, called him over and told him to report to brigade HQ that the bridge would be ready just before 06.00. "When you give the brigadier my compliments, try to mention that it was neither a miracle nor impossible. Oh, and, er, try not to tangle with a certain major over there. You know who. If you need me, I will be inspecting the road ahead."

Stock found a private who was not looking too busy and ascertained that he could drive. "Laker, sir. First name's Barry."

"Well, Laker, I may not need your driving skills but jump in the other side. Get your rifle, though."

Stock took the wheel of one of the two jeeps and drove off down the surprisingly smooth but narrow road, hemmed in by trees. They passed a few huts huddled together and saw elements of Oakham's troops half camped out by them, but it was nearly a mile before they came across a sudden dip. As Oakham had described, it would present lorries with a problem traversing it, with the probability of breaking an axle spring or two. It was only about ten yards across but enough to bring an entire motorised column to a virtual halt. He was about to U-turn when a thought occurred to him. What if there was another further on? Engaging low ratio, he tip-toed the jeep across the dry rocky bed of the stream. Not having a steering wheel to hang on to, Laker painfully banged his elbow on the unyielding metal side.

"Excuse my French, sir."

"Out here, Private, I will excuse you almost anything. Just make sure your rifle does not discharge."

Nearly three miles further on the road was blocked by a series of tree trunks. When they got out for a closer look, Stock noticed that they had been freshly hewn.

"You know what this means." It was a rhetorical question, clearly beyond Laker's understanding. "There is probably a body of the enemy up ahead and they felled these to slow us up. And they are organised, so that is something of concern." It suddenly occurred to him that they were probably being watched by the enemy where they stood. Perhaps they had been recognised as just the recce party and there were orders to wait until a larger body of men appeared. He tried not to look as though he was peering into the surrounding jungle. He had counted three hefty trees that blocked the road, even to tanks. Laker asked the inevitable question, "What do we do now, sir?"

"Now, Private Laker, we go back from where we came, advise Colonel Oakham of this ambush, prepare to fill in that dry river bed, then ready our saws to clear this lot." Although tired, Stock found it easy to make decisions. He looked at his watch again and saw they needed to get back sharpish. He wanted to be by the bridge - his bridge - when the first vehicles crossed over. It wasn't that he imagined that there would be any immediate appreciation from the brigadier or anyone else, but it would be most satisfying to see the look on their faces. Besides which, he had a battalion to organise making the route roadworthy. Then they needed to rest before heading off towards, what was the name of that place, Mansi, to create an airfield out of nothing.

*****

The site was perfect. The relatively short stubby grass had been cropped by unknown herds of herbivores roaming the elongated flat mound that protruded on an otherwise small plain. There would be no need to clear any trees. With careful orientation, drainage would be natural, with perhaps a few holes to fill in. From his elevated position on top of a wooded escarpment a couple of miles away, Stock steadied his binoculars and saw the provincial town of Lashio justabout within walking distance beyond his chosen mound. A short distance beyond that, the gently rising hill marked the start of the next barrier of dense jungle. It looked like it would be an easy piece of terrain to turn into a suitable runway. He focused on the town trying to see if there was any sign of the enemy. Other than a little dust being kicked up by a short mule train, it was quiet. He noted that the dust was being carried gently north and smiled at the tell-tale sign that would dictate the runway's alignment with the wind. Perfect.

He handed his binoculars to Tiffery who lay next to him. "Just this side of the road, itlooks like some sort of market. See any Japs?"

Tiffery put down his pencil and sketch pad and steadied the binoculars on the ground with his elbows while Stock cast his eyes left and right to see if there were any tracks running down from their elevated position. His thoughts started to wander as he looked at the skyline in the distance and he marveled at the silent beauty of the shallow valley that lay beneath them. He was thinking how pleasant the country would be if it weren't for the war when Tiffery interrupted.

"Not a sausage in the way of an enemy. Not even a temporary barracks, but you'd have thought they'd have some troops nearby. After all, it's as big a town as we've seen recently. Hang on a mo, that may be a camp hidden just in the treeline over there." He held his spotting position for a while before handing the binoculars back to Stock and pointing in the distance towards the other side of Mansi.

Much as he steadied his forearms, Stock couldn't be sure if the faded straight line he was looking at was the side of a tent or just a half-fallen tree trunk leaning against another one. "We had better send a section to recce before we go down there." He looked up at the position of the sun. "Make sure they have a mirror with them. And someone who knows morse code."

"Righto. On foot I presume." Tiffery edged himself back from the rim of the escarpment a little before getting up while Stock continued to pan the line of the forest for any clues as to what lay within. At a distance of over five miles and with the heat haze, he couldn't determine one way or another. He wished he still had the help of Oakham's battalion, but they had been ordered elsewhere and wouldn't be coming their way for a day or two. If they did come across any significant strength of Japs, then he would just have to withdraw. He glanced over his shoulder again to make sure his battalion was not visible from the other side of the valley and looked at the men as most of them lounged against trees and rocks, apart from the half a dozen men collecting their equipment for the recce. In his mind he tried to estimate how long it would take them to reach the forest via the circuitous route off to their left and thought they would probably have nearly three hours to wait. That would leave about an hour of daylight for them to signal. He half-kicked himself for not making sure one of them had a torch, just in case.

After a final look through the binoculars, he returned to his jeep which he had hidden under the leafy canopy where the remaining five Lieutenants were gathered. He ordered that they would make camp for the night a hundred yards further back into the trees. The last thing he wanted was for any camp fires to be seen if the enemy was across the valley.

It had been dark for some hours when Stock decided to check on the sentries, ending up at a point where the recce party were likely to return. There had been neither signal nor firing and he was beginning to wonder what he should do if they didn't appear soon. One thing was certain: there was nothing he could do until dawn. He smelt the faint whiff of the sentry's cigarette before he could see him and decided to test his alertness. Under the faint starlight and half-crown of trees, he silently got within two paces of the trunk that the man was leaning against. At least, he thought he was silent.

"Got a light, Private?" He had to wait all of five seconds before a response.

"Wrong side of the tree, sir, on your left." The sentry moved away from the tree just a little so he could be seen.

"Congratulations, Private. You had me fooled, but it's your cigarette that gave away your position."

"Not mine, sir. Don't smoke. And it's Corporal, Corporal Burton, sir."

Stock's instincts screamed in his head and he immediately retorted. "Then whose cigarette smoke is that, then?"

He had hardly got the words out of his mouth when a loud whisper reached them. "London."

Burton instantly had his rifle in the assault position and replied towards the more open space, "Derry." A few seconds later the recce section appeared out of the starry gloom led by Lieutenant Tiffery.

"Good evening, sir." The rest of them filed past. "That's quite a climb and steeper in places than it looks."

"Before you give me your report, was anyone in the section smoking?"

If he could have seen Tiffery's face, it would have portrayed a very quizzical look. "Not since I gave us all five minutes rest at the bottom of the hill almost half-an-hour ago. Two of the men lit up. Why?"

"Did you smell it, Corporal?"

"Not a thing, sir."

Stock wondered if he had been imagining it, but it had been the faintest of aromas and could have been the residue that had followed the party up the hill. "Just stay alert."

"Of course, sir."

He turned in the direction of Tiffery. "Come with me back to the jeep. By the way, whose idea was it to choose the password for tonight?"

"Oh, that would be Private O'Dennehy. He's got a lot to say about his extended family in Ireland and you'll know it if you ever come across him. I get the men to choose simple things like that and tonight it was his turn."

Tiffery explained that they had had to detour a very long way round to maintain tree cover which accounted for their overdue return, "It was almost dark by the time we reached the forest on the far side, but there's nothing there. I think I picked the right spot we saw from the ridge and we had a good look around while the daylight lasted. I think there must be a herd of elephants a bit further on as they were making quite a din. I didn't want any of the men blundering into them. It could have been the other way around, of course. In any case, we didn't start our return until it was dark, by which time it was too late to mirror our signal. I assumed you would want to wait until morning before move down there anyway."

Stock realised how useless a signaling torch would have been but gave himself a pat on the back for anticipating the potential necessity of their having to have one.

Once down the escarpment, they deployed around the chosen ground as ordered by Stock the previous night and set about their designated tasks. One of the more pressing jobs was to set up machine gun pits, predominantly facing South towards where the enemy were retreating. The exposed area with no tree cover for a couple of miles in any direction meant they were vulnerable to aerial attack and he still had a niggling feeling about the forest line to their south-east. Mid-morning, he got Corporal Burton to sit in with him and drove his jeep up to the edge of the forest to see for himself if what he had seen the day before was just a figment of his imagination or something else. In any case, it would give him another perspective on the runway.

"What exactly are we looking for, sir?"

"You start in that direction for a couple of hundred yards or so and meet me back here. Use your bayonet to search for any sign that the Japs have been here."

He looked past the dead tree that was leaning against two others, and then on the leafy ground beneath his feet, but there was no sign of anything untoward. He made his way through the thickening undergrowth, looking for any kind of disturbance, even that from Tiffery's Section the night before, but nothing. There were no sounds out of the ordinary and no residual tobacco aromas. In fact, nothing to arouse one's suspicions, but he still had that niggling feeling that the enemy had been here. Even if he did find something, it would probably not tell him when. He made his way back to the jeep, lent against the diagonal tree waiting for Burton's return and looked down on the battalion preparing the runway in the distance. It was a good vantage point to see for miles down the shallow valley, but in the other direction his view was partially blocked by the lofty trees. He took a few paces away from the tree line past the jeep and was rewarded with a similar view in the other direction. Then it dawned on him and he looked up. He was about to start climbing the half-fallen tree when Corporal Burton appeared and set his rifle down.

"Here, let me do that, sir. I like climbing trees."

"You see that kind of triple fork just beyond where it is resting on those others, see if you can reach that."

Burton was indeed a good climber and looked in his natural environment as he skillfully ascended the sixty or so feet. Once he reached the fork, he had the confidence to sit nonchalantly in the bowl with his legs dangling.

"Anything?"

"There's a herd of antelope or deer of some sort way off to the right, but other than that, nothing."

"Not the view." He watched Burton look around and then descend to the ground.

"You're right, sir. Someone's carved what looks like their initials into the wood up there. I don't speak Jap, and it's all hieroglyphics to me but it looks like a 'Z' with a sort of squiggle below it. Quite recent too I'd say as there's still sticky sap oozing out of it."

Stock smiled to himself. "Well done, Corporal. Where did you learn to climb like that?"

"Sherwood Forest. We lived in a village just north of Mansfield near Nottingham before the war. Me and my brothers, we used to play cops and robbers or pretend to be Robin Hood. Because my brothers were larger than me, I always ended up being the one hiding and the best place was up a tree." He stopped for a moment and laughed. "My cousin was a short tubby fellow and he usually played Friar Tuck, poor chap, but just before the war started he had the last laugh on us, as he married this gorgeous bit of fluff and her name really was Marion. Can you believe that?"

Stock was only half listening but returned the grin at the tale, his mind on where the enemy might be right now. "Come on then, jump in. Time we got back."

It was indeed time he returned. He found Major Gillard waiting for him beside his own jeep, which was parked adjacent to the lorries. "Been sightseeing, Captain?"

Both men knew that this was not the case. It was apparent that Gillard was going to continue to take every opportunity to needle Stock. He would just have to make sure he made no mistakes.

"As a matter of fact, I now have information concerning the enemy's recent movements, but I suppose you know about all of that already." He watched Gillard's face and was pleased to see him squirm at the insinuation that he, a lower ranked captain in the Engineers, knew more than one of the brigadier's intelligence officers about the whereabouts of the enemy.

After a moment of clear indecision, Gillard decided not to rise to the challenge. "Well, I'm sure we all have our own theories about where the Japs have been, but it's where they are now that's more important." He took the opportunity of pressuring Stock. "When can we expect this to be ready?" He looked around at the open expanse.

Stock was on a sure footing; just a couple of hours earlier, he had walked the entire length of the runway with a squad of men in a line search, covering every inch of groun to make sure they had not missed any cavities or undue depressions hidden in the grass. He watched as tar pots were being placed at hundred-foot intervals along both sides, ready to be lit in the event of night operations. "You can advise the brigadier that his runway is now open."

"Really?"

Stock thought it must have been Gillard's first time at a forward airfield and suspected that he would expect some sort of control tower and an official looking building to carry out the functions of administration and all that went with it.

"If you must know, the Japs are not too far away. Even as we speak, we are probably being observed. If they have a radio and report this location, how long do you think it will be before a couple of their dive bombers arrive? Even if they do not have a radio and send a runner, the Japs will still know shortly. If we erect any sort of tent out in the open, then it will be much more visible and an easier target, so it is best if we keep them guessing. Our pilots ought not to have any problem locating this runway as it is an easy approach from down the valley. The Japs can only guess because it is partially shielded by that jungle if you're looking from their direction. Especially at low level. You wanted an airfield right here and we cannot build it in the middle of the jungle in less than two weeks. Now, if there is nothing else, I must attend to the placement of the night markers at each end."

He was careful to offer a proper salute before marching away towards the far end, but Gillard wasn't finished.

"Just a minute, Captain."

They now stood some ten feet apart but neither of them took the first step to come within easier earshot of each other. Stock noted that a couple of his men had ceased their unloading tasks at the back of one of the lorries to earwig. He didn't mind.

"I have fresh orders for you so you'd better fetch your map."

Stock noted that Corporal Burton had been hovering at the back of the lorry that was being unloaded, chatting to the two other men within, and he ordered him to retrieve his map from the jeep.

Gillard continued, "You and I are going on a recce down to Mya Taung about fifty miles from here, because that's where we're headed next. Since you are now our bridge-building man, the brigadier wants your opinion on how best to cross the Irrawaddy there."

Burton returned with his map, "Sir."

"Put it on the bonnet of the jeep, then go and ask Lieutenant Tiffery to place the end markers two hundred and fifty feet beyond the last pairs." Placing the map was a task he would normally do himself, but he wanted Gillard to feel what it was like to command men directly, rather than relay orders like the functionary he really was.

Both men walked over to the jeep and Stock removed the map from its canvas cover, opening it on the relevant sector to spot Mya

Taung on the eastern bank of the Irrawaddy river. The scale of the map was not good enough to assess how wide it was likely to be at that point, but he traced the river back to just north of their position and guessed it would be a good deal wider further south than the water they had just crossed.

"I understand that there's a track that runs alongside the river on this side all the way down, so it ought to be easy enough to just follow that until we reach Mya Taung. Air reconnaissance reports that there's no sign of Japanese activity there yet but there is some sort of river crossing. That's what we're going to survey."

Stock looked more closely at the map. He suspected it was rather inadequate since it depicted the occasional settlement linked by what were supposed to be roads, but which he had an inkling would turn out to be little more than jungle tracks.

"One day to get there and another to get back, assuming we do not come across any Japanese."

"I agree, so we'd better leave before first light tomorrow. I'll have my driver join us just in case."

*****

Stock took the first turn at the wheel, driving his own jeep. Stock had kept his vehicle in good condition, whereas Gillard's jeep was from the pool of vehicles regarded as disposable, which is why they left it behind. There were four of them. He had ordered Sergeant Day to pair up in the back with Gillard's driver, a Lance Corporal Hopton. It wasn't that he wanted someone else from his own battalion with him to balance the 'them and us' situation, but if the track was blocked or the enemy did appear, then a man of Day's size and experience would come in very handy.

His suspicions about the state of the track were proved to be correct, but only in a few places. As they made their way along the south bank of the Irrawaddy mainly under the trees, Stock realised he was angry that he had somehow become embroiled in Gillard's plans. He ruminated that he had been manipulated and speculated that Gillard had somehow convinced the Brigadier to separate him from the battalion, thus denying him a further chance to demonstrate that he was capable of handling a body of men of that size. He had felt comfortable commanding a battalion of over five hundred men, and in his own mind had no doubts that he could continue to do so if Alfredson didn't recover. Stock speculated that it had been Gillard who had put his name forward to the brigadier but had been put on the spot when ordered to make this trip with him. Still, it would only be for two days and he had left command in the hands of Lieutenant Tiffery. There was little to be said between the two officers, and in the main, they kept their conversation to a minimum, but the pair in the back seemed to be getting on well enough.

Having changed drivers twice, had just one break for ablutions and taken wrong turns three times, by the time they reached the miserable looking village of Mya Taung, night was less than an hour away. The collection of shanty-style huts on stilts lay close to the river in what was obviously a flood plain. When the monsoon came in June, the whole area would most likely be denuded of all vegetation right up to the base of the buildings, some of which might even be washed away. A pair of lengthy jetties protruded into the water, attesting to the rise and fall of the river with the turn of the seasons.

"Just about enough time to do what we have to do before it gets dark. Come on, there's no Japs about so let's get down there."

As Gillard was driving at the time, they had little choice. Stock would have preferred to make camp for the night, check their immediate surroundings and recce in the morning, but it was a 'swings-and-roundabouts' situation. Stock remembered the adage 'Time spent in reconnaissance is seldom wasted.'

Gillard stopped them at the head of one of the two long jetties and they all jumped out, relieved to be able to stretch their legs. "Well, this is going to be a waste of time."

Stock immediately knew what he meant. The Irrawaddy had

to be getting on for half a mile wide and this was at the height of the dry season. Even a pontoon bridge would be out of the question because of the massive surge of water that would sweep it away when the rains came. Besides which, the army probably didn't have enough equipment in the region to build a bridge of that size.

Hopton and Day were ordered onto the far jetty with instructions to keep their eyes peeled for anything out of the ordinary, while Gillard and Stock walked to the end of the one they were parked next to. They passed several piles of rope and had to pick their way past some mouldy fishing nets. They came to a natural halt after three hundred or so paces, both men raising their binoculars to survey the far shore.

It was Gillard who spoke first, "Here, isn't that a big boat over there? Some sort of ferry?"

Stock had also spotted the squared-off shape berthed against a counterpart jetty on the far bank. "I believe it is a paddle steamer. No smoke coming from the funnel and nobody on deck."

"You're right. How many men do you reckon you could get on there?"

"Two hundred. Perhaps more. With it moored the way it is, it's hard to tell the real size of it."

They were looking almost directly onto the stubby bows and could only guess its length.

"It must be for carrying cargo of some sort otherwise it wouldn't be here. These jetties are obviously made for the job." Gillard looked back at the village. "But I haven't a clue as to what sort of industry goes on here. There's nothing big enough to warrant a boat of that size."

"There might be something on the other side."

They both panned their glasses past the few huts behind the ferryboat, seeing little in the distance other than more piles of rope stacked along another jetty. Something was niggling at the back of Stock's mind but he couldn't pin down what it might be.

"Off to the right and back about five hundred yards. Slightly up the hill a little. See it? It looks newer."

Stock tried to steady his binoculars to the spot that Gillard had described and saw a low-lying shed-type edifice open on two or three sides.

"Can't tell what it is but it's half-full of something." Gillard lowered his glasses and looked around. "Damn. There's not even a rowing boat around here we can use. Shame. We could do with knowing a bit more about that ferry."

A thought crossed Stock's mind and he looked back to shore. "If there were any villagers, we could ask one of them about a boat, but the place looks deserted."

They both looked hard at the fifty or so huts and then at each other. "Quick, back to the jeep."

They were both thinking the same thing. For a brief few minutes, they had put their differences to one side and become professional. Stock saw the other two men strolling back down their jetty and was about to shout out to them, when they too broke into a run.

Breathless, Gillard asked, "Anything?"

"Nothing, sir. And nobody about either."

"Quieter than a graveyard."

"Well, I can think of only one thing that would drive the natives from their homes and that's the Japs, which means that they can't be far away. What's your guess, Stock?"

"I agree. And I bet that if we look closely enough round here, there will be signs." They were all looking around, not just at the huts but in the distance. "You look at those huts there while we look in this direction. Meet back here in five minutes."

Stock had to stoop to enter the second nearest hut. The first had had its doorway smashed in. He almost gagged at the smell. The Japanese hadn't even bothered to remove the body. A teenager, covered with flies mainly around the neck. The buzz increased as Stock took a pace closer before thinking the better of it and exiting as quickly as he could, nearly bumping into Sergeant Day who was holding something in his hand.

"Found this in the dirt, sir." Day dangled a knotted rope-cum-wire from his hand. "Some sort of garrotte." He then noticed the ashen look on Stock's face. "You ok, sir?"

"No need to go in there, Sergeant. The Japs have been here alright." He noticed Gillard and Hopton walking towards them.

"There's half a dozen locals behind that larger shack. It looks like they've been executed from the way their bodies are lying in a row. Here. What's that you've got, Sergeant?"

"A garrotte sir."

"Yes. They used it on at least one person and he, if it is a he, is lying in that hut behind this one."

"Murdering bastards. What good's that going to do them?" Hopton spat.

"Have you ever heard the adage 'You hate the Hun but fear the Jap'? Well, these Japs certainly live up to their reputation. I expect that's why they've cleared the village - so that other villages will obey them instantly."

"Well, here's one man who's not going to bloody obey them and if I get the chance…" The others saw the whites of his knuckles gripping his rifle.

Stock interrupted Hopton, "Best if we spend the night elsewhere. I suggest that stand of trees on the side of that hill a mile or so back." He was looking at Gillard. "If the Japs do appear, it would be a mistake to have our backs to the river." His last comment made them all notice that night was all but upon them.

Under Gillard's orders, and with the help of a Coleman lamp, they set the two tents several paces back from the edge of the wood. Had it still been daylight, their position on the hill would have given them a decent view for several miles along the Irrawaddy. "Better not light any fires tonight, just in case, so….." He rubbed his hands gleefully. "Finest corned beef and wonderful K-rations again."

They sat in silence around the pathetic flame of the paraffin driven Coleman lamp, spooning the familiar rations,.

Scraping the last lumps from the tin, Gillard spoke first, "You know we've got to go back there in the morning, don't you?"

The two NCOs watched in anticipation as Stock swallowed a mouthful. "I know. It is not something we can leave undone. There must be a small boat somewhere on this side of the river so we can take a closer look at how serviceable that ferry is. How are your sculling skills?" He looked between the two NCOs."

"Don't look at me, sir, I can hardly swim, let along row a boat. You know that from Dieppe." From the tone of his voice, Day was clearly not looking forward to it, but Hopton was far more optimistic.

"Took the missus, well, before she was my missus, on a pond once in one of those new parks up near Bridlington. It's a doddle and you'll soon get the hang of it. You've just got to keep your rhythm. Back – down – forwards – up – and pull. Then you do it all over again. Until you get there. Wherever it is you're trying to get to," he laughed, more to himself than anyone else. "Still got wet feet, though, as it leaked like a sieve."

"Well, we can use the jeep to recce the banks for a boat in the morning. I think we ought to be alright rowing as the current looks fairly gentle. Here, pass me that water bottle, will you?" He pointed at one the other side of Hopton, who went to pass it over, but it caught on a frayed piece of string next to his belt and fell to the ground.

"Sorry, sir. Must attend to that but this webbing's in short supply at the moment so we have to use string and rope, which rots."

As Stock took a swig of warm water from the issue bottle, Hopton's words struck home. He put the lid back on and said, "Jute."

"What's that you said?" asked Gillard.

"It is jute. Across the river. That storehouse we spotted looked like it may have had jute in it. Why I did not recognise it straight away…" he shook his head side to side. "We sappers use it all the time for making rope and, as Sergeant Hopton pointed out, string when necessary. It does not rot like the bales from the stores and is a good deal stronger than ours. This must where they collect it ready for sending down river. Come to think of it now, the Japs will also have need of it, so perhaps that is why they commandeered the villages on both sides."

"I'll go along with that theory if indeed it turns out to be jute. But why squirrel away all the labour? They'd surely need workers to carry out all the menial tasks."

Stock thought about that for a moment. "A good question, so they must have them somewhere else."

"Maybe they've put them in one of their camps?" offered Hopton.

"And where's all the boats? There must be loads of fish in the river," Day contributed.

Only the night creatures made any sound as the suggestions gave them all something to think about, until Gillard spoke.

"The favourite's got to be that they're holding them in a camp somewhere but we won't be able to find that out until the morning. So, let's get some shut-eye. I'll take the first watch, you the second, Captain, you the third. 05.30 for reveille." He didn't need to add Sergeant Day for the fourth.

*****

Stock was settling down after his watch, making sure his head was fully under a flap of canvas, and looking forward to a little more sleep. He hadn't wasted his time awake and was sure that Gillard would have done likewise, trying to work out what was going on in the area. The only light had come from the half-moon which revealed the glistening path of the Irrawaddy in both directions for several miles. He hadn't seen any campfires through his binoculars, nor heard anything out of the ordinary. Even the crickets had been silent. His thoughts had wandered in the direction of Gillard. Whatever else, he seemed to be trying to be efficient at his job of providing first-hand intelligence but lacked the expertise in picking out important detail. He asked himself the question again: had Gillard put his name forward to the brigadier for this recce, or had it been the other way round? Perhaps the brigadier wanted more accuracy and ordered Gillard to bring him along. He could hardly ask Gillard, knowing full well that he would probably be rebuffed, and wondered again if he hadn't been too critical of the fellow, but then he recalled the errors he had made and satisfied himself that his criticisms had been right. Whether or not it had been appropriate to say so in front of Colonel Oakham was another matter.

He was just drifting off when he heard the first hint of thunder in the distance. He might have continued sinking into a sleepy abyss, had it not been for the little man in his head forcing him back into consciousness. Thunder was certainly not unusual, but this was the dry season. 'That's not thunder'. His eyes opened just a little, then fully at the sound of more 'thunder'. It reminded him of his first airfield in France. Then he was fully awake and up as Sergeant Day appeared. He had lit the Coleman lamp.

"Artillery flashes to the west, sir, but way off."

"I can hear it. Wake the others."

They both paused and looked through the trees as more flashes reflected in the clear night sky. A few moments later, they gathered round Stock who stood at the treeline, binoculars to his eyes.

"Anything?" asked Gillard.

"Nothing to see yet.It must be happening a good twenty miles or so away. Any ideas?"

"That'll be XXXIII Corps pushing the Japs towards the river. That's why I'm here - to find out if there's a way across, but I wasn't expecting it so soon. The brigadier said a radio would be useless miles from anywhere as there'd be no one to pick up my transmissions at this range. And in any case, they're not supposed to be here for at least another two weeks."

"With any luck the Japs have been overrun and are legging it over here," piped up Hopton.

"And there's just us four to stop them crossing." Day's suggestion was accompanied by his chuckle.

"The four of us are not here to do any fighting, Sergeant, and

I'll remind you that any information we collect here will be wasted unless we can report it back to HQ. If you haven't anything useful to add, keep your mouth shut," Gillard barked, asserting his authority again in his unsubtle way.

"Sorry, sir. I didn't actually mean we should try and fight them, it's just that….."

Stock interrupted him. "You are quite right, we can't possibly take them. But there is no reason why we should not *hinder* them."

"What do you mean?" Gillard's aggressive tone was meant to put Stock on the back foot.

"If that is a Japanese brigade or division over there trying to cross the river, it would be our duty to try and stop them."

"Our duty is to observe and report back to brigade, not go gallivanting about on some harebrained idea."

Stock was in two minds whether or not to pursue his instinctive idea. He felt he had to at least enlighten Gillard, even if it was in front of the two NCOs.

"You really do not understand, do you?" he challenged. He had turned and now stood directly in front of Gillard, their faces casting eerie shadows over themselves from the light of the Coleman lamp still held by Sergeant Day. "For once, use your initiative rather than just doing your job. What do you think will happen when they are pushed towards the river?" He waited for less time than he ought to have given Gillard. "The Japs will try to get across on the Ferry ahead of XXXIII corps, and to do that they will need those jetties, because the shallowness of the river will not allow disembarkation directly onto the banks. All we need to do is make the jetties on this side are unserviceable. Even destroy the last few feet and the ferry will run aground."

"Who do you think you are, addressing a superior officer in that manner? This will certainly go in my report. I wouldn't be surprised if you're not demoted back down to lieutenant again. Our orders are clear. They are to recce and report back, not take on the Japanese army." Gillard's anger towards Stock was not lost on the others. Had

Day had the chance, he would have melted into the night, but he was holding the lantern.

"Will you stop your bickering and think of the consequences?" Stock did not back down. "Just think for a minute if those Japs do manage to cross the river in some sort of decent order, where do you think they will be going? I can tell you where and I am not even an intelligence officer. They will be heading towards Mandalay which happens to be the target of our own brigade, only there will not be a decent enough gap between the Japs and us, all because we did not take the opportunity to prevent that happening. And then, just as our brigade is advancing, those Japs that ought to have been trapped on the other side of the river will be right up against our own right flank. Will you put that in your report as well?"

"Where are you getting all this information and how do you know our target is Mandalay? That's top secret."

"I have ears just like anyone else, and I use what I can in case it should come in handy. Besides which, the whole brigade has been talking about Mandalay." Stock was not about to reveal that he had gleaned what their objective was from Colonel Oakham. "If those Japs are allowed to cross, it will cause bedlam, and well you know it. So, are you going to let them do that or, with a bit of effort, help me remove the end of those jetties? Because that will be all that it takes."

He could see Gillard wavering, possibly because of the two NCO's standing right there. Whatever the reason, he thought just one more push and Gillard would concede. "Remember, I too will need to write a report."

"All right then, what have you got in mind? But remember our first priority is to report this back to brigade. That comes before anything else if we are threatened."

"Brigade will already know about XXXIII corps on their long-range transmitters and from aerial reconnaissance. Now that I think of it, it is likely we were sent down here to confirm there are no Japs on this side of the river, or hiding camouflaged en masse just round the corner."

If Stock could have seen Gillard's face more clearly, he would have seen a quizzical look come over it. Gillard's ethos was to blindly follow orders, whereas Stock's was more interested in understanding what the reasoning was that lay behind those orders in order to carry them out more effectively. He waited not only to let what he had said sink in, but to give himself time to think how to placate Gillard enough that they could work together to render the jetties useless.

"I suggest we recce the riverbank from south to north, say three miles in each direction, and then attend to the jetties."

"How are we going to do that? We don't have any explosives. All we have are shovels and mattock heads strapped to the jeep."

Stock sighed at Gillard's negativity. "That is one problem we have yet to resolve, but something will come up." He looked eastwards. "Here, dawn's just round the corner, so let's pack up and get going. You drive while I think."

*****

They came across three huts in a line parallel to the river, again with garrotted human remains within.

"Perhaps they're running low on ammunition," observed Gillard as they started their northwards track.

"Running low on human decency," retorted Day, and then instantly regretted his comment in view of Major Gillard's recent reprimand, but it wasn't repeated.

The track petered out just beyond the second jetty. Despite their efforts to survey further north, could not see an easy way other than by retracing their route inland.

"Satisfied?" asked Stock. He could see Gillard peering around for any sign that the enemy lay in that direction.

"Alright. Let's attend to those jetties, but we ought to be away from here sharpish. I am sure Brigade will want to know. How do you want to go about this?"

During their early morning recce, Stock had been musing over the problem of wrecking the jetties with the minimal equipment they had and had come to just one conclusion. "Petrol."

"Petrol?"

"Yes. All we need to do is tip some over those ropes and nets. Fire will do the rest." It had been Sergeant Day's comment about Dieppe and not being able to swim that had jogged his memory.

It was a very simple solution and one that none of the other three had thought of. It might take hours or days for it to burn through but, in the absence of any enemy on this side of the river, that wouldn't matter.

"Right, then. Let's do the nearest one first." Gillard, as well as the other two, were relieved that they would not have to spend hours hacking away at the timbers. Indeed, Day was almost looking forward to it but for his own memories of Dieppe and the airfield in France.

From the passenger seat, Stock glanced down at the notoriously inaccurate fuel gauge. They had just one jerry can of spare petrol clamped in its holder and would need most of that to return. "We had better put some in the jeep first but there ought to be enough left over. Jute is quite flammable once it gets going and I think I saw some tar pots back on one of the jetties."

As they drew up next to the first jetty, it was clear that the Japanese were indeed preparing to cross the river. Smoke was emanating from the paddle steamer's stack.

Stock drew out his binoculars and briefly surveyed the far shore. "We had better get a move on. Looks like they are getting ready to load their artillery onto the ferry."

"That makes sense. If they are retreating, they'll be able to lob their shells over the river onto our chaps without the risk of being overrun." Gillard commented and then added, "Corporal Hopton and I will attend to this one. You take the jeep to the other and we'll join you down there."

Hopton had already retrieved the jerry can from the rear metal clamps and was pouring it into the jeep's fuel filler. He then soaked a rag in fuel and left it in the back and trotted off to join Gillard who was already marching down the jetty.

The tar pots Stock had spotted the previous day had been mainly overturned, but they found a nearly full one half-hidden under netting at the base of the jetty. "This is the proof that there used to be small wooden boats working from here. They would have used this to waterproof them. Bring it while I drag some of that netting down to the end." He had to give up trying to shift the nets on his own because they were too heavy, and he called Day back to give him a hand. Between them, they managed to haul some of the nets and were sweating profusely by the time they reached an area just short of the pier's end. Despite their fitness, they paused to rest their hands on their knees while they caught their breath.

"Bloody Hell. I didn't know nets could be so heavy."

"Must be some pretty large fish they were after," replied Stock, who was looking sideways at the other jetty to see how the others were getting on. It was the cloud of black smoke that had caught his attention. "You're the nearest, go and get that tar pot."

Day stopped his panting and gave Stock a knowing look; neither of them was any closer than the other. Stock didn't waste his time while Day was gone. He chose a spot some twenty feet from the end as he had seen a half-rotten baulk of timber that spanned the supporting wooden frame. It wasn't too difficult to pry the plank away as it was fixed with similarly rotting timber pegs, and he dragged it so that it rested on the pile of netting. Waiting for Day's return, he looked towards the far shore. He was horrified to see that the ferry had started to manoeuver, but without his binoculars to hand, couldn't pick out any detail. He shouted back at Day, "RUN!"

Day was just picking up the tar pot when he heard his captain shout and started to run the few hundred feet towards him. Stock could see that the other pair literally getting on like a house on fire as they fed more of the jute and netting onto their bonfire and knew it wouldn't be long before they could abandon it to its own devices.

"That ferry's on the move and it's not going to take them long to get here," Day wheezed.

"Long enough. Tip it over this lot, then put it in here and set fire." Stock had created an aperture near the centre. He looked up again to see that the ferry was now heading in their direction. He estimated that they had but ten minutes. By that time, the fire would be well ablaze and the heat emanating from it would make it impassable.

Day was about to flick his lighter when they heard the first shots. They both ducked instinctively. They recognised it as a Japanese light machine gun and looked to where it was coming from, then over at the other jetty. They weren't the target, the other jetty was. For now.

"Quick. Light it." Stock reacted first.

There was very little wind to help fan the flames, but the fire readily took despite most of the petrol having evaporated from the rag. Initially, their attention was divided between the fingers of flames that followed the dripping tar, and the reactions of the pair on the other jetty. They were taking advantage of the dense black smoke and the heaped jute that only partially hid them from the almost continuous hail of bullets. The machine gunner continued to fire his bullets from the prow of the ferry. Then a second gunner started up, and between them they concentrated their fire on the jetty producing the most smoke. Gillard and Hopton were effectively trapped. If they stayed where they were, the ferry would simply have to maneeuver to one side as it approached and the gunners would have them clearly in their sights. If they ran back down the jetty, they would be out in the open. Even if they did manage to reach dry land, there was still open ground with little cover for more than a hundred feet before they could reach the first hut and any sort of shelter.

So far, Stock and Day's jetty was not on the receiving end, probably because their flaming pile was not yet producing anything like the amount of smoke as the other one, but it wouldn't be long before it did.

"The poor beggars. They can't hide and they can't run. And we can't help." Day watched as the pair cringed.

"Maybe we can. Help, that is." Stock waited for Day to look at him. "Unless you would rather wait."

"Wait for what?"

"Sooner or later, it will be our turn. If we run for it now, we may cause enough of a distraction, but if we wait, both of those guns will be on us."

It took Day all of five seconds to realise what Stock was saying. "Give me a head start, sir." And with that, he took off down the jetty. Stock could feel the heat increase from their own fire just behind him, and took one final look at it before haring after Day for all he was worth. It had been some while since someone had timed him over a hundred yards and it briefly crossed his mind that it ought to take him less than twenty seconds to reach dry land, and then several more to reach the jeep. He didn't count, but glanced across to see if the others had seen what they were doing. Somehow, he managed to register that they had both risen from their crouched positions and had started running. Stock's jetty was a little longer than the other one, but all four of them were now running in the open. The difference of fifty feet or so was unlikely to alter the odds from the gunners' perspective on the nearing ferry.

Probably because they already had their bearings and because the jetty they had fired was producing more smoke than the other, Gillard and Hopton were still the target of the machine guns as they sprinted towards dry land. First Hopton and then Gillard fell as bullets tore into them and Stock thought he heard a faint cry as his first footfalls reached the shoreline. He saw that Day had jumped into the driver's seat of the jeep and was trying to start it and he nearly fell under its wheels as his foot slipped on the metal side.

He finally found his seat as Day engaged the gears and looked back at the prone bodies of Gillard and Hopton. They had so nearly made it to the end of their jetty. Now the gunners were firing at the jeep.

"GO…..GO…..GO, and don't stop."

Day was indeed going for all he was worth. They both heard a clang as a bullet whined off the rear end. "Change gear." He shouted as Day wisely steered behind one of the huts and onto the track that they had first come down. "Keep going."

"What about Captain…?"

"They are both dead, now keep going behind these two huts, and change gear again."

Day was more at home on a motorbike but knew just enough about the four-wheel machine to maintain an increasing speed.

"Don't stop until we are well out of range."

Day followed their own tracks while Stock tried to look behind them. It was too difficult to focus as they followed the uneven path at relatively high speed. Upon reaching a small mound where the shrubbery thinned, Stock told Day to pull up.

"Before you ask, Sergeant, even if they are not dead, we cannot help them."

"I know. If only we'd had a few more minutes. I know you and the major didn't get on, and Corporal Hopton was not much to my liking either, but even so. It all happened so quickly."

Stock stood astride, binoculars in hand and surveyed their handiwork. To one side of the twin pillars of black smoke, he could make out the ferry gradually edging closer to their jetty between the fire and the shore. He let out a sigh of relief as it ground to a halt, a mere twenty feet short of the jetty, preventing it from docking. He then panned across to where Gillard and Hopton lay and steadied the glasses for over a minute.

"I am afraid to say that neither of them is moving. Here, see for yourself."

Day felt privileged to be looking through his captain's binoculars and needed to re-focus them a little. "They've thrown a rope over to the jetty and are trying to pull themselves nearer. Can't tell if it's working or not."

Stock retrieved his glasses from Day and saw more men

jump into the water to shin up the jetty stanchions. . Like Day, at this distance he could not tell whether the ferry was being pulled nearer the jetty successfully or not. "I doubt if it will make much difference." He lowered the glasses. "And as you say, if we had had a little longer, perhaps the fire would have consumed enough of the jetties, but I fear what we have done will just hold them up."

Day thought about this for a moment. "So Major Gillard and Corporal Hopton died for nothing. That could have been us on the receiving end of those machine guns, and us lying there, not them."

Stock had been concentrating on the ferry but, hearing Day's concerned tone, he lowered his glasses, half turned and stood facing him. "No, not for nothing. For one thing the enemy is now seriously delayed because that ferry has run aground. Until they offload their artillery, it is unlikely to float again. That artillery will have to be jettisoned into the river to allow the ferry to float again. While I am sure they have some more on the other side, at least two guns are now out of action. While there are trees on the far side, the nearest decent timber on this side is where were camped last night, over a mile away. They do not appear to have the necessary manpower or equipment on the ferry to chop down big trunks and even if they did, walking back with them would take an inordinate amount of time. So, they will need to get that ferry going and then manhandle everything on it across the river to repair the jetty. It will take them at least two days to make it usable, maybe longer. And that is only if they can refloat the ferry. All the while, XXXIII corps will be pressing them on the other side. What we have done has significantly delayed their evacuation, if not scuppered it." He paused. "So, I do not think they died for nothing and if that had been us and not them….. well….. that was in the hands of the gods."

He saw Day thinking over what he had just said and continued, "Think of it like this. We have just prevented two guns from killing two people, and most likely several more. That in itself justifies their death."

A look of understanding came over Day's face and Stock knew

then that he wouldn't be blamed for their deaths. "What do we do now, then?"

They both looked towards the jetties and could clearly see the ferry leaning over at an angle where the Japs had tried to pull it closer to the jetty.

"If we had more time, I would say let's try to sabotage that ferry under cover of darkness tonight. But, as the major put it, brigade will want to know about this. I think it is best if we do report back to the brigadier straight away."

"Do you want me to drive, sir?"

Chapter 8

Ambushed

Spring 1944

Wingate, recalled to Dhana, promoted to Brigadier General and ordered to take command of the 77th Indian infantry brigade which consisted of six mixed-nationality battalions, had trained them thoroughly to fight behind enemy lines. With one foray into northern and central Burma, he had successfully disrupted the Japanese extended lines of communication to such an extent during the previous year that the enemy's plans to take control of the Imphal plain had been abandoned.

Had Stock known it at the time, he would have been proud that his first Asian runway had been utilised and frequented by the Dakotas of both the RAF and the USAAF as a mid-way staging post to supply the three thousand men behind enemy lines. These men were to become known as the Chindits, famous for attacking Japanese troops, facilities and lines of communication deep behind Japanese lines. But the brigade's return to India was dogged by the vengeful Japanese who had boxed them in against a bend in the Irrawaddy River and forced them to split up into small groups in order to make their own way back to their own lines. Fewer than half were able to rejoin their units.

While the battle lines ebbed and flowed, Stock had been busy building airfields, sometimes in the most unlikely of places. Most were small and only temporary, but others consisted of twin runways capable of carrying heavy bombers and in need of hangars, workshops, Mess halls, perimeter fences, etc. etc. The supply of decent materials and equipment had been his biggest bugbear, but he had now honed the art of requisitioning down to the last detail and could usually get what he demanded in short order. Fifteen. That was the number of airfields he had built to date in as many months, and his skill had not gone unnoticed.

Away from the more civilized areas, where any amount of machinery was available, he had come across working elephants, and had utilised these endearing beasts, along with their handlers, in place of bulldozers. He soon learned that the mahout, one per elephant, was an extraordinary breed of person. They were mainly bachelors and would grow up with the female elephant almost from birth and were so attached to their charges were they that would groom, feed, water and even sleep with them. They were also highly protective of their lifelong charges.

"We name them after flowers, Sahib. This one is called Poppy and she's twenty-six years old. She will be your friend if you have any apples."

Stock had to shift the lower part of his torso to one side as Poppy's truck explored his nether regions. He liked the idea that they were named after flora, but their odour certainly didn't give credit to their names.

He had yet to come across the enemy again, but on two occasions when building single-runway forward airfields, he had heard artillery fire in the distance. Terrible stories and rumours about how the Japanese treated their prisoners filtered through and he prayed that if, or even when, the time came, he would not be captured.

With the expansion of operations against the Japanese and the creation of new regiments and battalions, he had been ordered to take command of the recently formed 103rd battalion of the Royal Indian Engineers and promoted as their lieutenant colonel.

"I'm going to miss you," said Alfredson sadly as he shook Stock's hand. "But I'm on my way also."

Alfredson had become one of those brigadiers who he had often disrespected in the past, but was now fond of. Stock, with hardly a moment to himself, found his new battalion waiting for him at the remote railhead near Singngat. This lay some fifty miles to the south of Imphal. To the west was India, while a few miles to the east lay the southern arm of the Himalayan mountains that separated India from Burma. The enemy wasn't far away, but unable to breach the broken ridges and disrupted by Wingate's Chindits. At the present, they were not an immediate threat.

He had felt breathless when he had learned of the appointment. He now had power of command over five hundred men. IT was such a big step at the age of thirty-four. He had learned that the command of their sister battalion, the 105th, was still training in Pradesh and likely to be assigned similar tasks in the near future, but right now he had been told to await further orders and prepare to move out of Singngat. Wisely, he took the opportunity to mould the battalion to his way of thinking. Starting with the British company captains and lieutenants in command of mostly Sikhs from the Punjab, he emphasized his primary concern was for their health. Rumours that the British and Americans were losing nearly as many men to typhus and dysentery as to the enemy could not be totally suppressed and he had already seen at first-hand how these diseases could destroy a company's morale, not to mention its effectiveness.

His only link with his old regiment was the retention of Sergeant Day, and he felt very lucky that he had managed to persuade Alfredson to release him. It was unusual that this was allowed and still needed to be ratified by central command in Delhi, but Stock had argued that he would need a competent aide to refine his new battalion's training and an experienced man such as Sergeant Day would be invaluable. His new command already had a full complement and Stock had had to post Day as Sergeant Major in charge of training. From Day's point of view this fitted in perfectly as he and Stock saw eye to eye on most things.

On his first day, Stock was delighted to learn that they had brought new equipment with them, including the much talked-about new hammock hook which they referred to as 'The Angel'. Up until recently, when the old-issue hammock broke, you'd end up sleeping uncomfortably on the ground and left open to attack from ground-crawling insects. Men would draw a thin line of salt around them for protection. But the new clew was much sturdier and made the hammock hang better so it had the reputation of helping one to sleep, dreaming of angels. Even those officers lucky enough to find a bed in some hut would fill bowls of water and place the four legs of the bed in them to stop the nastier little nippers from feasting on them while they slept.

While awaiting orders, he maintained the men's morale by joining in with their maintenance schedule and showing them one or two short-cuts with his mechanical skills. They cleared parts of the railhead area from the rubbish that had built up over the decades and replaced some of the more rotten timbers of the sheds. Upon learning that one of the old bridges across the river had been swept away during the previous year's monsoon, he had them rebuild it using some of the discarded rubbish, much to the delight of the townsfolk.

At first, it was impossible to distinguish between them as they all looked more or less alike with their beards and uncut hair hidden beneath their coloured turbans. Even worse, nearly all of them had the name, Ranjit Singh or Singh Ranjit, and sing they did, every night. Their homemade rababs and dilrubas, accompanied by small drums, seemed to bring them together as much as their daily prayers. Stock had come across a few Sikhs before and had just accepted them as another religious group, but now found that he needed to understand their philosophies, what their motivation was, and how to obtain the best out of them. He soon discovered that they were fiercely loyal and would carry out their orders to the letter, without delay or complaint, and he took the time to talk to them on an individual basis. Unlike British troops, they didn't drink or smoke and, as far as he could tell, never swore, but still they were happy and not just in themselves, but also because they were glad to be serving the King of England, some of the younger ones for the fourth generation.

Although baptised as a Christian, Stock was not a particularly religious man and had only tolerated the intrusion of an occasional visiting minister when under Alfredson's wing. The Sikhs had their own ethos when it came to worship and didn't need anyone to tell them what they should or should not be doing. It was as though they had already been indoctrinated and ready to face life, whatever it may throw at them. Elsewhere in the British army, friction between protestants and catholics was often the cause of ructions, but not in his battalion where their philosophy of 'live and let live' smoothed their way of life. They did not need to look to one of their own for religious guidance, although one man, unsurprisingly called Ranjit Singh, who was a little older than most of the others, was looked upon as their 'elder'. He was also one of the company sergeants.

Rather than eat in the officers' Mess, one night Stock joined them as they sat round their homemade spit that boasted a pair of freshly killed lambs roasting away merrily. They had clearly bartered some of their rations in the local town.

"It is an honour that you join us, Sahib, and we thank you." They addressed all officers as 'Sahib' rather than their rank. Ranjit handed Stock a rectangular tin of meat mixed with unknown vegetables. "We think we are ready to build whatever we will be building and are wondering when we will get to build it."

Stock told them that his specialty was airfields and drew comments of admiration when he told them the number he had built over the past few months. "I expect we will soon be called upon but I am afraid I do not know where. After all, I do not think we would have been posted so close to the enemy for no reason."

"Sometimes, when it is quiet, we can hear gunfire. It is a long, long way away but not so far that it doesn't concern us."

"I am sorry but I am in the same boat as you. Headquarters does not issue daily reports, but as far as I know, we will be going on the offensive well before the monsoon season." His reference to a boat had some of them flummoxed but the explanation went round those of them who understood.

Ranjit looked around for confirmation of what he said next, "We wanted to join one of the infantry regiments, Sahib, and we are a little disappointed that we are to be building things instead of fighting the Japanese." Murmurs and nodding of heads all round. "We do not like the threat of being ruled by the Japanese. If you look at our history, you can tell that we won't put up with that. I will give you an example. Many many years ago, the Mughal emperors and princes ruled us but we didn't like the way they treated us. They took our women when they liked, our crops, our sons to fight their wars, but then they tried to take away our religion and replace it with their Islamic Allah, and it was us Sikhs who led the rebellion to their downfall."

The crowd cheered at his last statement.

"We don't get excited easily but when someone else tries to steal our very identity, we can be a vengeful people." Another cheer. Once it had petered out, all eyes were looking at Stock for a response and he wondered if he was facing a rebellion.

"Yet you tolerate and fight for us Englishmen."

Ranjit had seen this coming. "You do not murder our women and children nor do you oppress us. You let us follow our own beliefs and even respect us, but the stories we are hearing about the Japanese are quite the opposite. If they beat you British here in India, then they will soon be at our front door which is why we fight with you and as long as you leave our religion alone, we will continue to fight to the last man."

Stock realised now that rebellion was not in their minds, but they were sounding out his ethics. He knew little about these people from the Punjab but did know that they had fought alongside their British rulers in the past and had excelled during the Great War a generation ago. He felt that they would judge him on what he said next.

"I believe I volunteered to fight our enemies for the same reason you did. To preserve our own way of life, to be able to make a choice for ourselves, to be able to see our children grow up without the tyranny of another, but above all else, to be able to live one's own life out with honour. Our ancestors lived and died according their own creed, right or wrong. For the sake of future generations, it is now up to us to maintain our own standards because one day they will look back on us, judge us on what we do now. If we do not succeed, then we are failing them."

Stock was relieved when the men cheered him and he felt a tide of relief that he had said the right things.

"You would make a good Sikh, Sahib. The essential teachings of our leader, Guru Nanak, are contained in the Mul Mantar, the opening verse of our holy book, which is called the Guru Granth Sahib. I will recite it for you to consider." The assembly hushed to absolute quiet at the mention of the Guru Granth Sahib, the Sikh equivalent of the Christian holy bible, although Stock did not know that.

Ranjit easily recited from memory "There is one supreme eternal reality: the truth. immanent in all things, creator of all things, imminent in creation. Without fear and without hatred, not subject to time, beyond birth and death, self-revealing."

He looked at Stock for a reaction, as did the others. "Do you understand, Sahib? One cannot escape the truth. Truth can kill you, but not as quickly as ignorance. That is why we hold honour to ourselves and others above nearly all else."

"It is certainly a fine principle and one that I agree with. I believe that one can judge a man by his honesty because everything else then follows." He paused to reflect upon the unexpected turn of the conversation. He hadn't expected to become embroiled in a religious debate, but on the other hand, realised that it was he who had been the instigator. Time to put an end to it before he put a foot wrong. "I am sorry you have not been allocated an infantry unit but what we are about to do will make it possible for others to carry the fight to the Japanese."

He left them soon after. The more he got to know them, the more he liked them.

He didn't often take an instant dislike to people, but his executive officer, Major Horton-Johns, had a natural aptitude for irking. Perhaps it was because of his small stature and his constant need to look up to people, his short arms or even his odd frame that somehow emphasised his rotund stomach, preventing him from easily accessing his shoelaces. Whatever it was, Stock decided he would be better placed elsewhere, preferably behind a desk a long way away. He was efficient enough and kept the battalion's records impeccably and that was where the trouble lay as he would not tolerate faulty equipment or attempt to understand the Sikhs. A pencil-pusher, not someone suited to field work.

The opportunity for Stock to discard himself of this annoying man came when their orders arrived by motorcycle messenger. Although he wasn't certain if he had the authority, he posted the man back to Imphal, suggesting in a circumspect way to his brigade commander, Alfredson, that he would be of good use in the logistics corps.

He had to choose from one of his five captains to take his place. Acting Major John Loveday from Hampshire was his ideal choice of a natural leader and stood easy in front of Stock's desk.

"Thank you, sir. I really wasn't expecting this, but I must say that I agree that Major Horton would be better off elsewhere. He never really took to camping out and if we're going where I think we're going, then it's probably best if he wasn't coming along. Where are we going, sir?"

As Stock produced a map, the tall fair-haired man took the liberty of joining him on his side of his desk. "A place called Indaw. Here, a few miles short of the Irrawaddy river. It is about a hundred miles or so as the crow flies but our interpreter says there are only two possible passes through these ranges. You can see the route I have drawn that will take us through the Moreh Pass, down this valley to Kale, and up a steep escarpment before we approach Indaw through this basin."

Loveday was not new to the region and knew what a journey through the mainly forested region entailed. He asked the obvious question, "Are we to be given transport or are we marching?"

"That is the rub of it. Logistics can only let us have twelve lorries and four transporters, arriving here the day after tomorrow. They are for the majority of our equipment and will be taking the long way round by road. The men will be marching nearly fully loaded."

Stock was referring to the heavy tools of their trade and the list was still on his desk. They had three D8's and one D10 bulldozer, the 8 and 10 designating the width of their blades in feet, two mechanical rollers, miles of wire hawser and other ropes, eight-foot tree-felling saws, oils, fuel. The list was extensive and that didn't include the rations or the two three-inch mortars with ammunition, nor the medical supplies and extra food. Each man would have to march carrying his own canvas pack weighing nearly seventy pounds, as well as a rifle and ammunition.

"We are to make our own way there by the 7th March, so that will leave us just two weeks to get there."

Loveday took an audible intake of breath. "What about the Japanese? I thought they were in that area."

"They are. According to reports, there are two divisions to the north while others are to the south. We will be passing in a gap between them along with other infantry battalions once we descend from the Moreh Pass, so we won't be alone. The report goes on to say that this 'gap' only exists because of the awkward jungle in that region. The only major road runs north to south which the Japs are using as their main line of supply. Our traversing west to east across two ranges is something that they won't expect. In fact, nobody in their right mind would expect."

Stock was about to add 'and when have you heard of a report being accurate before' but decided against it. He didn't know Loveday well enough yet to let him know of his reservations about reports that were all too often inaccurate or out of date. He needed to have Loveday pass on his positive attitude to the company commanders, who would pass it on to those below them.

"Look at it this way. If we aim for ten miles a day and only make eight, then we ought to arrive on time."

"Do you know what we'll be doing once we get there?"

Stock smiled. "That is the easy part: airfields." Stock stood up from his hunched position over the map. "Look, this is not just a minor assault like Wingate's Chindit brigade carried out last year. They will be coming on the journey with us too, but as part of a major operation codenamed Operation Oxford along with two divisions directly under the command of Bill Slim's Fourteenth Army group. Well over ten thousand men.

When we get there, we are to ensure that our particular airfield, codenamed 'Chowringhee', is fit for immediate use. It was used last year for the occasional airlift so we will not have to clear too much other than what has grown back, but we have to have it up and running by then otherwise the gliders won't have anywhere to land. There are two other airfields in the region, forming a rough triangle, and together they will form the centre of our initial thrust southwards. Once we have made sure that the runway is useable, we will need to set up perimeter defences for another battalion, as the Japs are bound to try and take it back."

"It'll be hot work filling sandbags in this dry heat. The ground's like iron now, but I'll make sure the men have enough shovels. What we don't have is more than a few hundred bags," Loveday said, in the knowledge they had used a significant number to shore up the local bridge.

Stock frowned at Loveday's last comment. It was quite correct that his new right-hand man should point out their deficiency in sandbags, but he felt he ought to have added that he would make every effort to have them replaced. He knew from recent experiences that minor negatives at this stage often turn out to be major difficulties in the field. On another occasion he would have berated him, but having just promoted him to major, decided that it could wait.

"Send three men in one of our trucks back down to brigade stores. Make sure they know to be back here in time. Before they go, I want to go through our list of equipment and see if there is anything else we are short of."

*****

Calcutta was hot and humid, even by its own standards, and despite the efforts of the punkawallahs next door to keep the room cool, the five generals that sat at one end of the long table didn't need a temperature gauge to tell them that it was over a hundred and ten degrees Fahrenheit. The dark marks emanating from their armpits attested to that. Major Generals Nicholson, Wingate, Cowan, and Roberts in command of their respective divisions, jumped a little as Lieutenant General William Slim's fist made the table jump.

"This has got to stop," he roared. The ferocity in his voice and the fury in his eyes betrayed his feelings on the subject.

He was Bill to his friends and immediate subordinates, including those now assembled in the Fourteenth Army headquarters deep inside the vastness of Fort William, but none of them would have dared address him by his shortened Christian name at that moment. Well, perhaps Wingate might have done. Slim's appointment the previous year had put him in command of over half a million men and he had but one objective: to drive the Japanese from Burma. It infuriated him that the men, with typical British self-deprecation, were calling themselves 'the forgotten army'. What the Fourteenth Army had been through – and would go on to achieve - was overlooked because the press and public's eyes were all on the theatre of war in Europe. Slim hadn't forgotten them, and he hoped to draw the world's attention once their offensive into Burma started.

He had earned the nickname 'Uncle Bill' in the lower ranks because they looked up to him as a child would look up to an Uncle who would protect them in the absence of a father. Much as Slim tried to look after his troops by making sure they had as much equipment to help them survive the conflict, there was not much he could do about nature's natural process of elimination. But now he had the authority and the means. Lieutenant General William Slim CBE, DSO, MC had not long been given command of the Fourteenth Army and he had been promoted over others because of his quick ability to grasp and recover from awkward situations. He also had that aggressive visage that only seemed to accompany commanders and he knew how to get what he wanted. Right now, he wanted more men.

"Look at this." He picked up a folder from the desk and waved it about. "Just look at this report." He whacked it down in front of him and opened it. "Even the first page makes grim reading and that's not the worst of it." He looked down towards the bottom of the page which was signed by the Chief Medical Officer. "Ignoring the combat losses, Rowland's brigade has less than fifty percent of remaining troops capable of fighting, and as for Bradford's...," he turned to the next page, "it's a similar story with only two hundred men out of nearly five, ready for combat. This must stop. Cowan, they fall under your jurisdiction, don't they?"

"Yes, sir, but remember they have just returned with Wingate's Chindits from behind enemy lines in the worst possible jungle. You can't expect men not to succumb to something or other."

"But his brigade has been there for three months. Yours for just three weeks, yet his medical losses are far less than yours. How do you explain that?"

"I'm not sure I can, but where we were training in the arid plains of Hyderabad doesn't compare with the jungles of Burma. The men just weren't used to it."

"Tommyrot!" exclaimed Wingate.

"Look, your men may have acclimatised themselves but mine hadn't had the chance. Besides which, there isn't enough salt to go round, let alone quinine."

"Nothing to do with salt and quinine. If the men follow orders and don't drink the water before distilling it then they've nothing to fear. It's the salt in the blood that the mosquitos go after and by giving them more you're just inviting the damn things to have a go." Wingate kept his arms folded as he leaned heavily on the back of his chair.

Cowan, on the other hand, was leaning forward with his elbows on the table. "That's not what we're being told and in fact it's been well documented for decades that if a man is short of salt, then he runs the risk of contracting jaundice. You can't have it both ways. Either you give him the salt he needs or he spends a month recovering in the hospital. We're particularly short of quinine and if my troops don't get it, then we're going to be short-handed."

It was common knowledge that Wingate considered the medical profession a waste of time in the army, other than when it came to tending to injuries inflicted by the enemy. His attitude was that if a man couldn't get better by himself, then he ought not to be there in the first place. Slim interjected before Wingate could reply.

"That's the conundrum and it's been sidelined for far too long. Ignoring your salt theory for the moment. "He glanced at Wingate. "These figures speak for themselves. Put a man in the front line for a month and he's got a one-in-five probability of needing treatment. Leave him there for three months and his chances reduce to one-in-three. And that's without any help from the enemy, thank you very much. The Fourteenth's got nearly half a million combatants but right now I can only field fewer than half of them and you gentlemen seem to be happy with that situation, but I tell you this will change. An experienced man is worth three recruits and if we can keep him in the field a month longer, that's the equivalent of a whole brigade. Just think what you could do with an extra brigade."

He glowered around the table, daring any of his subordinates to challenge him. They all knew Slim was picking figures that suited his argument, as in theory the vast numbers of support units were included in the half a million, but even Wingate decided not to interrupt.

"We've got Operation Oxford starting in two weeks and I want the majority of our medical units out there with them, right at the front where they can be effective. It's no good if a man contracts malaria or dysentery in the jungle and has to be airlifted back to base, that just uses up more and more resources. Let's get him treated where he can get back to his unit in short order. Once we've got those three airfields secured, I want full field hospitals set up, complete with enough medicines for three months and make sure those supplies keep coming, especially those new Halazone tablets. I want these figures halved by the time we retake Indaw. Wingate, you're the most experienced, who's in charge of those three airfields?"

It was Nicholson who responded, "That'll be me, sir. My brigades will be preparing for a Japanese counter-attack once they know we're there. The overland supply route also comes under my command, but once our sappers have made the runways useable, we'll be airlifting everything in except the tanks. They'll be taking the southern road as we can't get them directly over the mountains."

"Right. These three airfields that we're turning into one of the new defensive boxes and naming…" Slim thumbed through a different folder off to his left, "…Piccadilly, Broadway and Chowringhee. I want a hospital at each, not just one. Make your medical headquarters at Chowringhee, though, as it's more central. Who have you got there?"

Nicholson had to sift through his briefcase to find what he was after. "Lieutenant Colonel Anderson's Twenty-Third Battalion are detailed to guard that airfield. They're seasoned regulars, mainly from Scotland and the latest report shows they've got just under four hundred effective men."

"You see, that's just my point. There ought to be over five hundred men in that battalion, not four. Who's the sapper?"

"A Lieutenant Colonel Stock commanding the newly formed 103rd Battalion of the Royal Indian Engineers with a full complement."

"Can we rely on them?" asked Slim, concerned about a raw unit.

"I wouldn't worry about Stock," interjected Wingate. "Came

across him last year and he produced an airfield for me out of thin air in double quick time."

Nicholson frowned at Wingate directly across the table from him. It irked him that another general knew more about one of his battalion commanders than he did. Even though Stock had been under Nicholson's command for the past year, they hadn't met each other, mainly due to Stock's almost constant remote airfield-building activities at the extremities of the allied lines. On one occasion, he had even accompanied one of Wingate's Chindit battalions behind enemy lines.

Slim creased his brow and fingered his moustache at the mention of an almost forgotten name. "Is that the same Stock involved with that Karachi episode?"

"I'm afraid I don't know that, sir."

"Right. Get in touch with them both and make sure they know the score."

"I'm afraid that's going to be a bit tricky as both units left this morning and they are under strict orders to maintain radio silence. They've got a hard slog ahead of them."

"This is going to be the death of us, sir." Day removed his spade before heaving the pack off his shoulders and onto the ground next to Stock's. No training could prepare a man for this kind of terrain which so far had encompassed everything except for ice. Their march had started well enough, along a forested path that led to the upper pastures used by the townsfolk, and they even exceeded Stock's target of ten miles a day for the first two. Inevitably, the track became steeper and narrower as they climbed the first of three mountainous ranges that ran directly across them. The trees became sparse with altitude and their pace slowed. Certainly, the first ridge was the biggest hurdle, at one point only wide enough for one man at a time with a ravine on their right and a cliff on their left. Their descent was not much easier either. The entire column had had to halt while the forward units cleared away a rockfall. Their guide, a small man who claimed to have been born in the mountains but lived nowhere in particular, was always smiling. Stock had asked the town's equivalent of a mayor, if he could provide someone and, on the morning of their departure, this grubby looking man had appeared out of nowhere, pointed in the general direction, and left without waiting for them. He learned later that he was one of the Kachin people, who lived all over the northern part of Burma and had no love for the Japanese who were desecrating their temples as they advanced.

Stock feared that the Chindwin river was going to be their biggest obstacle if the advance Engineers had not provided a means of crossing in time. Sure enough, as the river came into sight on the morning of the fifth day, he could see that it looked like they had only just started and it wasn't even a bailey bridge but a series of what looked like tree trunks that spanned across to the sand bank in mid-stream. The river was just about at its lowest point due to the lack of rainfall but that would soon change once the monsoon started in a few weeks. Now, the Chindwin was a shallow trickle of water compared to the torrent it would become, but deep enough to prevent a man from wading across.

He had his men down their packs along the tree-covered bank, not just to shelter from the sun but also to provide a means of shelter should the enemy appear. The nearest tree was nearly four hundred yards away and marked the edge of the jungle. First impressions are often accurate and Stock's natural aptitude for quick assessment had rarely let him down. As he marched down the shingle towards the head of the crossing accompanied by Sergeant Day, he noted that the company of men building it were acting rather lethargically. It was only when he jumped up onto a rocky outcrop that he saw the officer in charge directly beneath him. His legs outstretched in front of him and his back leaning against the outcrop, his head was covered with his cap and Stock wondered if he was asleep but then he moved his arm to scare off a fly that had dared to land on his hand. There was a time when he would have considered being tactful, but this was not it and he decided to use his authority for once. He could see the two pips on the officer's shoulders that designated him as a lieutenant, but not the insignia of his unit on his arm epaulettes.

"Enjoying the scenery?"

The man below him tilted his head up and squinted in the bright sunlight. He still couldn't see properly. "Depends who's asking, but it's a nice spot for a picnic if it weren't for these damn flies."

"Colonel Stock is asking."

It took the man all of three seconds to get to his feet once he realised a superior officer was addressing him. Stock decided to stay on the rock where the lieutenant would have to look up at him.

"Name, rank and unit." He put an edge to his voice.

"Acting Captain Peabody 26845876 of the Twelfth Logistics Regiment, attached to the Thirty-Third Corps, Sir." He snapped to attention and saluted, which Stock returned.

"Report." He wanted to know the situation before he berated the officer.

"Er, we've been ordered to build a bridge across this river and the men are doing just that. You can see that they've nearly reached the sandbar in the middle, but just the other side of it, it's fairly shallow so we won't have to doing anything there."

Stock looked over at the sixty or so men, some of whom were just standing around and chatting, while others either pulled a steel hawser, or were affixing planks to the rough buoys mid-stream. None of them looked like they were putting their backs into it.

"You were supposed to have this ready by 06.00 this morning. Why isn't it?"

Peabody unwisely decided to start walking round the rock to get closer to Stock.

"And stand to attention when I'm addressing you." Stock could imagine what was going through Peabody's mind.

"Well, er…"

It seemed to Stock as if the man was stalling to come up with an excuse. "The riverside's quite soft in places and we had trouble finding secure fixing points for the hawsers, sir."

"When do you expect to have it finished?" Stock had already estimated it would take them at least another day at the rate they were going.

"The men got one of the lorries stuck at a crossing and we had to leave it behind so we're not quite sure if we've got enough stuff to finish the job, sir."

Stock cast his eye over the piles of timber stacked rather untidily off to one side. "What do you think, Sergeant?"

Day had been with Stock long enough to appreciate when his officer was asking for back up. During the past two years, together they had built over a dozen airfields and got to know that the most plentiful commodity in this part of the world was wood, apart for the seasonal rain that is. If you wanted something made quickly, then trees would provide. "I think if I knew we were short of timber, I would go and find some." He looked almost nonchalantly towards the raw material that grew a quarter of a mile away.

"Come up here, Lieutenant." He decided that the man didn't warrant the status of a captain.

Peabody almost jumped at the order and trotted round to join Stock on his vantage point.

"What the bloody hell are those men there doing?" Stock pointed at a group who seemed to be relaxing at the far end of the pontoon, some splashing around in the water.

"Er, I think they're looking for solid ground. At least, that's what I told them to do."

"And what about those men there?" Four of them were sitting on the sandbank in mid-stream, cigarette smoke betraying their lack of activity.

"They're doing the same. You see, we've got to find somewhere to fix the hawser to, otherwise the rafts will just float away."

"In that case why are you not out there yourself?"

Peabody tried to find an answer that would satisfy but didn't get the chance.

"Don't bother. I already know the answer." Stock knew the man was plain idle and couldn't care less. "Let me explain something to you, Lieutenant. When the army orders you to do something, the burden is on your shoulders to get it done because there is a reason behind that order. You do not question why, you just do it. In this case you are doing it because we need that crossing, but not only us. Right now, there are two infantry battalions that I know of converging on this point and expecting to cross, and if the Japanese find us here in the open and trapped against the river, then who do you think we are going look to for that reason?" He paused to let the logic sink in. "The burden is on my shoulders to get these men to their destination on time, and if an officer like you cannot carry out your orders, then you do not deserve to be one. What were you thinking by letting those men swan around while you decided to take a nap and all while you knew you were short of materials and up against a deadline? And worse than that, you tried passing the blame onto your men for your failing."

Peabody was beginning to quake but Stock wasn't going to let him off that easily. "Sergeant, take his name and number for my report, then ask the company commanders to join me over there." He pointed at the head of the pontoon. "You." He didn't address Peabody by his rank on purpose. "I want to see the anchoring points, the floats and the fixings. If you cannot build a simple pontoon bridge, then we can, and we are going to do it in double quick time."

Stock surveyed the crossing point from mid-way along the partially-planked rafts and cursed that they didn't have much equipment with them. God knew where their lorries were right now. The principle of a pontoon bridge was simple. You anchor a pair of taut cables each side of the river and attach them to several evenly-spaced rafts on which you lay planks for men to cross. He could see that at the western end, where they were, the two anchoring points were large rocks which ought to be sufficient, considering the meagre flow of the river, but the sandy island about three-quarters across the river would need stout timbers driven deep into it. He made his way back to the head of the pontoon where his officers had gathered and delegated differing tasks to each of them. Three companies would forage for suitable timber and prepare it, another would investigate the sandbar for insertion of anchor points and the last would assist Peabody's in positioning the remaining rafts and laying planks. He also ordered one section back up the hill to act as lookouts.

"You have not even posted any lookouts. You do realise we are in enemy territory?"

Peabody looked sheepishly at him and Stock turned away from him, with disgust, and went to join one of the foraging companies. He was about half-way across the open expanse of the riverside looking up at the trail they had recently descended, when he spotted men and mules coming down it, still quite a way up. He went over to his pack and retrieved his binoculars. He assumed this would be the first of the infantry battalions, and his scrutiny confirmed as much. He wondered if he could persuade their colonel to lend a hand.

That was three days ago and now they rested at the top of the final ridge. The ascent had been particularly steep and sapped the last of their strength, and he wondered how the muleteers of the other battalions behind them would manage. All of them had blisters including Stock, and it was becoming a nightly ritual for them to remove their boots and socks at the first opportunity. One of the Punjabi corporals had seen them doing this one night and had offered a small tin of salve. It smelt revolting but at least it cooled the burning abrasions. The man, who was one of the medical orderlies, claimed that its recipe was generations old and was good for all sorts of ailments.

"It is all downhill from here on in, I promise." Major Loveday had produced a map. "Our destination lies a mere seven or eight miles over there, at the southern end of this lake. See?" He had to slant the map askew in the gathering gloom of the oncoming night. "One thing's for sure, Sergeant, you won't be going back that way again. If we don't beat the Japs, you'll die and be buried here, and if we win, then we'll be going forwards."

Over the past few weeks, Day had been warming to Major Loveday's sense of humour. "Thank you for those inspiring words of encouragement, sir, but I don't think I'll pass them onto the chaps. They've a funny way of interpreting things like that. They're just as likely to turn around and go back, just to prove it can be done. Like a cat crossing a road just as it reaches the other side."

"Just for your benefit, Sergeant, but I must say, you do look fitter." Loveday was tweaking Day's tail. "Must be those lovely K-rations."

"Just as well we're nearly there because the men have just three days' of rations left. That's if you don't count the wildlife they seem to be able to catch at will."

"Any idea what's on the menu tonight, Sergeant?"

"Monkey surprise, probably. I expect we'll soon find out. Look, here he comes now."

Regimental Sergeant Major Singh came trotting up the track and rammed to attention in front of Stock. "Sahib. Pickets and sentries all set at four hours and the gemndah reports that there is sign of an old Japanese camp about five hundred feet up there."

Stock had discovered that the gemndah was their expression for the man who would lead the hunt, or scout ahead, and the rotating post was usually given to the one who knew the way. He had also found out that it referred to almost anyone who had not been anywhere before, but thought he knew the way. In any case, it was someone who the others would follow, and Stock had mischievously wondered what would happen if the gemndah had gone round in circles.

"Thank you, Sergeant Major. We will be breaking camp at 06.00 again." It was pointless leaving any earlier or they would only be blundering about in the dark.

Mid-way through the afternoon the following day, they came across the lake Loveday had promised would be there and followed its western shore southwards towards the airfield designated as Chowringhee. It was a great relief to be out of the hilly, overbearing jungle and, for once, have flat ground to stand on where you didn't have to watch your very next step, but even so, there were still a few trees surrounding the open fields. All Stock had on his small-scale map was a red cross which depicted the airfield's location. As he feared, it was not necessarily in exactly the right place. He had the companies fan out to cover a broad line nearly three miles across as they headed South with the lake on their left but it was only as the sun was setting that he received word from the company at the far end of the line; they had found it. There was no chance of carrying out a proper recce that night, but even so, with the aid of flaming batons, he joined one platoon walking its entire length.

It was undoubtedly a runway, but not one that could immediately be used and he knew they would have their work cut out to prepare it in time. He made a mental note to double check his diary later that night, but it would mean they only had one day to ready the runway to accept not just the Dakotas but also the Hadrian gliders that they would be towing. He'd not been in a glider before but had once had a good look over one, and given a choice, decided he would never take the risk. If rumours were anything to go by, their flimsy frame was apt to fall apart upon landing. He stepped over yet another large log and wondered why there were so many littered about the runway at odd angles. The real problem, as far as he could see in the dark, were the numerous pot holes and even small craters. He mentally multiplied the width by the length and the number of logs he had seen - and clambered over - and came up with a frightening figure. Perhaps the Japs had put them there to prevent them from using the airfield. He had been told that it had been over a year since it was last used as a landing site by the allies. Since then, it had endured the ravages of a monsoon season and two dry winters. In theory, their equipment should be arriving in the lorries tomorrow morning, but he had been sceptical from the outset if any or all of it would arrive on time, and therefore they would have to rely upon the few items that they had managed to bring with them.

Stock had ordered a meeting of all officers and senior NCOs at

21.00 in the open air, as there was nowhere large enough undercover. "Well done. I mean it, very well done and with only one injury. I doubt there are many other battalions who could have achieved what you have. Pass on my admiration to your men." He hoped that praise coming from him would be appreciated and help keep their morale up. "I hear only Private Paranji has suffered any significant injury." The day before, Private Paranji had been carrying one of the heavy mortar ammunition boxes when he had caught his ankle in some rocks and broken it. "I would like to be able to give you all a morning off, but I am afraid that will not be possible." He went on to describe what he had gleaned in the dark and allocated various companies and platoons their tasks. It was an extensive list.

The priority was to clear the runway and fill in any holes large enough to up-end a plane or glider, and to deal with that task he allocated four of his five companies. The fifth company he split up into their three platoons, one to set out perimeter markers that could be lit in the event of a night landing, the second to repair the latrines and shanty-like huts which would provide shelter, and the third was spilt up into sections to recce the area and provide some sort of early warning should the Japanese appear. They had orders to make contact with any locals and find a drinkable water source. He kept one section back to deal with communications. They were under strict orders not to break radio silence until the first of the air transports appeared, so in the meantime he would need runners. As the morning progressed, irregular reports came in, mainly from the runway, and it was not always good news. One particular crater had clearly been made by a bomb and would take an inordinate amount of stone and rubble to fill in. Another runner reported that there appeared to be a trench that traversed the runway, and when Stock inspected it for himself, realised that it had once been a water course. When the monsoon hit, it would become one again. Right now, rather than make a proper drain out of it, they would just have to fill it in.

Sergeant Day, accompanied by a private and another man, came trotting up to him. "Private Sanjid has something to report, sir. They were recceing off to the south down by the lake."

Stock looked at the man who he immediately surmised was a local. Before he could ask any questions, the man broke into a rapid explanation. He had trouble keeping up but got the gist of it. Nevertheless, Private Sanjid helped to translate.

"He says we are welcome and not just welcome but very welcome. I am sorry I do not know the words to describe how pleased they are to see us. He laments the absence of soldiers from the British Empire for so long. It has been nearly eighteen moons since we have been gone, and the Japanese have taken everything from their village and that includes their wives and children. And they rape them. Their holy man was taken one moon ago. One minute, Sahib," he paused to address the man and they jabbered away for a moment. "I asked him to keep his story brief as he was giving me a list that was without end. They hate the Japanese but love the British, and do we have any food, particularly rice?"

Stock was hoping to ask the same question and told Sanjid to tell the man that if they had had any, they would have been happy to share it with them. "Ask him how large their village is and how long ago the Japanese were here?" The man continued while Stock and Sanjid spoke, ignoring their own conversation. He was obviously distressed.

"Theirs is only a small village of nearly three hundred men, mainly men as many of the women have been taken and only the old ones are now left and the Japanese come often. They were here five days ago and shot two more men because they had no food to give them and he thinks that if they continue to keep shooting them, then there will be less food for them and more for the Japanese. They fish the lake, but the fish have to be hung out to dry and give away their drying place from the smell."

"Ask him how many Japanese there are, where they come and go from, and when he thinks they will be back."

The gibbering continued. "It seems there's about a hundred of them and it is always the same officer in charge. They come along the path that runs alongside of the lake from the south, stay for a day and a night, then depart to the north and then back round the lake. Perhaps they will return tomorrow or the day after. They are on bicycles."

"Bicycles!" exclaimed Day. "What do they want to go and use bicycles for?"

Stock had heard rumours that the Japanese equipped some of their units with the machines and their logic followed the principles that bicycles didn't need feeding like horses but provided a more rapid method of traversing flat ground. He grimaced at the thought of the British army having to lug the damn machines around, especially over the mountainous region that had just come through.

"He says that if we had not come when we did, then before the monsoon they would have left for the mountains as they can no longer sustain their way of life and he asks that you punish the Japanese for the evil they have done to his village."

"Tell him that we are here to stay and that we will deal with them, then I want you to go with him to show you the path of their approach and come back and report to me."

"Yes, Sahib."

"Oh, and ask him if he knows anything about those ruddy logs on the runway."

Sanjid translated. "The logs belong to a man from a place called Scotland, but they shot him and his friends when they first came. He says they are valuable teak, but he cannot understand why they are so valuable as there are many teak trees here. Before he was shot, he put them on there to dry out, ready for transporting down the river. He says that when they are dry, they can float easier. I will go with him now Sahib?"

"Yes." Stock watched the two of them depart but was worried that if the Japanese made an early return and found them clearing the runway without any significant infantry to hand, then they would be in hot water. "Sergeant, ask Major Loveday to meet me over there, and fetch my binoculars." He pointed at a rise a quarter of a mile away towards the lake. It wasn't exactly a hill, more of a hump, but it would suffice as it would provide a better view of the land that gently fell away.

When he got there, he kicked his boot around in the dust to expose dozens of empty bullet casings, picked one up and recognised it as the standard .303 supplied to all British troops. From the number of them, he surmised that they came from a Bren gun, thus confirming his thoughts that this was a good vantage point. From their corrosion, he assumed they were left there from over a year ago.

Loveday appeared at his shoulder with Stock's binoculars. "Trouble?"

"Trouble. I take it Sergeant Day has given you the basics?"

"Just the basics."

I have detailed Private Sanjid to go with a villager. Look, you can still see them." They were nearly half a mile away and about to disappear behind a line of trees, not far from the lake. "Looks like the Japs have a company strength doing the rounds on a regular basis and from what we are told, they go clockwise round the lake, feeding off the local villages in more ways than one. Likely as not, they will arrive tomorrow so we had better set up an ambush for them."

"How many men will you want down there, because we're struggling to shift these logs. They're not very straight and won't roll far. If only we had a bulldozer or a couple of elephants, that would make a difference."

"If necessary, we will work through the night, because it is now even more important that we have it serviceable by 09.00 tomorrow morning. If those Japs have a radio with them, we will have to make sure we take that out first, because we do not want them revealing our strength when it arrives."

"Makes sense, but it might also make sense to let the ambush party to have a rest shift beforehand?" Loveday enquired.

Stock pondered the issue. "Look, I will be frank with you, but do not let it go any further. I have never set up an ambush before and I take it you have not either, so I will take A company at 06.00 tomorrow morning and you remain here to finish things off. Post a couple of men with a Bren gun here, but make sure they keep out of sight. They can act as our relay station if things go badly. Place the mortar section just behind the Bren gun post."

"Are you sure one company will be enough? It'll be one to one."

"I know, but we will have positioned mortars and have the element of surprise." He looked down as his foot caught an awkward bullet casing and an idea came to him. "Have a couple of men collect these casings and get them to twist and sharpen them enough to puncture a bicycle tyre."

"Why a bicycle tyre?"

"Because that is how they are getting around," Stock grinned and Loveday grinned back.

*****

It wasn't cold, yet it felt like it, no doubt due to his tiredness. It wasn't the wind nor was it the temperature and Stock prayed that he wasn't about to go down with malaria, so he put it down to being just plain tired. They had worked on the runway through most of the night, filling in the smaller holes last, and he had managed only two hours sleep, which was now threatening to overcome him as he sat with his back against a tree, next to Captain Greenford. He was beginning to regret leaving Major Loveday in charge of the airfield as there were still many issues to attend to, and he would have liked to have been there to oversee them, but command meant delegation and he could not be in two places at once. He could not imagine the Japanese arriving much before 09.00 as they had no reason to. The next village was over five miles away and if the man from the village had been correct, then why would they leave it earlier, just to arrive at this one. Breakfast, perhaps?

He had learned from Private Sanjid that there was a wood which backed onto the lake through which the Japanese would be coming. Better still, it had natural ditches each side of the track. He had concurred with Private Sanjid's assessment that this was the best place for an ambush and made a mental note to ask his company commander if the man ought not to be promoted at the next opportunity. Indeed, it was just about the only place to catch the enemy unawares as either end of the wood were just fields with the occasional lines of trees. The site was as perfect as Stock could imagine and almost a replication of what he remembered from reading about in the field service pocket manual a few years ago. From their perspective, they held all the trump cards. They knew where the enemy was coming from and trying to go to and where they would stop. They knew when and they knew his strength. Stock had made sure they would be unable to retreat by placing nearly half of his force to the rear of where they would come to a halt. Going into the lake would not be a practical option nor would they be able to go forwards as he had detailed a firing platoon up front, which left just the direction of the airfield and he had that covered by the Bren gun. Better still, back-up was available should it be needed. He could picture the unsuspecting Japanese column of bicycles, perhaps in pairs and spread out over a hundred yards, cycling along a bright sunlit path and into the shadows of the wood where their eyesight would still be adjusting. Those at the front would be the first to suffer from punctures and stop suddenly, while those behind would concertina into their comrades and bunch up into a consolidated target. When the first shots rang out from unseen and differing directions, they would at first be entangled with their bicycles and it would take several moments before they could return any fire, and then only from an exposed position.

As is the commander's prerogative, Stock had given orders that no one was to fire until he did, and then to target anyone who looked like they had a radio transmitter on them, followed by officers and section leaders. Despite his inexperience at ambushes, he felt no qualms about what he was about to do. Even though he had considered the alternatives, he knew it was going to be a bloody affair. The warm day and the dappled sunlight that filtered through the trees as he leaned against one of them reminded him of his courting days back in England. No, not courting; cricket, and waiting to go into bat. Somewhere in the West Country, perhaps it was that sleepy hamlet in Somerset. He struggled to remember its name. Broomwood, no, Broomfield, or was it… As his eyes drooped and his head nodded forward, his tin helmet fell off and landed painfully on his kneecaps. He reacted by bringing his head back up quick enough to bang it against his tree. 'Damn fool' he thought to himself as he rubbed his knees rather than the back of his head, and looked to his left where Greenford ought to have been but wasn't. 'How long have I been asleep?' he wondered, as Greenford appeared.

"Just been checking the advance party again and they're really well hidden," Greenford commented. He looked down at his watch. "Nearly 09.00. Our chaps ought to be appearing any time now, but I suppose we'll hear them before we see them in these trees." He tried again to look up through the foliage into the skies for the first sign of an aircraft but gave up.

"Just because our orders stated that the airfield was to be ready by 09.00 does not mean that they will land then. It would not surprise me if someone misinterpreted the order to land at 9 p.m., not a.m." Stock looked up at Greenford. "I am sure the Japanese would love to come and shake you by the hand, but right now I think you would make a smaller target sitting down."

It took Greenford a second or two to understand that his colonel was telling him to sit, rather than make his presence known to the enemy. He sat.

"I know your record shows you were employed on the railways, but exactly what was it you did before the war? I have noticed you like standing up." Stock was looking for an excuse to try and stay awake as well as getting to know one of his company commanders better.

"I was the manager in charge of Paddington Station. Loved the job and you're quite right about standing. You see, although I was supposed to be behind a desk most of the time, had my own office, assistant, secretary etc. etc., I just couldn't ignore that gorgeous aroma of the trains, and anyway, someone needed to make sure the passengers were properly looked after. Used to meet dignitaries and the like personally as they alighted. There's a unique smell to a steam train after a long journey. Brings with it a taste of the countryside that it's passed through, and mixed with hot oils and grease and the sulphurous odour that clings to the drivers' clothing. I can almost smell it now." He shut his eyes and breathed in through his nose. "My father was a Director of Great Western Railways and it was he who helped me get the job. Quite a coup, really, as there were others who would have killed for such a chance. When war came, I volunteered for the RE as it was the closest thing to trains I could find. And those engines that took us across India. They're positively archaic, but they knew how to build things to make them last back then."

"It sounds like you made a sensible choice - joining the Royal Engineers, that is." Stock decided to test him. "Know how to replace the woodruff key on a tank's bogey wheel?"

"Er, well, it couldn't be much different from that of a 4-4-2 - that's the configuration of the latest…"

Stock held his hand up. A corporal from the forward position was running up the track towards them.

"They're coming, Sahib, about a mile away."

"On bicycles?"

"Yes, Sahib, and the sergeant says there's fewer than a hundred of them."

Stock looked hard down the track but couldn't see anything. He stood up, as did Greenford. "Remember, no firing until I do." He looked Greenford straight in the eye and held out his hand. "Look after yourself and your men, and good luck."

"Good luck to you too, sir." He briefly pumped Stock's hand, disengaged, saluted and beckoned the corporal to go with him.

Stock retrieved his binoculars from the ground next to where he had been sitting, stared through them in the direction of the Japanese for over a minute before he saw the first one appear round a bend, half-hidden by a line of bushes. At the pace they were cycling, he estimated it would take them nearly ten minutes before they entered the overhanging branches of the wood, and he took the opportunity to study their appearance while making certain he was mostly hidden behind his tree. It looked like they each had a rifle strapped across their backs and the counter-strapping across their chests seemed to hold their ammunition pouch but at this distance he couldn't see the size of their backpacks. About a third of the way down the column, which was indeed travelling in twos, he saw two soldiers whose bicycles had baskets on the front, with cargo inside which made their mounts less stable. He presumed these two would hold the radio and field generator, because directly in front of them was obviously their officer, betrayed by his peaked cap.

He knew he couldn't be seen, but nevertheless he naturally crouched as he retreated behind the shadow of his tree and made his way through the sparse undergrowth to the part of the ditch he had earlier designated for himself. Sergeant Day and eight others were waiting for him. The rest of the platoon was spaced out either side of him.

"Seven or eight minutes and they'll be here. Send a runner to the chaps at the back to warn them."

"Sir." Day turned and spoke quietly to a corporal next to him who disappeared before Stock hardly knew he was gone. He wondered if the Punjabis in his charge would live up to their vicious reputation when it came to the fight. Once again, he cast his eye over the part of the track some hundred feet further down and hoped that the leading pair of cyclists would not spot where they had scattered the bullet casings and half-covered them with soil. It looked alright to him and he ducked back down below ground level, unclipped his holster and palmed his Webley revolver, broke the chamber and for the third time that day checked to ensure all six chambers were loaded. Six minutes later, the first chattering voices of the approaching column could be heard, one particular voice louder than the rest. He risked a peek over the rim of the ditch: still a couple of hundred feet away and some twenty seconds. As he counted and the voices became louder, he now could hear the mechanical parts of the bicycles as chains revolved around sprockets and pedals strained underfoot. The doppler effect of the passing men told him they were about to reach his trap and he gave a look to his left then right to see how ready his men were. He need not have worried as they were all squatting down with rifles at the ready, all eyes on him and waiting for his signal. He held his hand up in case any of them decided otherwise and still he waited for that tell-tale exclamation from the enemy that must surely bring the middle of the column to a halt right in front of his position. The few seconds before the first cry of dismay seemed to take forever and he was just beginning to wonder if the casings were going to do their job, when it did come. Still, he held his hand up. He heard the application of the wooden brakes on wheels multiply, counted to three and dropped his hand.

Stock stood up, leaned his chest on the front to the ditch, steadied his right hand on the ground, and aimed his right eye down the barrel of the revolver looking for the two soldiers with radio equipment. By the time he had drawn a bead on the nearer of the two less than fifty feet away, the man was down, shot by someone else. He watched as the man jerked as two more bullets hit him, his machine toppling over into his compatriot. He had forgotten how loud rifle fire could be, especially as the sound travelled along the ditch from both left and right and it made him jump a little as he looked for their officer, but he too was down, his neck spouting blood onto the dusty track. A grenade, followed by several others exploded on the track. Everywhere he looked, the Japanese were falling, and so far, unable to bring their rifles to bear. He heard the platoon fire start from the head of the column and more of the enemy were writhing on the ground, tangled up with their machines. He looked to his left and saw that, so far, the rear section had not become entangled with their comrades but were beginning to organise themselves by dropping their bicycles and leaping into the ditch on the opposite side. He looked further down the track and saw a section of his own men get up from their hidden position, cross the track, and start circling behind the enemy. He turned his attention back to the battle in front of him and saw a few soldiers had just dropped to the ground and were beginning to return fire from behind the dubious shelter of their bicycles. He took aim at the nearest and was about to pull the trigger when a bullet threw up a spout of earth right in front of him, throwing dirt into his eyes, temporarily blinding him. And then there were bullets coming in his direction.

When he planned his ambush, he had envisaged that the enemy would not give up without a fight and while he rubbed the grime out of his eyes, wondered if he had not made a mistake. He heard another bullet pass close by and more exploding grenades brought cries of agony coming from ahead of him. He shook his head to clear his vision and to his horror saw an enemy soldier crawling directly towards him, no more than twenty feet away, rifle in one hand, a bayonet in the other. The soldier looked back at him, decided he couldn't get to his rifle in time, got up and started to charge Stock. He took no more than two paces before he collapsed as a bullet hit him squarely in the chest. Stock turned to see Sergeant Day standing upright a few feet away with his rifle at his shoulder, still aiming at the now dead Japanese. Then Stock recoiled in shock as a bullet smashed into Day's head, spraying his brains and blood out in an arc behind him.

By the time he blinked in disbelief, Day's now lifeless body crumpled, heaping itself into the bottom of the ditch. All Stock could do was watch helplessly as his Sergeant, who had been by his side from the outset of the war, lay there. When it came down to it, Day had learned almost as much as Stock during their time together in the Royal Engineers, and along with their affinity towards each other, meant that their time together, whether it be demolition or constructing, had made the war more bearable, indeed, enjoyable on several occasions. Day's favourite expression came into Stock's head. 'A proper job'. Well, some bloody Japanese had done a proper job on Sergeant Day and it took a few seconds before Stock took a pace sideways towards his friend. But then he looked up at one of his Punjabi soldiers who had taken Day's place, and saw the look on his face as he threw his rifle down and reached for his Kukri. It reminded Stock that there was still a fight going on. He looked towards the enemy who had taken his friend's life away.

The Punjabi jumped out of the ditch, shouting a blood-curdling war cry, and charged into the melee of men and bicycles. He was not alone. The entire section of men who had been standing alongside Stock just a moment ago were deserting their protective ditch and setting upon the enemy murderously, their razor sharp Kukri knives flashing up and down as they laid into the Japanese.

Wherever he looked there was death being meted out by his Punjabis. He climbed out of the ditch with his Webley ready and pointing at any movement from the injured. Fewer shots were being fired. The cries of the Japanese as their bodies were hacked by those razor-sharp knives, echoed off the trees. He saw a group of the enemy towards the rear, holding their hands up in surrender, walked towards them and was grateful to see Captain Greenford restraining those under his command from tearing them to pieces. He learned later that out of the eighty-seven, only fourteen of them had survived.

He had hardly had time to take it all in, yet he could not but help watch and admire the ferocity of the Punjabis as they heedlessly attacked the Japanese with their knives, oblivious to their own peril. He couldn't call out 'cease fire' because there wasn't any, nor could he blow a whistle to signal the end of the action, since he didn't have one. Instead, he called out to Captain Greenford to pass the word round for the fighting to stop, not that there was any fight left in the remaining Japanese. He stood in the centre of the track surrounded by dozens of dead, some still trapped under their now horizontal bicycles and grimacing in death. At first, there had been the overpowering smell of cordite, but now that was being replaced by the stench of human shit as eviscerated body parts released their pungent aroma. For no particular reason, he focused on a fly that eagerly took advantage of the new source of food. A thought came to him, 'Even in death, there is life'.

An oriental-like cry from further down the track brought his attention back to the moment. Time to take control again.

"Captain. One section to accompany the prisoners back to the airfield and make sure they stay alive. No more killing. Detail a burial party. Get the enemy fallen in the ground straight away and find out how many of our chaps are missing or injured. Then attend to Sergeant Day's body and have it taken back to the airfield for burial."

Greenford acknowledged the orders and turned to delegate, leaving Stock to put his revolver away and wander over to Day's body. He half-slipped down into the ditch, knelt beside it, straightened out his corpse and set his rifle by his side. He ran his hand over the one remaining eye, closing it. "Goodbye, old friend. You helped make my life richer and I am sorry it had to be you." Tears welled up in his eyes as he recalled similar emotions from his youth, when he had had to put down one of the horses on the farm. 'Bessie'. That was the horse's name. Before he knew it, tears were flooding down his face and he gripped Days' still warm hand, hoping for some sort of consolation. Even though he knew none would be forthcoming, he still hung on for a few moments, before standing up and wiping the tears from his face. He realised the only comfort he would get from this experience was the stiffening of his resolve. Once he had climbed back out of the ditch, he pulled his uniform blouse down, put his shoulders back, and marched towards Greenford.

"I'm sorry, sir, but I think Sergeant Day was the only casualty. Otherwise, we've three injured although one's not likely to make it. Private Amdihar Singh."

Stock really didn't feel like smiling, but he needed to show he was pleased. After all, the outcome could not have been better. "Congratulate your men. Once they have finished here, get them on parade by…" he looked at his watch, "13.00 after they have eaten. Remember, we still have an airfield to finish off." Stock looked past Greenford and saw a group of villagers standing still just watching them, and he hoped they had seen the retribution.

Stock returned to the airfield leaving Greenford in charge of the ambush site and was pleased to see that work had at last started on repairing the old dug-outs and even more pleased to see that Lieutenant Colonel Anderson's twenty-third infantry battalion was just arriving, complete with mules which looked nearly as weary as the men.

"Heard some shots a while back but they didn't last long. Need any help? After all, we're the ones supposed to be warding off any Japs, not you sapper wallahs."

Stock had never met Anderson but decided not to take umbrage at his use of the expression 'wallahs', as it was a common colloquialism. Nevertheless, he needed to establish their credentials as competent Engineers as well as being able to defend themselves. "You need not have hurried." This was an obvious jibe as he knew Anderson ought to have arrived sooner than he had. "We managed to take care of a scouting Patrol without the assistance of the Twenty-Third, but now that you are here, perhaps you might like to recce the area and tell us where you want your mortar pits. I might add that there are some existing ones already. My adjutant, Major Loveday, will show you their location on a map if you like."

Anderson was only half listening as his attention had been caught by a group of Japanese prisoners being herded towards them. "I see you found some prisoners."

"Yes. Those are the survivors."

Anderson assumed that the few shots he had heard had resulted in the patrol surrendering, but now a look of doubt crossed his face as he saw men moving in the distance at the ambush site. "Er, what size was their patrol? Are there any others around here?"

"Company strength and I think this is the only one hereabouts," Stock replied nonchalantly.

"Company stre…….. where are the rest of them?"

"Dead."

"Dead?" Anderson exclaimed incredulously as he added up the figures.

"Yes. All of them. I told you; you need not have rushed." Stock relished Anderson's reaction as it had only just dawned on the fellow that what they had achieved was significant. Not only was it unusual for an engineering unit to be found in a fight, but even more so for any unit to carry off such an engagement with so little loss. Up to that point and while he walked away from the ambush area, he had been consoling himself for the loss of Sergeant Day, but as he approached the runway, his thoughts had turned instead to the condition of the airfield. Anderson's arrival was more of an interruption to him, more than anything else.

"But what about your losses?" Anderson was obviously sceptical.

"Yes, that is unfortunate. Probably two dead and two injured." The ratio of men lost in achieving success was particularly good and he wouldn't need to point that out in his report.

Anderson couldn't but help himself let out a short laugh. "By the sounds of it, you don't need us infantry wallahs. Still, Coombes' battalion is just behind us, and as they're the last to arrive we'll get them patrolling the area instead of us, eh? Hello. Sounds like the first of the air transport's here."

*****

As the shadows lengthened in the afternoon sun, Stock was summoned to Alfredson's headquarters in the recently erected, elongated bell tent. He had submitted his written report only an hour or so previously and assumed he must have omitted something. Both men stood as it seemed someone had forgotten to include any chairs on the inventory.

"I'll have to think about giving you command of one of the soldering battalions if you carry on like this. You know I don't have the authority to do so, but it's my way of complimenting you on a magnificent achievement. Not only have you prepared the runway in good time, but you've prevented the enemy from reporting one of our positions and wiped out one of their patrols in the process."

Stock just stood there, wishing he could lay down on anything resembling a bed. He had been on his way to the hastily constructed officer's Mess when his summons had come.

"You're not after my job by any chance, are you?"

"Beats walking." It was all he could think of.

"It might well beat walking but it doesn't beat landing." Alfredson was referring to the dreadful landing the pilot of his Dakota had made in his haste to avoid skidding into one of the gliders that had crashed on landing. "You can see Wingate's Chindits arriving now and I gather he's due in on one of the flights shortly. Err, now that you're just about finished here, I think he rather wants you to move directly on to another airfield."

"Sounds about right to me. Any idea where?"

"I shouldn't be telling you this yet as it ought to come from Wingate himself, so don't let it go any further for the time being. I think he's managed to convince Slim that cutting off the Japs' supply route from the South will not only starve them into submission but deprive them of ammunition. Look." He moved some papers from on top of the map on a makeshift table. "The Japs have two divisions to the north of us. By landing at these three airfields, we will have cut off their primary major supply route from the south. There's another more minor route on the eastern side of the Irrawaddy. It's that supply route he wants to strangle at the same time."

Stock looked at the map that was, by now, familiar to him. What he had not seen before was most of the circles and arrows depicting locations, movements, objectives etc. At first, it was difficult to decipher, but Alfredson gave him the opportunity to study it in peace, yet however hard he tried, he could not see any references east of the Irrawaddy. "Which part?"

"You won't find it on any map as it was only discussed yesterday and not officially sanctioned by the time I'd left. In any case, I think Wingate likes to surprise the enemy just as much as High Command. Here, behind enemy lines." He pointed to the right of a small town with the name of Singu which straddled the Irrawaddy on the route to Mandalay. "And the good news is that he's planning to parachute in."

www.ingramcontent.com/pod-product-compliance
Lightning Source LLC
Chambersburg PA
CBHW061638190726
48289CB00006B/1655